The Day the Century Ended

Books by Francis Irby Gwaltney
The Yeller-Headed Summer

Francis Irby Gwaltney

The Day
the Century
Ended

Rinehart & Company, Inc.   *New York Toronto*

c.1

Published simultaneously in Canada by
Clarke, Irwin & Company, Ltd., Toronto

Copyright © 1955 by Francis Irby Gwaltney
Printed in the United States of America

Library of Congress Catalog Card Number: 55–6428

BL

c5-4-55

For M'Lou and Teejer

The characters and events in this novel are fictitious.

Book I

By Their Deeds

Book I

Sam Gifford, of the convict company on Luzon for striking an officer, tells of the shocks and strains and brutalities of war, of his love for his wife Jenny, and of the "ending of the century" with the dropping of the A-bomb. *Grim, frank, and full of raw power. Not for the shockable.* 55-6428

1

I awoke a few minutes before dawn. My guard was snoring raucously and his rifle was about to fall from his lap. Earlier, when he was told that I was a dangerous prisoner, he had gripped his rifle tensely, but now his huge hands were relaxed. One long, crooked finger, hooked through the trigger guard, kept the rifle from falling. And he was about to get caught. Sleeping on guard duty was a serious enough offense in the days of the National Guard army, doubly serious now in the army of the likes of Colonel Miles.

"Hey!" I called softly. "Hey!" The exertion of speech, even now when my bruised head was almost well, caused a faint throb in my temples.

The guard, such a young, innocent-looking boy, recoiled quickly and grabbed his rifle to keep it from falling. They trained them more carefully to respect their rifles than they had done during my days in basic.

"Goddamnit," he croaked, his throat filled with the phlegm of sleep, "I wasn't asleep."

"Just resting," I said. "It's getting close to daylight."

"What about it?" he said, attempting to be belligerent.

"I thought you might want to be awake when your relief comes."

"Don't worry about me," he said. "I can watch out for myself. You'd better worry about your own self."

"After you're over here a few weeks," I said, "you'll learn about watching out for people."

"Looks to me like you didn't learn so much."

The chains on my ankles suddenly pained me. "The trouble is, boy, I learned too much."

He didn't know what I meant; and there had been something said about not allowing me to talk. "Shut up," he said. "Just shut up."

Oh, my fine young man, I thought. My fine, innocent young man. "I'll be quiet."

"Now I told you, shut up!" He stood menacingly over my cot. "You hear——"

"Your relief's coming."

My guard straightened himself, rubbed the sleep out of his eyes, and hastened to the entrance of the guard tent. I heard the Sergeant of the Guard grumbling at his detail. My guard, still accustomed to training-camp discipline, obsequiously held the tent flap open for the sergeant's entrance. The sergeant, Kenny Carr, grinned.

"Morning, Sam," he said. "This boy here"—he thumbed at my guard—"now he's what I call a real fine soldier."

"Very patriotic," I said.

The boy didn't like that.

"Who went to sleep first?" Kenny said. "Him or you?" He caught the boy's start from the corner of his eye.

"He didn't bat an eye all night."

The boy appeared startled, then relieved, then puzzled by me.

"Glad to hear it," Kenny said. "He'd be taking your place if I'd a caught 'im even blinking."

And the boy believed him.

"Taking my place?" I said. "You got some news?"

Carr seated himself, after pushing my chained feet aside, on my bunk. "That hurt you?"

"Damn right! Take it easy. Circulation's cut off."

"Sorry, Sam," Kenny murmured.

4

"What about that news?"

"Well—it's news, all right, but I don't know whether you'll call it good or not. They ain't sending you to the stockade."

"That's good news."

"Guess so," Kenny said. "Ray Mosby talked to Colonel Miles, told'im what a fine young man you are and all. Ended up that they decided to send you to George Company."

"Oh." I had heard of George Company of course. And I had heard of its commanding officer, Captain Grimes.

After an awkward pause, during which my guard gawked stupidly at me, Carr dug into his cargo pockets for a ring of keys. He unlocked my chains, carefully keeping me from seeing his eyes while he worked, and helped me to my feet.

"That sonofabitch!" he said, meaning Colonel Miles.

"That's right." I flexed my legs gently. The sudden release of new blood into my feet caused them to throb and sting so sharply that I fell back on my bunk. "That hurts," I said.

"Just stay set," Kenny said. "Mutt! Bring me a C-ration. Hash! Sam, you still like hash, don't you?"

I nodded.

The hash was brought and while I ate my breakfast and drank warm water from the canteen the boy loaned me, Kenny gently massaged one foot. The boy, not at all tough now, worked with the other one.

George Company certainly wasn't something to which I could look forward. Convict companies had been abolished decades ago when penologists' protests had finally stopped the practice of taking volunteers from American prisons and putting them into suicide regiments. If they survived, it meant that they had paid adequately for their crimes. But there was still George Company. And the difference between George and those nineteenth-century outfits was not too great. The difference was the source of the men for the company. And they weren't volunteers.

"Anybody got an extra cigarette?"

Kenny produced a mangled, half-smoked butt. "Go ahead, take it," he said to my protesting gesture. "We're supposed to get a ration tomorrow."

5

It was a strong smoke, tasting of sweat, but it was delicious. "Can you walk yet?"

I lurched to my feet and tried a step before I nodded.

Kenny watched me give the cigarette butt a military funeral. He made a sound to express his disgust. "This goddamn outfit's more GI than many a basic camp."

"*C'est la guerre,*" I said.

"Yeah," Kenny growled. "Whatever that means."

I was marched to Regimental Headquarters, which was in a squad tent erected in the shade of a huge mango tree, where a sleepy major, sleepers still in the corners of his eyes, sat on an empty ammunition case. The major, a Regular Army officer who had been transferred to this regiment not long after the arrival of Colonel Miles, received Carr's salute and frowned at me. He had to clear the morning husk from his throat to speak.

"This is"—he looked at a slip of paper he held in his hand— "Samuel F. Gifford?"

"Yessir," Carr said.

"Stand at attention, Gifford," the major said.

"They had'im chained up, Major," Carr said quickly. "His legs is stiff."

"Oh," the major said. "Well, try to do better than you're doing now. The Colonel wants a soldierly appearance."

I tried.

"All right, Gifford," the major said. "According to the Articles of War, you ought to be in front of a firing squad right now, but Colonel Miles went to bat for you, just like he always does when an enlisted man gets into trouble——"

I thought, And when the old bastard's afraid of what General Hix will say about there being too many court-martials.

"——Now I don't know—or care—whether you appreciate it or not, but I want you to know that the Colonel has been very generous with you."

Carr twitched slightly.

"Can't you stand at attention, Sergeant?" the major said sharply.

"Sorry, sir," Carr said.

"All right," the major said roughly. "Now, Gifford, Colonel

6

Miles has offered you a choice. You can go to the stockade in Manila and await transfer to Leavenworth, or you can go to George Company as a buck private. Do you understand that?"

"Yessir."

"All right then, what's your choice?"

"George Company, sir."

"That's playing it smart, Gifford," the major said with great satisfaction. "Now you'd like to thank the Colonel for letting you off so light, wouldn't you?"

"Nosir."

The major was visibly shaken. His face reddened noticeably. "Did I understand you to say you don't want to thank the Colonel?"

"That's correct, sir."

The major turned white with rage. "Goddamn you! You drag your ass in there and tell Colonel Miles that you appreciate it, no matter how you feel. Either that or you'll be kissing stockade ass till you're a hundred years old. Now, get *in* there!" He shoved me toward the entrance to the headquarters tent.

Kenny caught me in time to keep me from falling.

Colonel Miles was waiting. The Colonel was five feet four inches tall. His skin was pink and stretched taut by the fat beneath it. Above his soft little mouth was a military mustache, a gray line seemingly drawn by a make-up expert straight across his upper lip. But the mustache failed to lend strength to the mouth, no matter how fond its hopeful sponsor had been of its possibilities. His round little belly protruded enough that it touched the edge of his field desk. The hands were small and, unlike the pink face, were quite white. On the third finger of his left hand was a ring which signified his graduation from the United States Military Academy. Behind him and to his right was a hatrack, which his orderly had carried from one place to the next as regimental headquarters was moved, and upon it hung a battered campaign hat, the Colonel's "trademark." Directly behind him, pinned to the wall of the tent, was a framed, greatly enlarged photograph of the man himself, clad in riding breeches and cavalry boots.

The Colonel was smiling benignly.

7

I came to attention in front of his desk and removed my fatigue cap.

"Salute, soldier," the major, behind me, said. "You're back in the army."

I saluted and said, "Private Gifford reporting to the Regimental Commander, sir."

Colonel Miles returned the salute. "Welcome back to the army, uh——"

"Gifford, sir," I said.

"Ah yes, welcome back to the army, Gifford." His voice was quite tenor and somewhat husky from many years of shouting military commands. Probably, I thought, the man had once been the victim of many a rough joke about his tenor voice. He leaned forward, grunting somewhat with the effort of lifting his belly over the edge of the desk, and offered me his hand.

As I took it, conscious of its softness, he massaged my hand while a photographer's bulb flashed.

He sat down quickly as soon as the photographer lowered his camera.

"The picture's yours," Colonel Miles said with his tenor voice. "You may send it to your parents if you wish—with the proper explanation, et cetera, et cetera."

"Yessir," I said. "Thank you."

Colonel Miles leaned back in his swivel chair and crossed his arms over his head. He was directly under his picture, which obviously had been made some years ago. "Gillum," he began, his sharp tone succeeding only in making his voice higher, "there are some excellent soldiers in George Company. During the two island campaigns they saved this regiment, and more than once too. They spearheaded both landings——"

How would you know? I thought; you weren't there.

"——At the present they're holding the most important sector of our line and doing a good job of it too. You should be proud to be associated with such an organization."

"Yessir," I said.

"Uh"—Colonel Miles looked questioningly at the major—"Was there anything else, Major?"

The major hurried around the desk and whispered in the

8

Colonel's ear. I saw what might have been muscle in the Colonel's jaw bulge like a pulse. He frowned and looked at me with something akin to hatred showing in his eyes.

"Thank you, Major," he murmured. "Gillum, I understand that you were the late General Cozzens' son-in-law."

You sonofabitch, I thought. You bastard! "Yessir."

Colonel Miles rolled the Academy ring around his finger. Suddenly he smiled; his eyes twinkled and the little mouth stretched into the abandoned grimace of a happy man. "Well!" he said happily, "I hope you have better luck than your late father-in-law did."

You bastard, I thought again. "Thank you, sir."

"All right, Gillum. Major Read will give you your papers and secure transportation to George Company. That's all." Still smiling, he dropped his eyes to his desk.

I pulled myself to attention and started to salute. I was stopped with a prod in the ribs by the major. He leaned close to my ear and whispered, "Thank him for keeping you out of the stockade."

"Sir," I said rigidly, "I wish to express my appreciation for your efforts in giving me a choice between the stockade and George Company."

Miles looked up and smiled. He had enjoyed my little speech. "Quite all right," he said airily. "You're welcome."

I saluted, made about-face, and marched out of the tent, conscious of the major's step directly behind me. A jeep and a driver were waiting. The major handed me an 8½ x 11 manila envelope, which contained a record of my military career, and led me by the arm to the jeep. The driver examined me closely.

"Get in," the major said. He beckoned to Carr, who handed him an M-1 rifle. "You won't cause any trouble with this, will you?" he asked doubtfully.

"Nosir," I said. I took the rifle and placed it between the driver's seat and mine.

The major tossed a bandoleer of clipped ammunition to the driver. "The driver'll give you the bandoleer when you're out of our perimeter." He nodded to the driver.

The driver and I both saluted.

9

"Take him away," the major said.

I waved to Carr, who gave me the thumb-and-forefinger sign, and the scene disappeared behind the cloud of dust from the wheels of the jeep.

2

We drove past the ammo dump, past the Negro truck company, past Service Company and over a Bailey bridge. The sun was up now and the Filipinos were going to the rice paddies. Several of them gave us the V-sign and the children, most of whom were burdened with farming equipment, grinned and yelled, "Geeve me wan seegarette, Joe." The driver drove slowly to prevent the dust from choking them. After we passed the Filipinos they continued to call after us; it was so peaceful that it made my throat thicken.

Less than three weeks ago I had been with the Recon Platoon when we had moved into this little town. The Japs had deserted it as we advanced, but Colonel Miles hadn't been convinced that they weren't still there. It was difficult to prove to Colonel Miles that there were no Japs around. It had taken the unnecessary death of Raker, Meleski, Saunders and Ralston to convince him of that much. Those four men, who would never have been my friends if the war hadn't brought us together, had died uselessly, but that hadn't been important to Colonel Miles.

And that had been only three weeks ago. I was thinking, as we drove along, that the yesterdays of a war are years ago in the civilian's measure of time. Twenty-or-so days ago, and it already seemed as if it had happened when I was a young man.

Once safely beyond the last outpost of spit-and-polish Regimental Headquarters, the driver, who had until now faced impassively ahead, removed his helmet and replaced it with a crumpled fatigue cap, which he took from one of his cargo pockets.

He was quite tall, this driver, and when he changed head-gear I saw that his hair was very short, blond and kinky. Now, after glancing back to see that it was safe to treat me civilly, he grinned and revealed a solid row of teeth which were stained by tobacco. His hands were long, so long that the steering wheel seemed small and frail when he gripped it. He was hawk-faced and gawky. His face and neck were burned to a leathery brown from so much sun. He looked, it occurred to me, like a share-cropper instead of a George Company jailbird. He tossed the bandoleer of ammunition into my lap, took a chew of tobacco, and said:

"Hell, go 'head and shoot somebody if'n you feel like it. I don't keer." Then he added: "Anybody but me."

It would have been impossible for somebody from Gray's Landing to doubt his accent. "You must be one of the old Guards-men."

"That's right." He spat, neatly so the wind wouldn't throw it back on us. "How about you?"

"Headquarters Company, Gray's Landing."

He gave me a quick glance that revealed the animosity the men in the line companies felt for us and our often soft jobs in Headquarters Company. "Walnut Creek," he said. George Company had originally come from Walnut Creek.

"You mean you're not . . ." I stopped, embarrassed.

"Hell no! I ain't no fukup."

"I'm sorry," I said. "I didn't mean . . ."

" 'S all right," he said. He offered his hand. "Willie Craw-ford."

"Sam Gifford," I said. I was certain now that he was a sharecropper. During the past few years I had come to like these people and know them as my friends, but the accent and manners of his kind had never been more welcome than they were now. I shook hands with him.

"Gifford, huh?"

I nodded. "Sam Gifford."

He pondered a moment. "Any kin to the Gifford that run a gin in Gray's Landing?"

"He's my father," I said. "Did you know him?"

11

"Yeah," he said, "I knowed'im." He spat and paused a moment before he went on. "Fact is, he knows me well enough to call me by name when he sees me." He chewed his tobacco twice. "Pretty good man. You'd a never knowed he was rich."

"He isn't rich," I said stiffly.

"He ain't no poor white."

"No, but he isn't rich either."

Willie suddenly grinned. Then he laughed. "I didn't go to hurt your feelings." He waved at a Filipino who gave us the V-sign. "Coming from an important family, how come you ain't an officer?"

I smiled. "I don't know," I said truthfully.

"Well," Willie drawled easily, "I guess living ain't *all* sweetness'n light, huh?" When he said huh, he poked me in the ribs with his elbow.

I laughed. "Not much of it, in fact." And I thought with some surprise, This man could've easily been one of Poppa's sharecroppers.

Willie grinned with the easy satisfaction that comes when a sharecropper unexpectedly finds a person with whom he can converse on even terms.

"Yep," he said, "not much sweetness'n light around this fuken outfit." He spat. And, safe with the knowledge that he could talk to me, went on. "'S getting so you don't see so many of the old Guardsmen no more. Most of'em's been wounded'n sent home or killed—or something."

"Yeah," I said, "or something."

Willie grinned at my oblique reference to the court-martial that had brought me here. And then his grin changed as he obviously remembered that we had become friends.

"Yep," Willie said, "your paw knowed me well enough to call me by name."

"Glad to run into an old friend," I murmured. "And you were in George Company back in Walnut Creek?"

"That's right," he said. "I ain't no fukup, like I said. I been in George ever since two years before we was mobilized."

"How many original Guardsmen are there left in the company?"

12

"One. I'm it." He spat. "When the Japs bombed us that time, me'n another guy'z the only ones that wasn't killed or wounded real bad. I'm the only enlisted man in the company't aint a fukup."

"Are they *all* jailbirds?"

Willie looked at me and shook his head. "Not a man in the company's ever been in a civilian jail. Every one of'em's been sent to us by the court-martials." Willie spat again. "We'n all get along all right in civilian life. It's the army we can't get along with, so they shove us all out to George." I liked him for automatically including himself with the men who had been court-martialed.

Comfortably friends now, we rode for a few moments without speaking. I took a drink from his canteen, which tasted of tobacco juice, and slumped in the seat to enjoy the sunshine. It was something to warm me to the core.

"What're they sending you to George for?" Willie asked abruptly.

"For doing like the man said, striking an officer under combat circumstances."

"What kind of officer?"

"Regular Army."

"Hurt'im bad?"

"I damn near killed him."

"Should a shot'im," Willie said. "That way you'd a been pretty sure of killing'im."

It was a fine morning. We drove along the banks of the Angat River and while Willie attended to his driving, I watched the Filipino women do their laundry in the cool-looking shallows next to the shore. Occasionally a woman passed on her way to the river. They carried their laundry on their heads. They were so graceful that they reminded me of the paintings Gauguin had done elsewhere in the Pacific. But these women ran to extremes: either they were duffle-bag fat and ugly or pencil-thin and pretty. They made me think of Jenny, but only because they shared a sex in common with her.

"College man?" Willie asked abruptly.

"Yeah," I said. "I went to the University. How about you?"

Willie was obviously pleased. "Naw. Third grade," he said, "that's all."

"That's enough sometimes," I murmured.

The river was like none I had ever seen before. Its waters were clear, almost blue, and it rippled over a stony bottom. The women, although busy with their laundry, didn't muddy it with their feet and the soap they used was quickly absorbed by the current, leaving no ugly, milky stain. It was more like one of the swift mountain streams back home than a river, but it was wide, while those fast streams at home were narrow creeks. I was feeling better than I had felt in a long time. I had forgotten that I had given up, had lost most of my courage, and would soon have to face combat again, face something that I had only recently tried to escape. Here on the peaceful banks of a clear, swift river, it was hard to remember combat, death and eyes opened wide by the sight of death.

The children, who flocked around the women, waved and shouted, "*Mabuhay!*" And Willie answered in kind.

"*Mabuhay* means they want us to live a long time," Willie explained seriously.

"Yeah."

One of the women was quite pretty and, standing by the side of the road near the water, she gave us a frankly friendly smile, which caused both of us to react.

"I'd pile out of this jeep and talk to that girl," I said, "if I weren't a married man."

"So'd I," Willie said, "if Grimes hadn't a told me to be back to the Company before nine o'clock."

We forded the river at a town Willie called Pollywog, his own personal corruption of an unpronounceable name. We had to disconnect the fan belt because, Willie said, the river had risen a few inches and the fan would throw water back on the motor and drown out the engine.

I wasn't aware that I was smiling until Willie said, "You won't be grinning long when you find out what you're getting into."

"Anything'll beat the stockade."

"That's probably right." Then he was serious. "But you'll

get along all right, Sam. The boys in George is a pretty good crowd. They're fukups, sure, but they ain't jailbirds. They just couldn't get along with the fuken army."

"Who can?" I said.

"Nobody can if he's got'n guts."

We stopped at a roadblock and Willie showed his trip ticket. The sergeant in charge handed the ticket back to Willie without looking at it. He was looking at me.

"What you got, Willie?" he asked. "Another fukup?"

Willie spat past the sergeant's leg. "Nope," he drawled. "This here's Sam Gifford from Gray's Landing. He's MacArthur's great-uncle."

The sergeant shook hands with me. "What'd they send you out for, Gifford?"

"Striking an officer under combat circumstances."

"You should've killed the sonofabitch."

"I tried to."

"Should've tried harder."

Willie put the jeep into gear. "How's the brown-nosing business, Anderson?"

"Fuk you, Willie," Anderson said good-naturedly.

Willie grinned. "Goddamn roadblock commando." He drove slowly away.

"Good luck to you," Anderson called after me.

"Anderson's all right," Willie explained. "But he just can't help brown-nosing himself into the good deals."

"Is the roadblock a good deal?"

"Yeah—well, let's put'er this way: it ain't a *bad* deal."

"George gets it that rough, huh?"

"If they's something Miles won't get'n a thousand miles of, or if they's a chance of somebody getting hurt, if they's a ditch to dig or a road to be built, George gets the job."

"The front's pretty quiet though, isn't it?"

"Yeah," Willie said, "if you want to call it a front, it's quiet. All they is up there's a line of outposts about a mile apart. Them Jap bastards could walk right into Manila and nobody'd ever known it till it's all over."

Some of the old fear was returning now. The three weeks I

had had under the care of Doc Wingate and his drugs had done a lot to restore pieces of what had been Sam Gifford during the early days of the war, but fear is malignant and after its damage is done repairs are impossible. It is somewhat like leprosy—it can be arrested by relief, but can't be entirely cured.

Willie stopped the jeep on a knoll and pointed ahead. "See that potato hill up yonder?" he said. "That's our first outpost. See that long hogback that drops off so sharp—shaped sort of like a pipe and stem? That's another outpost. That sharp drop off's where it hits the river. On most a them hills, we got outposts, six of'em anyhow. And one platoon's got to take care of all of 'em. Anderson's platoon gets the roadblock; right now Tom Thumb's got his platoon on the outposts and Little Joe Johnson's bunch stays around to guard the captain, Captain Grimes."

Willie pointed toward a clump of mango trees on the bank where the river took a bend. "See them mangoes? That's the *barrio*. That means 'little town.'" He spat into the dust. "That's where we got our company headquarters perimeter."

"What's this you said about a whole platoon guarding the company commander?" I said.

"Hard to believe all right, but that ain't no kidding. Most CO's keep a squad, but not Grimes. That ain't all either."

"What else?"

Willie spat. "He's got a couple of bodyguards."

"You're kidding?"

"Grimes is one human I don't kid about."

"Does he need bodyguards?"

"Well—I ain't got time to tell you all about it right now, but one of the boys tried to kill'im once, if that answers what you got'n mind." Willie chewed a couple of times. "He'd have'em though, whether the kid tried to kill'im or not. Grimes's the biggest fuken coward in the United States Army, and it's full of'em."

As we approached the company perimeter, Willie drove slowly to prevent dust trails from revealing us to artillery spotters. Two dirty, bearded soldiers were standing waist deep in a foxhole on the right side of the road. They were tending a .30 machine gun, which was equally dirty.

"*Mabuhay!*" Willie said from the corner of his mouth.

The two soldiers returned the greeting with a sour nod and then, together, turned their eyes upon me. I nodded, but they made no effort to acknowledge it.

Most of the *barrio* had been burned out. A few *nepa* huts still stood, and scattered about among the piles of gray ashes were strips of heat-twisted sheet-metal roofing, but there wasn't enough of the buildings left to call it a *barrio* now. The perimeter was plotted in a crude circle among the ashes. In the middle of the perimeter, on stilts, stood what had probably been the only frame building in the *barrio* before the fire. Its sheet-metal roof had been painted olive drab. Poked out of one of the windows was a radio antenna, the only sign that the house was occupied.

In various poses of indifference and boredom, stood thirty or so men and, like the two machine gunners, they were bearded and dirty. The gray ashes had covered them all. I had been in the army for almost four years and this was the first time I had ever seen a vehicle enter a perimeter without receiving a merry insult or a greeting of some sort. They merely stared—at me. I draped my bandoleer about my neck and, clutching my manila envelope, alighted from the jeep. While Willie hurriedly covered the jeep with a tarpaulin, I looked the men over.

George, the convict company of the twentieth century. The men were carefully concealing any reaction they might have had to my arrival.

Suddenly, in the dusty silence, a voice called out to Willie. The voice, I first thought, was foreign, but before it stopped, I knew that it was indeed American. The voice had sounded as if its owner wasn't capable of speech in the normal manner but rather produced the sounds of vocal intercourse by emitting, from deep inside, a belch, with which it formed words.

I located the owner of the voice. He was leaning from one of the windows of the house. He was a short, round-faced man whose hair had thinned back to the middle of his head and what hair was left had been cropped so closely that, for a moment, I thought he was completely bald. His mouth was quite wide and his lips were thick and amazingly dark, for which a slang term existed, "liver lips." His hands rested on the sill of the window and in one of them was a half-smoked, half-chewed cigar, about which was curled a stubby forefinger. He wore fatigue pants and an undershirt.

"Is that the new fukup, Crawford?" he said with that belching voice.

"Yes, Waco," Willie said. Willie, not long ago, had been cheerful in his own laconic manner, but now he was servile, visibly frightened.

"Well, goddamnit," the man belched, "send the sonofabitch up here."

"Now wait a minute——" I began.

"Shut up!" Willie whispered sharply. "Goddamnit, shut up! That's the captain."

"I heard what you said, Crawford," Grimes said. He didn't seem particularly angry about it.

"Sorry, Waco."

"All right, *all right*, quit acting like a damn Sunday-school teacher. Send that fukup to me."

"Yessir," Willie said. "I'll bring'im right up."

"I didn't tell you to bring'im up, Crawford," Captain Grimes said sourly. "I said, *send*'im up. . . . And Crawford——"

"Yes, Waco?" Willie's voice was actually trembling.

"Next time you call me sir, I'm going to send you to Norzagaray."

"Yes—yes, Waco."

"All right then, send that fukup to me." Captain Grimes popped the cigar into his mouth and disappeared.

Willie shoved at me. "Hurry up," he said, whispering again. "Get up there."

18

"Now what the hell's all this——"

"Goddamnit, shut up and get up there"—then he pleaded with me—"for your own good."

I slipped my rifle sling over my shoulder, crossed the yard, and started up the steps that led to a closed door. Before I reached the third step the door opened and a thin, sparsely bearded kid stepped into my path. The kid was carrying a tommy-gun which he held in both hands, almost in the firing position. I tried to brush past him, but he reached for my shoulder and pushed down, preventing me from rising to the next step.

"Just put your rifle down right here, buddy," he said.

I thought he was joking, for his manners were right out of a cheap gangster movie, including the narrowed eyes, the pursed lips, from which dangled a dead cigarette, and the surly voice. I tried to push on, but he moved the tommy-gun in a menacing manner.

"I said once, put the rifle down."

I couldn't take him seriously. "Shall I remove my shoes too?"

"Just don't get smart," he snarled. "Just don't get smart. Put it down."

I leaned the rifle against the house. "Okay?"

He opened the door and stepped behind me. Then he placed his hand in the small of my back and shoved gently. I stepped through the door, blinked in the sudden dimness, and stopped. He shoved again, and again, until I was standing in front of a battered field desk.

"Just wait," he said, and he leaned against the wall.

I waited for perhaps fifteen minutes. During the first few minutes I heard nothing but the croaking of a lizard, which seemed to be lodged somewhere under the eaves of the house, and an occasional word, quietly spoken, from the men in the yard below. This was the quietest perimeter I had ever seen. There were no friendly insults or laughter, and so little talk that it would have been difficult for me to believe that I was in the midst of an American military organization.

The guard, for he was obviously one of the bodyguards Willie had told me about, said nothing. He cradled his tommy-gun in his left arm and stared at the floor. Only once did he move; with a sudden, swift gesture he picked his nose and flipped a bugger on the floor. He ignored me completely and didn't move again after the business with his nose. Nor did he become at all impatient. The beard, a dirty blond frizzle, was thin, nonexistent in spots and told the truth about the age that it was trying to hide.

Another minute passed before the door into an adjoining room opened and Captain Grimes strode heavily up to his desk and sat down.

My first impressions of him—short, half-bald, small-headed, round-faced and incredibly broad-shouldered—were made curiously indelible by his eyes. They were gray, a lighter gray than the ashes outside; a gray, I could see, of the hue of smoke from burning grass. They were the eyes that one seems to see through, but at the same time, during the one brief glance he directed at me, I thought I saw eyes that look deeply into a man and discover his serious secrets.

Seated at the field desk, he stared unseeingly out the window and into the blue sky beyond the town's horizon. Then he moved; he scratched his groin. After another glance at me, which didn't chill me so much this time, he opened the desk drawer and chose, apparently from many, a cigar stub and put it as far into the corner of his mouth as it would go, where he clamped down upon it with his tiny teeth.

"Swanson," came the belching voice.

The guard sprang forward. "Yeah, Waco?"

"Get out there'n tell Crawford he ain't driving the jeep no more," Captain Grimes said. "I told'im once before about calling me sir and by god I don't tell nobody nothing but once."

"Who you want driving it, Waco?"

"That's my worry. Just do like I say. Now get going." But before Swanson could move, Captain Grimes halted him with a gesture. "Where's Millard?"

"Down't the river, taking a bath."

"All right, never mind about Crawford now," Captain Grimes said hurriedly. "Wait'll Millard's back."

Captain Grimes looked me over. And I saw that I had been

mistaken in one of my impressions of him. He didn't look into a man's eyes at all; he glared balefully at a spot on my forehead.

He held out his hand. "Give me them papers."

I handed him the manila envelope. He examined every form carefully and then went through them again. I suppose it took him ten minutes, interrupted only by the croakings of the lizard, to read everything in the envelope. Once satisfied that he knew as much about me as the army could put into its forms, he chose the record of my court-martial from the pile of papers and read it again. He stopped reading once to grin.

"Pretty good record," he said. "First you get a Purple Heart and a Bronze Star, then you get court-martialed. Rough, ain't it?"

"Yessir."

His voice clouded into a frown. "Didn't you hear what I told Crawford about calling me sir?"

"Sorry—Waco."

"Ain't no sniper potting me every time one of you guys call me sir." He read from the court-martial, " 'Struck an officer under combat circumstances.' "

I waited.

"What kind of officer?"

"Second lieutenant, Waco."

"West Point?"

"Yes, Waco."

"Should a killed the sonofabitch."

I swallowed. "I was trying to, Waco."

The door opened as Grimes started to make a comment, which, if his sarcastic grin was any indication, would have damned both me and the West Pointer.

The newcomer was clean and freshly shaved. He, like Swanson, carried a tommy-gun and on his face was the same impossible movie toughness that Swanson affected.

"Swanson," Grimes said, "tend to Crawford. Hey, Millard, we got us another fukup, name of Samuel F. Gifford. What's the 'F' stand for, Gifford?"

"Francis, sir—I mean, Waco."

"That's right—Waco," Grimes said. "Francis, huh? I got a sister named Frances. What're you doing with a girl's name?"

"It's also a man's name," I said and began to explain about the spellings, but he interrupted:

"It's a girl's name, ain't it, Millard?"

"Yeah," Millard said sourly. "You got a girl's name, Gifford."

I kept my silence and Grimes, seeing he wasn't going to make me lose my temper, launched into what I presumed to be his stock lecture to all newcomers.

"You want to know what we'd do with a guy that'd strike an officer in Texas, Gifford?" he said, and winked at Millard. "Well, I'll tell you what we'd do in Texas. We'd stomp hell out of you, that's what we'd do in Texas. Ain't that right, Millard?"

"Yeah," Millard said. "We got a way of taking——"

"But the army don't like our way," Grimes said gloomily. "And since the army's paying our way, we got to do like the army says. But I'll tell you something, Gifford, you won't hit no officer in George Company, 'cause if you do, it'll be the last *anybody* you hit. George Company's the end of the trail. We get the fukups and when they fukup here, they ain't no place to send 'em except home in a box." He chewed thoughtfully at his cigar stub for a moment. "You know radio procedure?"

"Some."

"Well goddamnit, how much?"

"I was platoon sergeant in Recon," I said. "We had to know radio procedure."

He spat on the rough planking of the floor and scuffed at the spittle with the sole of his boot. "All right," he said, "you're my radio operator till I get sick of looking at you. Them bastards at Regimental won't send me no operator. They think they're too good for good old fukup George Company."

4

It took Captain Grimes two days to get sick of looking at me.

Millard was the first sergeant, I discovered, and Swanson was the company clerk, although he held the rank of technical sergeant. Nobody seemed interested in discussing Swanson's rank. When I said something to Willie about a tech sergeant doing a corporal's work, he muttered, "That's how them things goes around here."

I never heard Captain Grimes address anybody by his rank, nor did I learn who the company officers were until three days later. When the morning patrols were sent out, Grimes went to his window, rested his hands on the sill (the cigar was always in the left hand), and, peering dully at the ground below, bellowed in his great, belching voice, to which I could never become accustomed, "Johnson, take six men to Baker Junction," or "Sellers, take six men to Parade Hill." Always it was a name, never a title. I never knew which of the two men he called the most often—Johnson and Sellers—was the platoon officer. Nor could I tell their rank by their appearance. All of the men in the platoon, as they stumbled out of the perimeter on the morning patrols, kept their heads down and didn't speak at all. They were all dirty, bearded and sullen. Several times I saw small groups of them, safely out of earshot of the house, talking and, a few times, smiling, but they never laughed.

Grimes, Millard and Swanson—and I—were the only ones allowed in the house.

I was told to sleep under the house, where four foxholes had been dug, and when time came to close the perimeter at evening, Millard or Swanson dismissed me with a curt, "Get'n your hole, Gifford."

I operated the radio, an SCR300, with as much dispatch as my casual training would permit and Captain Grimes seemed content with my efforts. He never used anything but code names for the outposts and I therefore didn't have to question him when he wanted to speak to any station in the net.

Insults and humiliations taken for granted as a part of my new military life, I was happy enough. I hadn't been called upon yet to demonstrate my courage, but I was quite certain that I had none. I brooded upon that aspect of the new situation, but, oddly enough, I didn't dread anything in the future. I was experiencing a kind of resignation, or fatalism, that one feels when he knows he is going to be hurt and can't do anything

23

about it; or, in the same vein, the way one feels when he sees a Jap shoot at him and knows only the fates of winds or the lack of the Jap's skill in marksmanship can save him.

My mail caught up with me the second afternoon. There was a letter from Poppa, one from the Sons of the Confederacy notifying me that I must pay my dues, four from Momma, one from Jenny's mother, and seven from Jenny. One of those from Jenny was a bulky, manila envelope which contained nothing but pictures. I read the letters, after carefully arranging them in the order in which they were mailed, and then, like a child saving the best until last, I looked at the pictures. She had had pictures taken in each of her various frocks and in the bathing suit she had worn the afternoon when we went swimming in the pool on Poppa's farm. The bathing suit was polka-dotted, two-pieced. I studied her body. It wasn't of the spectacular measurements of the billboard queens—not quite—but she was a beautiful woman and, separated by two years and thousands of miles, she seemed more beautiful than she had been on our honeymoon. She was seated on the huge, slanting rock above the pool. It seemed impossible that she was mine and that I was the only one who had ever had her.

The picture was jerked from my hand.

It was Swanson. "Goddamn, Gifford, that's real snatch!" He held the picture between his legs and groaned. "Give me that address and I'll be looking that little gal up, come rotation. How much you take——"

I charged him, rushed him into the corner and grabbed the front of his fatigue jacket and twisted. "Give me that picture," I fumed.

And, surprisingly enough, Swanson paled and handed it to me promptly. "She your wife?" he asked weakly.

"You ever act like that again," I said, "and I'll kill you."

He believed me. He believed me because he knew I was telling the truth. I folded the picture neatly, indeed tenderly, into my wallet, feeling now, my anger subsiding, somewhat foolish for treating a mere picture with so much tenderness. But then a soldier so long gone and so far from home. . . .

Swanson, after I released him, had fallen back slightly and

mumbled that he didn't know she was my wife. Even a bastard of Swanson's stripe feels the soldier's traditional respect for another man's wife. But he soon remembered his function in George Company and hurried out of the room. I heard him griping to Millard in the next room. I went back to sit by the radio.

"Let's see the picture, Gifford," Millard suddenly demanded authoritatively.

I was caught so short that for a moment I could do nothing but rise and gawk at him. Finally I managed a weak "No."

"I said once," he said arrogantly, "let me see the fuken picture."

"Go to hell." I jerked the telephonelike microphone-speaker out of the radio and, using it as a club, backed into a corner, ready to fight.

Millard advanced confidently on me. "You ain't got the guts to hit me, Gifford," he said. "George's the end of the trail, bud. Touch me with that once, and you're through."

"That's far enough, you sonofabitch," I said somewhat shrilly.

And Millard stopped, became momentarily confused, and then assumed his menacing scowl.

"Make any kind of face you want to, Millard," I said, "but try something funny and I'll beat your goddamn brains out."

Millard thought—a visible process—and then, leaning slightly forward, spittle jetting in a spray, shouted fiendishly, *"Give me that picture!"* An Old Army trick.

I was so startled that I almost hit him, probably would have if the great belching voice of Captain Grimes hadn't interrupted.

"What the hell's going on in here?" He stumbled through the door and flopped against the wall. Captain Grimes was very drunk. "What's all this yelling about a fuken picture? Sound like a bunch of goddamn schoolgirls."

I waited for Millard or Swanson to explain. Neither wanted to; they actually seemed embarrassed. Grimes glared drunkenly at them and then at me. For seconds, a decision, whether to hit me or one of the other two for not answering up promptly, was in the making.

Millard, wise enough to head the captain off, finally said, "He's got a picture we want to see."

"Christ on a crutch! A *picture!* That's all I been hearing all day long." He had only recently gotten out of bed and to his bottle. "A picture of *what?*"

"My wife, Waco," I said.

He stared stupidly at me for a moment. "*Wife?*" he said. "Oh, wife." He blinked slowly. And then: "*Wife?*" He glared at Millard and Swanson. "What the fuk you want to see the bastard's wife for? Ain't you two got enough on your minds without worrying about a man's *wife?*"

"Aw now, Waco, don't begin that again," Millard whined.

Grimes slapped him so hard that Millard would have fallen if Swanson hadn't caught him. Grimes himself did fall. He lost his balance and sprawled, with a heavy crash, at my feet. He looked up at me, somewhat foolishly, before he held his hand up for help. I lifted him to his feet. He was quite heavy.

Millard and Swanson began whining and imploring Grimes to "take it easy," advice he completely ignored.

"Gimme the picture," he said and held out his hand. "Don't argue, just gimme the damn picture." Then, as pathetic a figure as I have ever seen, he promised me: "I won't look at it."

I took the picture from my wallet and handed it to him. And he kept his promise. He turned it upside down, groped in his cargo pockets for his Zippo, applied the flame to the picture and let it burn, meanwhile glaring at the two whining bodyguards, until it scorched his fingers. Rocking gently, he watched it burn.

"You got a pretty wife, Gifford?" He silenced, temporarily, the whinings of the two guards with a roared: "*Goddamnit!*" The exertion made his face flush.

"I got a pretty wife," Grimes said. "The——"

"Aw, Waco——" Swanson began.

And Grimes swung on him, missed, and fell to the floor. I helped Grimes back to his feet, again aware of his weight.

"I got the prettiest little wife in Waco, Texas, Gifford, and I bet she's fuked more guys'n you'n count in a day. I know for a goddamn fact she's fuked more'n a hundred guys—including

26

some of my best friends—including that slick little sonofabitch right there." He pointed to Swanson.

"Aw, Waco——"

"SHUT UP!" Grimes roared. Grimes turned to me and started to say something, but instead, he mouthed, gestured, and left the room, growling, "Where's that goddamn mess-teaser?"

Swanson and Millard promptly decended upon me threateningly. After several "goddamn you's," Millard said, "You know what you done, don't you? Well goddamn you, you got'im started again and it'll take all night to get'im calmed down."

"He respects a man's wife," I said blindly.

"Shit!" Swanson said. "He ain't married. That's just what he starts when he's drunk. He just wants to get married, that's all. I fuked his girl once, but she was fuking everybody else on the post, so——"

"Shut up, Swanson," Millard said mildly. "You'n get'n your hole, Gifford."

It was only noon, but I left the room. And on my way through the house, I saw Grimes, his face in his hands, sitting on his foot locker. I think he was crying.

Walking across the yard, hunting for Willie, I was stopped by Millard's call.

"Gifford!"

I turned around. My duffle bag and combat pack sailed out of the window.

"Don't bother to come back, Gifford," Millard said. "We're tired of looking at your fuken face."

I picked up the pack and duffle and found my rifle, where I had left it, dirty with ashes now, leaning against the house.

5

"I thought for a while," Willie said, "that you'd took up with-
'em." And that was the only reference he would make to my stay
in the house. Nor did he have any comment to make about the
story I told him, except, "Any other outfit'd shoot an officer for
hitting an enlisted man."

I was assigned to the first platoon, which was the one
now guarding Grimes' perimeter, second squad, which was Willie's, although he was a private. The talk was that some time
soon, "ought to be any day," our platoon would exchange duties
with the third platoon, which was on outpost duty now. In the
meantime, beginning tomorrow morning, I would draw patrol.

Before I had a chance to brood on my cowardice, two
things happened that kept me occupied. The first one was the
reception I got. The sullenness of the first day, I was told, was
usual, for the entrance to the perimeter was next to Waco's
house and he didn't like to hear any kind of frivolity at all.
That afternoon, when I had settled down with Willie, who had
chosen me as his buddy, the men in the platoon gathered about
me and wanted to know about Manila, which I had seen not
long after the First Cavalry had liberated it and not long before
my court-martial. I enlarged somewhat upon my meager experiences in the city because the men were so fantastically eager
to hear about the women there. They were quite disappointed
when they discovered that I had sampled none of the fleshpots.
One of them, a big fellow with a friendly grin on his rather large
face, kidded me about being such a puritan. His name was
Johnson and, because there was something in his actions that indicated that he was accustomed to command, I presumed
that he was the platoon sergeant.

The second thing that kept me from brooding was the cigarette ration. The jeep brought the cigarettes in not long after
noon and, because we were short of them and had strict orders
not to smoke those in our K-rations, we gathered around the
house to wait for Millard or Swanson to pass them out. But Millard cursed us away. A few minutes later he got into the jeep

with most of the cigarettes and left the perimeter. Swanson distributed two packages to the man.

"Where're the rest of the cigarettes?" Johnson asked.

"Just never you mind, Johnson," Swanson said and smirked. "Just never you mind."

"To hell with that noise," Johnson insisted, "where're the rest of the cigarettes?"

Swanson paused and gave Johnson a curiously shaded, warning glance. "I wouldn't be talking out of turn if I——"

The belching voice of Captain Grimes interrupted from his window. "You heard'im, Johnson," Grimes said. "He told you never mind about the cigarettes."

Johnson shrugged—a defiant gesture, it seemed to me—but Grimes said nothing about it.

"Swanson," Grimes said, "you passed out what's left yet?" He was leaning against the window sill and Willie and I were probably the only ones in the yard, except Swanson, who knew he was drunk.

"Yeah, Waco," Swanson said.

"All right," Grimes said to us. "Get back out behind the house where you belong."

We withdrew and the men said nothing until they were safely out of earshot of the house and then they didn't really gripe; they muttered some among themselves, but the traditional army gripe was strangely missing.

As the day drew to a close we made preparations for closing the perimeter for the night. Millard returned, without the cigarettes, an hour before sundown. Nothing was said to him.

The wires for the powerphones, which were rolled onto drums during the day because the fragile stuff would part under the heavy boots we wore, were stretched from foxhole to foxhole. The men, following suggestions by Johnson, agreed who was to stand the first watch. Rifles were cleaned, clips were removed from bandoleers and roundabouts so they would be within easy reach during the night. The traverse of the machine guns was corrected to cover new lanes of fire we had established.

When the perimeter was closed and we were waiting for

29

darkness, Johnson came to my hole and sat on the edge of it with me.

"What'd they send you out for, Gifford?"

"I hit an officer in combat."

"Fist or did you shoot'im?"

"Rifle butt."

"You should've shot'im."

Amused by now at the sameness of the reactions I had gotten from everybody, I said, "That's a hell of a way for a platoon sergeant to be talking." I grinned at him. "You're supposed to tell me how wrong I was."

He chuckled and scratched the scab at the corner of his mouth. "Afraid I'm not qualified to speak as a platoon sergeant. I'm a goddamn second lieutenant."

"Jesus, I'm sorry, sir. I thought——"

"Cut it out, for christ's sake!" He gave me a dig in the ribs. "I'm really General Kruger, out acting like a second john so I can find out about George Company."

I laughed wryly. "Old General Kruger'd mow Miles and Grimes down to size if he knew about this." But before I could ask why Kruger didn't know about us, Johnson had to leave. Darkness was getting close.

And that night I had an opportunity to find out about my cowardice, for we were attacked.

My foxhole commanded a lane of fire which reached down a trail the men had used to go to the river for their baths. It was sometime after midnight and Willie was asleep when I heard the first sound that indicated there was somebody out there. The sound of rocks clicking together, which will carry far in the stillness of a tense night in a perimeter, gave the Japs away. They had swum the river and were making their way over the wide gravel bar below our *barrio*.

I was following my pattern, established during the first island campaign, in that I felt no numbing fear at the prospects of a fight. There was apprehension, of course, but it didn't paralyze me. I hissed softly into the powerphone.

"*Okay,*" came Johnson's voice promptly. "*What's up?*"

"This is Gifford," I said, "the new man. I heard somebody walking on the rocks down by the river."

There was a pause, during which I could hear the tightening breath of Johnson, before he said, *"Can't hear'em. How many does it sound like to you?"*

I listened intently and my ears, long accustomed to jungle noises, filtered out those that didn't belong. The Japs had cleared the gravel bar, however, and were moving up the trail toward us; now I could hear only a faint shuffle and that so dim and distant that I couldn't be sure of it.

"I can't tell now," I whispered. "They're this side of the rocks."

Calmly, from the bottom of the foxhole, Willie whispered, "Not more'n fifteen men."

"Willie says not more than fifteen," I said.

Even during such tension, it occurred to me that Willie's calmness was curiously savage, catlike.

There was another pause, and it was during this that I heard the breath of somebody else on the phone. There was Johnson's fast, steady breathing and there was that of somebody else, who was breathing wildly. Willie silently got to his feet and leveled his rifle down the trail.

"All right," Johnson said. *"Savage?"*

"Yeah, Little Joe."

"Sellers?"

"Okay."

"Crawl over to Gifford's hole with both machine guns." Johnson whistled sharply into the phone to attract the attention of the remainder of the perimeter. *"The rest of you guys, don't shoot. That's Sellers and Savage crawling around. Everybody get ready. They're coming up the trail from the river. Gifford'll be big brother when the shooting starts. Gifford?"*

"Yessir?"

"Do you think they know we're here?"

"I don't think so," I said. "They're coming along pretty fast."

"All right, Gifford, you take over," Johnson said. *"When you guys hear Gifford yell, start firing everything you got. I'll give*

31

you a flare to work by. Gifford, if I were you, I'd wait till they get pretty close."

"Yessir." Johnson was testing me.

The phone, except for the frantic breathing of whoever it was who was scared, fell silent. Savage and Sellers, neither of whom I had remembered from this afternoon's talk, were quiet enough. All over the perimeter there was a flurry of soft, hand-muffled clicks as rifle safeties were released. Willie didn't move.

The Japs were stumbling through the vines that littered the trail. Savage and Sellers were in position. Willie scratched his bottom. There was complete silence now. I held the phone to my ear in case Johnson had a command. His breathing and that of the stranger was all I could hear.

The Japs were closer now, no more than fifty yards away. They were talking, quietly, thinking they were in territory safe enough to permit their monkeylike chatter. I heard one of them stumble roughly on a vine and the others snickered. It amazed me, as it always had during the other jungle campaigns, how clearly sound will carry at night in such rank growth.

"*How close are they?*" Johnson said.

"Twenty-five yards," I whispered. "You got your flare ready?"

"*It's ready,*" Johnson said calmly.

My heart lurched slightly and I took a deep breath to make it beat steadily again.

"Twenty yards," I whispered.

Then I knew who the other man on the phone was, the one whose breathing I had heard. "*Fire,*" whispered Captain Grimes. "*Fire,*" he whispered frantically.

"*Shut up, Grimes,*" Johnson said, as sternly as a whisper would permit.

"*Gifford,*" the captain whispered fearfully, "*that's an order. Fire.*"

"*Get off the line, Captain,*" Johnson whispered. "*You're going to——*"

I put the phone down and picked up my rifle. I waited as long as I dared and then, without shouting, I said sharply:

"*Fire!*"

A split second before Savage and Sellers cut loose with their machine guns. I heard the flat pop of the mortar as Johnson dropped a flare shell into it. Before I fired my first round, I heard a high, strangely feminine scream from the direction of the house behind me, and then the fires of a thousand devils danced before my eyes as the machine guns, so close to my ears that they deafened me, blasted and spat at the column of Japs. Sellers and Savage fired a calm, even crossing fire, as if they were operating garden hoses instead of machine guns, and Willie was methodically pumping away with his rifle. I emptied my M-1 and had jammed another clip into it before the light came.

The flare, as it burst high overhead, threw the scene into a sudden, grotesque relief as its harsh, flat light fell upon us. The Jap column was revealed as a squirming huddle that had no faces recognizable as belonging to any particular bodies. In the midst of the wild tangle stood a Jap officer, a young, healthy-looking man, one of the few I had seen who didn't wear glasses, and in the one-dimensional glare of the flare burst, he looked starkly innocent, totally unlike the villainous Jap of the drawings in *Yank*. And he was in the act of throwing a grenade. Johnson had continued to dump flare shells into the mortar and now, with three-dimensional light, the young Jap officer's arm, cocked to throw the grenade, left shadows dancing on the writhing heap of men behind him. The streams of the tracers from the machine guns, busy crossing and recrossing the Japs, reached nearer the officer. It seemed that the tracers were moving altogether too slowly and I shouted wildly for them to cut the Jap down. The officer's arm was already into the act of throwing when the tracer stream from one of the machine guns reached him. The tracers disappeared into the Jap's body and emerged from his back and plunked into the twisting mass behind him, but the arm holding the grenade continued its seemingly slow arc of throwing. Then the tracers from the other machine gun struck him and the two streams converged at his chest and the arm dropped. The grenade fell at the Jap's feet and he crumpled and fell over it. I dodged instinctively, but the Jap officer's body smothered the explosion and no fragments reached me.

33

Johnson continued to send up flares and the machine guns hosed over the mound of men. Suddenly, from deep beneath the mound, there emerged a short, thin figure whose glasses were hanging from one ear. He ran wildly down the trail toward the river. The machine guns reached for him with such professional precision that it seemed impossible for him to escape, but the light of the flares was dancing in the leaves and vines of the jungle and the gunners couldn't see him well enough to kill him. He escaped, a wild, fleeting figure, into the shadows beyond our reach.

The machine guns stopped firing, leaving a silence so heavy it made my ears feel fuzzy inside. "Keep the flares going," I called across the perimeter to Johnson. "I'm going to see what we got."

Captain Grimes, I saw by the light of the flares, was peering over the edge of his foxhole. Even from this distance, I could see the whites of his eyes. Behind him, as pale as their captain, stood Millard and Swanson, tommy-guns cradled in their arms.

To the accompaniment of the rhythmic *thunk* of the mortar and the *splat* of the bursting flare shells, I waded into the stack of corpses, tugging and jerking at them as if they were sticks in a cord of stovewood. The Jap officer was a mess; the machine guns and his own grenade had done one of warfare's most notable jobs. As I disentangled the bodies, I discovered that each of them, except the officer, had died with his back to the guns, whether because of a submission to fate or from an attempt to retreat or from fear, I couldn't tell. It caused me to experience a sharp chill. Except for the noise of the mortar and flares, there was silence behind me.

I found two Japs who showed signs of life. Each I dispatched with a shot between the eyes. Both shots seemed terribly loud. Having satisfied myself that none of them was playing possum until he had an unchallenged opportunity to attack us, I returned to my foxhole and instructed Savage and Sellers to get busy. "Hose 'em down again," I said dispassionately. Experience had taught me that there is treachery in a Jap's last breath. The two gunners set about their chores with disinterested efficiency, firing until I waved for them to stop.

34

"That's it," I called to Johnson, who answered me with a short wave. The last flare popped, drifted down on its parachute and winked out immediately above the treetops. Groping about in the impenetrable blackness which followed the dead flare, I found my foxhole and sat on its edge.

I tried holding my breath, hoping that maybe it would stop what I knew was coming.

"Good job," Willie said.

The trembling began with what seemed a murmur in my heart and spread, evenly, the way whiskey does, until I shook violently all over, as if I were suffering from malarial chills. I slumped and hugged myself and writhed, but I couldn't stop it. Willie noticed that something was wrong when, unable to control the muscles of my jaws, my teeth began chattering.

"What's the matter?" he said.

"Nothing."

"What the hell you shaking for?"

I fell into the foxhole and huddled into one of its protective corners. "Oh jesus, Willie," I quavered. "Don't tell anybody about this."

He knelt by me. "I ain't going to, Sam. But what the hell's the matter?"

I moaned, deeply, without meaning to. "That's the way it happens." I took a deep breath. But I couldn't get enough air into my lungs. "It's almost as bad as it was before. . . . If that ever starts before the fight—I'm a goner."

"*Jesus!*" Willie said in awe. "Boy, Sam, you got it bad."

6

After daylight, when it was again reasonably safe to move about the perimeter, I heard the voice of Captain Grimes bellow for Johnson, who, busy directing the improvement of the lane of fire down the trail, frowned sourly and turned toward the house. Grimes was leaning out his window.

"Yes, Waco?"

"C'm'ere," Grimes ordered brusquely.

Willie, Sellers, Savage and I were digging graves for the eleven Japs we had killed last night. The bodies were beginning to smell, not rotten yet but with that first sweet bouquet of death, and we were hurrying because the sun, when it got hot, would quickly make the job unbearable. Johnson and Grimes could be heard talking. The belching voice was quarrelsome and irritating because Johnson, who was totally calm, was trying to give argument.

"Wonder what's ailing Captain Bly?" Sellers said dryly.

"D'you hear what Little Joe told'im last night?" Savage said.

"Yeah?"

"Well," Savage said, "you know what's ailing'im."

We continued to dig for a few moments. We could hear Grimes plainly when he raised his voice. The wind freshened and blew a cloud of gray dust from the ashes over us. We stopped to shield our eyes before we went back to work.

"Some of these days," Sellers announced, "somebody's going to catch Grimes out of reach of them two goons of his'n rip his belly wide open."

"Uh-hmmm," Willie grunted.

Sellers spat ashes from his mouth. "And I'm just the bird to do it, too." To prove this to me, he craftily turned his back to the house and extracted a long, slender commando knife from a sheath beneath his fatigue jacket. "I'n take this thing," he said tensely, "and shave the toughest whiskers in the Pacific. Wouldn't be no trouble at all letting air in Grimes' guts."

Willie, regarding Sellers with sleepy but amused eyes, bit a wad from his tobacco plug. "You been saying that for a long time, Sellers," Willie said around his cud. "When you going to get around to doing it?"

"I'll do'er," Sellers said seriously. "I'll do'er."

"Well," Savage said, the first word I remembered having heard him speak, "it's been tried before."

"Has it?" I was intensely interested. Many such stories had followed the First World War, but I had seen nothing of it in my years overseas. "What happened?"

Savage glanced at Sellers, then gestured with a nod of his head. "Let old Sellers tell you," he said with a certain affection. "He likes to talk."

Sellers, far from being insulted, immediately launched into the story.

"Guy's name was Shelby. Little guy, oh I'd say—five four or so—and he was always looking like he's about to break down and cry. I don't have no idea why he was sent to George Company, but anyhow he showed up around the beginning of the Leyte Campaign.

"Old Grimes used'im for orderly till the fighting got so hot Grimes got scared and moved his command post back a mile or so behind the main line, and he left Shelby with us. That was Grimes' big mistake, it turned out, because this little guy Shelby was one of them kind that's so religious—what you call'em's——"

"Conscientious objectors?" I said.

"Yeah, that's it," Sellers agreed. "Anyhow, maybe that's why he was sent to the Company. Anyhow, Bailey—Lieutenant Bailey—he got killed on patrol about a week or so ago—Bailey taken Shelby out on a patrol and Shelby screwed it up just good.

"Seems Bailey sent Shelby out to scout and when Shelby seen a bunch of Japs he never said a word—said later that he didn't want our boys to kill'em—and damn'f Bailey's platoon didn't walk right into them Japs and lose three men and four wounded.

"Well, if you'd a knowed Bailey, you'd know how he looked after his men so good, so this was something that he couldn't take. He got so mad I thought he was going to shoot old Shelby. Anyhow, he sent'im back to Grimes, but Grimes never said much about it, except a few of them cracks he makes about war being a good place to be killed. But somehow Cobb—that's the mail clerk—forgot and said something about it at Regimental when he went back to get our mail, so Miles found out about it and sent Grimes a radio message telling'im to put the screws to old Shelby.

"You know how it is, Miles brought Grimes into this outfit and all——"

I shook my head, but Sellers didn't pause to explain.

"——And Grimes never does nothing Miles wants in a half-

37

ass way. He put Shelby to digging a Triple-Six—" a hole which is six feet wide, six feet deep and six long—"right in the middle of the perimeter in that sun there on Leyte and you might know how hot that was. About every thirty minutes old Grimes'd come out and watch Shelby for a few minutes, then he'd cuss him for being one of them conscious objections. After a couple of days and old Shelby'd passed out three or four times from the heat, the hole finally got dug, mainly on account of a few of us sneaked around and done some digging at night.

"Old Grimes handed Shelby a Prince Albert can and told'im to put it square in the middle of the hole, and then he told Shelby to cover it up. Shelby got it done; it never took'im long to do that. Then Grimes come back out and got the whole platoon and made us stomp around till we had the dirt all packed down good and tight, then he got Shelby and told'im to find that P.A. can because there was a little message in it for him. Old Shelby went right to work.

"Dug all that day, with Grimes sitting around cussing'im and all, and Bailey and Johnson trying to talk the captain into letting Shelby take a rest. Not Grimes. Not that fuken bastard. He told Bailey and Johnson if they said one more word they'd rue the fuken day they'd ever saw Shelby. Hell, Bailey was the man who ought to be mad at Shelby, but he kept after Grimes till he got sent off on a patrol that was supposed to be suicide, but Bailey come back with not a man scratched. Grimes'll do that when he don't like a man—wants to get the man killed. Anyhow, Shelby kept digging.

"Finally Shelby got the P.A. can and Grimes told'im to open it. There was a note in it saying, 'You praying sonofabitch, put this can back in the hole and cover it up and dig it up again till I tell you to stop.'

"Shelby got to digging and Bailey and Johnson kept fussing at Grimes. And one day three or four snipers sneaked up close and started potting at us. Grimes sent Bailey to clean the snipers out and Bailey done it, but while he was doing it old Shelby come up to Grimes' hole and started saluting and yelling 'Captain Grimes' at'im, trying to show the snipers who the CO was so they'd pot'im.

"Bailey come back saying the snipers was all dead, so Grimes jumped out of his hole and beat the living shit out of Shelby. And that done it. That done it. Old Shelby crawled over to one of the machine guns and aimed it square at Grimes. He fired off a couple of rounds and knocked old Grimes' helmet off, but the gun jammed. Shelby didn't know how to clear it, so he jumped up and took out for Grimes with his trench knife.

"Well—from the looks of things, that was all for Grimes, 'cause he was so scared he just froze. But Bailey had missed a sniper and the bastard fired at Grimes just about that time and got Shelby right through the head, first time I ever seen a sniper hit anybody.

"Grimes wobbled back to his hole, taken a snort out of his bottle, run out to the jeep and taken off. Come back that afternoon with Millard and Swanson and told me'n Willie that we was busted. Millard and Swanson was taking our places. And ain't nobody got near Grimes since."

It wasn't an easy tale to believe, but Sellers had told it easily, without pause, as if sure of his facts, and Willie had nodded several times during its telling, so there was nothing for me to do but believe it.

"Does Colonel Miles know about it?"

"Hell man," Sellers said. "He *started* it!"

"What about General Hix?" I said.

Willie shook his head. "I don't much think he does. I talked to the General once. Seemed to be a pretty good guy."

"Yeah, but a full colonel in the U.S. Army——" I began.

All of them laughed at my naïveté.

"Miles knowed Grimes back in the Regular Army," Sellers explained, "when Grimes was a buck sergeant. Fact is, Miles commanded a fukup company in the Regulars and first thing he done when he took over the Regiment after Colonel Cozzens got killed was to make this a fukup company. That's the way they done it in the Regulars and Miles done'er that way with this outfit. Only, to Miles' way of thinking, anybody who's a National Guardsman is a fukup."

"Can't somebody talk to the Inspector General?"

"Nobody gets a chance," Sellers said. "When we're on the

line, Grimes, Cobb and the two goons is the only ones that ever gets to Regimental and Cobb's scared to death. When we're in garrison—well, everybody but George gets garrison, and we're out'n the woods somewheres digging ditches."

I nodded. But it was hard to believe. I had heard tales of George Company when I was still in Recon and they had been hard enough to believe then, but now . . . there was nothing here but the obvious truth. I keenly resented my old friends in Recon because they weren't believing the story and weren't taking it to MacArthur's Headquarters, where a sympathetic officer from the Inspector General's Department could hear it.

"*Gifford!*"

Willie spat at the sound of the voice.

"Jesus!" Sellers said. "Waco wants you!"

I dropped my shovel, grabbed my rifle and hurried to the house, ashamed of my frightened haste. Little Joe Johnson was leaning against the lister-bag tripod, staring at the ground. When Grimes saw my rifle at sling, he gestured and Millard and Swanson appeared at each side of him.

"Gifford, you was a real brave little soldier last night," Grimes said, "not obeying my orders like that. So I got a little reward for you. Instead of Johnson here, I'm sending you out for a little walk."

"You're doing the wrong thing, Waco," Johnson warned.

"Shut your fuken face, Johnson," Grimes said. "Gifford, I want you to take a little stroll up to Norzagaray. Nice day for it. Warm and balmly, like they used to say back in Honolulu."

I was scared, of course, but Grimes wasn't going to know it. "All right. What do you want to know about Norzagaray?"

"Let's see now"—he began, making a mock of pondering a serious problem—"I want to *know*—I want to know how many *whore* houses them Japs got up there." He grinned as Swanson and Millard laughed at his joke, although it was obvious to me that their laughter was forced beyond the mirth they actually felt.

Johnson looked sick. He had been picking at the fungus scab at the corner of his mouth and now, without a word, he took a piece of the scab from his face, which was left bleeding, and flipped it toward Grimes, who pretended not to have seen it. Johnson walked away.

And I will swear before my Maker that Grimes was suffering from injured feelings at the sight of Johnson's anger-squared shoulders.

"Another thing," Grimes said, recovering, "don't get the idea that you're going to hide behind a hill till this afternoon and come back with a lie about scouting the place either. I'm going to get the outposts to report on you every fifteen minutes. So when they can't see you—you better be damn sure you got a good excuse."

"How many men do I take with me?" I said.

"I told you once," he shouted in the manner of the old Regular sergeant, "you're taking Johnson's patrol." With that, looking for all the world as if he should have been wearing the five stripes and diamond of the prewar first sergeant instead of the two silver bars his rank entitled him to wear now, Captain Grimes turned and disappeared. Millard and Swanson stood at the window, their tommy-guns in hand, and stared sullenly at me until I turned to leave.

I found Johnson sitting, disgust showing in his very posture, on the shadow bank of his foxhole. He had applied a band aid to the corner of his mouth. He was idly crumbling clods of dirt and dropping the dust into his foxhole.

"Looks like you're stuck with it," he muttered. "He'll have the outposts reporting on you."

"It's all right," I said. "I'll do it."

"What do you mean, it's all right?" he flared at me violently. "It isn't all right. The whole goddamn thing stinks to high heaven." He stopped and wiped his hand across his mouth, flinching with the pain of touching the sore. "What was the matter with you last night after the shooting was over? I couldn't get Willie to tell me anything about it. What was it?"

"Nothing much."

"How much?"

"I get the shakes, that's all."

"After the storm's over, huh?"

"That's right."

He studied my eyes and then, with a quick glance, looked at my hands to see if they were trembling. "All right," he said. "I'll get your men." He stood up. "Willie, Sellers, Savage, Morgan and Terry. Rifles, extra ammo, no pack."

We waited, silently, while the men gathered around us. "All right, boys. Waco got his dander up about Sam last night and's sending'im to Norzagaray with the outposts reporting. Sam's big brother. He's got the word from now on."

They glanced uneasily at each other. Willie paused a lick in his chewing.

"Rifles, roundabouts, two extra bandoleers," I said. "And each man draw two grenades. Tape them to your suspenders." As they shuffled off, I called after Willie: "Bring me a couple of grenades, will you, Willie?"

Willie wagged his hand, in acknowledgment, without looking back.

"You won't have any trouble," Johnson said. "They're the best men I got. But watch Terry. He likes this crap and sometimes he'll start a fire fight just for fun."

"All right."

"I saw Norzagaray about a week ago. I figured there must have been about three hundred Japs bivouaced in the place."

"What kind of place is it?"

"*Nepa* huts, big church. No Filipinos; Japs ran'em all out."

"How far is it?"

He took a map from his jacket pocket and drew a rough line. "This way, six miles. That's the safest route." He handed me the map. "Don't lose that. It's the only one I got."

"Why don't they blast the Japs out with artillery?"

"It doesn't show up very high, but there's a pretty big hill right in front of it. Artillery can't hit'em."

The others came back with their grenades. I taped the grenades Willie had brought to my suspenders and, as thoroughly as possible, cleaned the ashes out of the action of my M-1. We were ready. Two of the men carried BAR's. One was Sellers, who handled the heavy weapon as if he had grown to manhood with it in his arms. The other was Morgan, a short, dark little man who was already sweating profusely.

Captain Grimes watched from his window as we filed past the house. His mouth, as he gave me that look of his, was distorted into a grimace of mirth. He was the first officer who had ever sent me out on a patrol without wishing me luck.

As we cleared the perimeter, I heard Grimes shout: "All right now, Little Joe Johnson, if you'll just step up here, I'd like to have a few words with you." The belching voice had spectacular carrying qualities.

The sun was brassy and hot, and it seemed closer to us than it was supposed to be. Our fatigue jackets were dark with sweat before we had covered the first hundred yards. These uniforms couldn't have been designed with tropical warfare in mind. And, I thought ruefully, my nerves hadn't been designed with warfare of any sort in mind. If we got into a position that would make it necessary to mix it up with the Japs, I knew what would happen, for it had happened last night. And the question remained: How long could I survive such attacks?

We each carried two canteens of water and Sellers had already started drinking from his. I had to warn him, but he took it gracefully enough.

I set a slow pace, as much to conserve energy as from fear. The hills beyond our outposts were already in sight and the road we were on seemed pleasant and safe. The hills, a sight that would make a tourist's heart race with ecstacy, were blue and blanketed by a fragile mist. My mind, however, busy trying to figure the angles as befits an almost professional soldier, was occupied with finding a pass that would let me and my men in and out without bloodshed.

We reached the burnt, blasted town of Angat, deserted now except for a carabao who was headed for the healing haven of the river, where his hide would find the water necessary to keep it from cracking from the sun; there we halted in the shade of the half-burned school building for a rest and a smoke.

The behavior of the men, in contrast to my own, was noticeably more cheerful, I suppose because they were out of earshot of the belching voice. Sellers and Terry, the two talkative ones, were exchanging jokes, most of which concerned the female sex organ. Savage and Morgan were both glum and quiet.

Willie and I were finding out how many mutual acquaintances we had. Willie twice said, "Mr. Gifford calls me by name when he sees me."

Norzagaray, according to the map, was huddled at the base of the artillery-proof hill and faced across a rather narrow valley, which was bounded by a smaller hill. I planned to circle the town and try to observe it from the hill across the rice paddies in the valley, a plan which Willie agreed was the only sensible one.

"Oh hell," Willie whispered, a protest against the intense heat.

I rested, smoked and thought about the patrol. It was impossible for me to figure how many I had gone on before this one, but it was important that I do this one right because I had to show the other men in my platoon that I could carry my share of the load. Several of them had come overseas with the Regiment at the same time I had and were as close to exhaustion as I was, so none of us, if we were to ever get home, could give less than his maximum effort. But, I brooded, how can a man give himself so freely when he is so exhausted by fear?

The men had followed me, so far, as readily as a comparative stranger could expect. I had dropped back into leading a patrol with almost as much ease as I had known during the early days of the war.

Willie, with as much enthusiasm as I had ever seen him display, said, "Boys, won't be long: outpost duty."

They all nodded and, thinking about it, their eyes looked far away, almost with the same dreamy glaze a man shows when he's thinking of the last woman he had, so long ago. The ashes and dust of the George perimeter—and Captain Grimes—and "the two goons"—seemed far away now and I quickly nodded when Sellers said:

"Hey, Gifford, how about making this an all-day patrol? It's right peaceful out here."

The next leg of the patrol wouldn't be so easy as it had been so far, for we would have to make our way through the trees that stood between the rice paddies and the jungle. I thought wryly of the pride the Filipinos showed when they said

44

there was very little jungle on this island. Maybe, in comparison with those tangled masses on the southern islands, and on Leyte, these weren't jungles, but they were thick enough to make a man fight his way through them.

The shortest route would be directly across the paddies, a saving of some three miles of walking, but such open country would bring observation and make it almost a certainty that the Japs would figure out our route and stage an ambush. And the Japs were quite skilled at the ambuscade. Often, during the early days of the war, before we learned the refinements of the profession, they would wait for days until a guard at a water point or a command post or an aid station fell asleep; then they would pounce. Well, to hell with you, I thought, you little monkeylike bastards; if you get me, you're going to have to pay for it with brainwork. Sam Cifford has hopes of outlasting this war if exhaustion doesn't overtake him—and he's not going to take a single unthought-out step.

A soft wind blew through the trees, which swished and whispered with movement, making us slightly more nervous than was necessary, but we traveled thirty minutes at a steady pace. I kept twenty-five yards ahead of the others and Willie, who followed me, kept trying to close the gap until I told him to keep his distance because I wanted to scout ahead with as little distracting noise as possible. Willie nodded tractably and passed the word back. Once, when I heard a sound I couldn't identify, I squatted and the others immediately rested on their haunches, without question, and peered tensely at me until I gave them the sign that all was well.

At the next halt I held up a cigarette and shook my head. Willie passed back a no-smoking order. Then I made a gesture of zipping up my mouth and Willie passed back a no-talking order. I was tremendously pleased that they had by no sign questioned my leadership. It made me remember the days when the first island campaign began, when we were still motivated by patriotism and respect for our officers, before Colonel Cozzens died.

The rest halt was a short one because we couldn't talk and we were too close to the Japs to want to kill time. The loafing would have to come later and in a safer place. As we came to the place where the rice paddies meet the hills, I stepped into the open long enough for the men on outpost to identify us. I didn't want to do it, because the Japs could have seen me too, but at the same time it was very important that Grimes know that I wasn't going to take anything from him. When I heard the shave-and-a-haircut signal from an outpost machine gun, I stepped back into the forest, satisfied that Grimes would get the report of our whereabouts.

I took an old, dim trail that wound in the general direction of Norzagaray and hoped that no Jap patrol would also think it was safe because it had obviously carried no war traffic. Nothing chilled my heart more than the thoughts of meeting, face to face, an enemy patrol. It had happened to me once, during the first island campaign, and I had been decorated for getting out of it alive, but the army could keep its medals.

Off to the south, only a few feet above the treetops, a flight of the new A-26's roared, strafing. They were two miles away, but in the stillness of the forest their motors, as they pulled out of their dives, were thundering loud. I considered halting my patrol until the planes were gone, but I decided that waiting them out was too dangerous; the Japs could have easily seen me when I stepped into the rice paddy a while ago.

So far, I thought, so good. The patrol had been so uneventful that it was almost like those absurd days in Texas when we had practiced scouting and patrolling on imaginary enemies. But the planes were making a terrible racket. And they almost caused me to lead the patrol into what I feared most, another patrol coming from the opposite direction. It was a faint noise; I wasn't even sure I had heard it. It seemed so much a part of the strafing planes. I quickly signaled my patrol off the trail and into hiding.

A Jap patrol of eight men, five wearing glasses, filed sedately past. They were silent but relaxed. The plump, moon-faced sergeant who was leading the patrol was actually smoking one of those little cigars the Filipinos make. For a moment I experienced a sharp, smothering in my chest, but the Japs were so unaware of any danger that I became easy again. I even pondered on what kind of people it is who will feed their officers and non-coms so well when the privates are so obviously hungry.

The Japs were no more than twenty feet from us and when the plump sergeant turned to spit I was certain he looked me directly in the eye, but he ambled, bandy-legged, on down the trail at the head of his men. I lay perfectly still, as much to make myself remain calm as to insure extra safety, until the Japs were a hundred yards away. I heard the Jap sergeant's saber bang against a tree and knew that was the noise I had heard before. Thank the good Lord, I thought, for small sabers; I almost giggled at my own wit.

I rose and motioned the men forward. They followed; I saw when I glanced back at them that they didn't try to bunch up the way recruits would have done. This, I decided, was a very professional patrol.

We reached the hill which overlooks Norzagaray when the sun was directly overhead. Sitting a few yards apart, we quietly ate our K-rations while I tried to find some signs of life in the little *barrio*. I watched until my eyes began to have the bulging feeling that comes with looking through binoculars too long. I finished the potted meat in my K-ration before I beckoned for Willie, who crawled silently to my side and waited.

"It looks deserted to me," I whispered and handed him the glasses. "See what you think."

Willie looked for a long time before he handed over the binoculars. He was obviously puzzled. "I came up here with Little Joe the other day," Willie said, "and that town was loaded with Japs." He ran his tongue between his lips and teeth. "They could be hiding out for an ambush. Or they could be clean gone." He hunched up to crawl away, but I stopped him. He waited.

I looked the place over carefully, not missing a hut. I studied the steeple of the church. The town was entirely innocent of any movement.

"Willie," I whispered, "we ought to look that *barrio* over, we ought to go right on in and find out what's up. Those Japs didn't pull out—if they pulled out—just for the hell of it."

Willie shrugged to show that it didn't matter to him; he was with me, ready to go. While I pondered, he picked his nose and said nothing.

"Tell the rest of them: we'll circle around the paddy and look it over." This, Captain Grimes, was going to be more than you bargained for.

Willie crawled from man to man, whispering shortly to each of them, and they in turn nodded to show me that they understood. Only Savage, in his peculiarly stolid way, gave a look which betrayed any alarm at all. Sellers simply glanced up shortly from his work; he was cleaning the BAR. Terry was more than ready; he was eager to get started.

They followed me, as good a group of men as could be found in the Pacific. And, I remembered, they were probably as near exhaustion as I was. I kept to the woods until we had walked an hour. I gave them a short rest and we were off again. At the end of thirty minutes of easy going, we were getting caution close to Norzagaray. The trees and undergrowth were not so thick here, sign that the Filipinos had thinned the woods out for materials to build their *nepa* huts. I signaled for the patrol to stop.

I listened for perhaps ten minutes, but I heard only the wind. The planes were gone. The church, a mass of gray stone that was similar to the churches the Spaniards built in early California history, loomed up squarely at the other end of the *barrio*. I beckoned Willie forward and signaled the others to wait. Willie and I crept forward. With a few minutes of stealthy winding among the bushes, we were in a position where I could see down the street that ran between the huts.

Norzagaray was indeed deserted.

I waited while Willie went back after the other men, and studied the huts. But I saw nothing, heard nothing.

Conditioned by the habits of war, I instructed the men to remain silent and we crept from hut to hut, trusting no shadow, fearing the sounds of the wind, until we reached the church, which, because it stood on a slight knoll, commanded a view of the *barrio*.

And it was in the church that we found the first sign of the Japs. Their headquarters had probably been here, for there were a few scattered bits of paper, which I carefully gathered and stuffed into one of my cargo pockets; the interpreters at Regimental Headquarters could possibly be interested in them. Further sign of the Japs was found in front of the altar: spaced in a perfect semicircle were several turds, dry and unsmelling now, a gesture I had come to know as typical of the Japs.

Morgan silently handed me two metal objects which were held together by a plastic neck chain and the others crowded around, for these were identification discs, dog tags. "Ralph M. Bailey, Protestant, Blood Type B, Serial Number 0-999224," I whispered.

"Lieutenant Bailey," Sellers whispered.

"How come they got here?" I said. "Didn't they take them off the body when he got killed?"

"They forgot it," Willie said. "They was pretty scared, I guess."

We stared at each other in wonder, for Willie went on to explain that Bailey had been killed—and buried—several miles away. The Japs must have been frantic for information to exhume a body in hopes of finding papers or code maps on it. The questions of the intelligence officers at RCT would be two: Why had the Japs evacuated Norzagaray when no effort had been made to dislodge them? And: Why were they so hungry for information that they should go to the trouble to dig up a body when they know that one of the primary rules of modern warfare dictates that no man is to go on patrol carrying information that might aid the enemy? It seemed possible to me that they were planning some kind of attack—a last, suicidal charge—before acknowledging that the war on Luzon was over.

"Let's go," I whispered.

We hurried past the silent rows of huts until we reached the crude road that had, during peacetime, connected the *barrio* with the outside world. There was a sign on the road that identified this as Norzagaray. Using my trench knife as a screwdriver, I removed the sign from its post and dropped it into a cargo pocket. I wasn't entirely happy about the sign, for it was a gesture, a childish one, directed at Grimes for sending us on what he supposed was an impossible mission.

7

Captain Grimes, when he was finally convinced that I had actually entered the *barrio* where, less than a week ago, Little Joe Johnson had reported a heavy concentration of Japs, was disappointed. He categorically called me a liar and said the man who claimed to have found his way to Norzagaray by means of a back trail, and without having been spotted by a Jap observation post, was a liar, that no such trail existed on any military maps of the sector.

"Maybe not, Waco," I said, "but I found it."

"If there's a trail, it'd show on the map. These maps was made by Regulars. I think you're lying. I think you ain't got the guts to go that far behind the Jap lines."

"I went to Norzagaray," I said, as emphatically as I could without being insubordinate.

"And I still call you a liar." Everybody in the perimeter could hear him. "You're so goddamn smart, why——"

I tossed Bailey's dog tags to him and I was dismayed to see the captain instinctively dodge away with alarm. Millard and Swanson, standing at each side of him, also dodged and Millard snarled like a cur before any of the three realized that they had been threatened by nothing more dangerous than two quarter-ounce dog tags. Millard was mad and his eyes glistened, but both Grimes and Swanson looked sheepish.

Grimes regained his composure and examined the dog tags. Although the discs didn't prove that I had taken a patrol to Norzagaray, they did show that I had been somewhere beyond the section of George Company's normal operations, for Lieutenant Bailey had been killed and buried at a place ordinarily called "behind the Jap lines." Continuing to hold the dog tags aloft, Grimes suddenly grinned broadly.

"They dug the bastard up!" he said in loud awe.

"Probably looking for information," Johnson said.

"Horseshit," muttered Captain Grimes.

"Any Jap officer would make a wild grab for information," Johnson said, carefully measuring his words for maximum sarcasm, "just before an attack."

It was lost on Grimes, who pretended that he hadn't heard. But it was somehow obvious—possibly by a stiffening at the corners of his mouth—that Johnson's comments meant more to Grimes than he wanted known.

"That still don't prove you went to Norzagaray," Grimes belched and tossed the dog tags back to me.

I removed the road sign from my cargo pocket and held it up for Grimes to read. The satisfaction he had got from baiting me was suddenly gone. His round face showed chagrin and both Millard and Swanson stirred uneasily.

"All right," Grimes said loudly, "all right, you've been to Norzagaray!" He gave Johnson an uneasy glance and added: "That don't prove nothing."

"It proves something to me," Johnson said.

"What?" Grimes said stupidly. Then, toughly: "Just *what?*"

"If Gifford could get in easy enough to get that sign without getting anybody killed," Johnson said quietly, "then the place is deserted. And the Japs don't pull back unless they got something else better in mind."

"Zat so?"

"Yes, it is and you know——"

"Shut up, Johnson," Grimes said. He paused and looked searchingly at Johnson. "All right, *all right,*" he said, although nobody tried to interrupt, "make the fuken report on paper. Maybe I'll send it to Regimental or maybe I won't. All according to how I feel when I get it." He retired into the mystery of his house.

"It appears to me," Johnson said as we retreated to the privacy of our foxholes, "that the U.S. Army has failed to learn one of the basic functions of its existence—how to handle men.

51

It's had more than enough practice, but it's failed to learn that one little item of psychology called leadership."

"This used to be a good regiment," I said.

"Sure it did," Johnson said. "I thought I was the luckiest infantry officer in the Pacific when I was sent to this outfit. These boys—or the boys we had then—they were right down my alley, just a bunch of simple civilians playing soldier. And damn if most of them didn't feel just about as silly as they would if they had been caught playing with kids." He grinned wryly. "They were smart. They knew it was a game that only idiots play in peacetime." He shook his head in disgust. "But damn if it isn't the peacetime idiots that take over when the wars begin. I wish there was some good smart way of getting around that little practice, but—oh hell." We sat down by his foxhole. "The worst thing that ever happened to this outfit was when——"

"Was when Colonel Cozzens got killed."

"That's right!" Johnson was red with anger. "And Colonel Miles comes along with his crowd of Regular Army goons. So—so we're not a civilian regiment any longer." Johnson snorted angrily. "Turned a bunch of fuken fascists loose on us." He seethed for a moment before he suddenly grinned. "I'm pretty good at popping off, huh?"

"Not bad."

"Well, anyhow," Johnson said, "I don't want to sound like a brass-hat snob, but——"

Willie interrupted by sitting down beside us.

"I don't want to sound like a brass-hat snob," Johnson repeated, "but you guys being enlisted men couldn't get to know Colonel Cozzens as well as I could. He was the finest man I've ever known. He's the kind of man I always wanted my own father to be. And when he got killed, I felt just about the same as I'd've felt if somebody in my own family had died."

I cleared my throat. "I know what you mean," I said and had to clear my throat again. "He was my father-in-law."

Johnson and Willie were stunned. Willie turned his head away and pretended to clear the stale tobacco from his mouth. Johnson peered into the ground with embarrassment.

"Jesus, Sam," Johnson murmured. "I didn't know that. Me and my big mouth. . . ." He fell silent.

And the loneliness and violence of three years away from my peacetime home, Jenny, Poppa, Momma, Bill Joe and Colonel Cozzens (his promotion to general would never become a part of the character he had left in Gray's Landing)—all of it caught up with me at once. Tears welled up in my eyes and I scrambled to my feet and hurried to the privacy of my own foxhole. There I could remember Gray's Landing—and my people—as I saw them in my dreams that night. They weren't quite as they actually had been, for the army had given me so much bitterness that I could remember only the sweetness of those misty days in Gray's Landing.

Book II

The Young and Sturdy Dreamers

1

It was spring and 1936. Hitler was a big talker and a small doer. And it hadn't been so long ago that the world had been made safe for democracy.

"Boy, Sam," Bill Joe said with disgust, "you ought to be glad that you don't have a sister." He glared at Jenny, who sat between us in the cab of the pickup truck. "What'd *you* have to come along for?"

Jenny, her braces showing when she opened her mouth, replied innocently, "Because I wanted to go swimming too."

"Then why in the hell didn't you go to the *Park?* They got a pool there too, you know."

Jenny nodded. "I know it."

"Then why'd you make Mother tell me I had to take you with us?"

"I don't like to go to the Park." Her eyes were getting slightly damp.

I studiously examined the rows of new cotton that fluttered past.

"*Why?*" Bill Joe fumed.

She didn't answer.

"Answer me," Bill Joe insisted, "*why?*"

And in a small voice, she did answer: "The boys make fun of me."

And that stopped Bill Joe. He was still mad, because we had hidden a case of cold beer near the Creek this morning and

Bill Joe swore that Jenny would tell if she found out about it. What had started as a magnificent intrigue was now a family brawl. Since early this morning we had been talking about the beer, the first we had had in any quantity, and now, as Bill Joe had said earlier, "that snaggle-toothed little devil was going to ruin the whole thing."

We drove deeper into the Bottom. The cotton was planted two months ago and it was beginning to make a good show now. The sprouts were very green and they looked tender enough to eat. A mile ahead the levee could be seen: a hunched snake, green with grass, that followed the lazy course of the River. The sun was warm, comfortably warm, for we had had a harsh winter and spring had been a little late this year. It was only now, late in May, that the Creek had become warm enough to swim in, and I suspected that we would spend more time basking in the sun than we would in the water.

Bill Joe, who was driving, hit a rut and Jenny bounced against me, where she stayed a little longer than was necessary. If, I thought, she would get rid of those steel-rimmed glasses and hurry up and make those braces straighten her teeth, she might be pretty. Her body was beautiful, even during this her awkward fifteenth year. I felt guilty and lascivious for thinking about her body; after all, she *was* two years younger than I.

"You didn't care if I came along, did you, Sam?" she asked me.

Before I could answer, Bill Joe shook his head.

"No," Jenny said, "don't look at Billy Joe. You didn't care, did you?"

"Well," I began, not wanting to hurt her, "maybe you'd've had more fun at the Park."

"I told you once," Jenny cried, "the boys make fun of me."

"I don't know why they'd want to do that."

"*I* do," Bill Joe said.

Jenny shook her head. "Billy Joe!"

"Damnit, my name is *Bill* Joe!"

"I'm sorry."

"I guess you're going to tell on me for cussing too!"

"No, I'm not."

"You'd better not."

"I won't."

We turned off the county road and took the field road that led across the fields of cotton. This was Poppa's land, someday mine, and I looked at it with a vaguely proprietary interest. But I wouldn't own it for a long, long time. Poppa was forty-seven and . . .

We drove past the pine thicket and Bill Joe stopped the pickup at the bank of the Creek. It was probably the most beautiful spot in our state. A small waterfall emptied into a pool, which was surrounded by the abiding pines. On the surface of the pool there floated a few pine cones.

"Okay," Bill Joe growled. "Jenny, you dress here and me and Sam'll dress in the thicket."

"Sam and I," corrected Jenny.

But Bill Joe wasn't going to be angered by the correction: our beer was in the thicket.

"Come on, Sam," Bill Joe said. "You'n be getting the picnic out," he said to Jenny. "And don't take that potato salad out of the ice!"

"Billy Joe," she called after us, "I'm not dumb."

Out of earshot, Bill Joe growled, "Like hell she isn't."

"You oughten pick on her like that," I said.

"She deserves all she gets and more."

We walked through the pines until we reached the hole we had labored over early this morning. Our beer was there in a number three wash tub.

"All my life I've been wanting to get drunk, just to see what it's like," Bill Joe said, "and damn'f *she* doesn't have to tag along."

I began unbuttoning my shirt. "I bet Jenny wouldn't tell anybody if we drank some of it."

"I bet she *would!* All she wants to do is tell on me."

"When'd she ever tell on you?"

"Why . . ." He couldn't remember. "Many a time," he said stoutly, "many a time."

I hunkered down so Jenny wouldn't see. "I'm going to drink one."

59

"She'll *tell*, I'm telling you! She'll *tell!*"

"She won't smell it."

I drank it. And Bill Joe took it as a dare. "But don't let her smell your breath."

We gulped it down—which, we were later to learn, was our most foolish act of the afternoon—and scrambled out of our clothes and into our swimming trunks. I was feeling dizzy and silly before we reached the pool.

Jenny was sitting on the huge, brown rock that slants into the pool. Fevered by the beer, my breath was almost taken away, for Jenny's body was nothing less than spectacular. I stopped abruptly and stared. Still gawky with adolescence, she was nevertheless beautiful. She sat sedately on the rock, legs tightly together, her hands cupped, with what she hoped was casual grace, over her lap.

She feels, I thought, like she's naked. And indeed, the bathing suit she wore fit too tightly. Mrs. Cozzens had forgotten to warn her daughter that she had grown during the winter until the suit was disgraceful.

"Come on," Bill Joe said.

And then he too stopped. "Sisto!"

"Now Billy Joe——" she began, and only then I noticed that she was wearing lipstick.

"Take it off," Bill Joe said roughly.

"I won't do it."

"The hell you won't," he said and rushed her.

She dived into the pool and easily outdistanced him in the water. She was shouting and blowing with the cold water, but she had no trouble outswimming him. She would have got away —to go where, I have no idea—if I hadn't intercepted her at the other bank. I held her, young and rigid, while Bill Joe rubbed roughly at her lips with his thumb.

It was then that the beer caught up with us. We belched almost at the same time. And Jenny jerked free.

"Y'all've been drinking!"

Without acknowledging Jenny, Bill Joe turned on me, his tough young face crumpled into a frown of anger. "See!" he shouted. "I *told* you she'd smell it." Then he whirled on his sister. "I guess you're going to tell."

"No," Jenny said pertly and ran to the truck, where she had hidden her lipstick. She applied a generous coating to her lips. I went back into the pine thicket and dragged the tub of ice and beer into the open.

"And that isn't all," Jenny said archly. "I'm going to drink some beer too."

"Nope," Bill Joe said bluntly. "Nope, no beer."

"Then I'll tell."

Bill Joe was shaken. Colonel Cozzens had never spanked his children, no more than Poppa had me, but the Colonel's gentle face, when drawn into a stern frown, was enough to chill even the most daring of seventeen-year-old boys. And not even Bill Joe had the nerve to incur that frown.

"All right," Bill Joe said grudgingly, "but I don't like threatening."

Jenny reached for a bottle of beer. I took her wrist.

"I'd rather get told on," I said.

She immediately let go of the bottle and, without a word, walked away and sat on the rock that slanted into the pool. Her back was straight and her shoulders were square and held back.

Bill Joe, his normal humor restored, said, "I know somebody that's got a C-R-U-S-H on you, Sam."

She stopped behind him and deliberately hit him with every atom of her strength. I should have warned him, but I was so embarrassed and startled by her sudden fury that it didn't occur to me. Bill Joe toppled over and, hysterical with laughter, shouted:

"That ain't all, Sam!" He dodged Jenny's flying foot. "She claims you're the man she's going to *marry!*"

He yelped with pain when Jenny's bare foot caught him in the ribs. And Jenny, her foot hurting, ran back to the slanting rock and sat down. Bill Joe, still gurgling with laughter, crawled to his feet and opened another bottle of beer.

From her slanted rock, Jenny said:

"Sam Gifford, I hope you die before morning!"

61

2

During the spring the oaks on our lawn were unbelievably green and strong. Their massive boughs drooped languidly over the slate roof of the house where I was born and where four generations of Grays and Giffords had been born before me. Poppa's mother had been a Gray.

Gray's Landing is the town, population 8,097, founded in 1818 by my great-great-great-grandfather, an adventurer whose adventures with the laws of Georgia had caused him to come off short for the first and only time in his life. First he went to central Louisiana, where he didn't like the malaria, and then to Texas, where he didn't like the wind, and then to New Orleans, where he acquired a "wanted" status for the second time—and a wife, Rene.

There is a legend that Cobb Gray said: "If I keep on having trouble with the law, there's only one thing I can do: I'm going somewhere and that's going to be where a man can make his own law."

And he did. He fled to Baton Rouge with his new wife and there he stayed until he managed—somehow—to buy a wagon and four mules. And he started north. He didn't stop until he had followed the Mississippi to the place where it is joined by the Arkansas. He followed the Arkansas almost three hundred miles until he found the Bottom where our farm is now.

"Rene, see that big flat of land on yonder side of the stream?" Cobb pointed to the Bottomlands on the north side of the river. "Floods won't reach that none too easy, Rene. And that's where we're going to live."

But he was wrong about the floods. He planted pines from Hogback Ridge around the pool with the slanted rock and built his cabin, vowing that a mansion would be built like the one he had lived in before his collision with Georgia's laws. But the flood got him. For four years the water came up with the spring and stopped, and on the fifth year Cobb Gray managed to get his wife and four children out of the Bottom minutes ahead of the highest flood the valley had known.

He built another place to live, the "mansion" he had spoken of, far away from the cruel river. And that was the house I lived in.

3

There is no pleasure quite so keen as that of loafing at the gin during the spring. There is the smell of last season's rotted lint, like the penetrating scent of recently dusty pavement cooled by a fresh rain; the rancid grease in a thousand gears; and the dry, foreign smell of the jute bagging. And in Poppa's office there is the smell of bookkeeper's ink; of tobacco; of Poppa's Dickens and Thackeray volumes which fill the bookcase against the wall; and there is Poppa's own smell, soap and shaving lotion.

Living was a heady experience this morning. My new manhood was accepted, symbolized by Poppa's careful explanation of everything he did around the gin. It was such a grand experience that I almost forgot the headache yesterday afternoon's beer had left me with.

Poppa was a deliberate man. All of his actions, the way he talked, walked, smiled and studied me with his cool blue eyes, were slow. But somehow, he made things work fast at the gin. I was enough like him when I was a boy that I was "Little Felix." But there was some of Momma's nervousness in me too and the nickname was dropped before I finished high school.

"Got a headache, Son?" Poppa's deep, gentle voice always sounded deeper and gentler when he was in the gin.

"Yessir."

"Seldom a man wakes up with a headache."

My face warmed. He knew; he always knew; there was nothing Poppa didn't know or couldn't find out about me. He saw through me as easily as if my soul were under glass—and he still loved me.

"Yessir."

"Something you ate," Poppa said. He was busy with some machinery orders and it sounded for all the world that he was making idle conversation, but Poppa knew about the beer. Poppa always knew.

I sat in the big, comfortable chair behind Poppa's desk. The gin office wasn't very large. There was room enough for his big, roll-top mahogany desk (Poppa got a good licking from Grandaddy Gifford for carving his initials on its surface when he was a boy), "the girl's" desk (she didn't work today—Saturday), and the two-shelf bookcase that held Poppa's Dickens and Thackeray.

The Dickens and Thackeray were the subjects of long, friendly arguments between Poppa and Colonel Cozzens. Both had long ago expressed their opinions on each writer and their arguments were difficult to follow. One was likely to remember something the other had said years ago and bring it into the argument as if it had been uttered only a moment before.

"Now Julian"—Poppa was the only one in town who still called Colonel Cozzens by his given name—"you know as well as you know your own name that Dickens was not a comic writer. He wrote for one reason: to right wrongs. . . ."

Those books gathered dust sometimes, for often Poppa would go through a phase during which he read nothing but the *Gazette*. But he always came back to the two Victorians. "A man gets hungry for some real reading," he would say.

I glanced over at the bookcase. Thackeray I could take and like; Dickens I left alone. Poppa had been a poor teacher with Dickens, but he had done excellently with——

"Hey!" Bill Joe said tiredly as he opened the door. He dragged himself across the room and seated himself on Poppa's desk.

"You have a headache too, Bill Joe?" Poppa inquired casually.

But Bill Joe wasn't embarrassed. His tough, young face showed no guilt at all. "Musta been something I et, like the man said."

"Must've been," Poppa murmured. He went back to his work.

64

Bill Joe sneaked me a questioning look and I nodded. "Jenny!" Bill Joe mouthed silently. I shook my head.

"Must be a very interesting conversation," Poppa said. "Only the young have important secrets."

"I'm sorry, Poppa."

"Me too, Mister Felix. We were just cutting up."

Colonel Cozzens entered, first poking his head inside with an inquiring expression; then, seeing Poppa, he smiled, as always, and stepped inside.

"Morning, Sam." He shook my hand. "I've been looking around for you since you graduated. Been thinking about doing a little recruiting."

I had never actually considered joining the National Guard, but I said: "I've been thinking a little about joining too, sir."

"Good!" he said. "We'll be glad to have you. I shanghaied Bill Joe this morning."

During the years immediately following the War Between the States, the carpetbaggers forced the dissolution of Gray's Rifles, a quasi-military social organization, which found its recruits among the wealthy families on Oak Street. But when the carpetbaggers were got shed of, Gray's Rifles was quickly reformed and soon regained its old social prestige. At the end of the nineteenth century, when most Americans were ready to forget pretenses, the Rifles continued to drill every Monday night. It wasn't until 1921 that old Colonel Jacob Cozzens, the present Colonel's father, put an end to it by making the Rifles the Regimental Headquarters Company of the state's National Guard. Most of the membership of the Rifles was commissioned.

The original snobbery was still alive to a degree. Colonel Cozzens chose his officers by recruiting young men and, four or five years later, commissioning them. Although more than half of the officers in 1936 were from homes other than those on Oak Street, I knew that Bill Joe and I had been chosen to serve the four- or five-year apprenticeship preparatory to a commission. There was a vague satisfaction in being aware that my future was so perfectly planned for me.

"Well, Felix," the Colonel said and jammed his hands into

his pockets. And I knew exactly what he was going to say next and what Poppa's answer would be:

"Well, Felix, have you heard?"

"Why no, Julian, I don't believe I have."

"Then let's go see if we can find out."

Bill Joe and I had been trying for years to find out what our fathers were talking about, but they never told us. Immediately after the Colonel would say they should go find out, they always left in Poppa's car and didn't come back for an hour or more.

This morning they paused before they reached the door.

Poppa smiled at Bill Joe and me. "Julian," Poppa said, "did you notice that Bill Joe woke up with a headache this morning?"

"Why yes, Felix, I did."

"And so did Sam."

"Uh-*hmmm!*"

"So maybe we'd better take them along so they can help us find out whether we've heard or not."

The Colonel smiled at us. "I suppose so." He ruffled my hair. "Come along, boys."

Bill Joe and I hurried out after them, both of us excited, even if we did call on every day of our seventeen years' experience to keep from showing it. We got into Poppa's La Salle and Poppa let me drive. With Poppa giving the directions, I drove through town and over the Ridge and into the Bottom. When we reached the road that separates our farm from the Cozzens', Poppa told me to turn into the yard of "that white house yonder."

I knew the white house. It was the home of old "Uncle Ben" Smith, a Negro who had sharecropped for my grandaddy and for Poppa until he was so old he couldn't follow a mule any more. He had been living, rent-free, in the neat, white little house for the past ten years and I had delivered groceries to him many times at Poppa's behest. I had never wondered, until now, why Poppa was more conscientious in seeing to the wants of Uncle Ben than he was of the two other old Negroes he kept rent-free on the farm.

66

Uncle Ben, his wrinkled old face alight with a completely toothless grin, was standing in the door.

"Wail, wail," he cackled, "'pears we is honored by some young gentlemen folks."

"Yeah, Uncle Ben," the Colonel drawled, "we figure we've held them off long enough."

Grinning with glee, the old man ushered us into his house. Aside from a table and four chairs and an old, tattered easy chair, there was another furnishing that caught my eye and held it. Against the north wall stood a gleaming white refrigerator.

"Well, Uncle Ben," Poppa said, as gay as I had ever seen him, "did it come?"

"It sho did! It sho did!" And the old man hobbled to the refrigerator and opened it. It was literally packed full of beer bottles. But these bottles didn't contain beer. They were capped by the kind of plain, white caps that you can buy in the hardware store, and there were no labels on the bottles.

Uncle Ben uncapped five bottles and, bidding us to sit down (while Poppa brought another chair from the little lean-to kitchen), he poured the amber liquid into five glasses.

When we were all seated, Uncle Ben between Poppa and the Colonel, the three older men held their glasses up and touched them in the middle of the table. At a gesture from the Colonel, Bill Joe and I held our glasses up too.

"It finally came!" said Uncle Ben, Poppa and the Colonel in unison.

And we drank. It was better than beer, smoother, stronger and it left a pleasant fizzy feeling in my throat.

"What is it, Poppa?"

"You like it, huh?"

"Yessir, what is it?"

"Home-brew."

Home-brew. I had heard of it all my life—Bill Joe and I had tried to make some last fall—but this was the first I had tasted. Since that day I have had my share of Uncle Ben's home-brew and I have drunk a goodly number of the mixtures various bartenders have concocted, but home-brew was and will remain the best drink ever made.

"You like it, Son?" the Colonel asked Bill Joe.

Bill Joe nodded and held out his glass for more.

"Whoa! Whoa!" Poppa said. "This stuff's strong. Two bottles in a seventeen-year-old and we'd have a mighty drunk boy on our hands." I had never known Poppa like this before. "Wait a few minutes and Julian and I'll let you two boys split a bottle."

"I still don't know why the Colonel always comes in and says, 'Have you heard?'" I said to Poppa.

"Tell'em, Julian," Poppa said. "You're the best storyteller."

While Uncle Ben and Poppa smiled happily, the Colonel took another drink of home-brew and leaned back in his chair.

"There's really not much to it, boys," the Colonel said. "When Felix and I were about the same age you boys are now, my father had some wine in the smokehouse and you can be sure that we sneaked in every once in a while to sample it. And of course we got caught.

"Now Father was a stern man and he used the razor strop on me on at least two occasions, but he had some pretty good ideas on how to raise a boy. So he went over to your grandad's house, Sam, and between the two of them, our fathers decided that we were going around sneaking a few drinks anyhow, so why not try to control it a little bit. 'Why not get Uncle Ben to make'em some good home-brew?'

"But the trouble was, Uncle Ben was out of malt yeast and he couldn't buy it in town. So Felix and I ordered some. Every morning for two weeks Felix'd meet the train, but it didn't come. I'd go over to the gin and, when your grandad wasn't in earshot, I'd whisper, 'Have you heard?' And Felix'd say, 'Why no, Julian, I haven't.' Well, that got to be a joke and when it finally came, we'd borrow your grandad's buggy and ride out to Uncle Ben's house to see how the brew was working.

"After it had worked itself up, Felix and I would go out in the morning for a few swallows and our fathers would go out in the afternoon. We've been doing it ever since."

Poppa patted Uncle Ben affectionately on his shoulder. "And no matter where you go or who makes it, nobody makes better brew than Uncle Ben. He's the king of them all!"

4

After chewing some mint grass that grew at the shady side of Uncle Ben's house, we got into the La Salle to go back to town.

"Uncle Ben, if you don't mind," Poppa said, "it would be all right with us if these boys come out for a little brew every once in a while."

"Das fine!" Uncle Ben grinned.

"But I charge you," Poppa said, "don't let'em drink too much. A little home-brew's good for what ails you; too much can be an ailment."

"Das a fack," Uncle Ben agreed. "Ah'll thump'em on da haid if'n they drinks too much."

I drove the Colonel and Bill Joe to their house and Poppa and I went on to the gin. We didn't talk while we rode; there was no need of that. I suppose neither of us boys had ever felt so close to our fathers before, and they were never distant from us again. And every morning that I was in Gray's Landing after that, I smiled when the Colonel opened the door to the gin office, peered inquiringly about, entered, and said, "Have you heard?"

At the gin, Poppa finished the machinery orders he had been working on before he said anything at all to me.

"Where'd you decide to go to school, Son?"

"The University, I guess."

"Uh-hmm." Poppa nodded deliberately. "Good enough, unless you want to be a scholar or something."

"Nosir, I'd rather not be a scholar."

"Uh-hmm. What'll you study?"

"Liberal arts, I guess."

"No law, no medicine?"

"Nosir."

"What do you want to do after you graduate?"

"Well—if you don't care, I'd like to work for you."

Poppa was tremendously pleased. "All right, Son, that'll be fine."

We never spoke of it again. At lunch Momma treated me

69

as if I were still a baby. She fussed over me, brought me my food and forced me to eat. She didn't know about the home-brew yet; I carefully held my breath when she was near. Poppa, now returned to his taciturn self, winked gravely when he thought Momma wasn't looking.

"Felix!" Momma said indignantly. *"You've taken him to Uncle Ben's!"*

Poppa didn't pause in his eating. He merely rolled his eyes over for a brief glare of disapproval. "Certainly," he said.

Momma slammed her hands into her lap and quivered with indignation. "Well!" she said. *"Well!"*

"Uh-hmm," Poppa murmured.

Momma, her sweet little face suddenly awry, shed a few brief tears before she decided that it was a man's world and I had recently become a member of the club and therefore another common idiot, and then she regained her slightly precarious composure. In spite of the fact that most of her hours in the past had been spent in devising ways of making a perfect gentleman out of me, she never mentioned the home-brew as something wrong again. It was many years later before I realized that the home-brew itself had meant nothing. It was only a symbol, the arrival of which she had long dreaded. But now it was a fact and I was accepted by my betters as a man and there was nothing she could do about it.

My mother was a great one for talking. And I was usually her conversational entree. While Poppa and I finished our lunch, she chatted gaily about everything under the sun that I had done, was interested in, or had said or seen. I almost let this slip by unnoticed:

"Of course you won't want to get married for a long time. . . ."

The home-brew had put some mighty worrisome thinking into her head.

5

The summer was a hot one. It was almost a yellow-headed, drouth, summer. But in late July, when the cotton needed it most, there was a good enough rain and everybody made a little money. But, as the Colonel said, "After six years of poor production and three major drouths, it's going to take three good years for us to recoup our losses." He was referring to the money he and Poppa had spent to keep the small farmers alive during those years when the wind blew so much of our good, clean dirt away.

I joined the National Guard and went to drill every Monday night. I learned little of the military tradition. Bill Joe and I were usually late after having spent the afternoon mixed up with what the Colonel called "summer devilment." Our names were constantly on the demerit list, a blackboard that hung on the north wall of the drill court. Of the thirty-odd men in my platoon, Intelligence and Reconnaissance, I knew but two, Raker and Carr, and them only because they both worked at the gin. I didn't know their first names. It occurred to me, years later, when these two and many others of their station became my close friends, that they must have thought that I was a terribly snobbish young devil.

Jenny spent the last two months of the summer with her aunt, the Colonel's sister, who lived in New Orleans. I left for the University without seeing her and wasn't to see her until four years later. I understood, from Bill Joe, that she graduated from high school and enrolled at "one of those fancy girls' schools in New Orleans." She was always away when I was home. She went to Europe the summer of my junior year. I never found out what she did during the other summers. I almost forgot that Bill Joe had a sister.

During my first two years at the University I was a poor enough student. The Dean put me on probation twice. Bill Joe, oddly enough, was an above-average student. He was studying aeronautical engineering with an energy that was surprising because he had never shown an intense interest in anything. Dur-

71

ing the summer of 1940 he changed his goal. Originally he had wanted to be an airline pilot, but when Hitler invaded Poland and there began to be heard some talk that the Army Air Corps was going to expand, he decided that he was going to be a fighter pilot. His tough face became a pale, brooding face as he applied himself to the difficult study of engineering. We were roommates and remained close friends, but we shared nothing in common except an abiding interest in girls. They never really left our minds, even after I stopped loafing and began studying during the final months of my sophomore year.

Both of us lost our virginity during our sophomore years and —an oblique proof of our friendship—at the same night and under the same roof. We picked up two slightly shopworn girls who liked to hang around the Student Union. After a few preliminaries, the girls suggested that we go to their apartment. We didn't realize that they were whores until we started to leave and they demanded payment.

"Damn!" Bill Joe growled. "If I'd known I was going to have to *pay* for it, I'd've looked somewhere else." He added heavily: "That's one thing I don't believe in paying for, 'specially since it's so easy to get free."

"Same here," I agreed gravely.

We were in our room and in bed before Bill Joe said, "That was your first time too, wasn't it, Sam?"

"Uh-hmmm," I admitted.

There was a full minute's silence. "Well," Bill Joe finally said, "we know where to find it next time we want it, don't we?"

"Yeah, sure do."

We never visited the two girls again.

When I think of it now, we were never typical undergraduates. Bill Joe was too busy with his studying and, during his junior and senior years, his flying lessons. Both of us had pledged a fraternity when we were freshmen, but the crude behavior of our fraternity brothers was too much for us. Bill Joe resigned with me and we took rooms at a boarding house off the campus. I went home more often than Bill Joe, but I liked for him to go too, because when he could find the time for a

72

home visit, he flew us down in a light plane that could be rented for the week end.

During the summer of our junior year, we fished a lot and, with Poppa and Colonel Cozzens, we set a trotline across the river. We caught so many catfish that Momma and Mrs. Cozzens finally protested. We started giving the fish to the Negro sharecroppers who lived in the north end of the Bottom.

I didn't understand the impatience of my senior year. College study became lifeless and, although I worked hard enough, I wanted to go home to stay. I had become solidly infected with the reading habit and I often dreamed of sitting in the big, comfortable leather reading chair at home, where, after a day's work at the gin, I could relax with a glass of Uncle Ben's brew and a book. I didn't know it then, but I was beginning to assume the conservatism that Jenny later chided me about.

So, when Bill Joe left for a summer of intense study for his commercial flying license and I boarded a train for home, bringing with me but two bags—proof that college hadn't burdened me with any souvenirs—I felt relieved of a vaguely irritating past, most of which I wanted to forget. As the early evening lights of Gray's Landing flashed past the windows of the train, I was elated and ready to take my place in the life I never wanted to leave.

The sight of Poppa, erect and quiet, and Momma, wiping her tears away with the corner of a handkerchief, as they stood on the station platform was enough for me. I had forgotten about Hitler and Poland and Hitler and England; I was home.

6

The First Methodist Church of Gray's Landing is more of a holiday house than it is one of worship. The women wear print frocks to their "coffees," "teas" and bridge parties, but they wear their "creations" to church. The men, most of whom wear net shirts and seersucker suits, stand gravely about the thirty-one steps that lead up to the five-pillared veranda, talking fishing. There is little shop talk. The men watch their women with a certain affection, for it is on a Sunday morning, with the bright sun and the colorful dresses, that a wife looks her best.

Poppa and I were half leaning, half sitting on the marble railing of the steps, smoking and enjoying a comfortable silence. The children of the Oak Street families were home from college for the summer holidays. I was amazed at the number of pretty girls of my generation. They were laughing and flirting and they were happy.

"Wonder where Julian and his family are?" Poppa murmured. "First time he's ever waited this long. Usually we have a good fish talk before the organ begins."

"Bill Joe's in Arizona."

"What for?"

"Working on his commercial license—airplanes."

Poppa nodded. From the babble of female voices that came from a group standing on the veranda, we heard Momma's quick laugh. Poppa gravely winked at me and I smiled. There are few things Momma enjoys more than the Sunday-morning gossip session. Poppa smiled to himself and I realized, now when I was twenty-one years old, how much he loved her. He saw her faults as clearly as he had always seen through my small pretenses, but he loved her in spite of them.

Suddenly the organ thundered out above the babble and, without saying a word to each other, Poppa and I dropped our cigarettes. Momma, still engrossed with her talk with her friends, stopped immediately and joined us promptly when Poppa stopped at the edge of her group and said softly, "All right, Cleo." With Momma between her son and her husband, the same formation that had been formed on a Sunday morning as long as I could remember, we entered the church.

Ray Mosby, an usher since his graduation from the University four years ago, greeted us: "Morning, Mister Gifford; morning, Miss Cleo; morning, Sam."

"Morning, Ray," Poppa and I said.

74

"Good morning, Ray Earl," Momma said and squeezed his arm.

The thunder of the organ made the church seem huge and open. Ray led the way down the aisle to the pew we had occupied since the days before I was born, when the church was largely supported by pew rental. Now rental was considered old-fashioned, maybe even feudal, but the church was never so crowded but that every family, from Oak Street to Railroad Avenue, knew for a fact it would sit where it always had.

We took our seat on the front row and Poppa glanced across the semicircle of the front-row pews to see whether the Colonel and his family were there yet.

The organist finished the Prelude and chorded softly while the choir filed in. The Cozzens entered as the choir began to sing. Ray Mosby escorted them to their pew. Mrs. Cozzens, a large stern woman, came first, then Jenny . . . and I didn't notice the Colonel.

Jenny was beautiful. She no longer wore her glasses and her teeth were straight and white; the braces had done their work and had been discarded. She looked cool and fresh and, standing by her tall father, I noticed for the first time that she wasn't a big woman at all. When I had remembered her during the past four years, I had always thought of her as somewhat of the same size as her mother. She was small, trim and very erect. I suppose it had been her breasts that had caused me to remember her as larger than she was.

The congregation stood for the Call to Worship and the preacher, Jack Gifford, my cousin, entered and watched the two sun-browned boys light the candles before the altar. Colonel Cozzens leaned close to Jenny and whispered. She immediately smiled and looked toward our pew. She dug in her purse and brought forth a pair of horn-rimmed glasses. She found me and the smile became radiant. I think I loved her from that moment on.

The choir finished and the congregation was seated—and old Major Gray entered. Jenny and I smiled at each other as we remembered what the old Major, my great-great-uncle, had done when we were children:

Old Major Gray, who had been one of Mosby's Raiders during the War Between the States, had entered the church that Sunday morning a decade ago, and had hurried down the aisle to his pew because he was eager to try the new hearing aid the congregation had installed to help his failing ears. With a great fuss and bother, the usher had helped the Major put the earphones over his head and adjust the volume. Then, as he had done for as long as I could remember, he had promptly gone to sleep, his hands cupped over the head of his cane, his chin resting comfortably on the backs of his hands. He slept peacefully until the preacher, a man of the old-fashioned hell-fire-and-brimstone school, whispered:

"But was Judas Iscariot a man of his word?" The preacher, fixing the congregation with a flashing stare, leaned over his pulpit and, with his mouth no more than an inch from the microphone that led to the old Major's earphones, shouted: "NO!"

The Major bolted to his feet, ripped the earphones from his head and slammed them on the floor. During that one breathless moment while both preacher and congregation were completely silent and still, the Major's gravelly old voice entered the ears of everybody present:

"Damnit, sir!"

The grownups, for the most part, had managed to control themselves, but the children couldn't. Bill Joe started it. He held himself in check as long as he could, and then, prefaced by a long, anguished groan, he exploded. I was next, then Jenny. And within five seconds every child in the church was giggling. Finally the preacher interrupted his sermon long enough to ask the parents to escort their children to the basement nursery. And down there we played, occasionally breaking into wild paroxysms of mirth, until our smiling parents came after us.

And now, this Sunday in 1941, Jenny and I smiled as we remembered.

But it wasn't the same Jenny. As soon as the preacher had finished the benediction, "And now may the good Lord bless you and keep you . . . ," I crossed the semicircle and joined the

Cozzens. I stood there, grinning foolishly, as Jenny grasped my arms and said:

"Sam, Sam, I'd just plain hug you if we weren't in church."

Vaguely, from the edge of the haze which seemed to surround us, I heard the Colonel chuckle.

Momma and Poppa joined us and we filed past the altar, each of us saying to Jack, "Enjoyed your sermon," and somehow I found that we were all standing outside in the bright sun. It was very important that I talk to Jenny and just as I started to beckon her aside, she took my arm and we walked away. We stood in the shade of the big oak that grows at the corner of the church lot.

"Jenny," I blurted, "you're beautiful."

She smiled. "Do you think so? Do my glasses bother you? I'll take them off if you want me to."

"No—" I stammered. Then: "Uh—you're beautiful!"

"I'm not too young any more?"

"No," I said. "No."

"Ask me for a date then."

"All right," I muttered, trying frantically to think of the right way to say it. "Swimming," I said weakly. "Swimming."

"All right," she said promptly. "This afternoon. Two o'clock."

"All right—two o'clock."

In the car with Poppa and Momma it occurred to me that this Sunday morning was the first time Momma had ridden home from church without talking. I stopped the car in the driveway and got out. I didn't want to go in the house. I wandered off into the back yard and sat on the garden-hose roll until Poppa came out to get me for lunch.

"Hmm," Poppa murmured. "I felt the same way the first time I saw your mother when she came home from college."

"Sir?" I said dimly.

"Did you ask her for a date?"

"Yessir."

Poppa shook his head. "Young men're a lot more forward now than they were in my time. It took me two weeks to get up the nerve." He smiled down on me. "Let's go eat lunch."

77

7

She drew her knees up on the car seat, her feet under her, and faced me. She wasn't wearing her glasses. She wore one of those crisp, eggshell-colored dresses, which gave her an almost completely innocent appearance. She chatted easily about several subjects, knowing that I couldn't talk. My face hurt from so much smiling, but I couldn't help showing the pleasure I felt.

"Are we going to the Park or to the Creek?"

"The Creek," I said, "if it's all right with you."

She nodded and suddenly laughed. "My reputation'll suffer on account of this. Miss Belle warned me." She smiled at something she remembered. "Do you remember the time you and Billy Joe let me wear lipstick because I smelled the beer you'd been drinking? I always wondered how that lipstick and my braces looked together."

"Fine," I said.

"Sweet Sam! You wouldn't hurt my feelings for the world, would you?"

The shade was deep and the water that fell over the lip of the falls was white and flowing furiously. This was a wet spring, the best one we had had in more than ten years, and the water was cool and blue in the pool. A few pine cones floated past to lodge on the gravel bar below the pool.

"Did you ever wonder why these pines are here," I said, "when you can't find 'em anywhere else in the Bottom?"

"Nooo," she said, "but I'd like to know."

"When old Cobb Gray settled this Bottom, he couldn't stand living without a few pine trees around his house like he'd had when he was a young man in Georgia. So he just hied up to Hogback Ridge and got 'imself a few saplings. Said the wind blowing through them made him sleep better."

We got out of the car. "You know a lot about your family, don't you?"

I nodded. "A little bit."

Jenny dressed in the car and I in the thicket. The tub, now rusted almost to nothing, was still there and still filled with beer bottles. It made me smile and feel much older than my twenty-one years. I quickly squirmed into my trunks and waited for her to call me. Feeling somewhat like a peeping Tom, I peered toward the car. She was sitting in the back seat, applying lipstick. I watched her run a comb through her hair before she stepped out of the car.

"Hey!" she called. "I'm ready."

I stared at her so hard that, walking out of the thicket, I got my feet tangled in a fallen bough and almost fell on my face.

"How you like my two-piece?" she said and pirouetted gaily. Her hair whirled about her head. She held her bathing cap in her hand.

I managed a weak whistle.

"In that case," she said and laughed, "it's better we didn't go to the Park. Too many wolves." She pulled the cap over her head and began stuffing her hair into it. "When I say go," she said, "run for it, podner!" She pretended to find something interesting in the thicket, and when I turned to look, she shouted, "*Go!*"

She ran down the slanted rock and dived into the water and I was right behind her. We came to the surface facing each other. Treading water, we looked at each other for a second, and suddenly, for no reason at all, we both laughed.

"Hi!" she said.

I kissed her. We both sank.

Again on the surface, she caught her breath and said, "Why, Sam!" with mock astonishment.

"What would Miss Belle say about that?"

"Wellll—since it happened to me," Jenny said, "she wouldn't like it. But if it'd happened to her, she'd probably think it was all right."

"What do you think about it?"

"I think it was fine."

I reached for her again, but with a laugh she kicked away from me and retreated to the rock. I caught her there and she let me kiss her again.

"You look funny with lipstick on," she murmured.

79

I wiped it off on the back of my hand, but before I could reach for her again, she was gone with a splash. We played all sorts of childish games. We dived for gravel to prove that we could go to the bottom of the pool; we sat behind the falls, where she let me kiss her again; we raced from one end of the pool to the other and she, the winner, received a water-logged pine cone as a prize. When we were tired we stretched out on the slanting rock to rest. She cradled her head in the hollow of my shoulder.

"Swimming makes me sleepy," she said.

And we both napped. It was late in the afternoon when I awoke with a sharp, stinging pain in my chest. Jenny had tugged out a hair to wake me up. I bolted upright and she laughed.

"Did you know you look like a young hawk when you're asleep?" she asked.

"I've got the beak for it."

She tugged at my nose. "You have a pretty nose!" Then she twisted it sharply.

Without a word I picked her up and tossed her, without ceremony, into the pool. She shrieked with laughter and when I sat at the edge of the slanted rock to help her out, she pulled me in with her, dunked me thoroughly and tried to get away. I grabbed her feet and pulled her under. She hugged me convulsively while we were under water.

When we rose to the surface she was suddenly serious. "We'd better go."

"Oh," I said. "Yeah, I guess so."

"*Disappointed!* That's the nicest compliment I've ever had."

"Let's stay."

"Daddy said that you're one of the bunch he wanted to come to non-com school before church tonight. He'd be put out if you didn't show up."

"Oh—all right. After non-com school?"

"All right."

I waited in the pool while she dressed. There was no sound but the gentle splash of the falls. Through the pines I could see the neat rows of young cotton, stretching seemingly without end into the blue mist at the base of Hogback Ridge. The spring sun of late afternoon baked into the dirt and made it smell strong and rich. She sat on the rock and combed her hair while I dressed.

"Daddy'll demote you if you're late tonight, won't he?"

"Not me," I called from behind the car.

"Why not?"

"You can't demote a private."

I heard her laugh. "Daddy said you could get a commission if you'd just apply for it."

"I'm not militarily ambitious."

We hardly spoke as we drove back to town. I knew though, that she was worried about her conduct today. If anybody discovered that she had been swimming—alone—with me, and in a two-piece bathing suit at that, there would be some talk.

"Do you remember the time Billy Joe said I had a crush on you?" she asked suddenly.

I nodded. It embarrassed me to remember it.

"I wonder what made me say what I did to you?" she murmured. "I cried like a baby when I went to bed that night. I even got up to call you and apologize, but Daddy talked me out of it."

"You shouldn't've worried about it."

"But I did because I *did* have a crush on you." She amazed me; the things she could say so easily.

I plunged in with: "What about now?"

She laughed. "Oh-ho! Trying to get me to commit myself, aren't you?"

"Yes."

"Oh I'm sorry, Sam. I didn't mean to be brazen."

"You weren't brazen."

"Yes, I was. But anyhow—the answer is yes." She touched her forehead to my shoulder. "Now, I *did* commit myself." She hugged my arm. "Miss Belle would have a fit. She says a girl should keep the men guessing until the very last minute."

When I stopped the car in front of the Cozzens' house, Jenny kissed me solidly; and when I drove away the curtains

81

of her neighbors' houses were dancing as hands hurriedly pulled them aside to get a good look at me. I drove directly to the armory.

Ray Mosby was rather apologetically conducting a panel on the responsibilities of "the non-commissioned officer" when I entered the upstairs classroom. He interrupted himself to say, "Have a seat, Sam," and went on with his talk. It was a dull subject and he knew it, but Army Headquarters had placed it on the training schedule and it must be done. When Colonel Cozzens entered the classroom, Ray stopped talking with a smile of obvious relief. We weren't called to attention.

The Colonel put his right foot in a chair and rested a hand on the upraised knee.

"Now boys," he said, "some of you want to go to church, so I'll make my talk short." He cleared his throat. "You sixteen men have been chosen for non-com schooling by me personally. I know your families and I know you and I know you're the kind of boys I want for non-coms.

"So, here're the few words I have to say on how to be a good non-com. You must never take anything for granted. You must see to it that your orders are carried out to the fullest, but if you have to shout or nag at your men to get your orders carried out, you're a failure. A kind but firm approach, seems to me, is about the only way you can get anything done."

The Colonel paused. "Now when we go to camp this summer, you men will be getting a couple of stripes. And I want you to understand this: the first time I find out that any of you're using profanity in giving orders or if you try yelling at your boys, I'll break you down to private again. I want a good regiment and I don't think I'll have one if I have loud, profane non-coms."

He cleared his throat. "Did Sam Gifford get here, Ray?"

Ray nodded and pointed to where I was sitting.

"I'd like a few words with you, if you please, Sam," the Colonel said. "All right, boys, thanks for coming. That's all."

Raker and Carr turned around as we got to our feet. Both of them started to grin, but changed their minds. I winked at them.

"When he gets through with you," Carr said, "you'll be wishing he'd a went ahead and bawled you out. I got one of them talks of his once. Makes you feel like two cents."

"I think I know what you mean," I said.

I followed the Colonel outside. Even in his uniform he was by no stretch of the imagination a military man. He looked like exactly what he was, a cotton planter. He had joined the National Guard in his youth because it was expected of him. He had done his work well because it was also expected of him. The promotions which came regularly always surprised him. And when the Governor offered him command of the Regiment, Colonel Cozzens debated a long time before he accepted. He wasn't sure he liked soldiering that much.

It was dark outside and there was a big cloud working up from the east. We leaned against one of the new six-by-six trucks. But now that he had me outside, the Colonel didn't know how to begin.

"Looks like we might have a little rain," he said.

I gave the cloud a thorough study. "Yessir," I said studiously, "looks like it."

"Wet summer."

"Yessir."

"Felix tells me he's taking you in partners with'im."

"Yessir, I begin in the morning."

"I sort of wanted to do the same with Bill Joe," the Colonel said softly, "but he got the flying bug." He cleared his throat. "Non-com school's pretty dull, isn't it?"

"Well. . . ." I stopped.

"Ray'll liven it up. He'll make a good officer, some of these days—when the time comes that we'll need good officers."

"Yessir."

"Jenny tells me y'all went swimming this afternoon."

"Yessir."

"Have a good time?"

"Yessir, I believe Jenny enjoyed it. The pool out there's a lot cooler than the Park."

"Very peculiar thing . . ." the Colonel mused. "Bill Joe and I've always been friends, but Jenny's always been my baby girl.

Hard to realize that she's a grown woman now." He cleared his throat. "I've always hoped that she'd be a lady."

"She is, Sir. And more too."

The Colonel chuckled in the darkness. "She likes you a lot too, Sam."

We strolled back into the armory and into the harsh glare of the lighted drill court. "Turn out some of these lights, will you please, Ray," the Colonel called. "Let's don't waste money just because it isn't ours we're spending."

We waited a moment while Ray went to the switch box and snapped out most of the court lights.

"I haven't been in the water in five, six years," the Colonel said.

"Go out and try the pool any time you want to, Sir. Poppa'd be glad for you to."

"I'll do that," he murmured. He glanced down at the floor. "How're you getting along at the gin?"

"A little slow, I think."

He smiled. "You'll catch on," he said. "By the way, Felix called my office to tell you he was taking his car. Uh—Jenny'll pick you up in Bill Joe's little car."

"All right, Sir. Thank you."

Jenny was waiting in Bill Joe's Ford convertible. She helped me fold the top back. As we started to drive away, Raker and Carr passed and Carr called out with strained heartiness:

"Hey, Sam! That the way you're going to get those stripes?"

"I couldn't think of a better way," I called.

When we had moved away, Jenny said, "Who were they?"

"Just a couple of boys that work at the gin."

She looked at me carefully. "Are you friendly with them?"

"Oh—I don't know," I said. "I guess so. Why?"

"They just acted like they wanted you to be friendly, that's all."

"Did they?"

She smiled. "Yes, they did."

I was vaguely disturbed. It had never occurred to me that

Raker and Carr, or any of the others who worked at the gin, would be any more interested in me than I was in them.

"Now, don't worry about them," Jenny teased. "It makes you frown."

I laughed. Anything she did pleased me.

We stopped at Wingate's Drugstore and then we drove to the Bottom, where the flat land and long rows of cotton gleamed under the moon. We drove to Hogback Ridge and parked.

"Do you always bring your girls up here?"

"No, I haven't been up here since I was fifteen."

She nestled comfortably under my arm and we talked about the possibility of a mobilization of the Guard. Sometimes we let minutes pass before we spoke and it was during those many pauses that I was most acutely aware of her warmth. She smelled of perfume and her hair was clean and sweet. Her arms were plump and round. We sat tensely still for a long time before she spoke.

"What time is it?"

I struck a match. "Two fifteen." I lit a cigarette.

"Daddy'll be upset."

"He talked to me tonight."

"What'd he say?"

"We talked about the weather, Poppa, swimming and Jenny."

"I told him we went swimming. What'd he say about me?"

"He said you were his baby girl."

She laughed softly. "I was seven years old before I would go to sleep without his rocking me."

"I think he was a little shocked because I took you out there instead of the Park."

She laughed again. "So was Mother." She looked up at me. "And so was Sam."

I said nothing.

She pinched my arm, hard. "Sam, stop being bashful with me. You don't have to—not with me."

I kissed her. "I won't be any more."

She murmured something softly and then, wildly, she hugged me.

85

The wind freshened with a heavy gust and the pine trees on the Ridge swished loudly. She shuddered with delight and when I asked her if she were cold, she murmured no and pushed herself closer to me. A few drops of rain fell on us and she sat upright until I put the canvas top back over us. I cranked the window up on the windward side and we sat in the rain until dawn. We were cool, cozy and dry.

She was so tender and gentle that my throat tightened and I wanted wildly to make love to her, but I was so stricken by her that I could make no move at all in that direction. We kissed until our lips hurt and she was moaning softly, but I could only foolishly keep my hands where they belonged.

We stayed there until the rain stopped and dawn came. The sun, when it first showed over the horizon, was clean and yellow after the rain.

"I'll bet the Colonel and your mother're beginning to worry about us."

She yawned. "Probably."

"I'll tell them you were out with an older man."

She yawned again and buried her face in the hollow of my shoulder. "As long's I'm with Felix Gifford's son, all is right with the world, Daddy, and Mother."

But we gave up and went home. Jenny was too sleepy to drive and I let her out at her house and drove Bill Joe's car home. Her heels pecked sharply as she hurried up the walk, stopped on the porch, made an exaggerated yawn, threw me a kiss and disappeared into the house.

Poppa, who always arises at dawn, summer or winter, was reading his *Gazette* when I entered the kitchen.

"Kind of late, isn't it?" he said casually.

"Yessir," I said sheepishly, "it's pretty late, all right."

"Who were you with?"

"Jenny."

"Jenny who?"

"Jenny Cozzens."

"Hmmm. I didn't know that little girl was old enough to stay out all night."

"Well—uh, I don't guess she really is. She's nineteen." Then

I remembered what he had said to me this morning. "Aw, Poppa, you knew who I was out with."

"Whom I was out with."

"Whom."

"Just joking, Son," he said and folded his paper. "Sit down and I'll fry you an egg. You look like you could use a little something to eat."

"Make that three eggs," I said. "I've never been so hungry in my life."

We were silent for a while, but Poppa, as he spooned sizzling grease on my eggs, gave me a few sly, examining looks from the corner of his eye. He put the eggs in front of me, put bread in the toaster, and got a tall glass of tomato juice from the refrigerator. He poured a cup of coffee for me. He went back to his *Gazette*.

"When I was a young man," he said from behind his paper, "not every young man wore lipstick." He ruffled the paper and turned a page. "Instead of beginning work today, you'd better get some sleep. I can't teach you much in your condition."

"Yessir. Thank you." I finished wiping lipstick off my face.

"I presume you'll be going out again tonight?"

"Yessir, I think so."

"If I were you," Poppa said carefully, "I'd try to arrange my hours so I could get a little sun. According to what I see in the paper here, sunshine is the only source of one of the most important vitamins."

"Yessir, I'll do that."

"And there's also the danger of getting your daily schedule so mixed up that you won't be able to sleep at nighttime as long as you live."

"I'll be careful."

He got up, folded his paper, went to his den and came back carrying several pages of legal-sized paper. He uncapped his pen and handed paper and pen to me.

"Sign."

"What is it, Poppa?"

"No need reading it. It's just something making our partnership legal. You now own half of the gin, half of the farm, a quarter of the Gray Chevrolet Company—half of my half—and half of my stock in the bank."

I signed.

He shoved another paper under the pen. "That's the deed to that lot in the next block. Not that you're going to be building a house, but now that you're a man of property, you can pay the taxes on it."

I signed again.

"You owe me five dollars. Pay up."

Stunned, I fumbled for my wallet and handed him the money. "Poppa——" I began.

That was the only time in my life that I had ever seen tears in Poppa's eyes.

8

Although Jenny and I didn't become a subject of gossip, we were somewhat a source of embarrassment to our parents. Both the Giffords and the Cozzens wanted to be as broad-minded as was possible about it, but when, for the three following afternoons, we swam in the pool at our farm, and when we stayed out until dawn for an equal number of nights, our parents looked at us with questioning and worried eyes. Bill Joe, who came home Tuesday afternoon, and in whom I had confided since we had been children together, was occupying a position he didn't relish at all. His sister's honor and our friendship were at fore and Bill Joe solved it in a manner typical of him. He avoided both of us.

"Has your family said anything to you yet?"

"Nooo," she said. We were resting on the slanting rock. "How about yours?"

"No, but they'd like to."

She was brushing her hair and when the breeze caused

the pines to part and let the sunlight into the pool, her hair glistened with the copper that only the sun could expose.

"They probably think I'm a fallen woman."

I felt my face warm and I quickly turned away and tossed pebbles into the pool. They fell with gentle splashes that couldn't be heard because of the murmuring falls.

She stopped brushing. "Oh Sam, did I embarrass you?"

"No," I said, "of course not." But I couldn't look at her.

She was strange and still for a few moments, and then with a laugh she put her feet in the small of my back and shoved. Before I could rise to the surface she was upon me, alternately enclosing me with convulsive embraces with her arms and legs and kicking me deeper into the water. If the water hadn't softed the blows, it would have been brutal. But whether I was hurt or not, I was about to drown. My lungs were aching sharply and I had to jerk hard at her arms and legs to break free so I could come up for breath.

"*Hey!*" I yelled. I had no idea of what had suddenly come over her.

As an answer, she splashed water in my face and laughed before she struck out in the direction of the thicket. I caught her on the gravel bar, but she pulled free and ran into the thicket. I caught her not far from the rusted beer tub and we wrestled briefly before we both fell. She was full length on the pine needles and I was on top of her. The merry smile on her face abruptly faded. Slowly she relaxed her legs and my wet body slipped between them.

"Jenny?"

She smiled dreamily and took my face into her hands and kissed me. "Will anybody see us here?"

I helped her to her feet and slipped the upper half of her two-piece suit off. Her breasts were free now and she held my head with the tips of her fingers when I stooped to kiss them. I watched her squirm daintily out of the rest of the suit, which she tossed aside, and she stood for a moment so I could see her —examine her; she knew her body was perfect and she was proud of it. My breath was so dry and harsh that it burned my throat and I couldn't seem to get enough air into my lungs. She lay on the pine needles while I frantically tore my trunks off and fell beside her.

It was a quick, piercing act that, at its height, paralyzed both of us, and Jenny uttered a tiny cry before she lay still. She had been a virgin.

We lay side-by-side for long minutes before either of us moved. Jenny fumbled for my hand and held it over her heart, which was pounding heavily. Then she dropped her hands to her sides and sighed quietly. After a long time—it might have been a half hour—she gestured for her suit and draped it over her stomach. She smiled lazily when I wouldn't let her cover her breasts.

"Did I hurt you?" I asked.

She took a breath and nodded. "But it's all right. It seemed to make me love you that much more."

I put my arm under her and rolled her against me. Her breasts were soothing and warm against me.

"Jenny," I began—and fumbled for the unfamiliar words: "I love you."

She ran her fingers lightly over my face. "I've always loved you, Sam," she murmured in my ear.

I got to my feet. "Come on," I said abruptly. "Get dressed."

She sat up quickly. "What is it, Sam?"

"I'm going to talk to the Colonel about us."

She smiled. "You scared me."

She let me watch her dress. She was self-conscious and she instinctively wanted to turn her back to me, but she let me watch. During the entire process there was on her face a happy little smile that made me choke with lustless love for her.

As we drove to town Jenny stretched her legs out and rested her head against the back of the seat. "That sure does make you relax, doesn't it?" she said wonderingly. "My arms and legs feel as heavy as lead."

I loved her so much that it made my heart pound. And she —relaxed here with an intimacy that had once seemed so remote—had given herself to me without a murmur of dissent. She—a virgin—had even thrust her body against me with a deli-

90

cate greed that had been so natural that I remembered nothing gross about it.

"Do you want to get married right now?" she said. "Or do you want a church wedding?"

"Right now," I said. "Uh—if you want to."

She nodded and laughed. "You're going to make an honest woman of me, aren't you?"

"Don't talk like that, Jenny."

She hugged my arm. "All right," she said. "I won't."

At her house she straightened in her seat and it was here that she showed the only sign of nervousness about us. "I hope they don't get upset," she murmured.

"So do I," I said. "You go upstairs and get a bag packed and—and I'll talk to the Colonel."

"How much should I pack?"

I had no idea. I didn't even know where we were going to spend our honeymoon. "Two weeks' worth, however much that is."

She nodded and, without so much as a glance down the hall, she kissed me passionately and hurried upstairs. I watched her run and when she stopped at the landing and kissed down at me, I found that there were tears in my eyes.

Colonel Cozzens.

Oh Lord! I said to myself. I squared my shoulders and took several deep breaths to steady my heart.

The Cozzens were in the dining room. I entered bravely enough, but I had no more than stepped over the door sill when I was drained down to a trembling coward. The three looked up at me, surely white with fear, and the Colonel and Bill Joe instinctively rose, but halfway to their feet my wild appearance prompted them to reseat themselves with a rather heavy thump. Mrs. Cozzens gave me a glacial smile.

"Colonel Cozzens," I began tremblingly, "I—Colonel——"

"Uh—yes, Sam, what is it?"

"What's the matter, Sam?" Bill Joe said.

"Colonel Bill Joe—I mean, Colonel Cozzens"— I took a deep breath and let it go with a gusty sigh,—"Jenny and I want to get married."

Mrs. Cozzens, whose calm had never been known to desert her, suddenly cleared her throat raucously. Bill Joe stared in horror (and I hated him because he was supposed to be my friend). Colonel Cozzens slowly placed his napkin on the table and then impulsively reached for it and dabbed at his mouth; he held the napkin there for some seconds while he stared raptly at his plate.

"Well now. . . ." the Colonel began. "Well—uh, *well!*"

"We want to get married," I blurted insanely.

Mrs. Cozzens was first to recover her composure. She quietly—and sternly, I thought—opened the door and called upstairs for Jenny. Mrs. Cozzens then walked with heavy, measured steps back to her chair, where she sat bolt upright, and the four of us waited in an awkward silence while Jenny came downstairs. She stopped beside me and took my arm with both hands. I knew then that I would always love her: she, by her very posture, gave them to understand that her mind was made up and nobody could change it.

"*Now!*" the Colonel said, feeling also that Jenny's arrival had suddenly lent sanity to the scene. "I'm to understand——"

"That Sam and I're going to get married," Jenny finished.

"Well—uh, *yes*, so I hear!" the Colonel said.

"And we're going to get married today," Jenny said.

"Can't it wait a few days?"

Mrs. Cozzens said, "It'll take at least five days to make the arrangements and——"

"Sara," the Colonel said firmly, "you hush."

Mrs. Cozzens subsided respectfully.

"Yessir," I said, "we could wait, but we're not going to."

The Colonel pondered that for a moment before he glanced, first at his son and then at his wife, to see that they didn't object, and said, "Well now, if that's the way you both feel about it—well then, I don't guess there's much for me to say."

"Nosir," I said weakly, "I guess not."

The silence that followed was broken by Bill Joe, who rose from his seat, sat down again, and said, "Well now, I'll just be damn!"

"Don't use profanity at the table," Mrs. Cozzens said automatically, and the crisis was over.

Jenny ran to her father; Bill Joe, still somewhat dazed but smiling, shook my hand and muttered his congratulations; and Mrs. Cozzens made her heavy way to the phone, where she called Poppa and Momma. I heard her say, "I believe it would be more proper if you came over here and let Sammy tell you about it."

"Sam," corrected Jenny as she flew up the steps to finish packing.

Bill Joe rushed out to the county clerk's office and the Colonel called Jack Gifford. "That is, if you want a preacher to marry you."

"Yessir, we do."

My parents arrived just in time to hear Bill Joe cuss the county clerk for not hurrying. The clerk, a bearded old man who had held the office since the close of the Spanish–American War, didn't like it, but Bill Joe was ready to get tough with him and the old man didn't seem disposed to talk back.

Poppa and Momma came in.

"Well, Felix," the Colonel, who had regained his composure and was conducting himself with a certain gaiety, said loudly, "Jenny and Sam've decided to get married."

Momma immediately collapsed in a deluge of tears and a barrage of sobs.

Poppa smiled. "Congratulations, Son." He didn't say another word, although he did frown at Momma's tears once.

Jack Gifford, wearing a sport shirt and his golfing cap, arrived with his Bible.

Momma managed to control her tears well enough to peel off the wedding band, a wide, thick hoop of yellow gold, that (the legend says) Cobb Gray gave Rene when they married in Baton Rouge.

A minute later, without music, Jenny and the Colonel marched downstairs, followed by Bill Joe, who carried her suitcase, and we were married.

We had reached the car before Jenny remembered. She glanced back at the house.

"Is your Poppa on the porch?"

"Yes, why?"

She jumped out of the car and ran up the walk. "Poppa Felix, you didn't kiss the bride!" she called.

Poppa, somewhat flushed, swept off his hat and kissed Jenny firmly. She ran back toward the car. "Bye, everybody!"

9

We spent our honeymoon at Poppa's hunting and fishing cabin at Lake Norfork.

I taught Jenny how to use a casting rod, a knack which she picked up with little trouble, and hoped that she would catch a fish the first time. She didn't, but we tried again before dark and she hooked a four-pound bass, a fish bigger by half a pound than anything I had ever caught. She carefully played the fish as I instructed; not once did she scream, which was a source of great satisfaction to me. And she insisted on removing the plug from the mouth of the fish and she did so without a single grimace.

"What'll I do with it?"

I tossed the stringer to her and told her how to run the holder through the lower jaw. Once the fish was securely locked on, she dropped it into the bottom of the boat, put her glasses on, and bent forward to admire it.

When I cranked up the motor to return to the cabin she crawled to me and sat between my knees, her arms resting on my legs, her head against my stomach, and fell asleep. I cruised about the lagoon in front of the cabin until she finished her nap.

Contrary to the impression I had when I took her swimming the first time (not yet a week ago), Jenny was very modest. We dressed in separate rooms and the only times I saw her naked was when we made love. She went to the spare bedroom and undressed and then she approached the bed, smelling of recently applied perfume, and with a little smile on her face. She was always flushed with excitement. She was very passionate. More than once, during the days that followed, she would pull my hair or hug me until I hurt, and cry feverishly, "Let's play!" And that was the word we used from then on.

I discovered that there was a mole in her pubic hair, which embarrassed her, and she said she was going to Little Rock to have it removed. I insisted that it was very exciting and she consented to let it remain, but she thereafter removed my hand quickly when I touched it.

Although she would permit me no more than an accidental glance at her, she wanted to examine me minutely. I was forced, following many minutes of argument during which she wouldn't listen to reason, to lie on my back while she delicately adjusted her glasses and went about the rather clinical business of appraising the first naked man she had ever seen.

"It's in *front!*"

"Absolutely," I said weakly. "That's enough."

"Be still," she said brusquely. "It's *growing!*"

"It sure is," I said, "and that's enough."

"Let's play."

"I was just about to suggest that."

We swam in the lagoon every morning, using the anchored boat as a diving float, and Jenny was soon tan, which made her even more beautiful. She was an excellent swimmer, better than I for short stretches. Once, after she repeated the performance of kicking and punching me as she had done at the pool, we made love in the boat and we snickered and giggled like two children when two fishermen went past and wondered out loud, over the noise of their motor, if somebody had deliberately left his boat this far from the bank.

After the fishermen were gone, Jenny giggled and said, "I'll bet they'd die if they'd known we were *playing* in the bottom of that boat!"

"We ought to be more careful."

"Oh Sam! Don't be so *dignified!*"

One afternoon, while it rained in torrents, we loafed on the screened porch and Jenny told me about the various misadventures that had befallen her at Miss Belle's and during her trip to Europe. Once, in a letter to her parents, she had casually repeated a comment concerning the food, that it was tasty but contained too much saltpeter, and the Colonel had written a letter in return that was filled with all sorts of fatherly advice associated with "the various controls of the basic instincts." She had suffered some embarrassment when one of the older girls explained the reactions people get from saltpeter. She also told me about a Frenchman who had taken her to the top of the Eiffel Tower and had tried to get his hand up her dress. "I knocked him down—completely down. I'll bet he thinks American girls're awful strong." It would have made me furious if I hadn't known that I had ended her virginity.

We sat quietly and watched the rain pour off the roof. It rained for more than two hours. Jenny moved her chair nearer mine and, finally, she sat astride me and rested her head on my chest. We were still and quiet for almost an hour.

After a few days had passed—I don't know the exact number—we exhausted Poppa's larder and drove to Mountain Home to restock it. The grocer couldn't keep his eyes off Jenny and he had a sly look about him too. On the way back to the cabin, she said:

"Sam?"

"Uh-mmm?"

"Have you noticed that I'm walking funny?"

I was alarmed. "No, why?"

She suddenly blushed. "Nothing."

"What is it, Jenny?"

She giggled. "I'm so sore I can barely sit down!"

And, of course, I blushed. "Well, maybe we'd better not——"

"Oh, don't be silly," she said.

When we reached the cabin the Colonel's car was parked there and Poppa and the Colonel were sedately sitting on the screened porch. Jenny hurried to kiss her father and then, murmuring "Poppa Felix," she kissed Poppa, who gave her a courtly bow in return.

"Anything wrong, Poppa?"

"Well—no," Poppa said. "We just thought we'd come up and see how you young folks're getting along."

"Uh—yes," the Colonel said. He smiled down at his daughter. Jenny was half hugging, half leaning against him.

Jenny and I exchanged puzzled glances.

"Y'all didn't drive up here for nothing," Jenny said. "Now *tell!*"

The Colonel cleared his throat. "I thought—we thought that since you've been gone so long, you might've drowned or something."

"Long?" I said. "About two weeks."

Poppa and the Colonel were very embarrassed.

"Two days short of a month, Son," Poppa said.

"A *month?*"

"A month," the Colonel said. "However, since you're both obviously all right, I guess the only thing Felix and I can do is retreat as gracefully as possible."

Jenny kissed both men again. "We'll come home in a week. We promise, don't we, Sam?"

The Colonel drove rapidly away.

Jenny watched them leave. "I've never seen two men so much alike before in all my life. No wonder they're such good friends."

We started carrying the groceries into the cabin.

"Daddy's always been worried about me," Jenny said. "He thinks because I can't see very well that somebody ought to be around to watch out for me. And he's right, a little bit. He doesn't know that being nearsighted is so nice. I live in a private little world all my own. The people that live in it with me are the ones I love. I don't have to worry about the others because if I don't like them, they aren't close enough to me to be a part of my world. Trees and things are blurred and they look very pretty. Daddy doesn't know about that. My whole world is pretty." She wrinkled her face in a happy grimace. "Sam, I'm so happy!"

A week later I carved "Sam loves Jenny" on the log about the fireplace, and added: "June, 1941," and we went home.

10

Because I had stored away a fair knowledge of the mechanics of ginning in the process of growing up with it, I found it not impossible to find my way about the maze of gears, belts and drive shafts. The grading of cotton—Poppa was also a cotton broker—was another matter. Although Poppa spent many hours plucking samples from the stacks of bales in the compress and pulling and tugging until he thought he had found a length of fiber or a kink that would demonstrate to my apparently unseeing eyes a certain grade of cotton, I remained unschooled. Cotton was cotton.

Old man Carr, Kenny's father, who had worked at the gin when my grandfather had owned it, put my slowness down to education. "'Pears to me them four years you spent at books is done you more harm'n good."

Jenny and I didn't discuss the building of our house as we should have. It never occurred to me that there were other styles of architecture. The barnlike colonial I had been born in was a good enough style for me to die in. Jenny protested, but not strenuously enough to make me change my mind. We drew a rough floor plan for a two-storied house and handed it to old man Kelton, who, having built a dozen on Oak Street almost exactly like it, glanced at the plan and threw it away. Our house was to have but one fixture not found in any other house on Oak Street: a forced-ventilation attic fan, which aroused considerable interest and made me feel that I might be building a house too modern for Gray's Landing. A glance at Ray Mosby's house, which was next door, should have convinced me of the opposite. Jenny was the one who could have kept me from building the house, but she kept quiet. Only once, jokingly, did she accuse me of glorying in my conservatism.

Poppa and the Colonel visited the site every afternoon. They stood on the lawn and assumed poses of genial satisfaction.

When old man Kelton finished the rough work on the house, we moved in. The finishing work was done with our new, Victorian furniture already in the house. We were glad to be sleeping in our own home because Jenny was very nervous about staying in the room where I had grown up. She was absolutely certain that Poppa and Momma could hear us, and our love making became so inhibited that it made us both somewhat afraid. When we moved into our own bedroom, our love once again assumed the intensity we had enjoyed during our honeymoon.

I continued to apply myself to the work at the gin and it wasn't long until Poppa expressed guarded satisfaction with my cotton grading. We thereafter bent our efforts toward getting the gin ready for a huge cotton crop this fall. Raker and Carr worked harder than any two men we had, but they didn't respond to my overtures of friendship. They were friendly enough during Guard drill, but they held themselves back at the gin. And it was Carr who brought about the only unpleasant incident I remember of those gentle days:

Every afternoon at two thirty Poppa gave the employees a fifteen-minute recess for coffee. I usually had my coffee in the office with Poppa. But one afternoon during the late days of July, Poppa had to go to Little Rock. I got my thermos of coffee and hunted out Raker and Carr, who always met near the press to drink and loaf. I noticed a quick exchange of glances when I sat down with them, but I thought it was an expression of surprise. I twisted the top off my thermos and filled it with coffee. Raker and Carr both kept their heads down. They said nothing.

"Wonder when the Colonel's going to give us those stripes he's been talking about," I said.

Carr raised his head and gave me a cool, level look. "I wouldn't know, Sam," he said. "Why don't you know? He's your father-in-law, not mine."

My heart tripped heavily and I knew my face had turned white. I was rejected for the first time in my life and I couldn't take it.

"I guess," I said tightly, "he's the one I ought to ask." I floundered and went on: "I'll see him before drill tonight and——"

"Look, Sam," Carr said tartly, "me'n Raker ain't came to your office to drink coffee with you. Looks to me like you ought to have that much respect for us and our private life."

It hurt me and both Carr and Raker knew it, but they both looked stubbornly determined to keep me at the employer's distance.

I opened my mouth to speak and said nothing. Then: "I'm —I guess—I'm sorry."

They both lowered their heads. I picked up my thermos and hurried back to the office. The secretary thought I was sick, but I made her leave me alone. I sat in my plush office chair and trembled with an emotion I had never experienced before. I was determined that nobody at this gin would ever again have an opportunity to treat me that way again.

I never mentioned it to Jenny. Neither Raker nor Carr ever showed sign that it had happened. We remained distantly friendly at Monday-night drill.

Aside from that momentary friction, I worked at the gin without incident. Poppa, without discussing it with me, gave me a good salary. He didn't like to discuss money because he considered it ungentlemanly.

"I deposited your salary at the bank, Son," he murmured when the first of the month came.

I received four hundred dollars a month and Poppa wrote me a formal letter to the effect that we would divide the remaining profits at the end of the year. That, with half of the profits from our other holdings, put me among the wealthy of Gray's Landing.

When I went to the bank to make the first payment on my house I was handed the deed, stamped PAID. Poppa, of course.

Colonel Cozzens gave us a Cadillac for a wedding gift and, although both Jenny and I felt self-conscious in it, we kept it for fear of hurting the Colonel's feelings.

Old man Kelton completed the finishing work on our house by the end of July and he hung around until Jenny had thanked him more than profusely for having it ready a full month ahead of schedule. The house was set back deeply into the lot and there were, of course, several—nine—oaks on the front lawn.

I carried Jenny across the threshold and we initiated, again, the master bedroom.

After Ray and Virginia Lou Mosby almost caught us making love in the downstairs bedroom, Ray and I devised a signal system. I wanted to tell him a system wouldn't be needed if he would learn to punch the doorbell, but the young married couples of Gray's Landing were going through one of those fads: it was somehow considered sophisticated to enter the home of a friend without knocking.

"Look now, Sam," Ray said, "I don't want you to get mad or anything, but since you'n Jenny haven't been married very long and all, maybe we'd better figure out some way so Virginia Lou and I will know—will know when it's—ah—*safe* to ring your doorbell." He paused and finished quickly: "Nothing upsets me more than a doorbell ringing right in the middle of things." He paused. "I won't say anything to Lou, so just you and me'll know about it."

We decided that a lowered shade in one of the kitchen windows meant "no visitors." Jenny was mystified at first but I discovered that she knew about it (I saw her let slip the smile she had for a man's elaborate safeguard for modesty). The signal system seemed childish after that and I discontinued it.

We bought a radio-phonograph, which was too expensive, but we excused ourselves by saying that it was better to buy the best if we wanted to enjoy our music. Jenny brought her own record collection from the Cozzens' house. It contained composers I had never heard of: Hindemith, de Falla, Berlioz, Stravinsky and Copland.

"So this's what you learned at Miss Belle's?"

"Yep. Like it?"

"I'm not sure. . . ."

I added my own Brahms, Beethoven, Handel and Schubert to the collection, which made it, we agreed, good enough for a start.

I insisted on doing the work in my den with my own hands. It was old-fashioned oak panels (stained darkly), a heavy, roll-top desk which contained a profusion of pigeonholes and drawers, and I covered the floor with a dark brown rug. I brought my old leather-covered reading chair from Poppa's house. The den brought some peppery remarks from Jenny.

My astonishment for my wife reached its zenith when I read some of her books: Joyce, Kafka and one of the modern Frenchmen. I resented them somewhat, for they seemed to intrude upon the comfort of my sanctuary, but Jenny enjoyed them too much for my heart to harden on them.

Jenny and Virginia Lou became close friends, close enough for them to share the secrets of the marriage bed with each other. It was from one of those gossip sessions that Jenny returned one afternoon in a state of almost complete puzzlement.

"Virginia Lou's a mighty peculiar girl," she said.

"Hmmm?"

"She and Ray were married more than a year before she—*before she had an orgasm!*"

"Oh? According to what I've heard, that's not so peculiar."

"Well, it's peculiar to *me*."

I smiled. "Yes, it would be to you."

She raced around the table and sat astride me. "Oh it is, is it!"

I laughed.

She locked her legs about me. "How do *you* like being married to a nymphomaniac, Sam Gifford?"

"*Jenny!*"

She ignored my reprimand. "I think we're both just a little bit oversexed, no kidding. Not much, but a little bit." She threw back her head and laughed. "You should've seen the look on Virginia Lou's face when I told her that *I've* asked *you*, lots of times."

"Virginia Lou's a very proper girl." I laced my fingers through Jenny's hair. "Not like another woman I know about."

Jenny ignored that one too. "She's still not crazy about doing it. She told me that she considered one orgasm a month proper enough—and that's about all she has." She squirmed on my lap. "I bet you could make her have one every time."

"I'll bet I could too," I said. "In fact, that's a good idea. I think I'll go over and find out."

"Stay right where you are, you stud!" She suddenly got very still.

On the first day of September, Colonel Cozzens had his orders from Washington. We National Guardsmen had two weeks to get our private affairs in order before we were called into federal service.

11

If I had been more solidly settled into my new role of husband and businessman, the sudden wrenching from my comfortable niche would have had disastrous results. As it was, I suffered enough. I had joined the National Guard as a favor for Colonel Cozzens—a pompous enough reason—and now I felt imposed upon. But I took it with grace. After all, Ray Mosby and I reasoned—and Colonel Cozzens agreed—this could only be regarded as an unpleasant eighteen-month interlude which could later be looked back upon as an experience for what it was worth—nothing. "Lots of people've wasted that much, just horsing around," Ray said. Our careers, our various degrees of domesticity would have to suffer an interruption, but it wouldn't last forever.

"I'm going with you, Sam," Jenny said. "Now I don't care what you say, I'm going with you."

But she didn't have her way. I was so much in love with her that she could talk me into doing almost anything, but I was dead set on her staying at home. And she stayed. That was the only time we ever came anywhere near getting mad. A fraction before her temper broke, Jenny suddenly smiled.

"You *can* put your foot down, can't you?"

"You bet your life," I said.

We worked three days loading our trucks and equipment

on flatcars, took a day off, and left the next afternoon. Jenny drove me to the train. We sat in the car and waited until Ray blew the whistle for assembly. Once, while she was chatting gaily, she stopped in midsentence and burst into tears.

"I promised myself," she sobbed, "I wasn't going to cry."

But I was pleased.

"I *hate* cry-baby women!" she said. "I *hate* them!"

I didn't dare tell her how her tears had pleased me.

The whistle blew. "Recon platoon, fall in!"

In the car next to ours, Virginia Lou wailed loudly. Ray was visibly embarrassed, but he couldn't leave to comfort her.

"Oh my god!" Jenny said with great disgust. "I'd rather die than be like that." She kissed me passionately. "Find a place as soon as you can, now, Sam. I'm coming to live with you. I didn't marry you for your name, you know. I want to live with you." She kissed me again. "Watch out after Daddy."

We reached the camp in Texas, located in a place where no sane people would live (such was our unanimous sentiment), and apparently the good rains which had fallen regularly on our cotton at home had not been heard of here. We were lined up, counted off, insulted, examined, filled with every conceivable antitoxin and cussed by Regular Army medics who had no use for us, civilian soldiers, and took pains to make it obvious. We retaliated by assuming an inertia that was broken only after we were again left to assume our identity as a civilian regiment.

Our training began two days later. Our arms were still sore from the shots, but the army was still on a half-day drill schedule and it didn't bother us unreasonably. Colonel Cozzens was admirably apologetic about the training we received: we were being taught no more than we had already learned at our Monday-night drills at home. If the army traditionally regarded everybody as stupid as it did its own men, we thought, then we must suffer.

"The trick to the whole thing," the Colonel told us, "is to bear up like gentlemen, smile and absorb what you need and shed the rest of it like water off a duck's back." The Regulars were absolutely certain that the Colonel was an insane man at the head of a lunatic regiment.

The Regulars hated us. Our non-coms didn't shout at us, didn't cuss us, didn't treat us as idiots and didn't consider the childishly simple maneuvers we were subjected to as grave tactical problems conceived by stern, benign brass gods from Army Headquarters. They jeered us, called us "Monday-night soldiers," but we retaliated by doing what hurt them most: we ignored them. They were particularly put out when our best soldier, Webster, beat their man at the rifle matches.

Early in October Colonel Cozzens stated that those of us who were married should advise our wives to visit us as much as possible, which was a move to "make for good morale," a phrase which the dull automatons from Army Headquarters liked to slide over their tongues. However, instead of periodic visits, we had our wives move baggage and everything to Texas. Jenny arrived in our car. With her were Virginia Lou, who, oddly enough, was quite composed (Jenny later explained that Virginia Lou was a changed woman, "in *every* way," because she was pregnant), and a plump blond woman of thirty-odd who was followed by four blond boys obviously on their best behavior. She was Raker's wife.

I rented an apartment in town and Jenny and I set up housekeeping. The apartment was four rooms in the home of a local family, the father of which spent a great deal of time extolling the wonders of beautiful, beautiful Texas and stealing glassy-eyed glances at Jenny's hips and breasts. "Texas!" Jenny said sharply. "It's the only state in the Union where ignorance is virtue and wealthy ignorance is saintliness." We learned to endure Texans with the same indifference I had learned for the Regulars.

The Regulars were getting almost frantic in their efforts to find better ways of expressing their hatred for us. Once, when Jenny drove our car out to camp to pick me up, a group of the Regulars, seeing the Cadillac, automatically popped to attention and saluted. I leaned out the window and said gaily, "Carry on, gentlemen!" The Regulars were terribly humiliated and there was much talk about "that goddamn smart recruit that drives the Cadillac." But their rage reached its zenith late in October.

Jenny and I had decided to give a party for the men in my platoon. I passed the word around. Only one man, Raker, said he couldn't come. We were sitting at one of the long tables in the PX, drinking beer.

"I'm sorry as hell, Sam," Raker said, "but me'n Sara Jo just can't make it."

A crowd of Regulars were seated near us, listening. And suddenly one of them shouted: "ATTENTION!"

The sudden shout made us all recoil. We peered about for the cause of it all.

"On your feet," one of the Regulars, an old master sergeant, growled, "you goddamn civilians."

It was Colonel Cozzens.

"Hey, it's the Colonel!" Webster yelled.

"Come on over, Colonel!" Raker called. "I'll buy you a beer."

The Regulars were speechless.

The Colonel, grinning broadly, crossed the floor and seated himself at the table. The Regulars stood at stiff attention.

"At ease, boys," the Colonel said to them.

They shifted to the formal at-ease position.

"Sit down," the Colonel said easily. "Drink your beer."

The Regulars sat down, but they were uneasy.

The Colonel's beer was brought to him and he sprinkled a few grains of salt into it. "Here's to a bale an acre!" he said. And we drank to a bale an acre while the Regulars stared.

"What're we talking about?" the Colonel said.

"Sam's giving a party," Bill Joe said.

"Who for?"

"Recon."

"How about me, Sam?"

"Jenny'll call you tonight," I said.

"Everybody in Recon, huh?"

The Regulars were listening so hard their ears were standing out.

"Everybody but Rake."

"What's your trouble, Raker?" the Colonel said. "Don't you like my son-in-law?"

The Regulars nodded knowingly to each other.

"Naw," Raker said, "he'll do. Sara Jo says we can't take the kids and we can't afford to hire somebody to stay with'im. I'm living up my savings too fast as it is. I just can't afford it."

The Colonel took a swallow of beer. "Tell you what," he said. "An old man like me would just slow up the party, so I'll go early and stay just long enough to keep Jenny from getting mad, then I'll come out and keep your family while you and Sara Jo make the party."

"That's mighty white of you, Colonel, but I don't want to put you out."

"Oh, hush that," the Colonel said. "I'm pretty good with children. I'll keep your kids."

The Regulars hurried out, with many "by your leaves, sir," and spread the latest, best story about the Crazy Colonel.

Jenny's spirits were somewhat dampened the afternoon before the party because Bill Joe received notice to report for duty as an air cadet. He left before dark. Jenny was absolutely certain that "those old airplanes" would be the death of Bill Joe, but as time for the party drew near she became interested in her first social meeting with people who hadn't lived on Oak Street and she soon forgot about her brother.

Several times during the hour we waited for the guests she jumped to her feet and pirouetted gaily about the room. "Sam! I think we're going to have a *wonderful* time!"

And we did. The party was a tremendous success. The Colonel left at eight and Rake and Sara Jo arrived at eight thirty, rather self-consciously driving the Colonel's car. Everybody got pleasantly tight before dinner and Kenny Carr was moved to sing "Beer! Beer! Beer!" He received an ovation. And Virginia Lou, as Jenny had said, certainly was a changed woman. She even drank a small highball, which made her giddy and funny. She danced, without coolness, with every man in the platoon. Ray was tremendously pleased. "All women," he told me, "ought to get pregnant."

And, during the party, I established friendships that would

have been impossible a few months ago in Gray's Landing. Raker and Carr went to the kitchen, made coffee, invited me to the back porch and we solemnly drank together. None of us, though, quite had the nerve to mention the incident at the gin.

Although I wasn't always to be included in the constant joking in my platoon, from the night of the party until the end of my military career, I was accepted as a friend. It was a long time until there were no reservations to the friendship between the men in the platoon and me, but I felt that I was getting as much as I could hope for.

And my marriage richened, which I would have thought impossible. Our love making became more practiced, less intense, yet is assumed a deeper, more satisfying passion. Jenny became alarmingly easy to arouse, but when I talked to Doc Wingate about it he laughed and said Jenny was nothing more than a healthy, passionate young American woman and not at all abnormal.

"I got another explanation too," Doc added, "but it isn't very scientific. She's in love with you. Why? Hell, I don't know. But with another man, she might be completely frigid. You're going to find out, young man, that women are just pretty damn strange about sex. So don't you worry about Jenny. She's just fine."

Poppa wrote regularly once a week and mailed my salary to me the first of the month. Momma wrote every day, long, worried letters that talked to a boy. It made me feel somewhat sad that I had never been as close to her as she had wanted me to be.

During the first week of December, Raker, Carr and I were promoted to corporal and I was made acting platoon sergeant a few days later when two of our old non-coms were discharged for overage.

"Say, Sam," Carr said earnestly, "does the Colonel have another daughter?"

I knew what he meant. "No, why?"

"I wouldn't mind being a sergeant myself."

I laughed. "You had your chance, buddy. She hasn't been married to me all her life."

Kenny pondered that one. "You think she'd consider leaving you for me?" He couldn't keep his face serious.

"I'll ask her."

"Okay, let me know in the morning, will you?"

Each Sunday afternoon, after Bill Joe was accepted for pilot training in the air corps, Jenny and I had lunch with the Colonel in the dining room of the local hotel, a small, frame building where the Colonel had established his private quarters. I was the butt of many a joke about those lunches and I told Jenny as much. She understood readily enough, because she had become a close friend of Sara Jo's, but she wouldn't hear of ending the lunches.

"With Bill Joe in the air corps and Mother at home, Daddy finds his only fun with us," she said. "If it makes him happy, it won't hurt us to take a little ribbing."

So I endured it with a grin.

It was on a Sunday in December when, during one of the Colonel's long stories of the messes he and Poppa had gotten into when they were boys, Ray Mosby hurried into the dining room and beckoned the Colonel to the lobby. Ray, who had in the past suffered something akin to a phobia about wearing an officer's uniform off post, was belted and brassed in his best. He was wearing a pistol too.

"Wonder what Ray's trouble is?" I said.

"Maybe Virginia Lou had a miscarriage," Jenny said. "I hope not. I don't see how in the world——"

She was interrupted by a hasty, nervous Colonel who, for a reason we didn't understand at the moment, suddenly stooped and kissed Jenny's cheek.

"Jenny," he began quietly, "I'm taking Sam back to the post with me. You take my car and go on back to the apartment and wait till you hear from us." He turned and addressed a group of officers who were in the other end of the dining room: "Will all military personnel present please return to their posts at once."

The officers stared at him.

"Promptly, please," the Colonel said crisply.

The officers hurried out.

109

"Daddy? What is it?" She was very pale, but she was calm, something I would later remember and love her for.

"Well," the Colonel said quickly, "it looks like we're in a war. . . ."

Jenny caught her breath quickly and looked at me.

". . . The Japanese bombed Pearl Harbor in Honolulu this morning."

Jenny was so pale she looked sick. But she calmly opened her purse and carefully slipped her glasses into place.

"Is the Regiment leaving?" she asked.

"I don't know," he said. "I'll try to find a way to let the married men see their wives before it does." He cleared his throat. "Let's go, Sam."

We walked outside. Behind us we heard the manager of the hotel hysterically shouting that we were at war. While we waited at the curb for Ray's jeep, I aimlessly patted Jenny's arm. The diners rushed past us and a hysterical woman blabbered something about us killing time while the country was being "all shot up."

"Texans!" Ray snorted.

The jeep arrived and I kissed Jenny, who clung to me desperately until the Colonel said, "Let him go now, Sugar." She released me and stood at the curb, and my wife was a pale, scared girl who seemed very small and innocent. Before we were out of sight I saw her get into the Colonel's car and drive away toward our apartment.

"What'd the orders say, Ray?" the Colonel asked.

"We have forty-eight hours, Colonel. Didn't say where we were going."

"Well," the Colonel said and absently fingered the silver eagles on his shoulders, "I guess we have to stop playing around now."

12

The Colonel had underestimated the situation when he re-marked about a future tightening up. At midnight we were told to discard all equipment and personal belongings that couldn't be easily carried in trucks. And at the same time we were given notice that our time of departure had been changed to tomorrow noon. At two o'clock the guards passed the word through the chilly night: "All married men with wives in town, report to Regimental immediately."

The Colonel was waiting for us. "I have here a three-hour pass for each of you. I hate to have to put it this way, boys, but I have to: If you aren't back by five o'clock, promptly, I'm send-ing the MP's after you—and you know what that means. Corpo-ral Gifford, front and center. Everybody else, dismissed. See you at five."

I came to attention and saluted. The Colonel returned the salute and smiled wryly. "Funny thing," he said. "Saluting still seems silly to me—even tonight."

"Yessir."

"Tell Jenny why I can't see her, will you, Sam?"

"Yessir, I'll do that."

"And tell her—well, never mind." He cleared his throat. "If I never do another thing right as long as I live, Sam, I've done a good job raising my daughter."

"I'll tell her that too, Sir."

He rubbed his nose absently. "Yes," he said. He handed me the three-hour pass. "Don't be late, Sam boy."

Jenny was sitting in the kitchen when I arrived. She was icy calm. She produced a plate of sandwiches and a bottle of beer from the refrigerator and watched while I ate and drank. She only nodded when I gave her the Colonel's message. When I finished the sandwiches, she got to her feet.

"Make love to me, Sam." This was the first time she had failed to use the word "play." In the bedroom she turned the lights on. "I won't be so modest tonight." She stood in the mid-dle of the room and turned slowly while I watched.

We didn't talk much. We sat in the darkened sitting room and she clung to me desperately. Once she shook her head violently, as if she were trying to dislodge something which bothered her. Only when I held her tightly could I feel that she was trembling faintly. Her body felt light and cool, a sharp contrast to the dry warmth I had known so well.

At a quarter to five, she drove me back to the camp. We were stopped at the gate. "Sorry, lady," the guard said. "He'll have to walk in. We've had orders to keep civilian cars out."

"But I'm Colonel Cozzens' daughter," she protested.

"I know who you are, ma'm, and I'm sorry I can't let you in." He looked at me. "You'd better hurry, trooper." He left us.

We were both silent for seconds and suddenly Jenny muttered, "Oh my god," quietly, and broke into shattering, convulsive sobs. I tried to comfort her and she again clung to me with startling strength, but she couldn't stop crying.

"I know I'm selfish, Sam," she cried, "but I can't help it."

The guard interrupted. "You'd better get going, trooper. AWOL's got a death penalty now, you know."

Jenny abruptly straightened. "Go on, Sam." She kissed me, hard and feverishly.

I stepped out of the car and watched her drive away. She drove very fast. I caught a truck that took me to our Regimental area.

"Sam!" Ray Mosby called as soon as he saw me. "You're in the second echelon jeep. Maintain a thirty-yard interval and use the siren when you have to get something out of the way."

We were served breakfast in the vehicles. We were rushed and cajoled, but still we didn't leave. An hour later we were still waiting. The Colonel drove down the line of trucks and told us to get out and rest in the shade, that we had to wait for a few more replacements. And we continued to wait.

At noon the replacements arrived. They were scared and disheveled from a long ride on a troop train. One of them approached me, said his name was Meleski and he was supposed to ride with me. I gruffly told him to get into the back seat and stay out of the way. A few minutes later we passed through the main gate of the camp and headed west.

The Colonel led us in his command car. He made his last consciously civilian gesture when he routed the convoy past our apartment. Jenny stood on the front porch with our Texas landlord and his family. I stood up in the jeep and yelled her name. She found me and, adjusting her glasses, she waved firmly.

I had no idea when I would see her again.

The speed of the convoy was set at forty-five miles an hour, faster by ten miles than an army convoy usually travels. The sense of urgency which dominated the convoy escaped me. I was thinking of my wife and I felt cheated by diplomacy and world politics. And I understood what Jenny had said about selfishness: I wanted my wife and the rest of the world could go to hell.

We had traveled perhaps twenty miles before I realized that the man in the back seat of the jeep was a stranger. He was swarthy and sharp-faced. His nose was tremendous.

"I'm a draftee, Corporal," he said. He was a Yankee; his accent fell harshly on my nerves.

"Don't brag about it," I growled.

He gave me a frank, level grin. "I'm bitching, Corporal." He wasn't so bad, I decided, for a Yankee. "Okay," I said. "Your wife back there?"

I nodded, again resenting him.

"Very pretty," he said.

"What's your name, soldier?"

"Meleski, Bernard L., Chicago, Illinois. Any more questions —Corporal?"

I was beginning to like him. He was cocky and his accent grated on me—and he had a rather evil face—but he had something else too, something I wasn't to appreciate until later.

"Okay, Meleski," I said.

"Okay, Gifford," he said right back.

We both laughed.

Rumors to the contrary, we did travel far. We passed through town after town and Americans who had for generations regarded soldiers as a silly, useless breed, turned out to cheer us as we roared down the main streets. Their attempts to make us feel like knights charging to join battle with the enemy embarrassed me, but at the same time it helped keep my mind almost free of selfish thinking.

That night we camped in the pasture of a friendly rancher who wasn't too put out when he was told that a visit to our tents would not be tolerated. Several of the boys pitched in and helped him with his milch cows and with the feeding of his beef herd. They returned to the camp and reported that they had finally found a Texan they liked. "But," they added, and I laughed, "he didn't move here till he was eight years old."

The next day we moved on, westward, and my buttocks were in agony. The December wind was cool and damp, but not too uncomfortable. The old round helmet gave me a headache and I was deafened by the deadly hum of the tires on the pavement, but I said nothing. Meleski told a few jokes and conned the pretty girls. The driver, a glum kid from Louisiana named Fromage, said nothing more than, "Yes, Corporal."

The second night we camped in another cow pasture, the owner of which had three loud daughters who passed out their patriotic passion at five dollars a meeting. Meleski, Carr and Webster visited them and told me that masturbation would have been easier. I awoke late in the night when the guard was changed. There was a light burning in the Colonel's tent.

And then into New Mexico. The wind was colder, but the sun blistered. We cotton-country boys looked at the endless desert with horror. Worse than Texas, I decided, but the people were courteous. And on into Arizona. My buttocks had developed small, painful sores that ached and burned smartly, but I was so tired that I had no trouble sleeping at night. And then California.

We were met in Riverside and rerouted through Los Angeles. "A morale gesture for the civilians," the Colonel said.

And I used the new army cuss word for the first time. "Fuk the civilians," I growled.

We were escorted through the city by motorcycle police whose sirens served to incite cheers that made me self-conscious and red-faced. In Hollywood the convoy was stopped by a public-relations officer with the rank of colonel, and four famous movie stars (the papers had long reported on the number of

114

husbands each of them had had) were photographed as they bestowed kisses on the embarrassed soldiery. One of them reached for me, but I drew back.

"My own wife's pretty enough for me," I said peevishly.

"Ahhh!" the public-relations colonel said with great satisfaction. He turned to the horde of reporters. "Good copy, huh, boys?"

The reporters crowded around me, asking my name and home town. I refused to tell them anything until the public-relations colonel directly ordered me to. "Bernard Meleski," I growled. "Chicago, Illinois."

"That's right," Meleski chirped from his perch behind me.

Los Angeles, I decided, was one hell of a town. I preferred Gray's Landing. Their cheers did nothing to change my mind. The sight of mass hysteria I found disgusting. Kenny Carr gave a spontaneous imitation of Hitler (he held a pocket comb over his upper lip for the mustache) and the crowds were crazy with laughter. I breathed a gusty sigh of relief when we at last broke free of the city and drove into the pleasant countryside.

That night we reached the end of our journey. This was what the army mysteriously called "an unknown destination." It was another cow pasture.

13

And there we stayed for nine weeks, "alerted" for a possible invasion. And it rained. And when there was no rain, there was fog. Our blankets, rolled up in our pup tents, were constantly damp and our fatigues mildewed and stank. We were wet, miserable and homesick. I seriously considered going AWOL to see Jenny. But the Colonel changed my mind.

"I'd give anything," he said, during one of the periodic visits I made to his tent, "if I could be home with my family. How about you, Sam?"

He made me feel weak and ashamed.

The new men, the draftees, who had been hastily assigned to the Regiment to bring it up to full strength, were mostly Yankees, men of a different breed. We neither understood nor liked them, and since we outnumbered them four to one, we left the burden of assimilation to them. Only Meleski, who attached himself to Carr and me, was readily accepted and he only because he was a natural mimic and was soon capable of talking to us in a language that only a sharp ear could differentiate from good, Southern English.

Our first day in the California cow pasture was somewhat soothed by an announcement that the Colonel had wired our APO address to the Gray's Landing *Gazette*. And before the first week was over we were getting mail. I was deluged with Jenny's letters.

She wrote a strangely literary language that, with a subtle twist of a phrase, conveyed to me exactly how she loved me, missed me and wanted "to play with my husband." She also managed to create in me something more than love. I felt a strong affection and admiration. And I surprised myself with my own letters. When I had been a student at the University, my English instructors had complained that I wrote too stiffly. But not to Jenny. I wrote long, nine- and ten-page letters and the words seemed to fall exactly into place.

We worked hard. The Colonel, although he never seemed to hurry, was everywhere at once, gently prodding us on. He encouraged us to get our new equipment into good shape and he set aside an hour after supper for us to write home to our families.

At the end of the ninth week in the cow pasture, we were awakened in the middle of the night and routed out of our blankets. I hurried the Recon Platoon into the waiting trucks. The abruptness of the move chilled me with cold spasms of apprehension, for it was a cold, black night, foggy, and as Ray Mosby gently chided, a good night for putting us aboard ships without our being spotted by spies who, several posters assured us, were ever with us.

Ray was as surprised as the rest of us when he was discovered, several hours later, to be entirely correct. Before dawn we were at sea. By daylight half of us were seasick.

Ray Mosby was the first of the responsible officers and non-coms in Headquarters Company to reveal the change that was eventually to come to everybody in the Regiment. Ray, who was my second cousin, knew he could talk straight to me.

"Sam," he said, "have I ever given you any brass talk?"

I shook my head, wondering what was the matter with him.

"Well," he said, "I'm fixing to right now. So listen close. You've got to get your mind off Jenny and start acting like a non-com. Lot of people're saying the war will be over before we get wherever we're going, but I don't think so and the Colonel doesn't either. So you've got to buckle down and hit it hard. Now Sam, I know I'm going to sound like a Regular, but you'll just have to take it. If you don't start pushing a little harder, I'm going to bust you and make Carr platoon sergeant." He smiled tiredly. "How about it?"

I hadn't realized before that Ray had more to worry about than I did. Virginia Lou didn't have the intellectual stamina that Jenny had and she was pregnant too.

I nodded. "I'll do it."

He grinned and turned to leave.

"Ray?"

"Yeah?"

"Don't you go off and worry about whether or not you've hurt my feelings," I said. "I'll do my work."

He grinned broadly. "Sam, you're a good man." He hurried away.

I watched him go, smiling to myself. There he was, the son of a hardware merchant who would own the store when his father retired. His future was almost as secure as my own, and at home he had taken his National Guard commission as somewhat of a joke. But now he was a second lieutenant whose responsibilities would eventually include the lives of thirty-six men, most of whom were his fellow townsmen. I had no doubts in my mind about Ray Mosby.

I went to work and before a week had passed I had relieved Ray of all of his petty responsibilities. Before we had spent two

117

weeks at sea, I was promoted to buck sergeant, in 1942 the highest enlisted rank in a platoon.

One day, during the evening alert, Ray and I lounged at our disaster posts and talked.

"Let's do a little confessing, Sam," Ray said.

"Hmmm?"

"Back in the days when you and Jenny were first married and Jenny and Virginia Lou talked about sex, did Jenny come home and tell you what Lou said?"

I grinned and nodded.

"So did Lou. She was horrified because Jenny was frankly in favor of a lot of sex. You know, having Jenny around and getting pregnant did Lou more good than anything I'd been able to do. She even went as far as to proposition *me* about three days before we left Texas. And when *Lou* does the propositioning, man, things've changed a lot." He shook his head in wonder and said, "Women're funny as hell sometimes, aren't they?"

"I don't know about all women, but I'll agree with you as far as my own is concerned."

"Jenny is a peculiar girl, all right. I've never seen a woman as screwy—pardon me—over a man as she is over you. Wish to hell Lou felt like that."

"I guess I'm pretty lucky," I murmured.

The weeks at sea became a month. The navy, called upon to do a job it had hoped to be able to do years later, did as well as it could by us, but living aboard the troop transport was, as Kenny Carr put it, "something that'd make living in that cow pasture seem like a Sunday-school picnic." We were stacked into holds intended to accommodate less than half our number. Our bunks, affairs made of pipes bent into rectangular shapes so as to hold, by rope lacing, a narrow piece of canvas upon which rested our hot, dirty bodies, were so uncomfortable that I often chose to sleep on the rusty steel decks. Colonel Cozzens helped our morale by offering a prize of fifty dollars—"and you can spend it anywhere you want to"—to the man who could grow the biggest cavalry mustache. At the same time, a measure of sanitation, he ordered that we weren't to grow beards. Kenny

Carr's mustache won the prize, which he promptly lost in a crap game.

The convoy of ships was pitifully insignificant in comparison to the mighty movements I saw later in the course of the war, but to me, who had never seen an ocean-going vessel of any size, it was tremendously impressive. The Regiment was carried in two ships and we were escorted by two destroyers and a smaller warship which the sailors identified as a destroyer-escort, a D-E.

The convoy's course was an erratic one; apparently this was an attempt to avoid submarine detection. And, according to the harsh, metallic voice on the public-address system which identified itself as the Captain, we were traveling almost completely around the globe and were coming to our destination, Australia, "through the back door." I never saw another ship during the entire voyage.

It was on the forty-second day of the voyage that a submarine spotted us. The destroyer which led the convoy was five or six miles astern of us, lazily tracking back and forth in the bright sunlight. I had begun to think that the Pacific war was going to be confined to the Philippines when I saw the destroyer's signal lamp suddenly blink madly for a moment before the ship heeled over sharply and dashed wildly to the south. The D-E answered the signal with several frantic squeals of its siren and, full speed, burst between the two transports and raced to the assistance of the lead destroyer. We were left under the obviously weak guardianship of the remaining destroyer. I was aware now of what sailors had meant when they described transports as sitting ducks, for we seemed slow and waddling. The PA system blared: *"When the warning is given on this PA system, every man aboard will stand on his tiptoes. If a torpedo hits while you're standing flat-footed it will most likely break your ankles."*

The episode, however, was anticlimactic, for the antisub mines made no earsplitting thunder when they exploded and the high tower of water the movies liked to picture wasn't present. There was a heavy vibration in the ship and a slight sucking sensation in the ears immediately following each explosion, and that was all. The sub was sunk; it seemed so easy.

The high, sunny days passed, each charged with fearful gloom as the PA system kept us informed of the progress of the war. The Japs had wrecked Allied shipping at Darwin; we had lost the Battle of the Java Sea; in March all of Indonesia and New Guinea were open to occupation by the little men who, we had predicted, wouldn't last more than six months.

On the last day of March we reached Australia and were soon camped in a meadow behind a small southwestern port town. In April Jap carrier planes demolished the British naval base at Colombo in Ceylon.

It was during the same month that I heard the first cheerful news of the year. Doolittle's B-25's bombed Tokyo, a gesture that wasn't as ineffectual as it was later thought to be, for it proved that the Japs weren't playing a game we couldn't play too.

During the voyage we had been almost certain that we were being rushed to the defense of the Philippines and when Bataan fell in early April and Corregidor in early May, we greeted the news with mixed melancholy and cheer. Those men were lost—but it might have been us.

"Goddamnit!" Ray spewed. "Are we going to let the slant-eyed little bastards push us all over the Pacific?"

Meanwhile, we trained. No longer did we laugh at the senseless maneuvering we were required to go through, even if we were doing exactly the same things we had done in Texas and at home, for, stupid as it was, we hoped with a dumb desperation that somehow it would stand us in good stead. We stood our guard with the minimum of griping and endured the endless night problems with some degree of grace, for the Colonel seemed to be at each man's shoulder, quietly urging him on.

Although he was outwardly the same man, Colonel Cozzens was no longer the prominent cotton planter and leading citizen of a small Southern town; he was a soldier. It was true that he didn't remotely resemble the traditional picture of the soldier, for he didn't cuss, carry pearl-handled revolvers or make colorful news for the press. He still loped about his regiment with that long, easy stride and his voice was gentle enough that when he reprimanded a man for some minor inefficiency, he sounded more like a father than a man of blood and iron.

"Now, son," he would say, "don't try to make it so hard. Do it slow till you get it right, then speed it up and, finally, you'll be plowing right down the middle."

It must have been his gentle approach that made the Regiment into what an inspecting general called "the best goddamn outfit in the Pacific." Even the Yankees and their less gentle approach to various problems were finally under the Colonel's spell. When he loped upon the crude wooden stage to address his regiment, he was cheered until my ears rang.

I talked to the Colonel only once during our stay in Australia. He called me to his tent one night when I was Sergeant of the Guard.

"Evening, Sir," I said.

He jerked erect. I hadn't noticed that he was asleep; he had seemed merely slumped in his chair.

"Looks to me like you might be needing a little sleep."

He blinked the sleep out of his eyes. "Sam boy!" he said quietly. "Sit down, sit down. I'm a little ashamed of myself. Jenny had to write and make me promise to check up on you. Sit down, Son, sit down." He handed me a cigarette and snapped his lighter for me. "Sam, you're taking good care of yourself?"

Before I could answer, he rushed on, "It's easy to see you are. Tanned, lean, eyes're clear, hand's steady."

"What about your own, Colonel?"

He glanced at his hands. "Oh, sleep'll stop that."

"I'd try it then, if I were you."

He shrugged. "Better be glad, Sam, that you never took a commission. Getting my friends' sons ready to fight—and possibly die—is no fun. We'll be getting in on an invasion some of these days. Somebody'll get killed and I'll be——" He stopped and took a deep drag from his cigarette. "You been hearing from Jenny regularly?"

"At least a letter a day, often two, sometimes three."

"Proud of it, huh?"

"Yessir, I am."

"Jenny's a peculiar girl, isn't she?"

I smiled and nodded.

"Do you remember the time she went swimming with you and Bill Joe? Well, she came back and cried for three, four days because she'd said she wished you were dead. I figured she just had a crush on an older boy, but it wasn't. I didn't know it till later, but she was a grown woman, in her mind, when she was fifteen. She swore she was going to marry you. And when she came home from Miss Belle's and we took her to church that Sunday, she told me—privately—that she was going to marry you." He crushed out his cigarette. "As good a job as I did with her, I never really understood her at all. I did Bill Joe, but not Jenny."

I waited for him to go on. He glanced at his trembling hands.

"Mother has written, asking if I might take you out of Recon and put you where you won't get hurt."

"Has she?" I said.

He smiled. "I thought you'd take it that way. I just wrote"—he picked up a sealed envelope and dropped it—"and told her there can't be any favoritism, even if you are Jenny's husband." He lit another cigarette and got to his feet. "Why, Sam, if I took my favorites out of the line companies—and out of Recon—there wouldn't be a single fighting man left. Why, my boys are sons of men I've known and liked all my life!" He puffed nervously at the cigarette.

"Now I know Mother meant well, but I also know that Jenny doesn't know a thing about the letter. Jenny probably wants me to do it too, but—well, she knows it wouldn't be fair." He mopped his neck with an olive-drab handkerchief. "How do you like the new M-one rifles?"

"They're fast, but not as accurate as the Oh-three."

He nodded. "Firepower's what they're looking for these days." He snapped the light out and I followed him outside. He carefully sealed the blackout flap behind me.

We stood and looked at the sky. The stars were as numerous as those in the sky at home, but there was a difference.

Colonel Cozzens, thinking the same, said, "I don't reckon I'll ever get used to seeing the Southern Cross up there."

"Nosir."

"How do the boys like the Australian girls?"

"They like them," I said, and added with some embarrassment: "They depleted our rubber supply, anyhow."

The Colonel chuckled. "That's modern times for you."

"Yessir."

"Ray Mosby's a good officer, isn't he?"

"He's the best."

"Yes," the Colonel said quietly, "he's the best I have. And I have a lot of good ones. All amateurs, thank the good Lord."

"Yessir."

"Ray's been saying some good things about you lately. In California he said he was going to break you. The other day he said you were all and more than he could ask for in a non-com." He laughed dryly. "I accused him of apple-polishing—uh——" He snapped his fingers, trying to think of a word. "What's that saying the new men brought in? Means the same thing as apple-polishing."

"Brown-nosing."

"Now I wonder," the Colonel mused softly, "how in the devil that ever got to mean anything." He chuckled. "Brown-nosing."

14

The island loomed in the distance, a blue hulk whose mountain made it resemble the silhouette of a grotesque, double-humped camel. It was formidable; it existed as a portion of that other world, the enemy's.

It was early dawn and, just as the tip of the sun showed over the horizon, the naval bombardment stopped and the huge convoy was pervaded by an onerous silence that made my hands and armpits sweat. The smell that came from the open collar of my fatigue jacket had a curious, acid edge to it. Through my binoculars I saw the beach, but the distance was so great that I could get only a suggestion of the damage done by the bombardment, which had gone on through the previous night and day.

"Sam!" It was Ray Mosby, interrupting a guarded conversation he had been having with the Colonel. "I told you to make the men keep their life jackets on." Then, in a gentler tone, he added: "Keep your eyes open, Sam boy."

Meleski, Saunders and Raker were sitting on their life jackets, waiting sullenly. It was odd, I thought, advancing on them, that these three men's reaction to fear was sullenness.

"Get those life jackets on," I said sharply. Then I grinned and added: "You have enough padding on your butt without them."

They hauled themselves to their feet and slowly dragged the jackets over their shoulders.

A flight of navy fighters roared, mast high, over the ship and with an insane snarl plunged at a shallow angle toward the beach. In a moment I heard, far away, the seemingly insignificant rattle of their machine guns as they strafed the island. A silence followed and the stench of armpits became fouler.

Four PT boats skittered past, headed for the beach, and after a minute I heard the quiet knocking rattle of their guns, which, to my tense ears, had a tone wholly different from the guns of the planes.

A destroyer glided gracefully across our port side, its bow wave reaching almost to its deck, fired a salvo, gracefully heeled over and rejoined the flotilla at our rear.

"*First assault wave,*" said a still-sleepy voice on the PA system, which sounded peculiarly dry so early in the morning, "*prepare to board landing craft.*"

"All right," I said quietly, my voice carrying easily in the morning air. I nodded to Kenny. "Eighteen men to the boat."

"I know it," Kenny said sharply, his temper frayed.

Ray Mosby called to me. "Sam! Make sure they keep their life jackets on."

"All right, Ray," I said, as irritated with him as Kenny had been with me.

We filed to the rail and stood quietly, waiting for the order to climb into the boats, which hung loosely from their cables.

"Wonder if we'll have it as rough as the marines did on Guadalcanal?" somebody murmured.

"Forget the marines," I said, mad as hell. "You'd be better off worrying about yourself." I heard no answer, only the scuffle of several pairs of feet.

Colonel Cozzens pressed forward, shaking hands with the men as he came through. "Now you boys listen to me," he said quietly in the early morning air. "Be sure you mind your officers and non-coms. It's going to be rough there"—he thumbed toward the island—"but you'll have a better chance of coming through if you'll mind your officers and non-coms."

"*First assault wave,*" came the dry PA voice again, "*board landing craft.*"

We filed into position. "Good luck, son," the Colonel murmured to each man filing past. "Good luck. God bless you, son. Be careful. Don't take any unnecessary chances. Good luck. God bless you, son."

I clambered up on the railing, but the landing craft chose that moment to sway away from the ship. I hesitated.

"Jump, soldier," the coxswain said quietly, encouragingly, from his perch. "You won't miss."

I jumped and tumbled into the bottom of the boat. I recovered and turned to help those who followed me. In the other boat I heard Ray encouraging his men.

"Just jump," I called to Kenny. "I'll keep you from falling."

Kenny jumped and I caught his arm in time to prevent his falling. He smelled strongly of sweat. He quietly made his way to the front of the troop well and stood waiting while I helped the others aboard. We were lowered into the water and the coxswain started the engine, which billowed diesel fumes over the water and into the troop well. The boat pulled away from the ship and the fumes were blown away.

"Can we smoke?" Raker asked.

125

"Go ahead," I said.

The ship was as large as a mountain from this vantage point, but I could see only the two humps of the island. Overhead, the sun had risen and grown into a ball as bright as stainless steel. Ray's boat was thirty yards away and I could see him peering, not toward the island, but at a dark, gray ship that had materialized behind us. It was a destroyer-escort, which slowly inched its way through the flotilla of landing craft until it was fifty yards ahead of us. A figure brandishing a megaphone appeared on the fantail.

"We—will—lead—you—in," he called. "When—you—are—close—enough—to—see—the—beach—wave—your—arms." His voice carried faintly, but clearly over the calm water.

Ray acknowledged with a wave. The D-E moved forward and we followed closely. From the bridge of the D-E a signal lamp blinked four quick dots and the bombardment began again. First there was the distant thundering roll of the guns, then the pause, the wild, roaring swish of the shells going overhead, and, far away, the crash of the explosion on the beach. Looking to my left and right, I counted twenty landing craft, which carried the men of the first wave; a pathetic few, I thought. As we drew closer to the island, the volume of the explosions grew until I thought the next one, if it were louder, would burst my head.

A wind rose and made the water swell and roll gently. Saunders vomited with a harsh, dry sound that immediately made Webster sick too. Although not a single one of the eighteen men moved, I said, "Keep your heads down." The coxswain, perched high behind his wheel, seemed to be in complete ignorance of the danger of the situation; he was preoccupied with maintaining the proper interval between his boat and those on each side of him.

The blast of the bombardment continued to grow until, with the same quick four blinks of its signal lamp, the D-E stopped it.

"What'd they stop shooting for?" Raker looked up at me and said.

"We're getting pretty close," I said.

126

"Oh god," Webster murmured wretchedly. He was pale, sickeningly gray, his lips were blue and his chin trembled.

From the corner of my eye I saw Ray wave toward the fantail of the D-E, which promptly dropped a smoke pot into the water and made a shallow turn toward the open sea. I peered at the beach through my binoculars, seeing it plainly now. From the water's edge to a distance of a hundred yards, there was nothing but twisted, splintered palms and heaped, tossed sand. A thin ribbon of smoke slithered gracefully, peacefully into the sky from a small fire the bombardment had started. The beach was less than a hundred yards away.

My throat was tight and dry and I swallowed with some effort, sensations which are similar to those one has immediately before he makes love to a desirable woman. But I wasn't sweating now; my hands were dry and warm. And I was steady and calm; icy, tautly calm.

"Okay, Sarge," the coxswain called—casually calm—from his exposed perch.

"On your feet!" I called.

Only Webster failed to rise.

"Kenny! Get Web up!"

"Get up, Web," Kenny said. "Get up, boy! *Goddamn you*, GET UP!"

Webster rose shakily and attempted to nod so I would know he was ready, but all he could manage was a few convulsive jerks of his head. He was so gray and blue-lipped he appeared to be a clumsily made-up clown.

"*Here we goooooooooooooo!*" The sailor was so calm that he seemed foolish.

There came a heavy crunch as the boat struck the sand, followed immediately by the metallic rattle of the ramp as it fell to permit our exit.

I took a deep breath. "*Let's go!*" I yelled hoarsely.

I sprinted madly over the fluffy sand and didn't stop running until I reached a heavy log, thirty yards from the water. Only then did I turn to see what the others had done. They were crouched behind me.

"Spread out!" I yelled.

They huddled closer.

"*Spread out!*"

They moved slowly, as if each of them drew behind him an inert, invisible shadow that dogged his every track. They glared at me with scared, accusing eyes, hating me viciously. I cursed them with every obscenity I had ever heard. To my right I heard Ray Mosby doing the same.

"Sam," Kenny called softly, "Web didn't come."

I glanced back at the yawning mouth of the boat and saw Webster, huddled into a corner of the troop well, his back to the beach. The coxswain waited patiently for me to come after Webster. I rushed across the sand and charged into the troop well, grabbed Webster by his collar and jerked him erect. He slumped. Carefully leaning my rifle against the bulkhead, I held Webster by his collar, at arm's length, and kicked his butt as brutally hard as I could.

"Get moving, you yellow bastard!" I gritted.

And he moved. Every time he stumbled, I kicked him again. Webster whimpered, but he didn't protest my kicks. I shoved him into Kenny's arms.

"Keep him moving," I said quietly.

Not a shot had been fired.

"*Now keep your interval, you goddamn stupid bastards!*" I shouted hoarsely. "LET'S GO!"

I sprang across the log and raced across the broken beach until I reached a depression, a shell hole, deep enough to shelter all of us. The men scattered themselves around the hole.

"That's more like it," I growled roughly.

For a brief instant I was amazed by the dreamy clarity of the scene and at my own calmness. Kenny, his hand clutching a twisted collar, was dragging Webster behind him. Webster dropped his rifle and Kenny, calmly, tenderly, looped the sling around Webster's neck and nodded that they were ready to go.

"All the way this time!" I yelled.

Before the murk of the jungle closed around me, I turned and saw the landing craft of the second wave hitting the beach. I tore through the jungle the way a drowning man flays at water and I didn't stop until I reached the abrupt rise of the thirty-foot ridge that was our first objective. We were, according to the briefing, two hundred yards from the beach.

I was totally exhausted.

Flat on my stomach, I looked down the ridge and saw my men. They were in position. I looked into the jungle ahead of me. There was nothing. There was no movement at all. And, except for our harsh breathing, a silence seemed to drift ahead of us and on into a deeper silence beyond. The final objective of the day was a hundred yards into that silence.

I could see it. Rather I could see a cone-shaped thickening in the jungle. I got to my feet, as much to take a deep breath as to impress my men with my bravery.

"All right," I said calmly, "we'll walk the rest of the way."

They docilely stumbled to their feet and obediently tumbled down the far side of the ridge. Calmly and easily, I hated them. Like sheep, I thought. If you had any guts or brains, you'd tell me to go straight to hell.

Webster collapsed at the bottom of the ridge. I rushed back, insane with anger, and jerked him erect.

"I'll kick you every step of the way, Web," I hissed, "if you don't straighten up and act like a man."

He slowly raised his head and gave me a bleary, exhausted stare that unsuccessfully tried to hide a hatred that would never dissolve. He nodded weakly; he stumbled forward. Kenny reached to help him.

"Keep your hands off him, Carr!" I said. "If he's not man enough to make it by himself, we'll leave him right here."

And then, a moment that burned itself into my memory so deeply that it will remain forever, Kenny looked at me with frank, open admiration.

"Yeah," I growled sourly, "I'm the boy, all right."

Kenny smiled, then grinned.

And so we walked to our objective. The strength it took to climb the hill, a cone-shaped knoll that rose out of the jungle to a height of forty feet, almost finished me. But when Webster again collapsed, with a loud wail akin to the sound made by a frightened rabbit, halfway up the hill, I forgot my exhaustion.

"On your feet, you yellow bastard," I called down to him,

standing completely erect, entirely forgetful of what a fine target I was making.

Webster moved, but he couldn't get to his feet.

"All right then, goddamnit," I called down, "crawl! That's more your speed."

Webster rolled over and pulled himself up on his hands and knees.

"That's it," I sneered, "crawl! *Crawl!*"

And he started crawling.

I turned to the men and snarled, "Get to digging."

The men had been waiting for me to give the order!

They fell to work quickly, but quietly, and I caught several of the admiring glances Kenny had flashed on me back in the jungle. Kenny went to work on the hole we were to share and before long he was drenched with sweat, but he dug steadily until he had a hole deep enough to hide both of us.

Ray Mosby's detail clambered up and set about digging holes which were to face inland. There were thirty-seven of us now and a change came over me. I had cursed my men, had even kicked Webster and had threatened him. And I was ashamed. I had done exactly as the Colonel had specifically instructed his non-coms not to do. I walked over to where Webster was frantically digging and squatted down beside him. He didn't acknowledge my presence.

"I don't know why I did it, Web."

He raised his head now. He was still gray and blue-lipped, but he was hating me with bright, steady eyes that seemed to go through me. His chin was trembling.

"Some of these days, Sam," he said, his voice somehow made more deadly by its unsteadiness, "you'll be sorry for treating me like that."

From the next hole, Raker said flatly, "I say you done right, Sam."

"I'll not forget you neither, Rake," Webster said and went back to his digging.

"That's all right with——" Raker stopped when I shook my head.

"That ain't all neither," Webster said, continuing to dig, "Carr'll rue the day he ever drug *me* around."

I went to the center of the perimeter, where Saunders was digging Ray's foxhole. Ray was setting up a mortar, its tube straight up.

"Hear you had a little trouble with Webster," Ray murmured absently.

"Yeah," I said, "I did. And I made it worse."

"Did, huh? How's that?"

"I kicked him. Cussed him too."

He glanced up. "I wouldn't worry about it. The other men told me you did a first-rate job."

"That still doesn't make it right."

He stomped the mortar base into the ground. "I did a little kicking and cussing myself. Fromage. Tried to yellow-out on us. I kicked his ass till he got so mad he dared me to kick him again." Ray dusted his hands. "I kicked so hard then that he fell down, but when he got up he got back in line and stayed there." He grinned suddenly. "Went over to apologize a minute ago and he didn't know what I was talking about. I think he thought *I'd* gone crazy."

As far as I was concerned, the first shot of World War II was fired immediately after Ray finished speaking. My neck was wrenched back and around; in my right ear was a heavy, clanging sound that I had never heard before. I landed on my back with a breath-jarring thump. My helmet was gone.

"*Damn!*"

There was nothing in sight but several protruding rumps, for the men had fallen into the half-finished foxholes. Ray appeared over me.

"You all right, Sam?" he asked anxiously.

I struggled to a squatting position. "What the hell happened?"

Ray handed me my helmet. A bullet had struck the front of it and, because of the angle of entry, it had followed the inside contour, making a complete circle around my head before it went out the same hole it had made in entering.

The firing began. Bullets zipped sharply across the knoll. I jumped into my foxhole with Kenny. There were four Japs shooting at us, but I couldn't locate them. They were inland from us, but that was all I could be certain of. Each of the four Japs fired five times and that was all. I crawled out of my hole.

"Get'em to digging, Sam," Ray said.

I made the rounds, urging the men on, but they didn't need it. Their holes deepened, the three machine guns were set up and the BARmen had established their lanes of fire quicker than the record had been in training. Only one man, Fromage, was loafing. He was seated comfortably in his half-dug foxhole and on his face was a silly grin, the kind he would have given a teacher had she caught him red-handed in some devilment or another.

He was dead.

I closed my eyes and, for no good reason, thought how I had remembered his name; in French, it meant cheese. A boy from Louisiana who had never had much to say, who had been scared but had forgotten the butt kicking Ray had given him. I was thankful—and ashamed of being so—that he wasn't from Gray's Landing.

"Ray," I called.

Ray hurried over and peered into the foxhole. "Oh my God," Ray prayed softly. He recovered quickly enough to add: "Get a detail and bury him. I'll make a record of the grave location."

Raker, Meleski and I dug a hole and, before we placed the body in it, I removed his dog tags and emptied his pockets, which contained a packet of letters, a penknife, a steel washer, an American twenty-five cent piece and a package of rubber contraceptives. Possibly, I thought wanly, an equally meek girl had met a boy here whom she could call her own.

"Hey!" Kenny said. "Where's Web?"

Immediately the fury of the beach assault came back to me. "If that yellow bastard——" I began. Then I remembered. "Forget about Webster," I said loudly. "If he wants to spend the night alone out there, it's his own business."

Webster burst out of the jungle and scampered up the

knoll. He was cursing wildly and most of it was directed at me. He wasn't carrying a rifle. I was waiting for him.

"If you're so hell-bent on getting revenge, Web," I said, "I'll see that you get your chance when the campaign's over."

Webster shuffled away to his foxhole.

The death of Fromage had frightened the others. They deepened their holes and watched the jungle with a fear so intense I could smell it. Except for occasional outbursts of a suddenly wild temper, I remained calm.

When we finished eating our K-rations, Ray asked for men to take on a patrol. He found no volunteers. He appointed two men from each squad.

They returned two hours later without having heard or seen another human, although they did find what had evidently been a Jap camp. When Ray reported his find on the radio, Colonel Cozzens himself, sounding stern and calm, answered with the information that the Japs had fallen back but that George Company had located them. "They're making their way back toward us," he added.

"Looks like we can expect a little trouble tonight," Ray announced.

Not a word was said. And I remembered the lectures on the Jap's prowess as a night fighter.

"Well," Ray went on. "Sam, send six men back for grenades; each man carry two cases. Send six men for flare shells; tell them to carry all they can."

I sent Ralston, Raker and Carr as the non-coms and they selected the men they wanted. They returned an hour before dark, only a few minutes before Ray planned to send a patrol out to check on them. They were loaded with ammunition. They reported that they had seen no live Japs, but they had found two dead ones on the trail.

"Just lying on the trail?" Ray asked.

"Yeah," Raker said. "Looked like they'd both bled to death. They both had some mighty big holes in'em."

"Probably the bombardment," I said.

"Jesus!" Kenny said. "All that shelling and we're sure it killed just two Japs."

15

We heard the voice not long after the darkness had become complete. I was supposed to keep watch while Kenny Carr slept, but we were both standing in the hole, alert and tense. It was so dark, at first, that it made no difference whether my eyes were open or closed; the clouds obscured the stars. It was almost two hours after darkness before my eyes became able to see vaguely the shapes of the trees above my head. The voice, when it came, spoke no words. It sounded as if someone were humming, open-mouthed, the first two notes of a minor-keyed song.

"*Eeeeeeeeeeeeeeeeeoooooooooooooooo,*" it said softly.

There was a storm of clicks as each man released the safety on his rifle. I reached for the row of grenades on the shelf of my hole.

"What was that?" Kenny whispered sharply from no more than two inches away. His breath left moisture in my ear.

"*Eeeeeeeeeeeeeeeoooooooooooooooooooo,*" it came again, sad and slow. "*Eeeeeeeeeeeeeeeeeoooooooooooooooo.*" It was so quiet, even sweet, that it made my ears strain and ache to hear more of it, to make certain that it was a human voice. "*Eeeeeeeeeeeeeeeee-oooooooooooooooooo.*"

There was a stirring and rustle of clothing in the hole to my right and I was afraid, for an instant, that someone had gotten buck fever and was about to run. I strained to remember who was occupying the hole, but I couldn't remember until, shatteringly, he bellowed:

"*Fuk YOU, jack!*" It was Meleski.

I wanted to kill him for giving away our position, but at the same time I liked the brassy little Yankee for it.

"Shut up," Ray Mosby said coldly.

"*Eeeeeeeeeeeeeeeoooooooooooooooo.*" And then, quietly, came the words: "*Foak you too, Yank.*" The voice continued without interruption from the words it had spoken: "*Eeeeeeeeeeeeeeeoooo-ooooooooooooo.*" And finally said: "Yank! Oh, Yank! Where you are, Yank?" I was strangely unafraid.

An M-1 rifle blasted into the night.

"You miss, Yank, but we are know your position." The voice spoke quietly, slowly, as if in great pain. But its weird peacefulness was terminated by several quick blasts—rifles—and flashes of fire, which were pointed into our perimeter.

"FIRE!" Ray roared.

The three machine guns, the three BARs and most of the rifles in the platoon opened fire simultaneously with a continuous roll of blasting thunder. It had never seemed this loud on the firing range. Our guns made the Jap rifles sound weak and ineffective. The Japs stopped firing and, after a few seconds, we did also and the jungle was once again as silent and dark as a cave.

There was no sound except that of our labored breath. The night was again, after the muzzle flashes, as dark as the face of the valkyrie.

One of our men moaned softly in the dark. The sound didn't come from the throat of a man in pain; it was the audible strangulation of fear. The moan came from the direction of Webster's hole.

"Easy, men," Ray called softly.

There was no sound from the enemy.

After a few moments had passed I again became aware of things closer to me. My acid armpits; my peculiar calmness. Somebody was gripping my arm, I became aware, and had been doing so for the past few minutes. It was Kenny. His fingers dug sharply into the muscle between my elbow and shoulder.

"You hurt, Kenny?" I whispered.

"No," he replied calmly. "Why?"

"Turn loose of my arm."

The grip relaxed and then was jerked abruptly away. I heard a quietly hysterical chuckle from him which is the kind of laugh he would muster up for an unfunny joke. Kenny shuddered violently. "By god," he whispered unbelievingly, "I'm nearly scared to death."

"Me too," I whispered.

"You damn sure don't act like it."

"I am, though."

Minutes passed in a silence so absolute that it was difficult

135

to believe thirty-six men could exist in such a small area without a sound of some kind escaping.

A small scratching noise was the first indication that the Japs were still there. When they had fired on us a while before, I realized now, they had been shooting from the trees, which had placed them on approximately the same level as we were. But this new sound came from below my foxhole.

Turning toward the middle of the perimeter, I cupped my hands over my mouth, making a megaphone, and called quietly, "They're climbing the hill, Ray."

"Roger," Ray said promptly, as calm as he would have been if he had been handing merchandise over the counter of his hardware store. "Yell when you want a flare, everybody."

I heard no further sound for a long time. I thought of Webster and Kenny and Ray, and I thought mostly about Sam Gifford. I knew what had caused my temper today, but I couldn't understand why it had taken that particular form. This calmness was almost a frightening thing in itself, for I knew I wasn't a brave man. And here you are, Sam boy, waiting calmly while Japs crawl around making scratching noises that sound like crayfish inching across linoleum. Nobody ever said you'd have to do this. You live in a small town, have a mapped-out future, married to the town beauty, and you're worried because you know you ought to be scared.

The scratch came again, once to my right, and several times directly in front of me. And this time I recognized it, cloth dragging across a sharp object, a twig or a stone. Kenny twitched and changed the position of his feet. He was standing on my foot and I jerked sharply to make him move. He uttered a short, quivering sigh. I patted his shoulder. The call came from my left:

"*FLARE!*" somebody shouted hollowly.

Immediately there was the solid *thunk* as the mortar launched the projectile and, for three excruciatingly long seconds, the expected light didn't come. There was a short screaming grunt from the other side of the perimeter and still the darkness remained. When the light finally came, poised two feet in front of me was a Japanese officer; a captain, my mind registered automatically. He held his saber high over his head, like a club, and his lips were drawn and distorted by fanatic courage, revealing his long, slender teeth. His eyes darted quickly in the sudden light and he saw me. He coiled smoothly, an oiled machine of destruction, and the saber began its seemingly slow arc toward my unhelmeted head. Equally slow, I raised the muzzle of my rifle and poked it, sticklike, at the face. As I pulled the trigger I saw another rifle muzzle enter the picture from my right. I heard neither mine nor Kenny's rifle fire; there was a silent blast of powdery flame from each muzzle, both pressed within inches of their target, and the face was revealed next as a round pulp of gore. The faceless head slowly fell backward and out of sight.

From behind the tumbling figure of the Jap officer appeared another face, a clean, smiling one that looked as if it should have appeared in the chorus of *The Mikado*. And to my right, another face, into which Kenny was firing. The mikado rushed at me, laughing merrily as my trigger pulled loosely on an empty magazine. I hadn't heard the ring of the ejecting clip when I had fired into the Jap officer's face.

Both hands clutching an alarmingly long rifle, the Jap sprang at my hole; and in the flat light of the flare, he appeared to me as an eagle swooping down to smother me. The rifle had, attached to its muzzle, a bayonet, which was pointed with sure accuracy at my stomach. I stepped slowly aside and, tangling my feet with Kenny's, made a graceful arc with the butt of my rifle, which crushed into the chin of the Jap, who sighed softly and fell on top of me. The bayonet was sticking into the foxhole wall behind me. I rammed a clip into my rifle and fired directly into the back of the Jap's head. I glanced down the slope. It was empty.

I whirled about for a look behind me and the rest of the perimeter was revealed in plateau: Ray, his pistol in hand, was preoccupied with dropping another flare into the tube; Webster's hole appeared empty until a Jap stopped directly over it and prepared to fire into it—I killed him with one shot; Raker, his mouth hard and grim, was springing out of his hole to meet, with rifle butt, the charge of a Jap lieutenant. I killed the lieu-

137

tenant and Raker jumped back into his hole, jamming a clip into his rifle as he moved. Five Japs raced over Webster's hole and headed for Ray.

The first of the five was within a yard of Ray when I fired. The Jap threw up his hands, as the villain in the movie does, grabbed his head and, screaming wildly, wobbled a few steps before he died. Kenny killed the second Jap. Ray himself killed the third and dropped another flare shell into the tube. Raker killed the fourth and fifth Japs.

I jerked back around and looked down the slope. Head down, clawing at the rocks and dirt, very intent on the mechanics of climbing the slope, was another Jap. I shot him squarely in the top of the head. He merely lowered himself to the earth and lay still in a grotesquely natural position of exhaustion. I heard a sudden flurry of firing from the other side of the perimeter, the mortar *thunked* again, and there was silence. While there was still light, I carefully examined the slope below me. I saw the tossed figures of the dead Japs, one of which had no face. Before the flare died, I saw Ray, standing in his hole with his hands dangling at his sides in the attitude of an exhausted boxer, wipe sweat from his face with his sleeve; I saw only a small part of Webster's back as he fearfully huddled in his hole. I saw Raker close his eyes and sigh. I saw Meleski, his face incredibly filthy, puff his cheeks with an exaggerated sigh of relief. On three of the corpses I saw the familiar dirty green of American fatigue uniforms.

The light from the last flare brightened momentarily and flickered out. Nobody spoke at all. There was only the thin whimpering of Webster to break the silence.

16

"Ray?"

"Not so loud, man," Ray said. "What is it?"

"Web's in his hole by hisself." It was Raker's voice.

There was a moment of silence. "Sam, do you have a man you can send?"

"I'll go," Kenny whispered.

"Kenny'll do it," I called softly. To Kenny, I said: "If he starts moaning again, slug him."

Kenny grunted acknowledgment.

"Hold your fire," Ray said, "till Kenny's settled." He waited until the rustle of Kenny's crawling had ceased. "You there, Kenny?"

"Yeah."

"All right," Ray said. "If you hear any crawling, everybody, shoot."

The perimeter was silent.

I noticed now, during the dark silence, that I was quivering. Not violently; it was more like the way I would have quivered in the first chill winds of fall, and my fatigues were dripping wet with sweat. I felt strangely self-analytical. The flaws of my heritage were showing now, for only when a man is truly frightened —when he is afraid he is going to die—does he really know himself. The vicious anger I had directed at Webster's failure showed me something, but I couldn't quite identify it. The experience offers the same frustration one suffers when he is within sight of the end of a problem, only to have one small, vital key completely slip his memory. And it seemed important —a duty, the failure of which was somehow rooted in Gray's Landing—that I do my share well and, in the military jargon, "with dispatch." My treatment of Webster this afternoon was indication enough that I had failed.

The night was suddenly riddled by the fire of many machine guns and rifles. It came so suddenly that I almost cried out and was already on my feet, ready to fire my own rifle into the jungle below, when I realized, with a peculiar self-disgust, that the firing was coming from Fox Company, fifty yards to my left. During a fractional silence, I heard Webster whimpering again and, beyond that sound, Kenny's voice comforting Webster in low, unfrightened tones. And I realized that I was the one who should have gone to Webster's foxhole.

The firing increased in volume, but the new firing wasn't

coming from Fox; it came from George Company, on our right, and from King Company, on the other side of George. The heavy blast of the M-1 rifles was punctuated by the light, seemingly chirping *plink* of the Jap rifles. The jungle shifted and writhed under the flares the three companies were sending up. Shadows crept about the large trees and swelled and dissolved into the darkness of the thick undergrowth.

From both the left and the right, the firing continued spasmodically throughout the night, but Recon didn't fire another shot. Once, an hour before dawn, we heard a Jap raiding party making its way through the jungle, but we didn't fire. A few minutes after we heard the Japs pass our position, the firing on the line stopped entirely. Then, with a cloudy sky, it was dawn.

At the same time an artillery-spotting plane buzzed over our position, looking for targets.

Ray hopped agilely out of his hole and stood erect. He stretched his arms over his head and yawned as if he had spent the night playing poker. There was a thick stubble on his face, which he idly scratched with his thumb and forefinger. He beckoned.

"Well," he yawned, "let's see about damages."

We hadn't taken a step when we heard the artillery coming. It was whistling—not as it does in the movies—and we dived for Ray's foxhole. The shell passed over us and exploded in the jungle, three hundred yards ahead. Ray grinned foolishly.

"Ours," he said.

As I pulled my right leg forward to get to my feet, I noticed a slight pulling sensation, but I thought nothing of it until I saw Ray's face change. He pointed to my butt. There was a circle of dried blood there.

"You wounded, Sam?"

Dumfounded, I lowered my trousers and looked at my hip. On the right pad of my buttocks was a four-inch gash, which, from a hasty remembrance of last night, I supposed had been made when the Jap had dived at me with the bayonet.

"I didn't even know about it," I said foolishly.

Four artillery shells whistled over and exploded ahead.

Ray smiled and unhooked the bandage packet from my rifle

belt. Chuckling merrily to himself, he quickly sifted sulfa into the wound and tied the bandage around my crotch.

He peered up at me. "Great weapon, the bayonet, huh?"

"Absolutely," I managed to say.

"Well—you're cured. Purple Heart, first night out, and didn't know about it." He gave me a hearty slap on the shoulder. "Sergeant Gifford," he said expansively, "you're a good boy."

I grinned, pleased.

We walked around the west rim of the perimeter. Webster was erect, but he seemed determined to stay in his hole.

"How's it going, Web?" I said.

"If you're still thinking I'm a coward," he said, a pathetic whine in his voice, "just jump down here with me and we'll find out."

"Aw, Web——"

"Look, Web," Ray interrupted, "if Sam hadn't done you that way, you'd be out there in the jungle by yourself, so get off that crap."

Without batting an eye, Webster said, "You heard what I said to Gifford. The same goes for you too—Sir."

Kenny walked up behind us. "Cut it out, Web," he said quietly. "Just cut it out."

Webster abruptly sat down in his foxhole and turned his head away.

"Ray!" It was Raker.

We hurried across the perimeter and found Raker peering into his foxhole, wide-eyed with fear. It was Bryant, slumped over the edge of the foxhole, and he was dead.

"Goddamn," Raker said shakily, "I didn't know he was dead." Then: "I was telling'im this morning that he'd sure been quiet enough." And, after a pause, he added: "I never thought much about him not answering me."

I didn't feel so strongly about this death. Fromage, yesterday, had numbed me, I suppose, and I was still concerned with Webster. And also, Bryant was one of the replacements who had joined us when we left Texas.

Meleski, who had so defiantly yelled at the Japs last night,

141

discovered—and yelled—that the hole next to him had been untended throughout the night, for the two men in it were dead.

"Jeez," Meleski said solemnly, "no fuken wonder that Jap almost got me in the back last night."

The corpses didn't impress me at all; I was only glad that nobody from Gray's Landing had been killed.

We counted the Jap dead. There were fourteen of them, stocky, bandy-legged little men with oddly shaped helmets and long, old-fashioned-looking rifles. They lay stiff and impersonal, like dead animals, in various poses of violence. I found the Jap officer where he had tumbled down the slope after Kenny and I had fired into his face. One of our bullets had entered through the bridge of his nose, the other through his upper lip. I hated him with a rich personal hatred that took no consideration of his being dead. In his pockets I found two maps, a compass and lewd pictures. I handed the bundle to Ray without comment. I gave the saber to Kenny, who had been eyeing it covetously. Ray gave the pictures to those who had concerned themselves with the stories of the peculiar structure of the vagina of the Japanese woman. They were disappointed to discover that only the eyes of the Jap were slanted.

We ate our breakfast—K-ration—and I compared, in my mind, the red meat of my food with the face of the dead Jap officer. The color was the same; only the texture differed. I ate all of my ration.

I put four men on a detail to bury our dead and Ray marked the graves on the map so the Graves Registration Teams would have no trouble finding them. I put Meleski in charge of burying the Jap bodies.

"All right now," Meleski called, mimicking our accent, "Ah'm a needin' fo' rot good men to hep me bury them theah Jayips."

"Hmmm," Raker drawled. "If ole Meleski keeps that up, he'll learn to speak real English some of these days."

"Come on, you Rebel bastards."

Carr, Raker and I pitched in to help him. We dragged the corpses into the jungle and dropped them. Meleski bowed to each of us. We bowed in return.

142

"Gentlemen," Meleski said gravely, "shall we return to yon wooded hill and carry away yet another load of shit?"

"Let's," I said.

"Let's *us*," Meleski said.

We started back toward the knoll, but Meleski stopped us. "I'm in charge of this detail," he said sternly. "You pigs will follow at my heels."

"Carry on," I said.

"Yeah," Carr muttered, "we're right behind you."

We marched back to the knoll, while Meleski whistled "Parade of the Wooden Soldiers," and dragged down four more Japs.

We were in the jungle, listening to Meleski conduct a short funeral oration over the Jap corpses, when we heard a column of men approaching. We ran.

"Japs!" Raker yelled, as we scrambled up the knoll.

"Live ones!" Meleski added.

"Take it easy," I said—almost growled.

There was a flurry of hustling bodies and abruptly all was quiet. We waited, rifles ready to pick out the first target that showed itself.

"Little Rock," came the call from the jungle.

There was an audible sigh of relief from our perimeter.

"Pine Bluff," Ray answered.

It was Able Company, sent forward to relieve us because the Colonel wanted to use us for reconnaissance—"For a change," Carr grumbled.

As we filed into the jungle, headed for the beach, I heard the Able CO hurrying his men into position and I smiled at his fear, probably equal to that of ours last night. I felt like an old, scarred veteran of many a bloody campaign.

From far to the left I heard the sullen rumble of artillery, 155mm stuff, I reckoned, and a flight of four P-38's roared over our heads, so low that the trees swayed with their prop wash. After a moment, I heard the ragged cackle of their strafing fifty-caliber machine guns. Without warning sign of any kind, it began to rain. It rained so hard that I could barely see the high,

143

square shoulders of Ray Mosby, who stalked through the heavy growth as if it were a cool, sunny day.

Kenny said somberly, "Hope them boys in the P-38's don't get screwed up by this rain."

17

Colonel Cozzens was seated on an empty ammo case, gently reprimanding somebody through the telephone he held tiredly in his hand. He glanced up as we filed past and held up his hand for us to wait. Ray halted us and we fell to the sand. The rain stopped and the sun came out; before the Colonel had finished talking, the sand was dry and hot. Colonel Cozzens handed the telephone to a waiting lieutenant. "Tell this man," he said firmly, "his orders are to wait where he is."

He looked at us. "Well now, you're as unsoldierly-looking a bunch as I've seen all morning." He was trying to grin, but his eyes were so tired that he managed nothing more than a grotesque twisting of the lips. "Any your men get hurt, Ray?"

"Lost three, Colonel. Two wounded."

The Colonel clucked. "Guardsmen?"

"Nosir."

"I'm sorry," the Colonel said. "I'm awful sorry." He looked at me. "How'd it go with you, Sam?"

"All right, Colonel."

"He's one of the wounded, Colonel," Ray said sharply. "Don't let him kid you."

The Colonel got to his feet. "What? What's this? Now, Sam, you told me—— Where were you hurt?"

"A Jap got him with a bayonet," Ray said.

"Where? Where'd he get you, Sam?"

I couldn't stop the grin. "My butt, Sir."

But the Colonel didn't return my grin. "Are you all right, Sam?"

144

"Yessir. I didn't even know about it till this morning."

His tired face relaxed. "Good, you're all right then." He looked at my men. "Pretty scarey up there, boys?"

"Pretty scarey, Colonel," Carr and Raker said. The others were asleep.

The Colonel clawed nervously at the stubble on his chin. "First time I haven't shaved in the morning in more than twenty years," he said. "Well—*fine!* Take them over to the tent, Ray, bed them down. Sleep hard, boys. I'll be calling on you before sundown. *Medic!*"

"Yessir?"

"See about Sam's wounded butt." He tried to grin this time.

In the tent I shucked off my pack and, using it for a pillow to keep sand out of my face, fell immediately to sleep. There was a sharp pain when the medic dropped something into my wound, but it would have taken much more pain to keep me awake. The last thing I saw before I slept was Webster's back; he was leaning against the tent pole, wide awake. My sleep was dreamless.

18

The trail was dim, hardly more than a ragged ribbon that threaded between two towering walls of green jungle. The foliage, still wet with the rain that had begun and stopped a few minutes before, flapped viciously at our faces as we slowly pushed our way ahead.

There were six of us: Carr, Meleski, Raker, Ralston, Washburn and myself. I had been steadily pulling them along for more than an hour now, so long without rest that my fatigues were spongy with sweat. Under my left arm a rash had broken out and the rough fabric of my fatigues caused me to grit my teeth every time I moved the arm. But I was determined to keep moving.

We wore fatigue caps instead of helmets because the undergrowth would scratch up a sizable noise on the metal. I hated the cap almost as much as I did the helmet, for, while the helmets were heavy and made my neck sore and stiff, the cap gave my scalp no ventilation and my head was itching madly. I finally put the cap in one of my cargo pockets.

Our objective, the base of the camel-back mountain, only four miles from the beach, still seemed as far away as it had been when we first sighted it, a half hour before. My feet, squeegy wet in my shoes, ached and smarted with the irritation of my wool socks. My legs itched under the heavy canvas leggings. My shoulder throbbed with the weight of my at-sling rifle. My fingers were stiff and swollen with the heat. And I had a headache. I was hurrying because the Colonel had told Ray and me that all five patrols (the entire Recon Platoon had been sent out in sections of six men) were to be back at the beach before sundown.

For the third time in the past thirty minutes, Kenny begged, "For the love of *god*, Sam, let's rest!"

"Maybe you'll shut up, Kenny," I whispered, "if I tell you we're two miles behind the Jap lines right now."

He said nothing more about rest stops.

I stumbled on with blind devotion to a duty that, as exhaustion crept upon me, became less and less sane. But I wouldn't stop; we couldn't stop. The slightest pause was wasted time and would spoil the margin of safe return I had calculated we would need if we made contact with the Japs. I had been ordered to fight only if it were absolutely necessary, but the only route of retreat was the trail we were on now, and it would have been simple for the Japs to let us march innocently past them and then cut us off from our own lines.

I wanted, desperately, to keep alert, but exhaustion deadens even the most desperate desires.

A right smart of a small-town gentleman, I was, I was thinking. One of those who owns a house on Oak Street (I thought of the bulky house, suddenly, with some disgust and wondered why I had been so stubbornly insistent on building one so much like the house I had grown up in). And I owned a Cadillac, the car only successful middle- and old-age men drive, and I was ashamed now because I hadn't had the will power to tell the Colonel that such a gift wasn't right for me. And I had married the prettiest girl in town. I wondered how many young men there were in America who were exactly like me. Somebody always gets the breaks in a small town, the secure future, the comfortable present and the pretty wife, and, except for the wife, it is never of his own doing. And it doesn't train him for squarely meeting a crisis; he finds that the only thing he can do, when his leadership fails, is curse and kick.

Jenny, I thought, what would you think of me now? I'm dirty, I'm bearded, and I stink. I don't smell, I don't have b.o.; I stink. And Jenny, you wouldn't believe it, but I'm so tired right now that I couldn't possibly play. I can't begin to tell you——

I was brought to my senses by the murmur of foreign voices ahead of me. Surprisingly enough, I moved calmly when I turned to my patrol and signaled the men off the trail and into the waiting jungle. We plunged out of sight, only a few feet, and lay waiting. My head was clear, startlingly clear; I was even sane enough to count the Japs as they marched past in single file. Ninety-six of them, a full company, led by a seedy-looking, bespectacled Jap lieutenant whose saber tangled in his legs twice before he was out of sight. Saner still, I wrote down that information in my notebook. The Japs were moving slowly, and they were silent. Then they were out of sight.

I waited a full minute before I pulled my feet up under me to rise. And I heard another Jap column coming. There were ninety-six men in this one too. Fresh companies, not a man missing. These Japs were new to combat too, I could easily see that, for I got a glimpse behind that fabled Oriental face that tells nothing to the stranger. These men were scared, afraid they were going to die. Maybe their officers hadn't given them the pep talk that lashed them into their peculiarly insane bravery.

Another company passed. They were maintaining an interval of a hundred yards between companies.

Somehow or other, I had to get the patrol back to Regimental. There would be a major attack tonight, all along the line, one that would make the attack of last night look like a mere reconnaissance clash. But reaching Regimental was a problem not often mentioned in the training manuals; especially small was the material telling one how to share the trail with Japs. Going through the jungle itself was impossible. There was but one thing to do; here must be what the generals like to call "a calculated chance."

I tugged and pulled my way, flat on my belly, through the growth until I reached Kenny. We froze as another company of Jap infantry marched past.

"Kenny," I whispered, "we got to get back and report. You stay behind me. I'm going to tell each man that we're falling in with these Japs——"

"We can't do——"

"They're a hundred yards apart and the trail's crooked. That's good enough."

"Oh my god, Sam."

"Hush," I said sharply. "That's the only thing I can do and that's what we'll do."

Kenny stared fixedly at my eyes for a moment, during which two drops of sweat fell from the tip of his nose, and he nodded. I heard him crawling behind me as I took my message to the other men. Each of them was alarmed, but I whispered the order, "Fall in behind me," with as an imperative an air as I could and they didn't protest.

The exhaustion of a while ago was gone. I had never felt better in my life. My heart was pounding steadily and my hands were still and sure. I let another Jap company go past before I rose and motioned the patrol to follow me.

I stepped firmly onto the trail, trampled now by hundreds of Jap feet, and turned in the direction of the beach. We marched steadily and without event. Only twice did I see the backs of the Jap column ahead of us. Only once did Raker pass up a warning that the column behind was gaining. It was stupidly, childishly, faultlessly perfect. The design of a genius. And, to add to the perfection of the plan, a heavy rain began to fall.

Even the problem of passing the Japs when they stopped was simple. When they reached a certain, probably prearranged place on the trail, a huge, vine-choked tree, they simply melted into the jungle. They were moving off the trail to wait for darkness. In the thrashing rain, we calmly walked past the vine-covered tree, probably watched from no more than a few feet away by eyes which didn't know whether we were aware of them or not. I turned to my patrol and was met by five looks of mingled astonishment and fear.

"Let's go," I said quietly. I broke into a run. Behind me I heard the heavy breathing and the pounding of canteens that told me the patrol had heard my command and was reacting with much energy.

If I hadn't given the order to run, the Japs would have probably thought we didn't know about them. They had a reputation for hiding and letting patrols pass them by. But our running told them. I heard a cry of alarm, followed by a shriek of rage, and one of their long rifles *plinked* a bullet over our heads, but we were too far gone for them to give pursuit. Somebody in the Imperial Japanese Army was going to catch hell. I laughed, but I was breathing so hard that it sounded more like a croak. I kept the patrol at a run until we reached the George Company perimeter. I hurriedly told the George CO what was up and we walked on toward Regimental.

After a few moments, I stopped the patrol and we took a two-minute break. We could spare it. It was during the break that the curious trembling came over me again. It wasn't violent, nor a sick trembling; it was hardly more than an awareness of my body.

"Damn'f it didn't work," Kenny breathed in wonder.

"Damn'f it didn't," Raker said.

"General Gifford," Meleski said to the others, "is quite the military man, right?"

I grinned at him. "You no-good Yankee bastard."

"Son," Meleski said, "I'm sure Robert E. Lee would be proud of you."

It was nearly sundown when I led the patrol into the perimeter at Regimental. The other patrols were already in and the Colonel greeted me with the information that he was getting ready to send another patrol after me. I quickly made my report and without another word, the Colonel hastened to his message center, where he sent warnings to the line companies.

"How'd you manage to get back through all that, Sam?" Ray asked.

I explained what had happened.

"Well," Ray mused, "looks like you might be getting a little ribbon to go with that Purple Heart ass-gash of yours."

I was too tired to laugh.

"Well, anyhow," Ray muttered, "we're going to have a little trouble on our hands tonight."

19

The first shots came from the direction of George Company, which had advanced to a position five hundred yards inland from where it had been this morning. I had heard much of George's combat skill this afternoon after I had returned from the patrol, and from the volume of the Jap rifle fire, George was going to meet a full test before the night was over. Soon the Jap and American weapons were firing so fast that it became no longer possible to distinguish one shot from another; the explosions rolled through the jungle in one, solid roar that made me shudder with the pictures my mind made up to go with the shooting.

The firing next came from the sectors occupied by Fox, How and King Companies. The thunder of the weapons rumbled back to us here at the beach with a strange, faraway sound. I wondered about that until I remembered the small ridge that ran between my position and theirs.

I heard Major Gates, the Colonel's adjutant, call out: "The Colonel has a one-man guard, Ray. Send two men."

"Hush, man!" the Colonel said sternly.

"Two men, Ray," Major Gates said firmly.

"Kenny and I'll get it, Ray," I called.

"*Shut up all this loud talking!*" the Colonel shouted.

"All right, Sam," Ray said.

"Hold your fire," I said loudly. "Kenny Carr and Sam Gifford're moving."

"No discipline at all," I heard the Colonel mutter as Kenny and I dropped into the big message center hole. "Sam?"

"Right here, Sir."

"First thing tomorrow morning," the Colonel said gruffly, "I'm going to have a few words with you."

"All right, Sir."

"Yelling all over the perimeter. . . ."

I smiled in the darkness. A very military outfit, our regiment, I thought.

The perimeter formed an almost-perfect circle. The Communications, Antitank, Pioneer, and Recon Platoons, rather doubtfully strengthened by the clerks from the headquarters section and a few cooks, made up a company of more than two hundred men. We were armed with rifles, machine guns of both thirty and fifty caliber, tommy-guns and, for the senior officers, pistols. Headquarters Company, if we received an attack, had the fire power to take care of itself. It wouldn't be long, I suspected, until we found out whether or not we had the right men.

The TG, a continuous-tone telegraph operating through the telephone wires and used when perimeter security won't permit talking aloud on the phone, began its weak chirping. The radio operator scrambled over and held the single earphone to the side of his head and listened carefully. He had to listen intently because he had to get the message correctly and keep it in his head; it was impossible to write in the darkness. After the chirping stopped, he tapped out a couple of letters and punched the Colonel.

"Colonel," he whispered, "company reports." He had a hard, brassy Yankee accent.

The Colonel didn't answer and for a moment I was afraid a Jap had sneaked into the hole and had done him in with a knife. I crawled over to the Colonel's side. He was snoring peacefully.

"The Colonel's asleep," I whispered. "What's the report?"

"King Company wants to fall back."

For a second I was too frightened to go through with it, but the Colonel was asleep for the first time in two days.

"Tell King Company," I said, "to stay where it is and keep fighting."

"Are you kidding?" the radioman whispered hoarsely. "That's for the Colonel to say. Who'n hell are you?"

"Look, you Yankee bastard," I whispered, "the Colonel's asleep and you're going to tell King to hold on, hear?" I poked a finger into his ribs and held it there.

"Fuk you, jack."

I poked harder. "Retreat impossible at night in jungle," I said. "Send that."

"Go fuk yourself, fella."

I cuffed him smartly across the cheek. "*Send it!*" I whispered harshly.

"You'll be sorry for that, jack."

"*Send it!*"

I heard the TG begin its weak chirp. When he finished, I said, "What'd you send?"

"White Horse not available. Have been advised retreat impossible in jungle at night."

"You're learning, son, you're learning."

"Go fuk yourself, jack."

I took my position again and waited. The stars glimmered brightly in the clear, dustless sea air and a cool breeze drifted in from the ocean. Some war, I thought, some regiment. A staff sergeant commands a regiment because he's concerned about his father-in-law's sleep. Too many kinfolks and friends, the heavy brass in Washington would think, should never be in the same regiment together. The National Guard Bureau had heard that argument for years. Well now, brass, to hell with *you!* I chuckled silently.

There came a quick, faint rustle in the jungle wall. The men made too much noise as they released the safeties on their rifles and the machine gunners pulled the bolts back. Goose-pimples rippled along my arms and shoulders; I leaned far over the edge of the hole to listen. The men of the perimeter were braced. The Colonel snapped erect.

"What's happening?" he whispered.

"Don't know yet, Colonel."

The TG chirped weakly again.

"What's the TG saying, son?" the Colonel said softly.

"King wants to fall back, sir." I noted with relief that he didn't say "again."

"Of course not," the Colonel whispered indignantly. "They'd get lost and cut to pieces. Nobody but Japs and fools wander around a jungle at night."

The radioman tapped out the message. I heard Kenny let his breath go with a gusty sigh. I turned back to the jungle.

There was no time to call for a flare. From the edge of the jungle came a sharp *pow,* then four more such explosions in rapid sequence. I had never heard this before and was standing erect, wondering, when there came five explosions, violent ones, followed by the weird whine of steel fragments. We were under attack from the "knee mortar" that had been talked about earlier in the Pacific war. We had heard recordings of its propellant's explosion during our training in Australia, but the Training Command hadn't given consideration to the difference between an explosion in the jungle and one in a recording studio. Our perimeter was in an uproar.

A few men, cooks and clerks who had been stationed on the side of the perimeter next to the sea, broke and ran, yelling hoarsely, down the beach. Major Gates sprang from his foxhole and took after them.

I huddled in the foxhole. I wasn't scared, at least not enough to run, but I was confused. I was in the act of turning to ask the Colonel what to do when he spoke for the first time since the mortars had fired.

"Ray," he called calmly, "can you tell me where the things are coming from?"

"About seven o'clock," Ray said, "in front of the first squad of the Antitank Platoon."

"First squad, Anti——" the Colonel began.

153

The *pow* of the knee mortars came again and I dived wildly for the Colonel and pulled him down with me.

"Now see here, Sam . . ." I heard him mutter.

He didn't finish, for one of the mortar shells exploded near the edge of the hole and we were caught in a deluge of sand, steel fragments and earsplitting sound.

"You all right, Colonel?"

"Certainly," he said stoutly and stood up again. He silently brushed the sand out of his fatigues.

"*NINE O'CLOCK*," somebody screamed. "*HURRY!*"

Immediately came the *thunk* of our mortar firing a flare shell and I scrambled to my feet. When the flare burst I saw a Jap, running with a curious crablike gait, hurtling across the sand directly toward our foxhole. I saw, too, that he held something, a round object, clutched to his breast. Hardly aware of the muzzle blast of the two-hundred-odd weapons, I raised my rifle slowly and fired. The Jap didn't halt or even hesitate. He flinched, but he continued in his headlong run. I fired again and hit him, but he didn't stop. I fired again. Then, frantically pumping the trigger, I emptied the remaining six rounds in the clip directly into the flying Jap's chest. On the last round the object clutched to his breast exploded with a deafening roar and the Jap disappeared. Pieces of human meat were blown all over the perimeter. I tumbled backward and landed solidly on the Colonel. The round thing the Jap had carried was a land mine. I stumbled to my feet, but there were no more Japs.

The machine guns were raking and lashing at the jungle wall and the truck drivers were peppering away with their tommy-guns. And the riflemen were emptying clip after clip as fast as they could reload. The perimeter was smothered with the roar. The muzzle flash of the fifty-caliber machine guns was startlingly long.

"*CEASE FIRE!*" Ray Mosby bellowed.

It took a full minute for the deafened gunners to pass the word around before, with one final ripping blast from a BAR-man, the perimeter was silent. I heard the soft moan of the dying and the urgent cries of the wounded. The silence made

154

my heart stumble a few beats before it took up its steady pounding again. I heard Webster cry out once, but I couldn't locate him. The last flare died out.

Major Gates called out that he was bringing some men back into the perimeter and, after the rustle of their hurried steps had gone, the silence was again solid. We waited.

The jungle rustled faintly and immediately there came a sound of dozens of grenade spoons being released, each with a sharp, slapping *pop,* and dim spark trails arched into the black wall. I ducked and hundreds of steel fragments whistled over my head. After a pause, during which there came a hoarse cry of pain from within the jungle, the knee mortars fired again. Their shells exploded all over the perimeter, throwing fragments and sand; we were safe from the fragments if we kept our heads down—so long as one of the shells didn't land in a foxhole.

"*MACHINE GUNS!*" the Colonel thundered, "*FIRE!*"

The gunners answered promptly with furious rolls of thrashing, beating fire into the jungle. The knee mortars stopped firing. Behind the crash of our guns, I heard the distant cry of wounded and dying Japs. Our own wounded cried out too, but with far less abandon.

For two hours there was no further sound from the Japs. Occasionally our machine gunners sprayed the jungle to discourage the setting up of the knee mortars and we heard the cry of their wounded, but that was all. Doc Wingate and his medics had tended to our men and had made them comfortable. It was the aid men who kept the perimeter at nervous edge by their constant crawling about. "Medic," they called softly as they inched over the waves of sand, "Little Rock." "Fayetteville," was their countersign. The Japs continued their silent waiting.

The silence was broken by a cry that began as a scream and, as the vocal cords ripped and gave away, degenerated into a loud gurgle as the man died. It came from behind me, toward the water's edge, where the cooks and clerks had been stationed. Our mortar launched a flare shell, but I saw the shadowy figures racing across the sand before the light came. They

155

had waded down the surf and had attacked us from the rear. The gunners hustled their guns around and the firing began again.

As the flare burst, I saw one of the Japs break free of the group, halt, and hurl something toward my foxhole. The Colonel, Kenny, the radioman and I all ducked with a startled grunt. The Jap missed. The object he had hurled was a Molotov cocktail, for it burst with a sizzling pillar of fire behind me. I killed the Jap.

There were Japs all over the perimeter, about fifty of them, and the machine gunners, forced to fire across the perimeter, were shooting high. I was momentarily sickened by the sight of the tracer bullets disappearing into the faces and chests of the darting Japs. They died with fierce cries, yelling until their hearts stopped beating, and I saw one of them, too torn and bloody to stand erect, feebly throw a handful of sand into the foxhole nearest to him.

The stubby, bandy-legged creatures raced into the lanes of fire, all of them shouting "BANZAI," and fell, with great head and chest wounds, into the cowering figures of the cooks and clerks who huddled fearfully into the bottoms of their foxholes. One Jap, his right arm completely blown away, didn't stop until a bright tracer disappeared into his face and spurted out the base of his neck. There were so many targets that I didn't bother to aim.

There were a dozen or more flares in the air now.

"Oh my god," the Colonel murmured.

Suddenly one of the Japs burst into flame. The Molotov cocktail he had carried was hit and the flame raced up his body and over his head. He halted and the firing paused momentarily too, but when he started running again the gunners followed him. He raced, silently, past me, turned, and ran toward the jungle. He was but a few yards from the undergrowth when the gunners finally got him. He crumpled, still burning like a huge torch, to the sand and the gunners went back to work on the Japs who remained. The smell of burning flesh was so strong that I vomited a gush of slime over the stock and rear sight of my rifle.

There were seven Japs left now and they organized, a miracle while receiving such fire, and rushed the foxhole where the switchboard was, probably thinking Colonel Cozzens was there. They stood and fired their long rifles directly into the three men below them until the gunners toppled them into the hole, where they fell on the bodies of the dead Americans. And the Japs were all dead; the firing ceased.

I fell to a sitting position. My head was aching so much that my eyes seemed to bulge. I clamped both hands over my face and rocked to and fro, trying to rid my memory of what I had seen. The headache went away when the trembling began. I took several deep gasps of breath before I was calm enough to see about the Colonel.

"Get some men on the switchboard, please, Major Gates," the Colonel said shakily. "Oh my god," he murmured to nobody, "what a horrible sight for young men to have to see."

20

The attacks the Japs had staged last night had broken their own backs. It remained for the Regiment to complete the conquest of the island, which, now, would be more of a mop-up than a hard strike. The next day George Company advanced boldly to the base of the camel-back mountain and radioed for permission to begin the scaling of its slopes. This operation, which was originally scheduled to begin a full week later, would seldom be bloody, sometimes dull.

"Tell George's CO," the Colonel said, "that he's not going to win the war alone. Send up Charlie, Dog and Easy Companies to relieve the ones that were mauled. Tell George to wait where he is till Fox joins him." The Colonel paused gravely. "Tell the King executive officer to take command of the company and have the CO come to my command post. He's relieved."

Last night Headquarters Company had killed ninety-one

Japs, King Company had killed twenty-seven, Fox Company seventy-eight, Able Company ninety-four, Baker Company eighty-eight, and the three reserve companies—Charlie, Dog and Easy—supposedly occupying a position out of reach of the attack, had killed more than three hundred. How Company, on the extreme left of the front, and Item Company, on the extreme right, had received only minor attacks, but they had killed more than a hundred Japs between them. George Company killed a hundred and sixty-one, a figure met with some disbelief until the Colonel sent Major Gates forward to the George perimeter to count them himself. The Colonel promised George a Presidential Unit Citation.

That afternoon there was a huge air battle to the north of the island. We saw only part of it, a navy fighter chasing a Zero, and a Douglas dive bomber screaming madly over the island to crash with a blossom of flame and smoke into the lagoon.

The Japs had retreated back to the mountain, where, aerial photographs revealed, they had taken refuge in the beehive of caves they had dug for the island's defense. The Colonel, with a grimace of distaste, ordered the flame throwers forward. The campaign's vicious fighting was actually over, for the flame throwers were mop-up weapons.

Navy fighters and P-38's roared over our heads, on their way to strafe anything that moved. A flight of dive bombers throbbed overhead, rose to an almost invisible height, and roared down at the mountains. As darkness came we received word that the air battle up north was won and we heard no more clattering Zero motors.

Recon was given a rest. Only the planes awoke me when they raced over the treetops. We were awakened in midafternoon of the following day to help move the command post deeper into the jungle. After the message center had been dug into a small cone-shaped hill, which was heavily pocked with grenade marks, I realized that this was the hill Recon had occupied on the first night of the invasion.

The nights passed, each with an isolated attack on one of the company perimeters by small bands of Japs, but the invariable report always read, "Attack repulsed," and added that one or two Japs had escaped.

The Regiment had taken a hundred and fourteen casualties (eighty-four wounded, thirty dead) on the night of the big attack, but there were only seven wounds and no deaths during the five days that followed.

Recon continued to rest. The Japs were all located and no reconnaissance was necessary. Our duties consisted entirely in guarding the headquarters perimeter. On the eleventh day a B-25 dropped bag after bag of mail on the beach.

"How many did you get?" the Colonel asked me.

My face warmed. "Thirty-one, Sir."

"That's Jenny for you," he murmured. "I got four from her myself."

"Dear Sam—

"We've been reading about the Regiment in the paper. *Time* magazine had a picture of Daddy too. He looked awful tired. Can you talk him into getting more rest, if possible?

". . . In reply to the question you so pokily asked, yes, I do want to 'play,' but somehow or other I've kind of suspended myself since you left. I must be terribly in love with you because the urge is controllable and not so intense as it used to be, although I dream about playing with you sometimes.

"Thirty minutes later—

"The mail just came and in it was your letter about the house. I knew that you'd get tired of thinking about it. It *is* a mausoleum, but I didn't think it would take a war to convince you of it. But I can't sell it right now. Bill Joe got married (he married a girl from *Texas*, of all places) and has sent her home to Gray's Landing. She's supposed to get here tomorrow morning. I'm going to keep the house so she can live with me until the war is over and you and Bill Joe come home. But I'm glad you want to get rid of the house. It's so pokey that I shudder every time I look at it. And yes, I *do* like the idea of building in the pine grove where Cobb Gray had his first house.

". . . Poppa Felix comes by every morning. He and Daddy are so much alike that it's sometimes hilarious. I made him read

159

some Kafka and he made exactly the same comment that Daddy did: 'Wonder what the man had in mind when he wrote it?'

"I've been doing a little needle work. I made a nightgown out of light gray chiffon. It doesn't cover a thing, but that's the whole idea. I'm going to wear it for you when you get home.

"Dream about me."

She added a postscript: "Bill Joe is a *captain* now!"

The letters caused a revival of discussion on sex, a topic which had lost its compelling interest in the violence and exhaustion of fighting. My thinking was filled with vivid pictures of Jenny's naked body and I regularly had wet dreams.

I heard Raker, father of four boys, talking to Carr and Meleski:

". . . You single bastards can talk about them glammer girls all you want to. I'll just stick with my wife. Didn't know what a good woman she is till I got over where I can't do no more'n talk about it.

"Funny way Sara Jo's got," Raker mused, "about fuken, I mean. When I start getting horny, she acts like she does when one of the kids gets sick, wants to hustle around and do her best to cure what's ailing 'em. She'd always save something for the kids to do and then she'd hurry in on the bed and act like I was going to die if she didn't get me done up right quick. Only thing about doing it in the daytime, though, Sara Jo always went to sleep after we got done." He shook his head in wonder. "Never knew what a good woman I got till I can't do nothing about it."

Kenny Carr, who wasn't married, made his contribution by telling about his experiences with an Australian girl who had eluded his advances for more than a month—until the night he happened to pat her bottom playfully. "Just that butt-patting got that old girl so hot she couldn't sit still."

"Greek?" Meleski asked.

"Huh?"

"Was she a Greek girl?"

"I'll be damn, Meleski," Carr said, "didn't I just get through telling you she was an Australian girl?"

"Greek girls like butt-rubbing," Meleski said with a worldly air.

We stared at him in wonder and, given the center of the stage, the ham in Meleski prompted him to tell of his adventures in pursuit of his civilian occupation, the selling of lingerie.

"You Rebel bastards don't know what fuken is," he began. "Back in the days when I was selling tit-holders and drawers, I used to get so much I didn't know what to do with it all. Some of them babes owning shops didn't have a chance to get out and scout around."

"Wasn't any of'em married?" Raker demanded.

"Oh sure, some of them were. I did my best work, though, on the ones about thirty-five years old. Now when a woman's thirty-five and ain't got a man anchored, she's a pushover."

"How'd you go about getting their minds on it?" Kenny asked. "Well, I mean, a man don't just walk in a women's store and ask'er for a piece of tail."

"Of course not!" Meleski said indignantly. "But there's a way. If they acted friendly, I'd say something like, 'Madam'—I always called my babes madam—' Madam, I don't want to be disrespectful or anything of that nature, but my clients have reported to me that this item has done quite well. They've stated that their customers' husbands have expressed more than an uncommon interest in the item.' So—if the old bitch giggled, I'd offer to give a pair free, 'a personal gift,' I'd tell them. Usually they'd say something like, 'Oh goodness, I don't have no man to interest with these!' And I'd say, 'Why, *any* man would be interested in seeing these on the woman of his choice.' '*Any* man?' they'd say. Then came my line and I'd say, boyish and sweet, 'Why, *I* know *I*'d be interested.' Nine times out of ten, the babe'd say, 'But *you* haven't seen me in them.' And I'd say, 'But that doesn't indicate that I wouldn't *like* to.' "

"Then what would they say?" Kenny asked, just slightly out of breath.

Meleski regarded Carr as an object of pity. "Sergeant Carr, how old are you?"

"What the hell, twenty-two. Why?"

"When you're my age, I hope you understand that point

161

where talk stops and action begins." Meleski picked at his teeth with great aplomb.

"How old are you, Meleski?" I asked.

"Twenty-three," he said, without turning a hair.

After a rather lengthy silence, during which Meleski stared, hands under his head, at the blue Pacific sky, Kenny spoke.

"Meleski?"

"Yeah?"

"I think you're fulla shit."

"Uh-hmmm," Meleski agreed, "but those were the days."

We watched a linen-white cloud drift over the lagoon. It was so white that it made me blink to look at it. The sand was cool and damp under my shoulders; my feet, bare, baked comfortably in the sun.

"Say, Sam," Meleski said, "you married a pretty babe, didn't you? These boys say so."

"Yes," I said.

From the corner of my eye I saw Raker and Carr exchange discreetly uneasy glances.

"How was it?" Meleski asked, still staring thoughtfully at the cloud. "I've shacked a few pretty ones, but not one you'd want to call a real beauty."

"Well. . . ." I began, and stopped. In Gray's Landing such a question would have obliged me to fight.

"Better take it easy, Meleski," Kenny murmured.

Meleski raised his head and looked questioningly at Carr and Raker. "Hell, what for?" Meleski said. "We're all friends, aren't we?"

And that was enough to make me answer, "It's fine, Meleski, just fine. Nothing like it."

Raker laughed.

Kenny said, "First time I ever heard one of you Oak Street bastards admit your woman's even got a————."

I tossed a handful of sand at Kenny. "Fuk you, Kenny!" I said. "Fuk both of you."

Kenny and Raker both rolled away and started laughing uproariously. Meleski failed to see the humor. He didn't know that Kenny, Raker and I had reached the ultimate of friendship.

Carr and Raker continued to laugh and I berated them until Meleski, pointing toward the beach, silenced us. "Hey! What the hell's *that?*"

Two plump marines, both sweating profusely in their fresh, starched khakis, were lugging a case of beer down the beach. I stared in wonder.

"Let's go," Meleski said. He composed himself into his most officious self and, as we followed behind him, threw over his shoulder, "I'll do the talking. Agree with me."

He called to the marines, "Hey, *you!*"

The marines stopped.

"That will be Colonel Cozzens' beer," Meleski said, "am I not right?"

The marines turned to go. "That's right, Mack," one of them said. "You're not right."

"*Just* a minute, my good man," Meleski said. "I'm Captain Miller. I have been sent, with these men"—he indicated us with a lordly gesture—"to wait for the Colonel's beer ration. I'll relieve you of it presently."

"Lay down, shitbird."

"Corporal!" Meleski said sternly. "You are addressing a commissioned officer. I bid you stand at attention and use proper military terminology. The penalty for insubordination in a combat zone is death. Please observe the courtesies due my rank."

The marine corporal thought that over. He was obviously no intellectual, but he finally got the point. "Sir," he managed, "you ain't got no bars on."

"Snipers, man!" Meleski said loudly and pointed toward the jungle. "*Snipers!*"

Meleski was so forceful the marines almost dodged a bullet.

"Oh, pardon, sir. But this ain't beer for no army colonel. This here goes to the navy lieutenant heading the beach party."

"We have no time to waste, my good man," Meleski said crisply. "You may wait here and take the next case to the navy." He gestured Kenny, Raker and me forward with an eloquent finger. "Take it, men. These uh—*marines* will wait for the next case."

"Yessir," I said brightly.

163

We took the beer and marched smartly toward the jungle. Behind us paraded Meleski, strutting like a Prussian major.

"*Hey!*" The Marine Corps had finally figured it out.

"*Fuk you, jack!*" Meleski yelled. "*RUN!*"

We plunged into the jungle and, a few yards up the trail, dodged into the thick undergrowth. The marines panted past, plump and sweating, still yelling "*Hey!*" After a while they returned, cussing, their neat khakis completely wet with sweat, and left us alone with the beer.

There were twenty-four cans, each beady cold. We drank all of them before nightfall.

21

The Japs in the caves held out fourteen days, during which the men with the flame throwers went about the business of extermination with horrible precision and the island became a pyre of bloated, roasted flesh. The corpses were found in a variety of grotesque poses, arms over their faces, wide, seared grins that exposed their long, narrow teeth; one had been caught, in a cave, in the act of urinating and there he stood, one hand supporting him against the wall, the other grasping his penis. A high-ranking general, in answer to protests from American humanitarians, stated to the effect that it was better to use the flame throwers than to lose the lives of American boys. The general was probably right, for entering the caves would have been impossible without them.

On the day the island was cleared and the caves no longer concealed effective fighting Japs, we grouped on the beach to wait for the landing craft to take us back to the ships. I saw the bombers coming, high, from the north, and it occurred to me, as I lounged in the shade of a splintered palm log, that they looked like no bombers of ours, but I had come to depend upon the navy as an almost airtight protective screen. It was a high, bright day and only a few moments before a flight of P-38's had rocketed out in the same general direction from which the bombers came. They were Bettys.

"*JAP PLANES!*" somebody shouted hoarsely when the planes, at five thousand feet, were almost directly over us.

I crawled under the log and Kenny Carr piled on top of me. The first bomb hit before many of the men even noticed the planes.

The bombs were dropped in sticks on the vast pattern of men and war equipment spread out on the beach. It was over in fifteen seconds. If most of the bombs hadn't been duds, the Regiment would have been erased as an effective fighting unit. There were four Bettys and they each dropped twelve bombs. Only nine of them exploded, four of them in the water, three of them in the jungle. The two which exploded in the regimental area killed most of the men in George Company and almost half of those in Able Company. The explosions were loud; rips of thunder that were so huge that my ears seemed unable to deal with their magnitude.

The duds plunked into the sand and disappeared, leaving small holes, into which oozed the hot, dry sand. One of them struck about a foot from my left shoulder and my arm fell into the hole it left. I lay perfectly still for perhaps a full minute before I became aware of Kenny's weight on my back.

"You hurt, Kenny?"

He rolled off me. "I'm all right," he said weakly.

I crawled from under the log and looked at Kenny. His own expression mirrored mine: we were both surprised that we were still alive. My hands began to tremble and I raked them over my face.

"*Recon!*" Ray called. "*On the line with the stretchers!*"

I took a deep breath and stood erect, trying to remember where Doc Wingate had established the aid station. I saw him busily directing his men into action. I gathered the platoon around me and hurried them to Doc.

George Company, which had received the Presidential Unit Citation for its work early in the campaign, was gone. There were three men, two privates and a second lieutenant, alive and unwounded. There were seven men whose wounds would heal. The remainder were dead, their bones and flesh thrown over a wide area. It was not until a year later when I was court-martialed and sent to George Company, that I realized one of the surviving privates was Willie Crawford.

Able Company lost twenty-eight dead and fourteen wounded. Headquarters Company had one casualty: an intelligence clerk was sliced neatly in two by one of the duds. He died instantly, without crying.

By midafternoon we had moved the wounded to the hospital ship in the lagoon and had buried the dead. Recon, the last platoon aboard the ships, was being drawn over the rail when the P-38's returned from chasing the Bettys. They had managed to shoot down one of the bombers. The convoy steamed away.

Looking over the fantail at the ugly camel-backed mountain, I realized that the huge gashes in the jungle would heal within a matter of days and nothing would remain except nightmares to arouse memories of violent explosion and fire. The island—already so far away that the scars were beginning to fade —was the end of the first episode, which makes the most indelible mark.

22

We were transported to a small island to the south which had been recently vacated by an infantry division now headed north to begin the invasion of another island. We noted, with great satisfaction, that one of the regiments had left its tents standing and we didn't have to suffer the exhaustion of making a decent place to live. Even the kitchens were left and the cooks served a hot meal, our first in almost a month, an hour after we landed. That night we were issued the beer which had accumulated during the campaign, twenty-one cans to the man. I got sluggishly, pissing drunk and awoke the next morning with a bloated, heavy head.

During the following two weeks, we stood reveille at nine o'clock, went through an hour of exercises, and we were through for the day. Raker, Carr, Meleski and I played bridge all afternoon, every day. Jack Gifford told me that he had never seen such a religious crowd of men in all his preaching experience.

Colonel Cozzens strolled about the camp with a lazy, benign air, stopping often to pass the time of day with the men, most of whom he knew by first name. Rested and relaxed now, the Colonel looked almost as well as he had back in Gray's Landing.

"Let's see now, Billy," he would muse and clear his throat, "you're Guy Chesterson's boy, aren't you?"

"Nosir, Guy's my uncle. I'm Elmer's boy."

"Oh, *Elmer!* Why, I know Elmer almost as well as I know Guy. Fact is, Elmer and I were sort of partners once."

"Yessir, during the Depression."

The Colonel's face reddened. "Ah—yes." He didn't like to be reminded that he and Poppa had acted as bankers in those days. "How'd you make out on the island?"

"Might' near got scared to death, Colonel."

"Same with me! Makes a man wish he's back plowing cotton, doesn't it?"

"Sure does, Colonel."

"We'll get back, some of these days." The Colonel cleared his throat. "Well, son, take care of yourself."

"You do the same, Colonel."

I couldn't help smiling. This was no twentieth-century military man. It would have been more in character if he had been in command of a regiment of Confederate infantry. His judgments came hard for him in this army, for he instinctively judged men as individuals. He had probably never used the word "masses" in his life.

I saw him alone once. I entered a screened latrine (the Colonel didn't like the idea of separate toilet facilities for officers) and found him sitting in deep thought over one of the holes.

He didn't notice me until I had lowered my pants, had

167

seated myself, and spoke, "You worried about something, Colonel?"

He roused himself quickly. "Sam!" Then he grinned. "I always do my best work while my bowels're moving."

"Poppa said that once."

The Colonel laughed. "Fine man, Felix. Wouldn't mind running out to Uncle Ben's for a glass of home-brew with him right now."

"I wouldn't mind it myself."

"Jenny writing regularly?"

"Twice a day, most of the time."

He nodded with satisfaction. "Been having any trouble with your men?"

I carefully looked away. "Webster."

"Uh-hmm, I've heard about that," he said. "Wasn't your fault, Sam."

"Yessir, it was too."

"I can't see why."

"If I hadn't been so scared, I'd've had enough sense to treat him right."

"Ray says you're calm as a block of ice in combat."

"I'm afraid Ray's not right."

We sat for a few minutes without talking.

"Tell you what let's do with Web, Sam," the Colonel said. "Just before we leave this place, I'll transfer him to—uh—can he type?"

"Nosir, don't think so."

"Hmmm. . . . He's too proud to be an orderly. How about trucks? Think we could make a mechanic out of him?"

"Yessir, I think so. But he's better with guns. He won the rifle matches back in Texas."

The Colonel nodded. "Good idea. Don't say anything about it. You might even act a little mad about losing a man just before an invasion."

"All right, Sir."

The Regiment was reorganized during the rest period. We had been designated as a "Task Force" during the island campaign, but the navy had made that name popular with the press at home and the army, having no intention of confusing itself with the navy in the minds of the taxpayers, changed our name to "Regimental Combat Team," RCT, it was usually called. A battalion of 105mm artillery was permanently assigned to us. Colonel Cozzens, in all likelihood a paradox to spit-and-polish brass because he had a good regiment without imposing any of the usual indignities upon his men, became heavy with brass himself, a brigadier general. However, aside from the small clique of Regular Army officers recently assigned to the Regiment, I heard nobody call him anything other than Colonel, which caused strong irritation among the Regulars.

After we were thoroughly rested, combat behavior became our prime source of conversation. Kenny admitted that he had almost bolted once during the first night on the island. Raker added to that by saying that he was already out of his hole when he happened to think that the hole was the safest place he was likely to find. I analyzed myself completely, but knew no answers. I had two reactions to fear: a vile temper fit or complete, slow-motion lucidity. My anger had caused the trouble with Webster; the lucidity has caused each fight to appear as clear as a well-photographed movie. The trembling fits after the fight was over went unexplained too.

For a few days I was given a nickname, "Stonewall," but it didn't last long.

It became my problem to help the replacements take their places in the platoon. At first they were awed by our combat experiences, but didn't dare ask questions about them. When they found out we didn't care, they nearly drove us crazy with their talk. Almost a month passed before they were assimilated, but it was their constant questioning that caused Webster's end to come prematurely.

I had steered clear of him as much as possible. The few contacts I had with him were always embarrassing. He wouldn't accept my apologies and I finally had to stop them because they were hurting me in the eyes of the replacements.

In Texas, Web had been rated an excellent soldier, especially with the rifle, and it was a surprise to us all when he failed so miserably in combat. But we were careful to avoid mentioning his failure.

However closemouthed we were with him, Web felt compelled to prove himself a worthy man. He started several fights and won them all. He was given extra duty because the replacements would get ideas. He tried to endear himself to all but me by telling long tales about his experiences with various women, but it was obvious that he was lying and, no matter how studiously interested the men pretended to be, their disbelief showed. Too often his tales ended with "Look, by god, don't you believe me?"

"Sure we do."

But he would carry it on until he started another fight.

I lost my temper with him but once. I overheard him berating me to the replacements and paid no attention until he said:

"Hell, boys, he'd be a buck-ass private if he hadn't married the Colonel's daughter. And that's the only reason he married her too. Why, she's screwed everything in Gray's Landing. *I've* screwed her, *after* Gifford married her too. And Carr did——"

I only remember spinning him around and smashing my fist into his teeth. He tumbled over backward and I was raising my foot to kick him when Carr grabbed me and pulled me away. Two days passed before I dared keep any ammunition near my rifle.

It was during the last few weeks of our stay on the island that Web finally folded up. I was sitting in my tent, making out the morning report, when Kenny entered and beckoned. I followed him outside.

"Web's at it again," Kenny said.

I shrugged. "That's nothing unusual."

"Look now, Sam. This's got to come to a halt. Them replacements're getting so they talk about you."

"Do they?"

"Damn right they do. If Web keeps on talking, you're not worth a popcorn fart."

"What's he saying?"

"Come on and see for yourself."

He hurried me to the wall of Web's tent, where he was talking to the replacements.

"Aw . . . don't pay no attention to what Gifford and Carr tell you. Don't tell nobody I told you, but when we got in a fight on that island, both them guys hunkered down in their holes, crying and yelling like they was about to die."

Kenny and I walked out of earshot.

"You planning on doing anything about it, Sam?" Kenny asked, insistently.

"Maybe if we sort of drift into the tent, he'll shut up."

"Yeah, but he'll begin again soon's we leave. I'm in favor of taking him to Ray."

"No, the Colonel's going to transfer him. Let's just drift in."

Kenny wasn't convinced, but he agreed. We strolled out to the company street and entered Webster's tent. His back was turned to us and he didn't hear us enter. Nor did he stop talking when the two replacements, boys, gave us stares of wide-eyed alarm.

Webster was holding his head in his hands and talking to the ground, not seeming to care whether he was heard or not. ". . . That fuken Carr, he's nothing in Gray's Landing. Had to get in the guard to make enough money to live on. Wouldn't be a sergeant if he hadn't worked for Gifford at the gin. And Gifford—that Oak Street bastard. All he had to do to get his stripes was marry the Colonel's daughter. Hunkers down in his hole while the real men do the——" Something, maybe instinct, warned him. He lifted his head out of his hands, leaving them in a curiously prayerlike gesture, paused, and jumped to his feet.

"Goddamn you, Sam!" he said hoarsely.

I acted surprised. "Hmmm? What's the matter?"

He stared sullenly for a moment before he grinned ingratiatingly and made a deprecatory gesture toward the two boys. "Just getting these men squared away," he said. He strolled casually toward me, a disarming smile on his tormented face. "I know that's your job, Sam, and I ain't a man to take your job away from you. You don't mind, do——" He leaped at me like a monkey, his hands clutching for my throat. At the same time he

171

uttered a strangely animal cry. His hand closed around my Adam's apple.

"*Web!*" Kenny shouted.

Somehow we broke his hold on my throat and he fell heavily on his back. Both of us dived on him and the two boys, white with fear, raced out of the tent, yelling, "Lieutenant! Lieutenant Mosby!"

It was impossible to keep Webster down. He was a powerful man and rage multiplied his strength enormously. At the moment when Ray entered, Webster saw him and shrieked a long scream of agony. And he broke free of us. He stumbled to his bunk and snatched up his rifle. He pointed it directly at Ray's chest and, without a word, his lower lip drawn down until it revealed his tusks, he gathered three bandoleers of ammo and looped them about his neck. The tent was filled with the sound of his breathing. Without having spoken a word, he wheeled and bound across the stretch of sand between the coconut grove and the jungle.

That was the last we saw of him until the day we left the island. And I was the only one who ever heard his voice again.

The Colonel was deeply moved by Webster's desertion, but he made it plain that he didn't blame me, although I knew that in part it was my fault. The Colonel insisted to the contrary, but I wasn't convinced. Each day the Colonel sent a patrol into the jungle with instructions not to fire. The patrols stopped every few yards and shouted, "Web, the Colonel says come back! You won't have to go to combat again. *Web, come back!*" But nobody found him.

We knew he was alive, for, on the third night of his absence, a noise was heard in the kitchen tent and the next morning two cases of ten-in-one rations were missing. The next night a rifle and four entire cases of ammo were missing. Thereafter, under orders from the Colonel, a man's weekly ration was left standing unguarded in the open and there it stayed until it disappeared, to be promptly replaced again. Rifles and ammo were to be kept strapped to our bunks. On three occasions the S-4 officer reported that the warehouse tent had been raided for fatigue uniforms.

"Getting fixed up for a mighty long stay, seems like," Carr murmured.

We saw nothing more of Webster until the day we left the island, although I talked to him the night before.

It was late at night, sometime between midnight and dawn, and I was asleep. I dreamed that somebody was in the tent with me, but I couldn't wake up. A hand clamped down tightly over my mouth and I tried to sit up. I felt cold metal against my temple.

"Don't say a word, Sam," Webster whispered in my ear. He was so close I could feel his breath.

With a heart-lurching bolt of fear, I realized that the metal against my temple was the muzzle of a pistol. I lay perfectly still, hoping that I wouldn't excite him enough to cause him to shoot.

"Are you awake, Sam?"

I nodded.

"All right," he whispered, "don't be scared. I'm not going to shoot you unless you yell. The only reason I got the pistol on you's so you'll be quiet. Will you?"

I nodded again.

The hand and pistol were taken away. "All right now, Sam?"

"Web," I whispered, "you got to come back."

He uttered a whispered laugh. "Not me. No more combat for me."

"The Colonel was going to transfer you to the ammo section the day before we leave the island."

He said nothing. I heard him breathing. Finally: "You should've told me, Sam."

"I didn't want to hurt your feelings, Web."

"Well, too late now."

"No, it's not. The Colonel says——"

"I'd never be able to hold my head up again long's I live. I just came to tell you that I'm sorry for talking about you, Sam. And—I know Jenny's a fine woman." He took several sharp breaths before I realized that he had begun to cry. "I must a been crazy, talking like that."

173

"That's all right, Web. I knew you didn't mean it."

"Did you?"

"Yes," I said. "Look, nobody blames a man for being scared, Web."

"You're all right, Sam." He got to his feet. "Tell the Colonel I appreciate what he's been putting out for me."

"I'll tell him."

Webster was gone.

We left the next day at noon. Stacked at the edge of the abandoned camp were more than a hundred cases of ten-in-ones. There was a wall tent, a couple of new ponchos, five pairs of boots, underwear, soap, socks, shoelaces and a carton of storm matches. There was also a note from the Colonel, telling Web that the Colonel would help him as much as he could if he ever got a chance to return to civilization.

We saw Web again, and for the last time, when we were boarding the landing craft that was to take us to the transports anchored offshore.

"*Look!*" Raker cried.

Standing in the middle of the deserted company street, his rifle at sling, his legs planted far apart, his cap in hand, was Webster.

"*Web!*" Ray shouted joyously. "Thatta boy! Let's go, fellow! Let's go!" Ray ran a few impulsive steps toward Web.

But Web quickly trained his rifle on us and Ray halted. Web motioned for him to go back to the boat, which Ray did. Standing there, dumb with sadness, we stared at Web for a long time before he motioned us to leave.

As we pulled away from the beach, he slowly walked toward us, all the while giving us friendly waves, and he watched us until he was merely a lonely figure on the beach of a deserted island. I had never been so ashamed in my life, nor would I in the future.

Web was the first of us to give up.

Book III

The Old Men

1

The invasion was absurdly easy, even on the first day. We landed under a bright, friendly midday sky instead of in the gloom of dawn. There had been no resistance. We pushed ashore from the landing craft and plunged unchecked into the familiar jungle. This time the navy had known what to do; for a week their dive bombers had pounded at the island. The bombardment had lasted three days. I saw hundreds of corpses thrown about the jungle. Able, Baker and Charlie Companies pierced the jungle and rammed three miles inland before they stopped to form the night's perimeter. The new George Company, the patched-up King Company and How Company, forming the other half of the nutcracker maneuver, covered an equal distance. Only four shots were fired during the first twenty-four hours of the campaign. It seemed absurd that it was on such a quiet afternoon that Colonel Cozzens was killed.

Recon was in perimeter with King Company and Ray was talking on the radio. "This is King," he said, "repeat your last transmission."

"*This is Big Red,*" the radio replied. "*Send the Recon platoon sergeant—Gifford—to this headquarters immediately. Over.*"

My heart lurched. It was something of extreme importance when a radio operator was in such a hurry that he didn't stop to look up my code name. "What is it, Ray?"

He lowered his head and pinched nervously at the bridge of his nose. "The Colonel's been hit by a sniper."

The blood drained out of my head. Without even picking up my rifle, I whirled and ran into the jungle.

I heard Ray shout, "Meleski, Raker! Take Sam's rifle and follow him!"

I didn't stop until I reached the beach. Grouped around the message-center foxhole were more than fifty men. I burst through them and jumped into the hole. Major Gates grabbed me, but I jerked free of him and knelt by the Colonel. I suppose I was crying; my eyes ached for two days afterward. I alternately shook him and pleaded with him to answer me.

"Ease up now, Sam," Major Gates muttered.

Oh, certainly, I thought, act sane. Men die every day out here. By all means, ease up now, Sam.

"Where in the hell was the guard?" I shouted into Major Gates' face. "Let me get hold of the sonofabitch. Where's the guard?"

"Now take it easy, Sam," Major Gates said soothingly. "It was nobody's fault, the Colonel said so himself. It was his time, that's all."

"Yeah," I said coldly, "that's all."

The enlisted men were embarrassed and were slowly leaving. Soon only a few officers and the radio operator were left.

"*Where was the guard?*" I asked.

A young second lieutenant, who had been observing me silently, stepped forward and spoke up. "Shall I put this man in arrest for insubordination, Major?"

Major Gates had been a gentle man all his life, but his fury was as explosive as the most violent of men. He half rose, choked with anger, and then jumped out of the foxhole. He gave the lieutenant a shove. "Get out of my sight, Lieutenant Baxter!" Major Gates said. "Do you hear me? Get out of my sight!"

The young lieutenant hurried away.

"We got to bury'im, Sam," the Major said. "Where'd you want the grave?"

"Nixon," I said, "that's where."

178

"Now Sam. . . ."

I got to my feet and looked down at my father-in-law. He wasn't mutilated; his face was in repose. His eyes were closed. And, my mind starkly clear, I thought that it had been foolish for him to become a military man. A man like my father-in-law, I was thinking, couldn't expect to live. The good men always are the ones to die.

"All right, Mister Gates," I said. "I'm sorry I talked like I did." Nixon was the name of the cemetery at Gray's Landing. "We ought to bury him someplace where it'll be easy to find after the war."

Major Gates nodded. "Pick the spot, Sam, and I'll have the intelligence section draw a detail map of it."

We buried the Colonel at sundown. Jack Gifford, his strong Arkansas accent strangely alien in this air, read over the grave. And while Jack talked shortly, I realized that this day had wrenched me still further away from that gentle, innocent life at Gray's Landing. Jack's words were more than a funeral oration:

". . . We bury a friend here. Julian Cozzens. Most of us knew him as a civilian, and he was that. He died a civilian, still aware of the virtue and honor of being a gentleman and hating this criminal war. He was a civilian to me and he was a civilian to all his friends. It is the shame of the twentieth century that such a man had to lose his life to the bitter, pagan gods of warfare." Jack paused to regain his voice. "I pray to God," he murmured, "that the man in this grave isn't the Regiment's last civilian."

Jack's prayer was given a negative answer the next morning. Flown in aboard a navy PBY flying boat, Colonel Miles arrived to replace the Colonel. He was a short little man, fat-fingered and pink. His mouth was red and soft. His butt quivered with every step he took. His orderly unfolded a canvas chair and Colonel Miles eased himself into it.

"Well, gentlemen, I've spent a comfortable year in the replacement depot waiting for such an assignment as this. Let's get to work." He deliberately scratched his chin with his left hand so everybody could see his Academy ring.

As we walked away, Ray Mosby muttered, "Not very smart

of him, admitting he's waited a year for a regiment. Most colonels're sent overseas with their outfits."

2

The next morning, after the Regiment had spent an uneasy but quiet night, the fiasco began.

Able, Baker and Charlie Companies on the left, and George, How and King Companies on the right jaws of the nutcracker were preparing to begin the slow closing motion that would trap the Japs between them. It was perfectly planned, a little gem of strategy, the first such maneuver executed in the Pacific because this was the first time space had been found to do it. In the center of the jaws was a high ridge and there the Japs would be, holed up in their inevitable caves, and the fierce charges on our perimeters would never happen. The Japs were purely on the defensive from the day of the landing.

But before dawn had become daylight, it happened.

Colonel Miles, for reasons that must have been his own, for Major Gates advised strongly against it, ordered Able Company to break off and retreat to an area which had been covered yesterday. Miles offered only one explanation to Major Gates: "I've a hunch that we'll find the enemy—right—there!" He directed his swagger stick to a spot which had been, yesterday, deserted.

"Colonel Miles," the Major said, "we covered that sector yesterday."

"Major, I'm a peculiar duck, you might say. I have hunches, and nine times out of ten, those hunches have proved correct, if twenty-seven years in the army will back me up. And I have a hunch that you let the enemy slip through your fingers yesterday. The enemy is quite clever at infiltration."

"So we hear," Major Gates said wryly.

Colonel Miles tapped the map with his swagger stick. "The

enemy is—*right—there!*" He turned and gave the Major a glassy look. "You're not disagreeing with me, are you, Major?"

So Able Company broke off and retraced its steps—and found nothing. It spent the day crashing through the jungle, looking for Japs like a bunch of kids on an Easter-egg hunt. The men were exhausted and their officers had no explanation to offer.

But Colonel Miles' hunch did finally prove correct. During the day the Japs sneaked through the hole left by Able's breaking off maneuver and that night, as Able occupied a lonely perimeter, four miles from the nearest company, the Japs attacked it in strength. Colonel Miles, who had called in Dog Company to strengthen his own company perimeter, could contemplate the situation in complete safety. He was tremendously satisfied.

"Well, Major, wasn't my hunch correct?"

"Yessir, they're there, but you gave them the entire day to make the journey." Major Gates was relieved a few minutes later.

I listened to the firing all night and as midnight came and passed, it was obvious that most of the firing was coming from Jap rifles. At two o'clock, Able radioed that it was down to half strength and it was then that Colonel Miles made a mistake that no regimental commander had made before him and none afterward.

Colonel Miles ordered Easy Company out of reserve and dispatched it to the rescue of Able Company.

All the staff officers protested that Colonel Cozzens' policy had been to keep a strict perimeter at night.

"Quite right," Miles answered. "But I'm happy to report that I'm not the late *General* Cozzens."

Easy Company moved forward without incident until it passed within fifty yards of Baker's perimeter, which, thinking it was under attack from the Japs, opened fire with machine guns and mortars. Easy Company lost fourteen men before the firing could be stopped.

After that, the whole thing fell apart. The trails, dim enough during the daylight hours, were impossible to follow after dark. Somehow Easy's first platoon took the right fork in the trail and the second platoon took the left fork, but floundered into the jungle a hundred yards later. The third platoon missed the fork altogether and stumbled on, trying to follow a compass bearing through the dark tangle of undergrowth. Only the first platoon, because it reached the far side of the island and followed its ears toward the sound of the firing, reached Able Company at dawn, in time to help the sixteen survivors, counting seven walking wounded, bury the dead.

During the following day, the Japs launched the first daylight attack we had ever seen. They charged out of the jungle and flowed into Baker Company's exposed flank and, before Baker could get itself into a position for defense, it lost twenty-one dead and twenty-nine wounded. The Japs also found the two lost platoons of Easy and, of the seventy-two men in the two platoons, thirty-three returned.

Colonel Miles, of course, had an excuse: "Nine times out of ten, my hunches are correct." And here he made a gesture that signified that he had written off the losses. "That must have been the tenth hunch."

As sundown approached, Colonel Miles began to look worried. Immediately around his foxhole, he ordered Recon to dig a ring of holes. Around us, the remainder of Headquarters Company. And around Headquarters, Fox and How Companies. He had built a three-ring perimeter and he was snugly in the middle of it. He gave no orders at all to the companies which remained in the jungle. They sat. And that night the Japs attacked each perimeter—and each company reported that the attacks were of battalion strength.

The attack on the Headquarters perimeter was the only one that failed. Our tremendous firepower cut the Japs down before they could penetrate even the first ring. But the other companies weren't so lucky; they were already weakened by the vicious daylight attacks. Nobody was ever certain how many casualties the Regiment took that night, for Colonel Miles didn't let it be known.

The Regiment spent the next day fighting off a few isolated attacks, but they were weak and sporadic. The Japs, weakened by the attacks themselves, were saving their strength for the night. Colonel Miles, under persistent heckling from Major Gates, Ray Mosby and the rest of the staff, finally gave orders for the companies to come out of the jungle. Two huge perimeters were formed on the beach and that was how the Regiment survived.

The next morning a Major General was brought to the island by PBY and for four hours he and Colonel Miles sat in a tent and talked. The guard, before he was ordered out of earshot by Lieutenant Baxter, the one Major Gates had shoved the night of Colonel Cozzens' death, reported that he heard the Major General say, "My *god*, Colonel, does it make any *difference* what Grant did to Lee at Fredericksburg? Those boys in that jungle were *Americans* and they're dead!"

"General," Miles was heard to say firmly, "I'm a man of hunches and nine times out of ten they're——"

"Hunches in a pig's asshole! You're the stupidest——" And the guard was permitted to hear no more.

The Major General left at noon. Colonel Miles sat in his tent for the remainder of the afternoon, unseen by anybody. At dusk he emerged, cocky and fat, to order his tent struck and the perimeter closed for the night. And we took more attacks.

The Japs were unable to break our big perimeters, but we took casualties. During the height of the attack an American grenade exploded in Miles' foxhole. I know it was one of our grenades because it left a spark trail as it arched up from one of the Fox Company foxholes. Miles was shaken but unhurt because, huddled behind Major Gates, none of the fragments could reach him. Major Gates, who had been relieved, but remained as adjutant until a replacement could be found, died the next day at noon.

The next afternoon a regiment from a famous army division relieved us. We boarded transports and were taken to a rest camp in New Guinea.

3

The full impact of the Colonel's death didn't hit me until a few days after I landed in New Guinea. And yet, the loss remained vague and misty. It was a severance with a part of my past, but I couldn't make myself articulate enough to spell it out in words. After his death my memories of Gray's Landing existed in the sweet mist of a strange nostalgia. It made me ache longingly for my innocent past and at the same time, fear for my future.

The loss of the Colonel took symbol in the map the intelligence section had drawn showing the location of his grave. Lieutenant Baxter found out about it and demanded that I hand it over to him, so "it can be given to the proper authorities; there's no place for sentiment in the army." I stalled him for two days until the intelligence section could draw another one. Baxter accepted the map with undisguised glee.

I tried to explain to Jenny how her father had died and the strange effect the death had had on me, but it was no good. I destroyed the letter. I wrote many letters, but I finally had to settle by repeating, as best I could, the words Jack Gifford had spoken over the grave. And I added:

". . . I know that you and your mother aren't likely to agree with me, but I think the Colonel's body should be left in the grave. He's buried only a few feet from where he died and every Guardsman in the Regiment has left a rock or some sort of memento on the grave. . . ."

I dropped the letter into Ray's mailbox so he could censor it. I noticed that, in the box, there were several letters, almost all of which were addressed to either Jenny or Mrs. Cozzens.

We drilled. Close-order drill. The sun was so hot that many men, still exhausted from the ordeal of the last campaign, fell under it. And Colonel Miles, swagger stick in hand, watched the non-coms closely. He called us together:

"I don't know who trained you men for non-commissioned duties, but you're a failure. Didn't anybody ever bother to tell you that drilling is a serious business? You must *shout! Shout* your commands! *Shout* orders! *Shout!* You understand? The only thing a private understands is a loud voice!"

I drilled Recon all morning and during the afternoon I worked them like a chain gang until the camp looked like a permanent Stateside installation. We fell into our bunks at night, exhausted and insane with anger.

Around Colonel Miles' tent a stone wall was built, four feet high, by sweating, cussing men from Service Company. White paint was found for the stones. Bordering the company streets were hunks of coral and each tent sergeant was instructed to have his men plant some sort of jungle flower at each side of the tent entrance. The flowers, taken from their natural habitat by rough hands, soon wilted and died. The new Colonel stated that he had made his men plant flowers on almost every army post in the USA and Hawaii, a practice he could see no reason for discontinuing.

Colonel Miles put out a special order that officers were no longer to refer to enlisted men as gentlemen during the training lectures. "The U.S. Army," the order read, "allows the existence of gentlemen only in its commissioned ranks."

Colonel Miles lectured the Regiment:

"All right now," he began, "this isn't a civilian outfit any longer. I understand that most of you so-called Guardsmen have taken it upon yourselves to write to the family of General Cozzens. I have instructed all censoring officers to destroy those letters. The United States Army has a system for handling such matters, as it has a tried and true system for handling everything, and it needs no help from its enlisted men. Understood? If General Cozzens got killed, that's too bad, but there's no need crying over spilled blood."

As he talked, he paced back and forth across the platform built for the occasion. A staff sergeant was detailed to follow, squatted so the Regiment had an unobstructed view of Miles, and hold a microphone up to the man's lips. Each time Miles' right foot came down, he slapped his leg sharply with his swagger stick.

"I have also been told," Miles went on, "that many of you have called your officers by their first names. I have instructed the officers of this command in that little matter, and it is my desire that no enlisted man is to call any commissioned officer by his first name. Understood?"

Whack went the swagger stick.

"Now, something else. It has been the practice in this command for everybody to refer to the late General Cozzens as 'the Colonel.' He was not a Colonel; he was a Brigadier General in the United States Army and it is my desire that he be referred to as such. However, I see no need of talking about him. He's dead and no talk will bring him to life. Understood?"

Whack!

"Now, something else. The matter of uniforms. In the future, it is my desire that you wear khaki, cotton, sun tans. This is the army—*now*—and you're going to dress like soldiers. Understood?"

Whack!

"Now, something else. The matter of this command's designation. This is not, repeat *not*, a National Guard regiment. It is my desire that you call it a Regimental Combat Team, exactly what it is. It was at one time a National Guard regiment, but it is no longer a National Guard regiment. Under——"

"*You fuken right it ain't, Miles!*" arose a shout from one of the line companies.

"What? What's——"

The voice roared out: "*It ain't no National Guard outfit no more because you killed all they was left, you murdering old sonofabitch!*"

Miles purpled and choked—and dropped his swagger stick. "Arrest that man!" he finally shouted. "Arrest that man! Put him in arrest! Every man here's a witness! You heard what he said to me! Every man here's a witness! Put him in arrest! You'll regret the day you ever talked to William C. Miles like that! Put that man in arrest! Every man here's a witness to what he said to me!"

While Miles ranted, the man was dragged, kicking and clawing, through the crowd of seated enlisted men. Four officers, each with the cold, blunt face of a brutal cop, were holding him. I had never seen the officers before, although I later knew them

186

as the first of many Regular Army officers Miles was to get into the Regiment.

The commander of an RCT was supposed to hold the rank of Brigadier General, but a week later Miles' hopes of becoming a general officer were obliterated. Brigadier General Carl S. Hix was given command of the RCT and Miles was left to command the Regiment. He had been in command no more than six hours when the telephone operators had overheard enough to tell us that he was in charge of all tactical situations and Miles was to be nothing more than an administrator. Miles retreated to his tent, where he stayed four days, coming out only when Hix called for him.

General Hix was a big man, dark and scar-faced. He looked like, and was, a slightly aged All-American. He charged about the camp, greeting our salutes with a casual gesture and a "How's it going, son?"

But we couldn't completely trust somebody who would tolerate Miles. Hix was going to have to do some tall soldiering to convince us.

He discontinued the drills, issued our overdue beer and put us back in fatigue uniforms, but Miles was ever present with his "little talks."

"The only thing we can do," Ray told me, speaking of the treatment Miles was handing out to the National Guard officers, "is stay away from him as much as we can. When we get around him, he gives us a lecture on how 'real officers' act. And for an officer that's never seen combat, he sure's to hell sets himself up as an expert on it. I'd hate like hell to be on a patrol he would lead."

The man who had called Miles a murderous old sonofabitch was court-martialed. But instead of being sent to the stockade, he was kept in the Regiment. He was transferred to George Company, which seemed a ridiculous punishment, for the man had been in King Company, which had received its share of the bloody fights. However, a few days later, Lieutenant Baxter caught one of the regimental clerks masturbating and the court-martial sent the man to George Company. Thereafter, the pattern was clear: men were sent to George for a multitude of sins, some bad, some petty, some, apparently, for no reason at all; some were sent for rape (laying with the New Guinea women, by consent or purchase, was rape), brawling, uniform careless- ness, dusty rifle, lack of personal sanitation and insubordination (calling officers by first names).

And so, until the invasion of Leyte, the Regiment did noth- ing. We rotted in New Guinea. We were weakened by malaria, jungle rot, dengue fever, jaundice, and elephantiasis. But mostly we were weakened by the court-martials, which had become an almost daily occurrence. It finally got so bad that General Hix called Miles (with a telephone operator listening) and put a stop to it.

"Get this straight, Miles. You're not commanding a fukup company. This is a regiment, and not every man in it is a fukup. This is a wartime regiment and these men are here to fight, not run through close-order drill, which reminds me: stop screwing up that training schedule I send over to you. You might also remember that every man in the country can't and doesn't want to be a soldier. . . ."

The court-martials leveled off. Recon lost four good men to George and they were replaced by men from the replacement depots. The replacements came in with stories about a certain colonel, commanding a replacement depot, whose punishments were so cruel and unusual that several attempts had been made to kill him.

"It seems like a hundred years ago," Ray Mosby said, "but I can remember when we had the best regiment in the Pacific."

4

I took refuge in thinking of Jenny. She continued to send bun- dles of pictures, but I asked for more. I couldn't get enough. Sometimes I would steal looks at a favorite picture and have an erection so full that it made me ache.

And, as we continued to rot in New Guinea, I developed a strange inferiority complex. Jenny became too good for me. It seemed that she should be married to an officer. She was too pretty and too wealthy to be the wife of a mere enlisted man. Such thinking must have become apparent in my letters, for her own letters took on a tone of frantically trying to cheer me up.

Finally came the invasion of Leyte. But we weren't a spearheading regiment. We were nothing more than security troops. Miles lectured: ". . . There'll be good hunting, men." But as much as we hated the Japs, we couldn't help thinking of them as humans. The idea of their being game sickened me.

Ray and I had Recon on outpost and we talked during a drenching downpour:

"Ray?"

Although we were ten miles from Regimental Headquarters, he automatically glanced around to make sure nobody had heard me call him by first name. "Yeah?"

"How long've we been overseas?"

"Two hundred years, give or take a year."

I wiped rain out of my eyes. "Wonder what it's like to be a civilian."

He snuggled deeper into his poncho. "I have a wife named Virginia Lou and a daughter named Anna Louise, I have a business that nets eight thousand a year, I have three thousand acres of good cotton land, but mostly I have a wife and a daughter. They're the ones that'll get me home—sooner or later." He gave me a searching look. "You're not thinking about giving up, are you, Sam?"

I shrugged in the rain. "I'm getting pretty tired of this crap we're taking."

"I'm going to outlast this fuken war, no matter what I have to do, short of getting myself killed."

Ray was the next one to give up.

It happened on a routine patrol. Ray was leading us and I followed him. We were alert but relaxed, glad to be away from Regimental Headquarters. Ray was the first to hear the scream. I halted the column and waited for his instructions. He crept forward and I advanced a few feet so I could keep him in sight.

He was no more than thirty yards away. Suddenly the scream came again and this time it was obvious that it was a woman, or a girl. Ray stiffened and brushed a palmetto aside. Then, roaring like a lunatic, he plowed through the jungle. I quickly signaled Carr to bring the men and rushed forward to see what had happened to Ray. I found him standing over three huddled bodies, two Japs and a tiny Filipino girl. Ray was chopping at the Japs, axe-fashion, with his rifle. He was talking insanely to himself. The girl was motionless. There was no need of my making sure the Japs were dead. Ray had beaten their heads to a pulp with the butt of his rifle.

I jerked him away. He glared at me, white-faced and blue-lipped, before he groaned pathetically and collapsed. I left him on the ground while I examined the girl. She was about six years old and the Japs had tried to rape her. She had probably bled to death; there was a pool under her buttocks.

Leaving the first squad with Ray, I carried the girl to a village and her parents were found. The mother screamed and wailed until some of the older women took her to the priest. The father followed us back to where we had found the girl. He was very angry because the Japs were dead. He had plans for them.

We were on the way back to Regimental with Ray when the fit hit me. Before this, I had been able to control the trembling that came after the fight, but I couldn't now. I could walk, but Raker had to help me. I knew that I was going to be the one who followed Ray.

He didn't speak during the return trip. He stumbled along, a man holding each arm, and when we sat him in a chair at the aid station, he stared stonily into the wall of the tent. Doc Wingate gave him a shot in the arm, which put him to sleep.

But Ray wasn't sent home. That wasn't Miles' policy. Officers were given assignments that weren't such a drain on their morale. Doc Wingate argued and pleaded with Miles, but Ray stayed. He was promoted to captain and became commanding officer of Headquarters Company.

Only during those times when it was absolutely safe did Ray emerge from his foxhole. He kept a demolition grenade handy and he swore that he was going to blow himself up if the Japs got too close to him. Once, when he had to leave the hole to go to the latrine, I sneaked in, found the grenade and removed the fuse from it.

It was soon after that I began to feel myself slipping. I began to have nightmares and my trembling fits were more violent each time it happened. I was still as good in combat as I had ever been, for when we were fighting I operated with the same, seemingly slow-motioned precision. I became obsessed, however, with the thought that maybe this slow-motion idea was false: it could be true, I thought, that the Japs are actually that slow. A really fast-moving Jap, I thought, will some day run a bayonet through my belly.

So I was falling apart. It was now a matter of which could last the longer, the war or Sam Gifford. The answer soon came: Lieutenant Baxter took Ray's place as CO of Recon.

"Now let's get a few things straight, Gifford," he told me. "You used to run this platoon the way you wanted to. You can make up your mind that *I'm* running it from now. Mosby might have been satisfied by telling you to take a look at so-and-so and take your word for it. But I'm not Mosby. You'll bring back proof to me or I'll call you a liar. Understood?"

All you need, sonny, is the swagger stick. "Yes," I said patiently, "I understand."

"Say sir when you're addressing a commissioned officer!"

"Sir," I said.

"Repeat your answer and add sir."

"Yes, I understand, sir."

"And *stand at attention!*"

I stood at attention.

"And something else. You might be a big shot in that hick town of yours, wherever this Guard outfit came from, but here you're just another tech sergeant and you'll take orders the way I give them. Understood?"

"Understood—sir."

"You're dismissed, Sergeant."

I turned to go.

"*Come back here!*"

I faced him.

"Salute, make about-face and leave."

I did as he wanted me to.

"Come back here!"

He made me salute, about-face and leave five times before he was happy enough to let me go.

And I led patrols. For a man who had chosen the army as a career, Baxter was mighty leery of fighting. Contrary to what he had told me, he did take my word on reports, for he stayed away from the dangerous patrols. But Miles didn't know about that. Baxter used "I" when he turned in my reports; Baxter even got a Bronze Star for a patrol he never made.

The trembling fits were taking their toll. I went to Baxter, armed with the proper army regulation, and told him I wanted to turn in my stripes.

Baxter was dumfounded. He had never heard of this. Soldiers, by tradition, covet those stripes and won't give them up easily.

"What for, for christ's sake?" he said.

"I'm worn out, sir," I said. For some silly reason, I needed to cry.

"But what about your wife?" The old army mind working now. "Do you want her to live on private's pay?"

"I have a private income, sir. So does my wife."

He might have let me turn them in if I hadn't said that. He was in a rage. An enlisted man with a private income! Of all the crap.

"Sergeant, the answer is unalterably no! You've got experience that I can use and I'm going to use it. Understood?"

"I'm trying to tell you, sir, I'm worn out. I'm asking to give up before I ruin myself."

"*Give up?*" he shouted. "*Give up!*" He got hold of himself. "Sergeant Gifford, we're in a war, in case you didn't know it. And something else, when you give up—as you *civilians* insist on putting it—cowardice is a better name—when you give up, you'll go directly to George Company. Understood?"

"Sir, there're fresh men in the platoon who could do a better job of——"

"Shut up, Sergeant. Do you hear? Shut up!"

So I continued to make the patrols, although I was never any good as a leader on the return trips. Kenny Carr always brought us back.

"Remember how scared you got when you'd almost have a car wreck?" Doc Wingate explained. "Well, your trembling fits are an exaggeration of the same thing. But be careful. You can no more keep this up than you could continue surviving a near wreck every day. If this damn army weren't so ridden by pseudo virtue and puritanism, you could take a good jolt of whiskey after each patrol and you'd do better. Aw hell, this fuken army. . . ."

5

The Luzon Campaign was easy fighting. Other, better outfits were making the bitter pushes and we moved in behind them to guard against infiltration and snipers. Our contacts with Jap patrols never lasted more than three or four minutes, but each little fight left me with a minutely more violent fit of trembling. I developed a tic in the muscle of my right cheek, immediately under my eye. A crusty rash broke out on the backs of both hands. The same rash covered my crotch. My feet were both infected with fungus.

During the actual fights, I still fought well enough, but I was haunted more than ever by the fear that a Jap was going to move faster than I anticipated. . . . I stayed in my foxhole and wrote long, often clever letters to Jenny. The act of writing became a ritual and the contents of my writing kit, the paper, the pen, became objects of very jealous affection. I kept the kit at the bottom of my jungle pack and anybody who tried to borrow it was met with cold rejection. I heard Raker, Carr and Meleski talking about me:

"Sam's pretty far gone," Raker said.

"Those fits of his," Meleski said, "give me the creeps."

"All right then, goddamnit," Carr said, "don't watch'em."

"Funny thing," Raker said. "Ray, then Sam. You think them Oak Street boys ain't got what it takes?"

"Shit!" Carr said. "They're as tough as anybody else." He paused. "It's just that they've had it easier than we have. Sort of like not getting enough basic training."

The battle lines tightened and locked; the campaign was stale. Manila was free and in that blasted city American soldiers were whoring and brawling. Miles had no pass system, but the mail truck needed guards and those of us who were lucky were put on that detail.

Raker, Carr, Meleski and I were four of the lucky ones. We went into Manila like four country boys going to town on a Saturday. At one of the Red Cross canteens, we saw the first American women we had seen in almost three years. One of the women thought of herself as The Girl Next Door, another was The All-American Co-ed, another was The All-American Older Woman and there was also The American Mother. They pretended great interest in the infantrymen who were in town to see the sights. It wasn't long, though, until they left us in favor of a crowd of Air Force flying sergeants.

Carr and Meleski toured the whorehouses while Raker and I found some whiskey. I poked my pistol in the bootlegger's ribs and made him drink from both bottles to make sure it wasn't poison. It wasn't, but the margin of safety was thin. I awoke the next morning, big-headed and sick, and discovered that I still had my wallet, but it had been rifled. The four of us met at the post office and bummed a breakfast from a quartermaster company nearby. I was glad to see the truck, loaded with mail, ready to take us back to the Regiment.

"Think you'll make it through the war, Sam?" Carr asked.

"They say it'll last till forty-eight," I said. "I can't last that long."

"Bad."

"I tried to turn in my stripes, but Baxter wouldn't listen to me."

"Fuk Baxter."

"That's right, fuk Baxter. But you're the one who ought to be wearing five stripes, not me."

"Fuk your stripes."

"That's right, fuk my stripes."

"Back in forty-one, Sam, what'd you think'd happen to you?"

"I thought I'd be a respectable married man by now, kids, stuff like that. How about you?"

"Back in forty-one," Carr said, "I never thought me and you'd be making the town together."

I grinned. "We're doing it though, aren't we?"

A few days later the first rotation plan was announced. I had more than enough points, but Baxter listed all his non-coms as "essential to the war effort," and I stayed. Baxter became the object of an emotion the intensity of which dominated much of my thinking: I hated him, the first person I had ever hated.

I took no pains to hide it from him. When it was necessary for me to talk to him, I looked him squarely in the eye and let my hatred flicker as brightly as it would. It made him squirm and it wasn't long before he developed the habit of finding something for his eyes to do when I faced him. If he hadn't been aware that reduction in rank was what I craved, he would have broken me to private immediately.

During the final weeks of the campaign, with the fighting at an almost complete standstill, Miles decided it would be safe enough to move his headquarters nearer to the front. He chose a small town in Central Luzon; the choice was made after Recon examined several towns and found one where Miles could be comfortable. Squarely in the middle of the town was a huge brick house, around which were several smaller buildings that could house the various platoons and sections of Headquarters Company.

As we approached the town, Miles stopped the column. "*Baxtah!*" he shouted.

"Let's go, Sergeant!" Baxter said immediately and jumped out of the jeep. He trotted back toward Miles' command car. I followed at a walk.

"I have a hunch," Miles said, "that there might be a few of the enemy left behind to bother me. Baxter, send some men forward."

"On your way, Sergeant!" Baxter said crisply.

I took four of the newer men with me; no need of bothering the experienced hands with trivialities. There were a few civilians picking at the ruins in the south section of the town, but nothing else. When I reported back to Miles, I led the men down the middle of the road, our rifles at sling. Baxter, waiting for me, took my report and told Miles that he had found nothing. I followed Baxter to the command car and stood behind him.

But then one of the sagging walls in the south ruins chose that moment to fall. Miles blanched white and stopped the column.

"Get that Recon sergeant up here!" he shouted angrily.

Lieutenant Baxter became a whirlwind of military ambition and started running down the slope, yelling my name. He had forgotten that I had been standing behind him.

"Right here, Lieutenant," I called dryly after him.

The lieutenant, as he made his way back up the slope, was burning red with embarrassment.

"Sergeant," Miles bawled at me, "didn't your report state the enemy had withdrawn?"

"That's right, sir."

"Then how do you explain that falling wall?"

"It was weak, sir, ready to fall."

"Goddamnit, I know it fell!" He studied the town through his binoculars. "I have a hunch," he said, "there's still enemy troops in there."

"I think you're right, Colonel," Baxter chirped promptly.

"I don't think so, sir," I said.

"Your opinion wasn't asked for," Baxter said.

The Colonel, who held his binoculars with a high-elbow grip as movie heroes do, said, "Baxtah!"

"Yes, *sir!*"

"Two men in there to make sure. Cover them with the machine gun on your jeep. I have a hunch that we'll find a little something."

"Yes, *sir!*" Baxter hurried down the hill to his jeep. I followed patiently behind. By the time I had reached him, he had dispatched Raker, Meleski, Ralston and Saunders, double the number Miles had wanted, toward the town. The lieutenant then crawled into his jeep and made much show of pulling back the bolt on the machine gun. "You men stand clear there," he said pompously. "I'll need a clear lane of fire."

Oh certainly, I thought.

The men, sullen with disgust, scrambled slowly to their feet and stood with me behind the jeep. The four-man detail, Raker in charge, strolled casually down the road and I could see Meleski talking; I could tell that he was making his usual caustic remarks. Baxter knew it too and his mouth tightened. No doubt Meleski would be Sergeant of the Guard tonight.

With Raker in the lead, they disappeared into the ruins. None of the four men had unslung his rifle. Behind me, the binoculars held dramatically to his eyes, Miles watched. Baxter was breathing tensely. The rest of us were relaxed, bored.

A wall, which stood at the end of the street that we were looking down, suddenly collapsed with a crumpling roar and Baxter, his tense finger on the trigger, let loose a burst of fire. The tracers disappeared into the cloud of dust the falling wall had stirred up. The men in the Recon platoon winked and grinned at each other. I remained bored; if the fool kid wanted to waste ammunition to show off for Miles, I didn't care.

Raker, Meleski, Saunders and Ralston, running to escape the rolling bricks from the falling masonry, ran directly into Baxter's lane of fire. The lieutenant stiffened and turned sickeningly white—and froze on the trigger.

The four men, looking over their shoulders at the falling wall, failed to hear the machine gun firing. Raker and Meleski fell first. Ralston and Saunders turned in time to see the tracers coming at them, but they were running too fast to stop or fall. Both of them were shot through the head.

The scene became like the one the night I had fired into

197

the Jap officer's face. It was very plain and slow and bright. I moved with the same calm slowness, grasped my rifle by the muzzle and methodically chopped at Baxter's head with the butt. I hit him twice before he let go of the trigger and fell off the back of the jeep. He tried to roll away from me, but I followed him relentlessly.

"I'm going to kill this sonofabitch," I said plainly.

I beat at him with the rifle until he was still, then I put the butt against my shoulder and, slowly, punched at the safety with the back of my trigger finger. I had my eye to the sight, making sure I didn't miss, when I saw Kenny's huge, gnarled fist coming toward my forehead. Baxter's face tilted out of sight and I struck the ground heavily on my back.

6

A strange captain was standing over me when I opened my eyes. My forehead was so swollen that I could see only that part of him below his Adam's apple. I was in the aid station. Doc Wingate, his face worried, stood behind the captain, who was shaking me roughly.

"Gifford, you awake?" the captain said.

"Keep your goddamn hands off him," Doc said. "I told you about that once."

"Colonel Miles has commanded me——"

"And I've commanded you to keep your fuken hands off my patient too, and this is my hospital." Doc knelt beside me. "You awake, Sam?" he said softly.

I tried twice before I could croak, "Yes."

"You're in arrest," the captain said. "A guard is posted at the head of your bed. He has been instructed to shoot to kill."

"Baxter," I said, "that murderous sonofabitch. . . ."

"You're charged with striking an officer under combat circumstances," the captain said coldly. "That is all I'm allowed to tell you." The captain executed a brisk exit.

Doc rubbed cool alcohol on my arm with a dab of cotton. "Sam, why'n hell'd you have to do that?" He jabbed me with a needle.

"He killed the . . . only good friends I've ever had."

Doc regarded me curiously. "Oh," he said. "I see." He cleared his throat and I was reminded sharply of how Colonel Cozzens had done it the same way. "Carr came in to see you. They ran'im off."

"Carr's . . . good boy."

"He's that," Doc said. "Ray came by too."

"Good."

"Carr really poled you a good one."

"He should've . . . let me kill Baxter."

"You damn near did anyhow." Doc smiled benignly. "I'm going to make you sleep a little while, Sam."

"Doc . . . you the best doctor in . . . Gray's Landing."

"All right, Sam, go to sleep."

I slept for two days, waking only when the needle stung my arm. Then Doc put me on a strong sedative and I stayed on my bunk, suspended in a dreamy fog. This lasted for many days, I don't know exactly how many.

"All right, guard," I finally heard a voice say from the fog, "wait outside, please."

A man knelt at each side of my bunk. "This's Doc Wingate and Ray Mosby, Sam. Can you talk?" He lifted me until I was sitting up.

"A drink of water, Doc," I said.

A canteen was placed at my lips. I had never tasted anything so delicious before. My head cleared considerably.

"Can you answer some questions, Sam?" Ray asked.

"I think so."

I answered Ray's questions. He wanted to know how long I had lived with Jenny, how much land Poppa and I owned, the value of the gin, the value of all my holdings and my home, seemingly unimportant things about my life in Gray's Landing. When I had given him all that information, he leaned closer.

"Now look, Sam," he said, "I'm your lawyer. Miles passed down word that you're to be found guilty, but I'm going to give them one hell of an argument. If General Hix keeps his word—and I think he will—not another man's going to be sent to the stockade unless it's for a good reason. So you'll get a transfer to George." He paused. "Now. I want you to go over—word-for-word—every rub you've had with Baxter. Don't skip a thing. I want to know how he acted on patrol. I want to know how he treated the men. I want to know everything you've ever noticed about him. But more than anything else, I want to know how he acted under fire, under extreme conditions, stuff like that."

I talked for a long time. I began with the death of Colonel Cozzens and told Ray that Baxter wanted to put me in arrest for the way I had acted. I told how Baxter took credit for all patrols Recon ever went on, even for those that he didn't make. And I told him that Baxter got a medal for a patrol he didn't go on at all. I talked for a long time before I had told everything.

Ray listened carefully, interrupting me only when he wasn't clear on what I was talking about. Finally, when I was through, Ray said nothing for fully five minutes.

Then he said, "Why didn't you give up long time ago, Sam? Just so much can be expected from a soldier and no more."

"I tried to," I said. "I tried to turn in my stripes, but Baxter wouldn't let me."

"That sonofabitch," Ray breathed, "that Regular Army sonofabitch. But I can use that too, not letting you turn in your stripes."

Ray was silent again before he clasped my shoulder and got to his feet. "Doc saw to it that you got a good long rest, so maybe you can outlast the war. Think so?"

"No responsibility," I said. "Maybe I can."

"You want me to write to Jenny?"

"If you will, please."

"I'll do it. Just tell her the plain truth, huh?"

"I suppose so," I said.

At eight o'clock the next morning I was escorted by a heavily armed guard to the squad tent which served as a courtroom. The court was composed of Regular Army officers. Ray muttered something about "a hell of a way to think of it as a jury of your peers."

The court was called to attention and the charge was read. I was charged with striking an officer under "circumstances of combat." Ray protested, saying there was still no proof that the enemy was in the vicinity, but the charge stood because we were in a theater of war.

Lieutenant Baxter, still heavily bandaged, was called first. He didn't look at me the entire time he was in the tent.

"Lieutenant Baxter," the prosecuting officer began heavily, "you will state your name, rank, serial number and organization."

Baxter called out the information clearly but it was obvious that the effort made his injured head ache.

"Now, Lieutenant Baxter," the prosecuting officer said, "you will tell, in your own words, exactly what happened on the date and time specified in the charge."

Baxter paused, cleared his throat with a thin cough, leaned forward and said, "On the date specified in the charge, Technical Sergeant Samuel F. Gifford, the ranking non-commissioned officer of this regiment's Reconnaissance Platoon, was ordered to reconnoiter the town located at the grid co-ordinates of——"

"Did he reconnoiter?"

"He so reported, sir," Baxter said. "But the Regimental Commander saw some activity which he thought might possibly be action on the party of the enemy. The Regimental Commander ordered me to dispatch another reconnaissance party to the scene and find out if his suspicions were correct."

"Was the veracity of Sergeant Gifford questioned in any manner?"

"It was not, sir."

"What was Sergeant Gifford's reaction?"

Baxter glanced at Ray before he answered the question. "It appeared to me, sir, that he was angry and sullen because he thought his judgment was being questioned."

Ray Mosby called out, "Objection, sir."

"The defense will state his objection."

"Sir, the lieutenant stated that Sergeant Gifford thought his judgment was being questioned. The lieutenant had no way of knowing what Sergeant Gifford was thinking."

"Sustained."

Ray took his seat and permitted himself a smile.

The prosecuting officer frowned to show Ray that he didn't appreciate the interruption. "Very well. What happened next, Lieutenant Baxter?"

"I dispatched my best men, Staff Sergeant Raker, Line Sergeant Meleski, Corporals Ralston and Saunders, to the scene."

"Why wasn't Sergeant Gifford given this detail? Didn't you state that he was the ranking non-commissioned officer in the organization?"

"Yes, he was, sir. But I wanted to send my best men and I didn't consider Sergeant Gifford one of my best. I planned—I planned to reduce him to the rank of private as soon as the campaign was over." Baxter's face suddenly reddened and he coughed thinly again.

Ray wrote this on his pad of paper: "Lies." Beside it he put a mark.

The prosecuting officer had seen Ray writing and waited for an objection, but when none came he hastened on to say, "Ah —then what happened?"

"With Sergeant Raker in charge, the party was dispatched for reconnaissance. Because I could not trust Sergeant Gifford with a machine gun——"

"Objection!" Ray shouted.

"Captain Mosby," the court's CO said, "it isn't necessary to speak so loud. We're not on a parade ground. State your objection."

"Well—it isn't really an objection," Ray said. He blushed slightly. "I just think the lieutenant's loading his testimony when he says something like 'I couldn't trust Sergeant Gifford. . . .'"

"Denied," the court said. "Proceed."

". . . I didn't *feel* that I could trust Sergeant Gifford," Baxter went on, "so I chose to cover the detail with the machine gun myself. When the detail reached the village a wall of masonry fell and, at the same time, I sighted two enemy soldiers running through the ruins."

Ray made another mark beside the word "Lies."

"I opened fire," Baxter said. "Sergeant Raker's detail also saw the enemy——"

I put a mark down beside those Ray put.

"——and Raker began an immediate retreat under the protection of my covering fire." Baxter was having a difficult time of it now. He was sweating and occasionally he glanced imploringly at the officer commanding the court. But he wasn't to stop.

"Go on, Lieutenant Baxter," the court's CO said coldly.

"I am, sir," Baxter said, rather plaintively. "I heard a shout behind me, but I couldn't turn to investigate because of the fear of hitting Sergeant Raker's detail. Then I was hit on the shoulder by the butt of a rifle. I saw the tracers from the machine gun turn toward Sergeant Raker and his men, but before I could correct my fire—" He stopped.

The court was silent fully ten seconds before the prosecuting officer spoke. "Go on, Lieutenant Baxter," he said sternly.

"——Before I could correct my fire—which was now hitting among the men of the detail—because the rifle butt had knocked it in that direction—I was hit by the rifle butt again. I fell and, before the rifle butt hit me again, I saw Sergeant Gifford standing over me. He hit me again and I lost consciousness. I—I remember nothing else." Baxter was trembling and plainly anxious to get off the stand. He suddenly got to his feet to go.

"One moment, Lieutenant Baxter," Ray Mosby said. He was pale and trembling. "Did I understand you to say that you planned to reduce Sergeant Gifford to the rank of private at the end of the campaign?"

Baxter took some time getting back into his seat. "That is correct, sir."

"It is my understanding, Lieutenant Baxter," Ray said, "that Sergeant Gifford requested to be broken but you refused him because you stated that you needed his experience." Ray paused until he caught Baxter's eyes. "Is that correct, Lieutenant Baxter?"

Baxter lowered his eyes. "That is not correct, sir."

Ray paused a long time before he said softly, "I see." He

203

let Baxter squirm a moment before he asked, "Lieutenant Baxter, did you receive a decoration—a Bronze Star—for a patrol you were on a month and two days ago?"

Baxter's head remained lowered. "I did receive a decoration, sir."

"Was it given to you for a patrol sent out a month and two days ago?" Ray was pressing hard now, but he didn't like what he was doing.

Baxter suddenly flinched. "I suppose so."

Ray paused a moment. Then he leaned forward and said softly, as if to a child, "Were you actually on that patrol?"

Baxter had already started to shake his head, when the prosecuting officer shouted, "Objection!"

"Sustained! This has nothing to do with the case. You are trying to discredit an officer who has served with honor, Captain Mosby. You are reminded that such behavior in a military court is insubordinate."

Ray didn't take his eyes off Baxter. "Why is it that nobody else saw the two enemy soldiers you mentioned, Lieutenant Baxter?"

Baxter squirmed. "Sergeant Raker saw them."

"But Sergeant Raker is dead."

"The other men saw them."

"Which other men?"

"The men on the detail."

"Lieutenant Baxter, those men are also dead."

"The men around the jeep saw them."

"We'll see about that."

The officer commanding the court stood up. "This is the last warning, Captain Mosby. You're trying to discredit an officer."

"I apologize," Ray said. "I have no more questions."

"You're dismissed, Lieutenant Baxter," the court's CO said quickly.

Baxter got to his feet, saluted the court, made about-face and stopped. He was directly in front of Ray. I believe there was a plea for forgiveness in the look he gave Ray. Baxter ignored me. The tent was quiet for a moment and then Kenny Carr was called.

The prosecuting officer wanted nothing from Kenny but his name, rank, serial number and organization. "I have no questions."

Ray stood in front of Kenny. "Sergeant Carr, on the date and time specified in the charge, did you see the enemy soldiers Lieutenant Baxter was shooting at?"

"They wasn't none to see, sir," Kenny said promptly.

"What kind of non-com would you say Sergeant Gifford was?"

Kenny, his face set and stubborn, said loudly, "The best they was, sir. I'd a follered him anywheres."

"Have you ever doubted his honesty?"

"Nosir, I ain't."

Ray cleared his throat. "Sergeant Carr, will you tell me, in your own words, your personal impressions of Sergeant Gifford?"

Kenny was getting nervous. But he was stubbornly determined to have his say. "Well—" he began. "Well, I've knew—I've knew Sergeant Gifford just pretty near all my life. His folks lived on Oak Street and mine lived on Railroad Avenue, but Gray's Landing is a little town and everybody knows everybody else.

"I ain't saying that Sam—Sergeant Gifford was snooty'r nothing like that because folks on Oak Street was never that kind of people. But they never knowed much about anybody but theirselves. And Sam knowed me, but he never knowed nothing about me." Kenny paused to rub his hands. "We was acquaintances when we both joined the Guard and I started working at his paw's gin."

"When was that, Sergeant Carr?"

"The summer right after I quit high school."

"All right, go ahead."

"After we got federalized, Sam wasn't an officer like everybody thought he'd get to be and us boys in his platoon got to liking him all right. After the first island campaign, he was as good as being one of us. We was all close friends, I mean. And he made one of the best non-coms anybody could ever ask for. He had lots of guts and he wouldn't ask us to do nothing he

205

wouldn't do hisself. And he liked us, too. So we couldn't a asked for better.

"But—well, when we landed here he started coming apart. He tried to turn his stripes in to Lieutenant Baxter, but the lieutenant wouldn't let'im on account of he needed Sam's experience."

Ray cleared his throat. "Are you sure Lieutenant Baxter wouldn't permit Sergeant Gifford to turn in his rank?"

"I'm plumb certain of it!" Kenny said sharply, in the manner of a man not used to having his word doubted.

Ray pressed on, "How were you so certain?"

"Lieutenant Baxter told me so hisself."

"Did he give you any reason for telling you this?"

"He told me I'd better not get my eye set on Sam's stripes because Sam was going to keep on being the platoon sergeant."

"Exactly what were Lieutenant Baxter's words?"

Kenny pondered a moment. He rubbed his hands. "He said, 'Sergeant, I realize you would like to carry—would like to carry Gifford's stripes, but Gifford's . . . generous offer to break hisself—himself so you can get a promotion won't work. Gifford's got to learn—got to learn that his father-in-law doesn't command the regiment no—any longer and he can't get everything he wants.' "

"Those were his exact words?"

"Yessir."

One of the officers of the board asked, "How can you be so sure of that, Sergeant Carr?"

Kenny's jaw hardened. "I got a good memory, sir."

"Very well," the officer said, "carry on."

"All right, Sergeant Carr," Ray Mosby said, "how many enemy soldiers did you say you saw when Lieutenant Baxter fired on Sergeant Raker's patrol?"

"I told you, sir," Kenny said roughly, "I never seen none."

"Why didn't you see some?"

Kenny looked at Ray questioningly, frowned, and said tersely, "They wasn't none to see."

"How can you be so sure of that?" Ray asked.

"I was *there!* I was standing right behind Lieutenant Baxter!" Then Kenny said flatly, "They wasn't no Japs to see."

"I see," Ray said. He cleared his throat. "Did you see Sergeant Gifford strike Lieutenant Baxter?"

Kenny nodded reluctantly and glanced at me. "Yessir, I seen'im."

"What did you think Sergeant Gifford was trying to do?"

"I *knew* what he was trying to do, sir," Kenny said bluntly. "He was trying to keep Baxter from killing those men. If Sam hadn't a hit'im, I'd a did it myself. Sam just got to'im first, that's all."

"Then what happened?"

"Well, Sam seen the men'd been hit and it must a made'im purty mad, because he started trying to beat Baxter to death. Then he started trying to shoot'im."

"What did you do?"

"I was afraid Sam might really kill'im, so I hit Sam."

Ray nodded. "What did——"

"I didn't like'im either," Kenny said suddenly, "but I couldn't see no need of killing'im."

The court's CO said, "Unless otherwise directed, Sergeant Carr, you will answer questions and not answer out of turn. Proceed."

Ray said, "What did you hit him with?"

Kenny was startled. "Why, I hit'im with my fist, sir." He held up his fist.

"All right, Sergeant Carr," Ray said. "Did you think the circumstances warranted Sergeant Gifford's striking Lieutenant Baxter?"

"They sure did, sir. He'd already killed Raker and Meleski and——"

"Objection!"

"Sustained," the court's CO said quickly.

Ray sat down. "I have no more questions."

Kenny was dismissed. Each of the men in the Recon Platoon was called and all were asked the same questions by both the prosecuting officer and by Ray.

"Was Sergeant Gifford a fair and good non-com?" the prosecution asked.

All of the old men answered in the affirmative, but the replacements were still possessed of the fears and disciplines of training camp and they gave negative answers.

And Ray asked, "How many enemy soldiers did you see on the date and time specified in the charge?"

Only one man, a replacement, gave an answer other than "none." He said he had seen five Japs.

The prosecuting officer said, among other things, in summing up his case:

". . . Sergeant Gifford was from the privileged class of a small town. He was spoiled and accustomed to having his own way. When the Regimental Commander doubted the validity of his report, Sergeant Gifford was angry and vindictive. Those were the circumstances under which he struck his superior officer. And when he struck that officer, he indirectly caused the death of four men. The prosecution demands the death penalty."

Ray Mosby rose to sum up his case and I watched him in awe, often forgetting that he was there in my interests. I was thinking, as he talked, that he was the first of us from Oak Street to come of age. And he was the first of us to give up.

"I want to comment briefly on the prosecution's comment concerning Sergeant Gifford's civilian social status. At the same time I'd like to say that he's not being tried for his civilian life too. This court must mind its own business. If Sergeant Gifford was used to having his own way as a civilian, I'd like to know how. I lived next door to him and I've known him all his life. I want you to know this: Sergeant Gifford's father has made it a part of Sergeant Gifford's thinking that the other man has a will too. So, for that reason, the prosecution's contention that the Sergeant was angry and vindictive because he didn't have his way is not, I repeat not, valid."

The members of the court looked uncomfortable. They weren't sure that they understood what Ray was talking about.

"Now," Ray said. "This court-martial must deal with issues.

"We have heard what Sergeant Carr had to say and I'm sure we can do no less than agree that he is a man of uncompromising integrity. He has stated that Lieutenant Baxter fired the machine gun that killed Sergeant Raker and his patrol. Sergeant Carr and thirty-one other men have stated that no enemy soldiers were in the area. Therefore, it seems to me that Sergeants Raker and Meleski and Corporals Ralston and Saunders were nothing less than victims of Lieutenant Baxter's hysteria.

"So I don't think there was any doubt in the minds of those immediately present that Sergeant Gifford was justified in striking his superior officer under the circumstances. Sergeant Carr stated that he himself would have done the same if Sergeant Gifford hadn't beat him to it.

"At the same time, I think the prosecution's contention that Sergeant Gifford had been looking for a chance to act as he did because of friction between him and Lieutenant Baxter—I don't think such a contention was justified. It boils down to this: Sergeant Gifford was overwrought because Lieutenant Baxter had killed four men who had become of great importance in Sergeant Gifford's life. And it *is* true that the men wouldn't've been important in Sergeant Gifford's civilian life. But you must understand that he had lived with those men for a long time, had been near death with them, had had the same good times and bad times they had had. So they were close together, very close. It makes no difference—*now*—that they didn't share a common background because they had all become close friends.

"I want to point out something else: Lieutenant Baxter stated that he intended to break Sergeant Gifford, but the same lieutenant told both Sergeant Gifford and Sergeant Carr that he had no intention of breaking Sergeant Gifford. The truth was ignored—either at this court-martial or in the presence of Sergeants Gifford and Carr. I think that fact should be taken into consideration.

"Let me make one last observation. And in making this observation, I know I'm guilty of contradicting myself somewhat in bringing up Sergeant Gifford's background. He is a wealthy man; he has a pretty wife of splendid character. Do you think he would turn down a chance to return to his wife and his wealth by deliberately striking an officer? Absolutely not. I have known him a long time, as I've said. He was my platoon sergeant when I commanded this regiment's Reconnaissance Platoon and I knew him as a calm, even-thinking man even under the stress of combat. It would take an awful lot to cause him to act as he did when he struck Lieutenant Baxter. And there was an awful lot. Lieutenant Baxter had killed his friends. When we bring in anything that asks why the men were his friends, we are both confusing the issues of this court and ignoring the fact that the tensions of combat bring men closer together than they could possibly be as civilians. If Sergeant Gifford would not have been the friend of these men in peacetime, it makes no difference. The important thing is that they *were* his friends.

"And, I suppose, the crux of the whole matter is this: what kind of man is it who will stand idly by while a hysterical officer shoots down innocent men?"

Ray sat down. He was pale and sweaty, but he managed to clasp my shoulder and wink. "All that fancy talk," he whispered ruefully, "for nothing."

The court retired to ponder its decision. While we waited for them we smoked. The court didn't stay out long, no more than ten minutes, but we became restless. Ray said nothing. He remained pale and his hands began to tremble. Kenny Carr said, "Oh hell," several times, but he said nothing else. I sat in my chair and thought about the things that had been said about me. And those vague mists of the day of Colonel Cozzens' death were dissipated and the importances of today came into sharp focus. I understood a lot of things now. But there were still areas of ignorance.

7

The court-martial found me guilty. But, possibly with the warning of General Hix in mind, nothing was said of the death penalty the prosecution had asked for. I was called to attention before the court.

"Technical Sergeant Samuel F. Gifford, 19099225, you are found guilty of striking an officer under circumstances of combat. By the authority of the Commanding General, ——th Regimental Combat Team, you are sentenced to ten years of hard labor at the federal detention facility at Fort Leavenworth, Kansas, United States of America." He cleared his throat. "Further, you are reduced to the rank of private, and, upon the completion of your sentence, you will be dishonorably discharged from the United States Army. You will forfeit all privileges commonly due to the honorably discharged soldier.

"The findings of this court are subject to the review of the Regimental Commander. If the court's sentence is approved, it will be subject to review by the Commanding General of this Regimental Combat Team. If, however, the Regimental Commander sees fit to commute the sentence, no further review by higher authority is necessary.

"Private Gifford, what have you to say?"

"Nothing, sir."

"This court-martial is dismissed. All personnel are reminded that the information heard here is restricted. Dismissed."

I was escorted to the guard tent. My head was strangely clear and I was unafraid. Ray sat on my bunk with me for a few minutes.

"I wouldn't worry about that ten years and dishonorable discharge business, Sam," Ray said. "Miles wouldn't dare send you to the stockade because that would mean Hix would review the court-martial. He'd find a few things Miles doesn't want him to know. Worst you'll get'll be George." He smiled. "Bad enough, huh?" He rubbed his pale face with trembling hands.

Book IV

The Seasonal Eternity

1

Savage stood guard while Johnson, Willie Crawford, Sellers, Morgan and I bathed in the river. The water was clear and cool, a healing balm to me. It removed a stubborn layer of filth from my skin, which had become as black and dirty as the others now. I found a shallow place and sat on the pebbled bottom, letting the water tumble over me. The water was so clear that I could see my naked self plainly. It fascinated me; I had never seen such a beautiful sex organ. I had never loved anything so dearly. It floated and bobbled in the water. It was so beautiful, but it was also so useless.

I shook my head sharply. Don't let your loneliness turn to ego, son, I thought. You're no worse off than the others.

Willie and Sellers were trying to catch Lieutenant Johnson, who was fighting them with fists of gravel and splashes of water. They were going to duck him because he was a goddamn officer and all officers should drown.

"Stand away, you fuken enlisted pigs!" Johnson said grandly. "You should be honored that an officer will even bathe in the same river with the likes of you."

Willie and Sellers stood at attention.

"Well now," Johnson said. "That's more like it."

"Sir," Willie said, "I got a question."

"Speak up, man, what is it?"

215

"It's real personal, sir."

"All right, all right, out with it!"

"Would the Lieutenant mind kissing my ass?"

"Why, not at all, Private Crawford, I'd only be too happy to do——"

KA-WOOONG!

Savage had fired directly over our heads. I hustled out of the water, grabbed my clothes and dashed for the small protection of the bush the others had hidden behind. I turned to see what was going to happen.

"What's going on, Savage?" Johnson asked.

"Four Japs was getting ready to pot you guys from the other bank."

"All right, get your clothes on, boys." As we dressed, Johnson continued: "That's the second patrol they've sent this far down. But that's the first daylight job I've seen since Bailey got killed."

"I saw one yesterday," I said.

"Not this far down," Johnson said. "They must be planning to bust out or something. God knows, they wouldn't have any trouble doing that. We could hold this line just about like we could stop the river from running."

Grimes, when we returned to perimeter, was standing in his foxhole under the house. We had no sooner appeared than the great belching voice summoned Johnson. I dropped to the edge of my foxhole and tried to control my trembling.

"Goddamn, Gifford," Sellers said, astounded. "What's wrong? They never fired a shot at us."

"Leave'im alone, Sellers," Willie said sharply. "He gets shaky after it's all over."

Sellers and Savage regarded me curiously for a moment before both nodded understandingly.

It had been the patrol that had done it. The rest Doc Wingate had managed for me had been enough to last out the patrol, but the trembling had returned enough to make me sick with it.

There's one way to tell when I'm really done, I thought for

the hundredth time, and that's when I stop waiting till it's over to start trembling. A really fast Jap . . .

"*Second platoon!*" Johnson called. "Full field pack. C-rations for a week, three hundred rounds, poncho, blanket, extra socks; march order in ten minutes!"

"Hot damn!" Willie exclaimed gleefully, but not so loud as to be heard by Captain Grimes. "Outpost!"

"Best thing I've heard in a month!" Sellers said.

Savage and Morgan were both solemnly pleased.

The line of outposts began four miles from Grimes' company headquarters perimeter and that was a distance which pleased us. He was too much of a coward to come up to the outposts. And outpost duty was doubly desirable because, aside from the patrol clashes of the last few days, there had been so little action.

We hustled enthusiastically about the perimeter gathering the supplies Johnson had called for. I too had caught the feverish desire to get away from Grimes.

We gathered around the house, ready to leave, and stood in the shade of the lister bag while Grimes surveyed us with that grin of his. Swanson and Millard stood at each side of him, the tommy-guns cradled in their arms. Grimes had opened his huge mouth to speak when the first *crunch* came from the direction of the river. Sudden, sick alarm hit Grimes' face as if had been thrown there like a glass of water. He visibly recoiled.

"*Artillery!*" Swanson gasped.

There was a rushing clatter as Grimes and his two guards hurried through the house and down the steps toward their foxholes. I sped across the perimeter and made a flying dive into my own foxhole. The second round of the barrage hit a hundred yards to the south. There was a pause while the Jap spotter corrected the fire, and the next round hit squarely in the middle of the perimeter.

This was the first time I had ever been under artillery fire.

The second shell in the perimeter exploded only fifteen yards from my foxhole. I was jolted and shaken as the earth jerked around me. Dust sprang up from the ashes. Thereafter, at precise, ten-second intervals, a shell exploded in the perimeter. Far away there was the sound of the gun and, following a hardly perceptible pause, the approach of the shell could be heard. As each shell came closer its sound sharpened, but it never attained the pure whistle I had learned to expect from the movies. It was a sizzling whistle, and then there was a terrifying *KA-RAAAAASH!* It seemed that each shell was arching up to land squarely on me. I wanted desperately to jump free of my foxhole and run for the safety beyond the perimeter.

I was enveloped by great clouds of gray dust from the ashes. I hunched, face down, in my foxhole and held my helmet over my loins. I grunted just before each explosion.

I heard somebody rush past my foxhole and run toward the river. As he passed he was talking to himself in a frantic, tenor voice, urging himself to get away from here before he was killed. When the next shell exploded I heard him scream and soon the medic crawled past. I was strangely conscious of the sun's intense heat on my back. Another explosion showered me with dust and rocks and I braced myself again. The next explosion never came; I slowly let my muscles relax.

For perhaps two minutes I didn't try to move. Finally, with a heavy groan rising unbidden from my throat, I crawled sluggishly out of my hole and flopped in the dust.

"Who's hurt?" I heard Johnson call.

"Millard," the medic answered.

There was another silence before Sellers breathed from somewhere nearby, "Maybe the sonofabitch'll die."

I rolled over to look, but I was trembling so hard that the scene, four or five men huddled over the sprawled figure of Millard, danced spasmodically.

"Dead," the medic announced.

"Good!" Sellers breathed triumphantly. "The bastard's had it coming for a long time."

"Who is it?" another voice called. It took some time for me to realize that this last shaky voice belonged to Captain Grimes.

"It's Millard, Waco," Johnson said.

"*Millard!*" Grimes shouted unbelievingly. "Millard? Millard?" Grimes walked dreamily across the perimeter. "Millard?" he called. "Millard!"

"Take it easy, Waco," Johnson said gently.

"Hey, Gifford's hurt!" Sellers cried.

I waved my hand negatively. "Just shaky," I said.

"Leave'im alone," Willie said. "He'll be all right in a minute."

"Hey, Savage, Morgan," Sellers called softly, but failing to keep the joy out of his voice, "Millard got it! Fragment cut his throat from *ear to ear!*" He cackled a soft, triumphant laugh.

"Well I be goddamn!" Savage muttered solemnly. "First time the Japs ever done anything to please me!"

Willie knelt over me solicitously. "About through, Sam?"

I took a deep breath. "Just about."

He lifted me gently to my feet. "Millard's dead."

"I know it," I said.

Willie grinned through the dirt on his face. "Ain't that the berries!"

The talk suddenly stopped. Captain Grimes passed carrying the limp corpse of Millard. The feet dangled loosely and the head, half-severed, bobbled crazily. Captain Grimes was crying silently.

Ignoring us, he carried the corpse to one of the foxholes under the house and quietly went to work burying it. He didn't use a shovel; he removed his helmet and scooped dirt into the hole until the corpse was no longer visible. Grimes turned, still without seeing us, and made his way unsteadily up the steps and out of sight in his house.

"The sonofabitch," Terry said unbelievingly, "was crying!"

"Yeah!" Sellers said.

For perhaps ten seconds nothing happened. Johnson leaned calmly against the scaffolding of the lister bag, his head down, saying nothing, answering Terry's insistent questions with a keep-still gesture of his hand. I squatted on my haunches and waited, still slightly sick from my fit of trembling.

"We going on outpost, Little Joe?" Willie asked, using the code name in deference to Grimes.

"Don't know, Willie," Johnson said. "We'll just have to wait to find out." He sounded tired and irritated.

We waited. Johnson continued to stare at the ground, but the waiting was telling on him. He nervously fingered the band aid on his chin.

"Waco!" Johnson called. He raised his head and, eyes closed, called sharply, "*Waco!*"

Swanson, very pale and blue-lipped, appeared at the window. "Go ahead and man the outposts," he said, surprisingly civil.

Johnson turned away without appearing to notice Swanson's civility. "Double column," he ordered. "Keep close to the ditch and keep your ears sharp for artillery. Move out."

With no noise other than the flap of canteens and the creak of leather rifle slings, the platoon filed out of the perimeter, strangely silent men whose elation over Millard's death and the job of getting to the outposts was unconsciously chilled.

"Wonder what made'im want to cry?" Terry said.

"Shut up, back there," Johnson said coldly.

"Jesus! Little Joe, you——"

Johnson stopped him with a hard stare. The other men stared a second before they forgave Johnson with a shrug.

The road, once black-topped but now pitted and torn by explosion and war traffic, crossed a bare flat expanse of land, before it turned south and entered a shallow draw, where Johnson halted us.

"All right," he said evenly, giving no indication of his previous bad humor, "we'll wait for the jeep here."

We lounged in the shade and smoked. My jacket was wet with sweat and when it dripped from my elbows the water was muddy. A slight breeze pushed across the rice paddies and funneled through the draw. I removed my jacket and fanned it in the air, trying to dry it out before we started moving again.

". . . We're the fukup companeee of the whole Pacific sea. . . ." Terry sang gaily.

"And you're the greatest fukup of us all," Sellers finished.

The jeep rounded the bend and stopped. The back seat was loaded with ammo and it pulled a trailer, also loaded. Without

220

waiting for the command, six men from the first squad stepped forward and took cases of mortar rounds, flares and machine gun ammunition out of the jeep. The jeep rolled on ahead.

We marched through Angat, which had once been a town of considerable size, but leveled now; only the huge mission church was left standing. It was a hot day, a high, bright, cloudless one, and my fatigue jacket was soon soaked again. I put my wallet and bundle of pictures into a cargo pocket so they wouldn't be stained by sweat. The straps of the heavy pack—laden with three hundred rounds of rifle ammo and a week's C-ration—bit into my shoulders. Behind me Sellers was grunting with the weight of his pack, the BAR and its extra load of ammunition.

The jeep was waiting for us at the base of a hill which paralleled the road and, while the driver listened nervously for artillery, the remaining six men of the first squad unloaded more ammo. They climbed the hill with their load. The jeep moved away.

"How long do we get outpost?" I asked.

"A week," Willie said.

"Just a week?" I said, disappointed.

Willie grinned. "You're catching on fast, Sam boy."

The next outpost—a hill roughly shaped like Poppa's big English pipe with the front part of the bowl cut off sharply by the river which flowed below it—was where I would stop. I helped unload the ammo, but Willie shook his head when I started to carry my share. He handed me, instead, a couple of radio batteries.

"I'm not sick, Willie," I said.

But Willie had seen my trembling fits. "We'n managed all right," he said gruffly. "Batteries's enough." He refused, by sharply clasping my wrist, to let me pick up anything else.

With Johnson in the lead, followed by Willie, we labored up the hill. Sellers, already overloaded with his BAR and its ammo and his pack, couldn't handle the two cans of machine-gun belts he carried. I took the cans. "Thanks," he breathed heavily.

The heat wasn't so bad in the trees, but the trail, littered with rocks washed loose by generations of rainstorms, was hard going. I fell twice when I stepped on rocks that rolled under the stiff soles of my combat boots. This would be a bastard, I thought, to make a fast retreat on; a man could start running and not stop until he reached the bottom.

We were stopped at the top of the hill by the call of "Hallmark." The column stopped. I flopped down easily on the trail.

"Jesus H. Christ!" Johnson stewed. "I forgot to get the fuken sign and countersign." He raised his voice: "Hey, Tom Thumb, this is Little Joe. I forgot the fuken sign and countersign."

I heard a chorus of laughter. "Come on up, Joe."

We trudged on up. There were six men at the top of the hill, which was completely bald of trees. Ponchos had been stretched over a small ring of foxholes to hold off the blinding sun. The men weren't glad to see us and several of them roughly remarked that they had entertained the hope that we would be ambushed on our way up here. They didn't want to return to the George perimeter and Captain Grimes.

One of them, a big-handed giant, appeared to be the officer, Tom Thumb, for it was with him that Johnson talked while we exchanged places with the men who had been occupying the place. As soon as we were settled, Tom Thumb led his men down the hill and we were left alone. Johnson squatted by the radio so he could hear when the rest of the platoon had relieved the other men and were in position.

If a West Point upperclassman had been asked to imagine the perfect hill for a defensive outpost, this would have been it. The back of the hill dropped straight down to the river, four hundred feet below, and the sides of the hill were so steep that climbing them after dark would be such a noisy maneuver that an ambush would be very easy. Only the stem of the pipe-shaped hill would offer a comparatively easy route of approach, and it was in that direction that the main firepower of the outpost—two thirty-caliber machine guns and a Jap fifty-one caliber —was directed.

And we were provisioned to stand off an army. Resting in one of the big holes was a stack of some twenty cases of ten-in-one rations, which, together with the C-rations we had brought, would last out almost any siege. Tom Thumb's men had left almost all of their ammunition, taking only a few rounds with them in case they ran into trouble during their return to George. There were two mortars, with stacks of antipersonnel and flare shells.

Johnson said, "Tom says they haven't heard a shot all week, except the artillery that hit the perimeter this morning."

"That," Willie said cheerfully, "is the kind of talk I like to hear."

"But what about the patrols we've been running into," I said.

Johnson gave me a sideways flip of his head and said to the others, "Cold-blanket Gifford they called him in college."

"Fuk it," Terry said. "Let's eat."

"Your fuken stomach!" Morgan growled.

"Your fuken *ass!*" Terry said placidly.

"This is Little Joe," Johnson said into the microphone of the radio, "Wilco, roger. Out." He turned to us. "Grimes wants us to listen for artillery."

"You don't say!" Willie said.

"So the sonofabitch started talking again," Terry said.

"Lay off," Johnson said. "Millard was Grimes' best friend."

"Some friend," Willie said.

"His only friend," Sellers said. "None of the other officers would have nothing to do with'im. Had to get a poor fuken enlisted pig to——"

"All right," Johnson said quietly.

The joking stopped. Somehow, they seemed to understand exactly what Johnson had meant. Friendships, I was rapidly learning, were respected here, even Grimes' friendships.

While I sat and thought about this strange man Grimes, Willie urinated over the cliff and commented that it would make the water rise a whole foot.

The men hated Grimes; it was more than a common dislike of a man. Their daily living was taken up mostly with hateful contemplation of him. A company commander is bound to have a few men who dislike him or doubt his intelligence and courage, but hatred for Grimes was like a disease. Aside from a certain respect for his friendship with a now-dead buddy, they gave him nothing but hatred. Later, when Johnson went out to pace off the lanes of fire, I went with him for no other purpose than to ask about Grimes.

Johnson smiled. "That's a long story, Sam. I'll tell you as much as I know in the morning, if you're still curious by then."

I had learned something of hatred on my own; there was certainly no doubt that I would still be curious tomorrow morning.

2

"Well, in the first place," Johnson said, "the boys are too hard on Grimes. They don't know all of the story and most of them haven't been too interested in hearing the rest of it. But I want you to understand this much: I don't like the sonofabitch any more than anybody else does. I've known him about seventeen months and if there ever was one, Grimes is a bastard.

"But I've always had the feeling that he wasn't always that way, and not long ago I found out I was right. You know how it is: you can't hide anything in the army. There'll always be somebody around that knew you back-when. And Bailey, the guy whose dog tags you brought in, served in the same regiment with Grimes back before Pearl Harbor.

"Grimes was a buck sergeant in those days and that explains why he still acts more like an old peacetime non-com than he does an officer. He was tough, but nobody ever said he was anything but fair. He expected the best from his men, even if they were making only twenty-one bucks a month. If he didn't get the best, Grimes rode hard till he got it. But once a man started delivering, Grimes let him alone.

"Incidentally, Grimes doesn't understand why the Guardsmen and draftees can't take rough talk like the boys in the Old

Army could. Back in those days, a sergeant called you a bastard on the drill field, but he was your friend in the rec hall. Sometimes Grimes looks like his feelings are hurt when somebody looks mad about being called a sonofabitch or something like that. His trouble is, he doesn't understand civilians.

"Anyhow, back in the old days, Grimes was always in trouble with women. In fact, he still brags about the size of his tool. The way I heard it, he got a girl knocked up and the girl was underage. So he got a transfer to Honolulu. He did all right there and was about to get promoted. But he got into more woman trouble. Back in those days, it was SOP to put guys in fukup companies. Sometimes, if they broke an army regulation, they got busted.

"Grimes got sent to a fukup company, George Company of the ——th Regiment, and the CO was Miles, a captain then. Millard was company clerk and Swanson was a supply clerk. Maybe that'll explain why they're such big buddies and why Grimes was so crazy when Millard got killed yesterday."

"Yeah."

"So Grimes did a good job with the fukups, and when you find a fukup in the Old Army, you really find one. But Grimes really made a fine platoon out of his men. Finally, after a year, he'd served his time. Miles made a deal with Grimes: if Grimes would stay in the fukup company, he'd make him first sergeant. Grimes stayed.

"Now Miles must've been more of a prick in those days than he is now, to judge from what Bailey told me. He could do almost anything he wanted to because he was commanding a convict company, for all practical purposes, and the rougher he was, the better the CO liked it. You know, white-glove inspection, revoking pass privileges for no reason, drilling men till midnight just for the hell of it—stuff like that.

"Grimes wasn't that rough. He insisted on a man's best and when he got it, he was happy. The whole thing boils down to this: Grimes liked discipline and good soldiering. It was the only thing he had ever done in his life that he really liked. And the more he soldiered, the easier it was to stay away from women.

"But that screwed him too. He went back home—Texas—on furlough and while he was there he met a girl he wanted to marry. But she wasn't interested. He nailed the girl every night, but she told him she was going to marry a civilian, another reason he doesn't like Guardsmen and draftees.

"So when Grimes came back to Honolulu, he was one hell of a sour character. Along about that time, a new fukup came to his outfit and somehow or other the new guy found out about Grimes and the girl. He started riding Grimes about it. Now Grimes had a temper then, just like he has now, but he took top kicking seriously and managed to control himself. That kept on, the riding and all, and Grimes kept holding himself back.

"The night after the Japs hit Pearl Harbor, Grimes' company was bivouacked on the beach, waiting for the Japs to try a landing. Along about that time, the new fukup started riding Grimes again about the girl. Miles was along and he told Grimes that no first sergeant of his was going to take that crap from anybody. Grimes said okay to that, gave the new fukup an ass-chewing and forgot about it.

"Late that night one of the men reported something in the water a few yards off the beach. They sent up flares and saw something out there all right, and fired into it. It turned out to be a log, but that isn't the story.

"When daylight came, the new fukup was found dead in his foxhole.

"Nobody knew how it happened. The guy's neck had been broken by a pretty strong man. Grimes hated the guy, was strong enough to snap his neck like a match stem, so he was the most likely suspect. Grimes would've been court-martialed right then, but Millard swore that Grimes hadn't been near the dead man since he'd given him the ass-chewing.

"A week or so later, Miles came around and told Grimes he'd recommend him for a commission. Grimes said no. He didn't like officers much more than any other Regular. But Miles said take the commission or stand trial for murder. Grimes took the commission, of course. Miles couldn't stand to be refused, even when he was offering to do a man what he thought was a favor.

"The way it sounded to me, Miles hated to give up the fukups because he liked to push the men. The next best thing was to have a man along to do it for him, someone he was sure he could force into being as chickenshit as he himself had been. And Grimes was the man.

"Well—it's been eating on Grimes till he's the king of all bastards. Every day and in every way, like they say, Grimes gets meaner and meaner.

"But he isn't all bad. The trouble is that Grimes loves the army and the army's using him for a screw-boy. To Grimes, that's sort of like his mother using him for a pimp."

Johnson raised his binoculars and studied the expanse of rice paddies to the south. "It's a damn good thing," he murmured, "that there're men smart enough to get past those bastards like Miles and go on to the top, or this country couldn't hope to win a war with—well, something."

He swept the binoculars toward the east. "So, if I were you, Sam, I wouldn't be too hard on Grimes. He's a bastard, all right, but it isn't all his fault."

3

The night was a calm one. Two guards were posted and five men slept. Johnson took his turn at guard without seeming to think much about his rank, and he stood it alone. Not once did the warning device, M-1 clips strung along an ankle-high telephone wire, jingle its merry note of danger. Nor did any dogs bark with excitement, another excellent warning. Johnson even gave permission to smoke, if we hid the glow of the butts carefully.

Below, in the gleam of the moon, the river flowed merrily along and not once was there any break in its reflection to indicate that the Japs were trying to float down it. The stars, seemingly close, twinkled peacefully, as gently as they had the night

Jenny and I had parked on Hogback Ridge before the rainstorm. I spent the two hours of my guard duty thinking of her. I had a dull semierection during the entire two hours.

The next morning Willie, Sellers and Savage went out on a short patrol and returned before noon with the word that they had seen nothing. We ate our lunches and threw the cans over the cliff and watched them sail, seemingly without end, until they splashed gently into the river. The sun was bright, but it wasn't too uncomfortable under our ponchos. In the middle of the afternoon there came a rain which lashed furiously at us for a few minutes before the sky cleared and the bright, hot sun came out again. I kept my foxhole dry by digging a small trench around it to catch the drippings from the poncho.

Terry, the youngest of us, was eager to find out what the rest of us had done for a living in civilian life.

"Sharecropper," Willie said.

"Railroad section hand," Morgan said.

"Welder," Savage said.

"Loafer," Sellers said.

"Cotton business," I said.

"And," Willie added, "Terry was a pimp."

"Fuk you, Willie," Terry said and rushed on: "Hey, Little Joe, what'd you do?"

"Hell, man," Johnson snorted, "haven't you heard? All officers were janitors in civilian life."

"No kidding," I said, "what'd you do?"

"I," said Johnson, "was one of several personnel directors for the Union Oil Company of California."

"Where'd you go to school?" I asked.

"Oklahoma U. How about you?"

"Yawnock University," I said. "How'd an Oklahoma boy get way out to California?"

"Gathering material for a book. I was going to call it *Grapes of Wrath*, but that fuken Steinbeck beat me to it. I lost heart and never wrote it. Went to work instead."

"Hey, Little Joe," Terry said, "hey, what does a personnel director direct?"

"Hire people, mostly."

"Women too?"

"By the droves."

"How'd you go about it?"

"Well now, gentlemen," Johnson said seriously, "I'm glad you asked me that. But it's a long story."

They immediately lost interest, which embarrassed me. I said, "Let's hear it."

"It was this way," Johnson said, his eyes twinkling. "When we needed help, we advertised, set a time for the interviews, stuff like that. I'd take their credentials and pick out the four or five that had the best qualifications, then we'd interview them again. Then I picked the one I wanted."

The eyes giving him away, I stooged by asking, "How'd you decide on which one you wanted?"

"Well, some guys did it one way and others did it another. Me, I always picked the one with the biggest tits and the best-looking butt."

The others, realizing their legs had been pulled, exploded with a barrage of obscene language. All but Willie, who waited for silence before he said:

"Don't let Joe kid you, Sam. He's an old married man. Writes to his wife every day."

"That's right," Johnson agreed. "Married my secretary."

"Prove that," Morgan said heavily.

Johnson hauled out his pictures, and we crowded around. If he had hired the most shapely of the crowd, he had certainly married the cream of the crop. She wore a bathing suit. . . .

There followed several carefully polite remarks. I didn't hear what they said. I had drifted off in a dream of my own.

"Hey, *Sam!*" Willie said, and shook me.

I realized that he had spoken to me several times. "Yeah?"

Johnson laughed good-naturedly. "My pictures make you think of home, Sam?"

I gave them a red-faced grin.

"All right, goddamnit," Johnson said, "let's see some pictures of your old hag."

I produced my bundle of pictures and, with a blush of pleasure and embarrassment, spread them out on the dirt. I was promptly aware of a new aura of respect about the men: civilian accomplishment of any kind is keenly appreciated in the army and a pretty wife makes a man cast a dark shadow.

"Funny thing," Johnson mused, "us ugly bastards always get the best-looking women. Of course, I'm not quite as ugly as you are, but——"

"Fuk you, Joe," I said.

"Speaking of pictures," Sellers said, "did I ever show you boys any of my baby pictures?"

"Whose baby?" Willie said suspiciously. "You ain't married."

"I mean pictures of *me* when I was a baby." Sellers fumbled in his wallet for a picture.

"Bet it was took at a zoo," Morgan mumbled heavily.

Sellers handed the picture to me and, as the others crowded around, we studied it. A baby picture, all right, but it was a composite. It showed a baby on a velvet pallet. Superimposed on it was a huge penis at full erection. Beneath the baby was scrawled in ink: "John Sellers, age four months."

"Of course now," Sellers said modestly, "I've growed considerably since then."

"All peter," Willie said and gave Sellers a shove that sent him over backwards, "and no brains."

"He ought to have a big one on'im," Morgan mumbled, "he raised it by hand. I seen'im the other day out behind——"

"Target!" Johnson said quietly.

We sprang toward our rifles and machine guns.

"No guns needed," Johnson said. "Man the mortars."

Willie and I took one mortar and Morgan and Terry took the other one. We waited for Johnson to call the target.

"Let's look at these birds a while before we fire," Johnson said. "See down there in Angat. There's a ditch running behind the church. Now follow that ditch to where it comes out into the rice paddy. I've been watching six Japs sneak up to that church."

I looked carefully, followed every move he told my eyes to make. "Can't see them, Joe."

The others shook their heads.

"I can't either, right now," Johnson said. "They acted like

230

they were going to lay low for a while—till dark maybe. Don't we have a mortar zeroed in on that church?"

I hastened to examine the tags on the rows of stakes in front of the mortars. "Yeah," I said, when I found the one marked "church."

"All right," Johnson said quietly, "they're about a hundred yards this side of the church in a direct line. See if you can't take up a hundred yards' worth of slack. Zero both tubes." He waited while we made the adjustments. "Hold your fire," he said quietly. "Let's just wait a minute."

Johnson handed the binoculars and I carefully studied the ditch he had pointed out. For a while I saw nothing suspicious. There was some heavy growth and any one of a thousand shadows could have been a Jap, but I failed to see the target until a smudge of brown moved. It was a Jap uniform. They were stretched out on the floor of the ditch and they appeared to be asleep. It was their guard who moved. He was squatted behind a thick bush, but he wasn't looking at us. He appeared to be watching another hill, our Parade George three. I handed the binoculars to Willie.

"Parade George Able," Johnson said into the radio, giving the call sign that alerted the entire radio net, "this is Parade George. Little Joe speaking. I have a target. Information only to Parade George one, two, four, five, six, and seven. Action only to Parade George three. Over."

"This is Parade George three," came the metallic reply. *"Locate the target. Over."*

"Parade George," Johnson said. "The target is hidden in the ditch running behind the church in Angat. Can you see the ditch from your position? Over."

"Parade George three, wait—" The radio hissed as the operator released the butterfly switch that controlled the power on his set. *"Parade George three. No, we can't see the ditch. The church stands between us and the ditch. Over."*

"Shit," Johnson said before he pressed the butterfly switch. "Parade George. Do you have a mortar zeroed on the church? Over."

"Parade George three. Yes, we have. Over."

"Parade George. Roger. Raise your elevation a hundred yards. The target is in the ditch that far this side of the church. Over."

"*Parade George three. Roger, wilco. Wait—*" The radio hissed again. "*Little Joe, we have two mortars. Do you want both of'em zeroed? Over.*"

"Parade George. Yes, zero both mortars. Over."

"*Parade George three. Roger, wilco. Wait—Mortars zeroed. Over.*"

"Parade George. Roger. Now listen to me carefully. We're not going to try to drop them down their throats. I'll have both my mortars do that. When I give the command, you will commence firing and keep it up till I command cease fire. The idea is that we'll scare them out and your stray shots might get a few. Is that clear? Over."

"*Parade George. Affirmative. Over.*"

Johnson glanced to see if we were ready. "Parade George broadcast. Stand by to fire." He released the butterfly switch. "Fire!" he said to us.

We dropped a shell into each tube and with the familiar *thunk* they were on their way. We watched the ditch, waiting for the explosions. One of the shells, mine, burst twenty yards long and thirty wide. I quickly adjusted. The other shell hit somewhere near the church. Terry adjusted the other mortar.

"Hurry, boys," Johnson said. "They're up and ready to run."

"Ready," I said.

Johnson depressed the butterfly switch. "Parade George. The command is—fire!" He paused. "Stand by for command to follow. Out."

While we dropped shells into the tubes as fast as we could, Johnson watched through his binoculars. When I had time to glance up I saw the Japs burst out of the bushes in time to run into the explosions, which blossomed thick and fast around the ditch. Four mortars, firing together, can lay down a considerable barrage, and the Japs, caught in a sudden hell where peace had reigned only moments before, were wrenched into the open, where, of course, they panicked.

They scattered like a covey of quail. Two of them dropped before they had taken ten steps. And, in another second, one of them disappeared in a puff of smoke as a shell exploded on top of his helmet, the only time I had ever seen a mortar make a direct hit. The other three, running with that queer, crablike gait which never ceased to fascinate me, escaped back up the ditch and toward the church.

"Parade George, cease fire. Good work, men. Out." He nodded to us. "Good work."

I sat down to rest. The others rushed to the edge of the cliff to see what damage we had done.

"Well—" Johnson mused, "not bad, not bad at all. Three out of six—and with mortars at that. Not bad. Well—Willie, take Sam and Terry and go down there. See what's——" He looked at me. "What's the matter, Sam?"

"He gets the shakes, Joe," Willie explained. "After it's all over."

"Oh," Johnson said understandingly. "Okay," he said, "Morgan, you take his place."

"Wait a minute." I got to my feet. "I'll do what I'm detailed to do."

Johnson glanced at Willie, who nodded. "All right, Sam," Johnson said. "Does it make you sick too?"

"Not much," I said. "Shaky, mostly." It was easy to lie about it. It did make me sick, but the mortars didn't seem to bother me as much as the more personal act of firing a rifle.

Willie and Morgan horsed the Jap fifty-one caliber machine gun to the edge of the cliff and trained it on the ditch behind the church, five hundred yards away.

"Ready, Sam?" Willie said, and spat over the cliff.

"Yeah," I said, "let's go." I wasn't ready, not at all, but it was more than important for me to carry my share of the load. I wasn't going to let them take risks that were as much mine as theirs. Scared men have to live closely, or they don't live at all.

"Okay," Johnson said. "We'll give the trees around the paddy and the town a good hosing down with the fifty-one every once in a while, so don't get excited—unless Savage or Sellers fire a shave and a haircut. Sellers'll be on the BAR. Okay?"

We nodded.

"Willie'll be big brother," Johnson said. "Hurry back—and goddamnit, be careful."

Willie led us down the trail. As we were leaving I heard Johnson begin his report to Grimes: "All right, all right, take it easy. They're not headed your way. I'm sending a patrol down to check on . . ." And that was all I heard.

We slithered and skidded down the rock-strewn trail, cussing and sweating, and by the time we had reached the deep gully at the bottom of the hill, I was calm and steady again. Willie dropped back to check on me and grunted with satisfaction when I held my hands out to show they weren't trembling.

We found the three bodies sprawled at three different points of the compass, mute indication that they had panicked. Two of them were face-down in the rice straw, spraddled, their hands clutching tufts of yellow straw in that one final desire to grasp something before death. The other one lay on his back, his eyes half shielded by the short visor of his cap, as if he had drawn it over his forehead to protect himself from the hell-ball of a sun.

The Jap who had received the direct hit was scattered over the entire area. One arm lay nearby, its fingers extended in the sensitive gesture of an orchestra leader.

I stood guard while Willie searched them. Before he touched them, Willie thumped each of them solidly on the bridge of the nose with his trench knife. Terry uttered a grunt of elation when he found three gold teeth in the mouth of the first Jap we searched. He gleefully took a pair of rusted pliers from one of his cargo pockets and unceremoniously extracted the teeth, which he tenderly dropped into a Red Cross ditty bag, already heavy and bulging with wealth. He found another tooth in the second Jap.

Willie bent to thump the third Jap. "A fuken sergeant, no less," he grunted. He brought the handle of his trench knife down with a little more force than he had used on the first two.

He recoiled with alarm when the Jap jerked and, before subsiding, sighed loudly.

"Well now," Willie said wonderingly, "I be damn! The little bastard was playing possum on us." Willie stood erect and kicked the Jap at the side of the head. While the Jap sighed again, Willie said, "That'll hold'im for a while."

"Jesus!" Terry whispered loudly. "D'you see the gold in that bastard's mouth when he opened it?" He clicked his rusty pliers with the same professional preoccupation I had seen in dentists' offices. "Hurry up, Willie!"

Willie removed a packet of papers from the pockets of the dead Jap.

"Hell, Terry," Willie muttered, "you got more gold than Fort Knox already." He stood back to let Terry get at the teeth.

Terry pried the Jap's mouth open and propped it with a stick obviously whittled for that purpose. "All right, Willie," Terry said. "When you're back staring a mule in the ass, I'll be owning my own business back in good old Tulsy." He peered at Willie. "You want me to shoot the bastard?" He dropped a tooth into his bag.

"Might as well," Willie said.

Terry pulled another tooth, examined the mouth carefully to see if there were more, got to his feet and said, "Best haul I've had"—he shot the Jap between the eye and the ear—"since that night we found them fukers in that cave."

There was a rattle of bullets in the line of trees behind us, like a flurry of hailstones, which had come from the fifty-one and the BAR's Sellers and Savage were firing.

"Guess we might as well go on back," Willie said.

We started retracing our steps toward the hill. "I figure," Terry said, ignoring the gunfire from above, "that I got about a thousand bucks' worth of gold, counting what I have in my jungle pack. Before this fuken war's over, I ought to have at least five thousand."

"You think it'll last that long?" I said.

"Shit yes! Them Japs don't know when they're whipped. Only way we'n put an end to this war's to kill every one of the little bastards." He pondered for a moment. "Maybe we ought to leave a few knocked-up women alive. No need of killing them."

Willie spat. "Right generous, ain't he?"

There was another rain of fire from the hill.

"Captures the real spirit," I said, "of the Regular Army."

"All right, all right," Terry said, "you guys'n make fun of me all you want to, but you'll be learning the hard way by the time you've been overseas long's I have."

"Get off that shit, Terry," Willie said mildly. "Me'n Sam was in this outfit long time 'fore it was took into federal service."

"Well, anyhow," Terry said stubbornly, "I damn sure know I'm right."

Willie laughed, spat, and slapped Terry's back. "Old Terry! If MacArthur knowed about you, he'd make you a full colonel before breakfast tomorrow morning."

Terry couldn't hide a grin. "Fuk you, Willie," he said, pleased.

Sellers and Savage, enjoying their workout on the fifty-one and the BAR, didn't stop firing until we reached the top of the hill. They stopped with satisfied grunts and fell to discussing the superior merits of the Jap machine gun.

Willie handed the Jap papers to Johnson. "Not much," he said. "Terry got a few teeth, though."

"Some of these days," Johnson said, "Terry's going to get a hold of a possum-playing Jap that'll bite a few fingers off."

"Aw hell, Joe—" Terry said.

"Almost did this time," Willie said.

"Just a poor country boy," Sellers said, "trying to work his way through dentist's school."

By the lack of response I figured that Sellers had only repeated an old jibe, one so old that even Terry and his quick grin didn't react.

4

"*Parade George, this is Parade George Charlie.*" Even the metallic rasp of the radio couldn't disguise the great, belching voice of Captain Grimes. "*Waco speaking. Let me talk to Little Joe. Over.*"

Johnson took the microphone from my hand and, with a grimace of irritation, said, "Little Joe. Over."

"*Waco. Get your map out.*" He paused to give Johnson time to unfold the map. "*Look at the sector of these coordinates.*" He gave the code for the hills behind Norzagaray. "*Indian Chief has another one of his hunches. Wants to know what's up there. His hunch says there's nothing and we can establish our perimeter in Norzagaray. I tried to talk him out of it. No go. Can you send a patrol up there to see? Over.*"

"*Can* you!" Sellers said. "Get that! Most of the time the bastard says *send* it."

"Little Joe," Johnson said. "Uncle Sam was up there a couple of days ago, if you'll remember. He saw a patrol, but the town was deserted. **Over.**"

"*Waco. I told Indian Chief that, but he's getting hunches again. Over.*"

"Little Joe. He might be right. Norzagaray would make a good perimeter site. Over."

"*Waco. Maybe. But why move? The campaign's too near over to bother with all this moving around. Over.*"

"Little Joe. From the action we've seen during the last three days, I wouldn't say the campaign is that close to being over, would you? Over."

"*Waco.*" He actually laughed on the radio. "*All right, you send the patrol for your reasons, I'll order it because Indian Chief said so. Let me know soon's the patrol's back. Out.*"

Johnson dropped the microphone into its cradle and stared thoughtfully toward the rice paddy this side of Norzagaray. For almost a minute he said nothing.

"Grimes's getting awful considerate all at once," Willie said suspiciously. "When a sonofabitch starts acting human, I always figure he's——"

Johnson got to his feet. "You'd probably soften a little yourself, Willie, if your best friend got killed right in front of you." He took a bandoleer of rifle ammunition from one of the opened cases.

Willie shrugged and dropped his head. He was squatted on his haunches and now he picked up a clod of dirt, crumbled it slowly, and let the dust sift lazily through his calloused fingers. He shrugged again.

"If that's the case," Savage said, "next time Grimes starts cussing me out, I'm going to turn old Sellers loose on Swanson with his knife."

"I'll get Grimes," Sellers said menacingly, "some of these days. You wait and see."

"I'll wait," Willie said.

Johnson paused a moment and pursed his lips before he began buckling on his cartridge belt. "I'll take this one," he said. "Sellers, get your BAR. Morgan, you'll come too." He handed the binoculars to Willie. "You're big brother, Willie. If we don't get back before sundown, I'll try to make it to George four. Okay?"

I said, "You don't have more than two, two and a half hours, Joe."

"We'll hurry." He beckoned to Sellers and Morgan. "Let's move out."

The three men, silhouetted against the falling sun, their canteens bobbling at their hips, their caps pulled low over their foreheads, paced swiftly down the trail and disappeared into the trees. I heard them rattling over the rocks for a few moments, then there was no sign of them. While Willie, Savage and Terry hustled the fifty-one and the thirties to the edge of the cliff, I adjusted the mortars for maximum range; it wouldn't be possible to cover the men all the way to their objective, but if they had to retreat, we might be able to give them help of some sort.

Soon they appeared below us and, without hesitating, waded into the river. With the binoculars I could see that they were holding their rifles and cartridge belts above their heads.

In the middle of the river Johnson and Sellers had to tow Morgan, who was too short for the deep water. When they reached the distant bank, they hurried along until they were at the line of trees that bordered the rice paddy. Johnson was taking much the same route I had taken a few days before. We settled down to wait, glancing occasionally toward the place where the three men had last been seen and then measuring the distance between the sun and the horizon.

"Hope they don't run into nothing," Savage muttered. "With all them patrols the Japs been sending out the last few days, I ain't anxious for'em to spend the night up there'n leave just the four of us here."

"Think they'll make it back, Willie?" I said.

Willie shrugged. "Joe ain't the kind of officer that leave a post undermanned if he'n help it. He'll get back if he'n make it."

We sat very still for a long time, listening, before Willie took his plug from his pocket and bit off a sizable chew. Before he replaced it, he measured it with his eye and, satisfied that it would last him until the next PX ration arrived, grunted one word: "Nasty."

"Why'n hell you chew it then?" Terry said.

"Tastes good."

"Thought you said it was nasty?"

"I did."

"Well?"

"Tastes good."

Willie raised the binoculars and looked for a sign of Johnson and the patrol. I glanced at the sun. About an hour was left. I lit a cigarette. I passed the time by shaving the ash off the cigarette with a sharp-edged stone.

"Jesus!" Savage said glumly. "They'd better be showing up pretty soon."

Terry smiled. "I wish I'd a went with'em."

Willie spat dangerously close to Terry's boot. "Terry," Willie said, "you talk too fuken much."

"Fuk you, Willie."

Willie glared coldly at Terry. "I told you once, Terry, you talk too fuken much."

Terry said nothing.

The first explosion was so faint that I wasn't even sure I had heard it, but Willie, followed by the two others, all of whom were more accustomed to the distant sounds one hears on outpost, became rigid with listening, their heads turned, their faces intent. There was another explosion, still faint. Willie sprang to his feet and stood at the edge of the cliff.

"Rifle fire," Willie whispered. "Jap rifle."

The other two nodded tensely.

The next explosion was one which I could recognize. It was a grenade, a Jap grenade, I could tell, by the flat crack of its explosion. The next sound was the heavy, burring rip of our BAR and several rapidly fired M-1 rifle shots.

"Run, you bastards!" Willie muttered. "Come on out where we'n see you!" He clinched his fists at his side. "Come on, Joe, you old bastard!" he whispered. "Come on out of there."

We strained and made our hands into fists, rooting for the patrol as if we were college cheerleaders. "Hurry," I whispered. "Hurry."

The rifles stopped firing, but I could still hear the comforting burr and rip of the BAR, and the quality of the explosions was changing. "They're moving!" Willie said. "Hear that?" The BAR, being fired in bursts of six, was moving, definitely moving.

"Keep coming, keep coming!" Savage muttered.

We didn't see them the instant they cleared the hill which stood between us and them, for, instead of following the tree line around this side of the paddy, Johnson had elected to take a chance and cut directly across the paddy, which would put him under the most distant edge of the fifty-one's range.

Willie sighted them first and with a cry of "There they are!" he trained the binoculars on the rice paddy. For perhaps a second he watched them before he said dejectedly: "Somebody got it." His voice was flat, suddenly weary.

I said, "Let me see." I took the binoculars. One of them was wounded and another was helping him along. I studied the hurrying figures intently until I made out that it was Morgan who was wounded and Johnson was half carrying, half dragging him along. Morgan's short stature told me that much. Sellers was bringing up the rear, stopping every few yards to spray behind them with the BAR. Sellers was a cool one; each burst of the BAR was six rounds long, no more, no less. And at the end of each second burst I could see that he calmly dropped the empty magazine into a cargo pocket and reloaded. The fire from the Jap rifles, contrasting with the heavy BAR, sounded like pop-corn popping.

We saw the Japs. There were nine of them and they ran and stumbled about like drunks, for Sellers, although he wasn't hitting any of them, was spraying the kind of harrassing fire that kept them from doing any damage. Sellers and his BAR made me feel pretty good about their chances of survival.

"Sam!" Willie said. "Maximum range on the mortar."

I stuffed the celluloidlike explosive between the fins of several mortar shells. "Okay," I said.

"Fire one and let's see where it'll go."

I dropped a shell into the tube.

It seemed to take the shell an eternity to get there. I had never fired a mortar at maximum range before and didn't know the flight interval could be so long. Finally, in the distant dusk, *crunch!*

"Two hundred yards right," Willie said. "Range is short too, but keep firing when I tell you to. Maybe the little bastards'll run into it." He glanced to see if I was ready. "Commence firing and don't stop."

I dropped a shell into the tube and ducked away from the curiously ear-hurting *thunk!* Drop. Duck. *Thunk!* And, far away, *crunch!* I scooted around so I could watch the shells fall on the Japs.

"Get that fifty-one going!" Willie called.

Savage began firing in bursts of ten. The barrel of the gun wasn't aimed directly at the paddy. From its angle of fire, it appeared that he was trying to hit the top of the high mountain far to the east. But, after the tracers of the first burst showed him that he was hitting quite close to the Japs, he hosed them methodically.

The Japs ran directly into my mortar fire and raced through it without losing a man. Cursing bitterly, I reached for the thirty-caliber machine gun, but Terry, who had been busy calling ranges for Savage, beat me to it. Still cursing, I jerked the other thirty-caliber into position and began firing. The thirty-caliber tracers arched high into the sky and literally fell on the Japs because the range was so long.

I saw a Jap drop. From this distance he looked like a half-empty gunny sack thrown carelessly aside. The tracers bounced among the little figures like tiny fireballs.

Suddenly Johnson tumbled and for a moment I thought he was wounded, but when Sellers fell beside him and continued to fire toward the Japs, I saw that they had taken cover behind one of the waist-high dykes at the end of the paddy. The Japs immediately stopped and sent flankers out to the right and to the left. Without waiting for a command from Willie, Savage trained his fifty-one on the left flankers and Terry and I took those on the right. The flankers took cover, but not before Terry had dropped one of them.

"Mortar!" Willie called.

"I got it," I said.

Estimating the range quickly, I adjusted the mortar and dropped a shell into the tube. The explosion was fifty yards behind the Japs. I adjusted again and dropped another shell. This one was behind them too, but the force of the exploding propellant would drive the mortar base into the ground, shortening the range. I dropped another shell and it hit close enough to give the Japs a shower of dirt and steel.

The tracers from the thirty and the fifty-one converged again on the main body of the Japs and from the corner of my eye, I saw that the four flankers had been dropped. The remaining four Japs tried to huddle against their protective dyke, but our angle of fire was so high that they gave it up and ran, leaving one of their number a flung, brown clot on the yellow straw of the rice paddy. My mortar killed another one. The two surviving Japs raced away behind the hill. I ceased firing, but Savage continued to arch fire over the hill in hopes of accidentally hitting one of them.

Far below, Johnson sprang from behind the dyke. With a great, sweeping gesture, he pointed toward the road that ran through Angat. Sellers joined him and between the two of them they carried Morgan out of sight. Willie rushed to the radio.

"Parade George Charlie. Over."

"Parade George Charlie. Over."

"Parade George. Get the jeep and bring it up to that big gully about two hundred yards this side of Angat. Morgan's wounded. And goddamnit, hurry! It's getting close to sundown. Over."

"Parade George Charlie. Roger, wilco. Out."

Willie slammed the microphone back into the cradle. "You're big brother, Sam. I'm going down to see if they need any help." He grabbed his rifle and hurried off down the trail.

"Parade George, this is Parade George Charlie," came the voice of Captain Grimes. *"Over."*

"Parade George," I said. "Over."

"Waco speaking. What happened up there? Over." He sounded more interested than scared, a fact which brought a gesture of surprise from Savage and Terry.

"Parade George," I said. "I don't know yet, Waco. Little Joe will be back in a few minutes to report. Over."

"Waco. Did Morgan look bad hurt? Over."

"Parade George. I couldn't tell. Over."

"Waco. Roger. Have Little Joe call soon's he gets back. Out."

Terry said, "Damn'f the sonofabitch don't sound almost human." He added judiciously: "But not quite."

I saw the jeep race through the cut and soon it returned, bearing Morgan. I didn't see Johnson, Willie and Sellers at all and, after a while, I became slightly frightened with the thought that Johnson had decided to spend the night at another outpost. But it wasn't long until I heard them stumbling up the rocky trail. They appeared at the line of trees at the head of the trail just as the sun fell out of sight behind the hills. Johnson and Sellers were exhausted and Willie, with his plodding, oxen strength, took a hand of each man and actually pulled them the last few, steep yards. I took the BAR from Sellers and give it a hasty cleaning while there was still light. Terry used the ramrod on Johnson's M-1.

For minutes, Johnson and Sellers sat on the edge of their foxholes, drooping figures, pale and trembling. I handed my canteen to Johnson, who, when he saw that my hands were trembling slightly, smiled wanly before he emptied the canteen. He gestured toward the radio. I carried it to him.

"Parade George Charlie, this is—Parade George. Little Joe speaking. Give—me Waco. Over."

"*Waco. Over.*" Grimes had been waiting.

"Little Joe. Full report. . . ." He stopped to take a full breath, still winded from his task. "There is a strip of woods east of Norzagaray, about where Indian Chief had his hunch. We stumbled onto a big crowd of Japs there. I don't know exactly how many of them, but it looked like they were pretty close to regimental strength. The ones I saw had full field packs, but they were getting ready to bed down for the night, so it doesn't look like we can expect the roof to fall in tonight.

"We were hiding in a little gully when a Jap came up behind us and dropped a grenade. Morgan killed the Jap, but the grenade got Morgan. It looks like he lost his manhood. The Japs sent a squad after us when we ran. I figure they didn't send more men because they didn't know that we knew they were so strong and thought they'd fool us with the squad business. The boys on the outpost got all but two of them.

"Can you get some artillery on that area? Over."

"*Waco. Stand by*—" There was a long wait, almost ten minutes, during which complete darkness came, before Grimes started talking again. "*Waco. I called the artillery, Little Joe. They say the strip of woods is just like Norzagaray, can't be hit because of the hill that George four's on. But I'll tell you what I'll do. I'll call Indian Chief and see if he'll try to get some planes up there first thing tomorrow morning. Over.*"

"Little Joe. Roger. That's about all we can do. But if the Japs are still there, they're even dumber than I gave them credit for being. Over and out."

Johnson handed the microphone to me. "I'll bet you two pesos those Japs are far gone by tomorrow morning. But I'll be damn if I'll send or take another patrol out to see. We'll just let the planes shoot the woods up, *then* go down and see. I wouldn't mind seeing those air corps bastards fight the war for a while."

Using his helmet for a pillow, Johnson stretched out on his back, his legs dangling in his foxhole. He looked up at the new stars. "Boys," he said, "that was one hell of a shitstorm."

5

In the bright moonlight I felt exposed and defenseless. The bald knob of the hill didn't seem such a perfect defense setup now, for the earth, a pale yellow in the sunlight, seemed to glow from the rays of the moon, which was bright enough to make me the perfect target for an infiltrating Jap. I wore my fatigue cap because the helmet formed a too solid silhouette. Johnson's wrist watch, its dial glowing where it hung suspended on the mortar sight, told me I had a few minutes over an hour before my guard duty was done. The others slept peacefully, trusting that I would warn them early enough in case of an attack. I longed for the time to hurry so I could give the responsibility to Sellers, my relief.

At thirty yards, the line of trees that marked the edge of the hill's bald knob reposed peacefully, but behind that black façade was an even darker silence. My fear seemed to rise and fall in cycles. For long minutes I would freeze in dry-throated terror. The silence was filled with mute, stalking figures of bandy-legged Japs. At the edge of the woods, I knew, was the telephone wire on which were hanging M-1 clips that would jingle if the wire were disturbed; and I heard nothing. But I couldn't conquer one of my senses that whispered to me that something was wrong. Silent, treadless Japs were out and stirring, I was positive of that, but I still heard nothing. I stared at the trees until spots danced before my eyes, but the blackness remained unbroken by nothing more than the purple orbs which appeared because I looked so hard. There was nothing. Yet, my senses were reaching for something.

The river.

Of course, I thought with mild hysteria, the goddamn fuken river. I studied the bar of light the moon made by its reflection on the water. During the fifteen or twenty seconds I watched, I saw four specks drift across the light. My head swam briefly because the specks seemed suspended in mid-air. I blinked the mirage away and watched again. This time I saw three specks.

I tossed a pebble into Johnson's foxhole. He immediately sat up, soundlessly, and by the bright glow of the moon I saw the questioning expression on his face.

"The river," I whispered.

Immediately following my whisper, I heard the sleeping breath of the four other men alter. They were awake.

With no more sound that the rustle of his clothing, Johnson crawled to the edge of the cliff and looked down. A few seconds passed before he whispered, "Willie."

Willie promptly joined us.

"See what you think."

Willie studied the bar of light across the river. "Floating downstream," he whispered.

"Everybody else awake?" Johnson whispered.

"Yeah," Terry said.

"Ummm," Savage grunted.

"Yeah," Sellers said.

"All right," Johnson said. "No flares; give our location away. Set both mortars to fire downstream from us. Sam and Willie, take the mortars. Sellers, watch the shell bursts. Terry and Savage, watch the trail behind us."

I set the mortar up. I wasn't sure I was lined up on the right stake, but it didn't make much difference so long as I dropped the shells into the river. As I reached for my shell, Johnson said, "Don't fire till I give the word."

"Parade George Able," Johnson said into the radio, giving the net call, "this is Parade George. I have a target. Information only to everybody but Parade George three. Over."

"*Parade George three. Over.*"

"Parade George. The Japs are floating down the river. Set both mortars up to fire two hundred yards downstream from my position. Over."

"*Parade George three. Roger, wilco. Wait—we're ready to fire. Over.*"

"When I give the word to George three," Johnson said to us, "get busy. All right, here we go: Parade George. Fire! Stand by to cease——"

I heard no more. The solid *thunk* of the exploding propellant made my ears ring. I dropped shells into the tube as fast as I could find them. I had dropped six before I heard the first *crunch* below, but then they came so fast that I couldn't count them. The intensity of the barrage was increased suddenly with the arrival of the shells from George three.

We fired steadily for more than a minute before Johnson gave the cease fire. The mortars both glowed a dull red near their base and the heat made me pop out with sweat. After a few seconds, while the last shells hurtled through the air toward the river, the explosions stopped. The night was instantly silent.

"Probably didn't hit anything," Johnson whispered, the need for silence seeming absurd after the racket of the mortars, "but we stopped them from sending any more of the little bastards downstream." He sighed with dying excitement. "Sam, you all right?"

"Trembling," I said.

"Think you're going to make it, huh?"

"I'll be all right."

I heard him chuckle. "I can hear you shaking."

"*Little Joe, this is Waco. Over.*"

"Little Joe. Over."

"*Waco. What's going on? Over.*"

"Little Joe. I was just getting ready to report, Waco. You can expect some infiltration pretty soon. We were firing mortars at some Japs swimming or floating down the river toward your perimeter. Over."

"*Waco. Roger. Out.*"

"Well now, I'll be damn!" Willie said. "He didn't get excited, didn't yell a bit. Must be sick."

"Yeah," Johnson drawled thoughtfully. "Something to think about all right." He sighed. "Well, keep your eyes peeled, Sam. Good work, by the way." He eased himself back into his foxhole.

After a short time, during which there were the sounds of the men adjusting their bodies to their foxholes, I heard nothing but the various rhythms of their breathing, a sound my ears soon dismissed to listen for others more alien.

I shuddered convulsively once and my trembling lessened enough for me to be no longer uncomfortable. I let Sellers sleep a few minutes past relief time because he had had such a vicious workout on this afternoon's patrol. He grunted his thanks when he looked at the wrist watch. I curled up in my foxhole and waited for sleep.

When I get home, Jenny, I thought, you might have a little trouble sleeping with a man who hasn't slept full-length in almost three years. But that won't be much of a problem—if I get home.

Johnson awakened me with his talking on the radio. ". . . What kind are they sending? Over."

"*Waco. Twelve B-twenty-fours with five-hundred-pound bombs and right behind 'em will be eight B-twenty-fives. The B-twenty-fives're the new kind with all the guns in the nose. I think they's a seventy-five millimeter in 'em too. Over.*" Grimes' manner had certainly undergone a drastic change.

"Little Joe. Roger. Do I talk to them or do they just drop bombs and shoot at whatever moves? Over."

"*Waco. You'll talk to 'em. Wait.*" There was a short pause. "*The B-twenty-fours' call sign is Blue Nose one. The B-twenty-fives are Blue Yonder one. They'll call you first. Your channel is number six. Over.*"

"Little Joe. Roger. Out." Johnson stooped to attend to the calibration of the radio. "I always get a kick out of watching an air strike," he mused. "This'll be the closest I've even been to one. Tried to get in the air corps myself once."

"What happened?" I asked. There was always the twinkle in Johnson's eyes to tell me that he wanted somebody to play straight man to him.

"Well, it was like this. I passed all the exams, mental and physical, had good eyes, good coordination, wasn't too tall, and —hurrrmph—was handsome enough. But they washed me out. They had me try on one of those go-to-hell air corps hats—

248

and that's when they washed me out. I looked too much like a bus driver." He paused to listen to the radio. "Seems that the air corps was rather sensitive about some remarks the navy had made about their fliers looking like the glamour boys of the army bus drivers corps."

"I talked to a bunch of them guys once," Willie said. "They was all juned up because they'd been under AA fire for seventeen minutes once. I told 'em we were under fire for a week at a time, sometimes. And damn'f they didn't want to know how long we stayed under fire before we got a medal. Fuken flight-pay bastards!"

"My brother-in-law's in the air corps," I said. This was the first time I had thought of Bill Joe in more than a year.

"What's his rank?" Johnson asked.

"Major, I think," I said. "We don't write to each other. My wife said he was expecting to make his majority pretty soon."

"Only a major, huh?" Johnson said. "How long's he been in?"

"Almost four years."

"Hmmm," Johnson said. "Must be a fukup like us. After four years they're usually lieutenant generals. Friend of mine had a pet monkey in New Guinea that made major after only two years. He'd've made lieutenant colonel, but he was only sixteen years old. Seems like they have a rule that you can't make anything higher than major unless you're eighteen or over. But you know——"

"*Howdy, Parade George, old man,*" the radio began—and Johnson made a belittling gesture toward its youthful voice, "*this is Blue Nose one, coming to rescue the ground forces. How do you read me? Over.*"

"This is Parade George, sonny. Being an infantryman and not getting flight pay, I don't know how to read. But I can hear you roger-five, sugar-five. Where are you? Over."

"*Blue Nose one. I'm riding a bicycle down the middle of the Angat River; where'd you think I was? Over.*"

"Parade George. Oh, how clever you bus drivers are getting these days. I still can't see you. Over."

"All right, dad. We will buzz your position in precisely thirty seconds. I would also like to take this opportunity to express our appreciation for your invitation to come to your party. At the same time, I'd like to caution you about keeping within jumping distance of your foxholes. We have an apprentice with us today. Over."

Johnson winked at us. At the same time I heard the distant rumble of constant thunder, and, away to the south, a line of specks appeared.

"Okay, sonny," Johnson said. "What's the apprentice's rank? Major or lieutenant colonel? Over."

"He's a field marshal in the navy's submarine corps. Can you see us yet? Over."

"Affirmative. Over."

"Don't dodge the question. Answer a simple yes or no. Over."

"Yes, we see you. Aren't you a little low? Over."

The heavy, slender-winged B-24's roared over the river, so low that we were looking down at them. Blue Nose one didn't answer Johnson's last transmission. But when the flight reached a position which seemed to be directly over the rice paddy, he called, "Bombs away, dad!" Surely, I thought, this was going to be another example of the air corps' practice of dropping bombs where they weren't wanted or needed. For the bombs, visible now against the yellow straw of the rice paddy, seemed to race parallel to the ground. There were so many bombs that I couldn't count them. They disappeared against the line of trees and, a second later, came the first explosion. It was followed immediately by others in so rapid a sequence that it was one constant explosion.

The earth trembled violently and dust sprang up on the bald knob of our hill. The woods erupted in a turmoil of huge fireballs and deafening sound. Shock wave after shock wave pushed fiercely and then tugged at us with unbelievable force. It was impossible for anything to live in those trees. The sky, hundreds of feet into the air, was filled with debris, whole trees and huge stumps that rose and fell, revolving slowly, and landed with a crash that would have been tumultuous enough had it not

250

been for the awesome comparison of the explosions of the bombs.

When Blue Nose one said lightly, *"Ta, ta, dad,"* I felt a kind of shame because a man, after having exercised the power to unleash such tremendous destruction and violence, could have regarded his own doing in such a foolish, bantering farewell.

"Jesus!" Willie said solemnly. In the silence that followed the bombs, Willie's voice sounded pitifully small and weak.

Johnson grunted with disgust. Sellers and Savage regarded the still boiling woods with eyes that plainly mirrored their sickness and awe. Terry, a happy grin on his face, his eyes dancing with excitement, stood at the edge of the cliff and watched the retreating B-24's with complete satisfaction.

The B-25's arrived ten minutes later. The familiar shape of the bombers, the same type Doolittle had used to bomb Tokyo during the bleak months at the beginning of the war, had been altered somewhat by the blunt metal which replaced the shapely bubble of plastic in the nose. There was a cleft in the nose where the seventy-five-millimeter cannon was placed. The remainder of the space there was taken up by the clustered muzzles of fifty-caliber machine guns. There were eight bombers and, while seven of them circled lazily in the sky overhead, one of them, Blue Yonder one, prowled around among the hills while Johnson tried to vector him onto the target.

"Now it's behind you!" Johnson said, beginning to sound irritated. "Can't you see that strip of woods smoking? Over."

"Roger. Got it." There followed a string of instructions delivered in the jargon of the air, stuff as much calculated to make good reading in popular magazines as to facilitate rapid action. Then the second part of the air strike began.

The planes, in shallow power dives, roared overhead, coming so close to the top of our hill that their propwash blew clouds of dust into our faces. And, as they reached a point directly over our heads, they began firing. I huddled, miserable, buffeted by the roar and the air blast from this monstrous, miraculous product of man's ability to wreck punishment upon himself, and feeling a vague, disturbing sympathy for the targets of this insanity, I prayed for it to end.

But it wouldn't end. Again and again came the nerve-rending thunder of the engines as they roared a few feet over our heads and then began spitting their evil cackle of gunfire into the trees. As each plane neared the bottom of its dive, the seventy-five-millimeter cannon in its nose punctuated the diatribe of depravity with its dull crack. It was strange that I felt no desire to run, nor was I questioning my own safety. All I felt was that this must stop. Surely, I reckoned hopefully, Americans, not sunny American boys could be this methodically brutal.

It did end. Forming into squadron boxes, the B-25's bored away to the east, leaving a quip of a good-by from a young innocent voice trailing in the speaker of our radio. I clambered from my foxhole and blinked in the bright morning sun as if I had risen from a long, dark sleep.

"Jesus!" Willie murmured. "That's what I call just a little bit too close." His Adam's apple jerked convulsively twice and then he spat a long stream of tobacco juice over the cliff.

Sellers swallowed repeatedly and he continued to direct curiously doubtful glances toward the torn and twisted woods. Terry's eyes were alive with excitement. Savage stood, grunted, and shook off the tumult of the past few seconds before he calmly began going about the task of cleaning the machine guns and BAR of the dust the planes had thrown into them.

On Johnson's face there was no expression at all, until with a tiny convulsion, his mouth tightened and relaxed.

"I could've done without that," I said.

"Did it make you have the shakes, Sam?" Willie asked solicitously.

I managed a croak of a laugh. "Only around the asshole."

"Them bastards think they got it so——" Willie began.

"*Parade George Able*"—the net call for everybody—"*mail call. Mail call. Out. Parade George, this is Parade George Charlie. Send Little Joe down to the jeep with your mail detail. Over.*"

"Parade George. Wilco. Out."

Johnson got to his feet. "Wonder what the hell he wants?" he said. "Anybody want to go with me?"

"Not me," Willie said.

"Fuk it," Sellers said.

"Nope," Terry said.

Savage shook his head.

I slung my rifle sling over my shoulder and buckled my cartridge belt. "Okay if I go?"

"Sure, Sam," Johnson said. "Willie, you're big brother. Send a water detail down to the river, will you?"

"I'll do'er, Joe," Willie said, looking at me as if he wanted to ask why I would like to go to the George perimeter. He shrugged.

Walking on our heels in an effort to act against the steep trail's rolling rocks, Johnson and I bounced down the hill. Johnson said nothing; he was entirely preoccupied with something else and I made it my business to maintain a lookout for stray Japs. They weren't likely to bother us during the daylight hours, when our superior marksmanship was most effective against them, but they had shown a degree of uncharacteristic aggressiveness lately. And the Japs liked to do, occasionally, what was unexpected of them.

Johnson stopped at the river to take a hasty bath and I felt somewhat better after having unmatted my hair and beard. The water was cold and, when I stretched out on the gravel to take a drink, it tasted strangely sweet, much like the taste of iced tea and saccharine. One swallow was enough to change my mind about drinking it right now. I filled my canteens and put two purifying tablets in each one.

"That air strike," Johnson said, rousing from his preoccupation, "was one sonofabitch, wasn't it?" He wagged his head with disgust.

We walked toward Angat. "Yeah, I guess it was," I said. "But it didn't give me the shakes."

"You felt safe, I guess," Johnson suggested. "It didn't scare me either, but it—well, I'm damn glad I didn't get in the air corps now. It'd take a lot of glamour to make me get a kick outta being able to kill so many people at once." He wasn't sure he should have said that to me and, having once let it out, he didn't look at me until we had walked several yards.

"That's about the way it got me too," I said.

Johnson gave me a sidelong glance and walked along in

silence a long time before he finally formulated what he wanted to ask. "Sam," he said, "didn't you used to be quite a soldier?"

I was angry and humiliated. Looking doggedly straight ahead, I said, "I can still do enough to get by."

"Oh, I didn't mean anything by that," Johnson said hastily. "I was talking about that Bronze Star. Grimes made a sarcastic remark about it the morning he sent you to Norzagaray."

"Yeah, I got it." I briefly explained how I had led a patrol down the trail the Japs were using. "Those things'll happen. I had to get back or spend the night in the jungle."

"When Grimes first came to George Company," Johnson said, "he tried to get some medals for a few of the boys who'd done a good job or two."

"What happened?"

"Miles called him on the phone and gave him an ass-chewing, said the only medals George could have was Purple Hearts. And we've got plenty of them." Johnson wiped sweat from his face with his sleeve. "Grimes tried a couple of times after that, but Miles just sent the citations back stamped 'not recommended.'"

"Somebody ought to tell the boys about things like that. Maybe they wouldn't hate Grimes so much."

"Naw, they'd hate him just as much. Grimes is a sonofabitch and nobody loves a sonofabitch."

We walked on. "How'd you get sent to George Company, Joe?"

He smiled. "Remember the night after Colonel Cozzens got killed? Miles sent Able Company on that wild-goose chase. When I got back—with three wounds—I got madder than hell, told Miles off and the next morning I found myself in George. Grimes got there a few days later."

"And you've been hearing him yell ever since."

"No, not quite. When Grimes first came—the first couple of months, that is—he wasn't so bad. He of course acted like an Old Army non-com, but he did some good soldiering. It was not long after Miles refused the medals that Grimes started acting like a number one, gold-plated prick."

6

The jeep was waiting in Angat. Johnson reached it first and left the front seat for me. The driver eased around and we drove through the ruins of the town, moving no faster than five miles an hour because a little dust is a fine target for artillery. Two P-38's roared past, a few feet over our heads, and gave us a friendly waggle of wings before they thundered into a shallow climb.

"Bastards!" Johnson said.

The George perimeter had undergone a change. Nothing was moved; the jeep, when we dismounted, was parked in its usual position; the lister bag still hung from its scaffold; the stack of ammunition, slightly reduced in size, was still there. But something was missing. Johnson paused and glanced at me. With a slight grimace of puzzlement, he raised his eyebrows and lowered them into a frown. Then I knew what it was:

Instead of sullen faces, I saw men standing about with various expressions of alarm.

Then I saw the cause. Captain Grimes, who left his orderly room in the house only when an emergency drove him to his foxhole, was seated on an upturned grenade case squarely in the middle of the perimeter. He was bareheaded and his half-bald head glistened sweatily in the bright sun; his sleeves were rolled up close to his armpits. The massive shoulders sagged and the head was bowed. In his hand was a three-foot length of rope, which he twitched endlessly in the dust at his feet. Between his legs rested the radio; the telephone was in his lap.

Johnson shrugged and motioned for me to follow him. We stopped in front of Captain Grimes, who for a long time continued to stare woodenly at his feet.

Our presence was finally acknowledged by a weary, sideways lift of his head as Grimes peered at us. His eyes didn't focus promptly and it appeared to me that he didn't know, during the first brief seconds, who we were.

"How's it coming, Captain?" Johnson said.

I waited expectantly for the inevitable insult that followed the speaking of Grimes' rank.

Captain Grimes mumbled unintelligibly and then, without lifting his head, offered a tentative hand to be shaken. Johnson, caught with the unexpected, hesitated awkwardly before he shook it.

"Morgan lost his balls," Grimes murmured absently. The great, belching voice was softened.

"Yeah," Johnson said hesitantly. "That's too bad."

Grimes swallowed. "I'd just about as soon get it like Millard did," he said. "Man without balls ain't much. . . ." His voice trailed off.

"Did any of those Japs floating down the river get to your perimeter last night?" Johnson asked, trying to change the subject.

"One," Grimes said. He started to ask something, hesitated, shook his head, and said, "How old do you figure Morgan was?"

"I wouldn't know, Waco," Johnson said. "About thirty, I'd say. Swanson could tell you."

The rope stopped twitching. "No," Grimes said, rousing himself slightly. "No. No, he can't. I transferred Swanson back to Regimental this morning." The rope suddenly snapped at the earth. "That sneaking little bastard!" he thundered. He subsided. "Nothing but a fuken spy, that was Swanson." The rope resumed its twitching.

"Well, I guess he couldn't tell us then," Johnson said awkwardly. He cleared his throat. "You want me to send a patrol out to see what the air strike did?"

"Aw——" He stopped, undecided. "Aw, I don't know. Do what you think's right. But if you do, be sure nobody don't get hurt."

Johnson glanced absently at me. "I'll go myself, Waco. But there won't be any trouble. The air strike was pretty rough."

Grimes nodded until his vague eyes fell on my boots. With the same sideways lifting of his head, he peered into my face. "Who's this with you, Joe?"

"Gifford."

Grimes nodded and said, "Gifford," but he didn't remember

256

me for quite a few seconds, during which he continued to nod. "Yeah," he said, "the new man that took the patrol to Norzagaray."

"That's right," Johnson said.

"That was a good patrol, Gifford."

"Thank you," I said and finished: "sir."

"I'd like to give you a cluster to go with that Bronze Star, Gifford," Grimes mumbled, "but don't nobody get medals in this fuken company."

"Yessir, I know. . . ."

There was a pause, during which Grimes continued to switch the rope across the dust at his feet.

"You come down for any special reason, Joe?" he said. He had forgotten that he had ordered Joe down.

Johnson started to speak, stopped himself quickly, and began again, "No, just a little change of scenery, Waco. Came with Sam to get the mail."

"Cobb's got the mail," Grimes said absently.

Johnson dismissed me with a nod. As I was leaving, Johnson seated himself on the ground beside Grimes. I found the mail clerk, Cobb, in the house. He recoiled with alarm when I opened the door and a packet of letters fell from the desk.

"Jesus christ, fellow!" he said sharply. "Do something, make a noise, next time before you come in. I thought you were Grimes."

"Sorry."

"Hell, don't apologize to *me!* I'm just a fuken flunky around here."

Unable to think of a balm to Cobb's irritation, I plunged in: "Look. How about letting me in on what's going on around here."

"That sonofabitch out there"—he gestured violently with a thumb—"he's going to get us all killed. Last night! Jesus! After you guys warned us to look out for Japs, Grimes crawled off his fuken grenade case and started walking around the fuken perimeter! Right in the middle of the fuken night! Popping that fuken rope he's been carrying all the time. The bastard! Had to see how the men were getting along! Talking too! Stop by a hole, look at the moon. *Mumbling!* If the fuken Japs'd found us, he'd be one dead captain, and that would be oh-fuken-kay with me."

"How long's this been going on?"

"Why, ever since Old Army Buddy got it in the fuken ass. Got a grenade case, walked out in the middle of the perimeter and sat down. Hasn't moved since, the bastard. Playing with that fuken rope. Hasn't slept! Tom Thumb made him eat a fuken K-ration this morning.

"Walked in on old Swanson and started yelling to beat hell: 'Get out of my sight, you fuken spy!' Hit old Swanson and kicked him down the steps. I drove Swanson to Regimental and damn if old Swanson wasn't saying he was going to get Colonel Miles after Grimes. Grimes ain't said a word to nobody since."

"That's better than being insulted, isn't it?"

"I'd rather be insulted by the fuken bastard than have him drawing sniper fire. And he was the one that was so fuken scared of snipers too."

"Did he try to draw fire?"

"You fuken right, he did! One fired at us a few times yesterday. Every time he fired that fuken Grimes would stop popping his rope for a little bit, then *swish, swish!* That cocksucker! I hope he gets his fuken head blown off."

"So Swanson got kicked out, huh?"

"That's what I said."

"How'd Grimes act when he kicked him out?"

"Just walked in and started yelling. Swanson started that whining crap he pulls. Grimes backed him into that corner and knocked the shit out of him. Old Swanson's head hit the wall like a ton of lead." Here Cobb paused to chuckle. "I thought he was going to get killed, but he didn't. And when Grimes kicked him down the steps, he yelled, loud as hell, 'Go see what Miles thinks about *that,* you fuken spy!' Then he turned around and looked right at me. 'I always told Millard, Swanson was no goddamn good. That fuken spy.' Then he walked out and stood on his box and yelled, 'From here on in, men, we're going to do some soldiering around this fuken company!' And he's been sitting on that fuken grenade case ever since."

"I see."

He tossed me a packet of letters. "No packages worth delivering. Wish those fuken women in the States would stop sending the damn things." He tossed a couple of crushed packages into the wastebasket. They had at one time contained cakes. He clumped angrily out of the house. "First platoon!" he yelled. "Mail call!"

I waited by the lister bag while Johnson finished his talk with Grimes. The men had gathered at the house to get their mail. I noted that, when they crossed the perimeter to approach the house, they made a rather wide detour around Grimes and his grenade case. I sorted my mail out by the date on the postmark and read it while I waited for Johnson.

Jenny was still shocked by her father's death, but she tried in one letter to be lighthearted. Enclosed in a very passionate letter was a key to the front door of our house. ". . . Just whistle when you come in so I'll have time to run upstairs and get in bed." The letter, designed to cheer me up, caused me to experience such a violent surge of desire that I felt dizzy. I became aware of a dull ache in my forehead.

The letters were all addressed to T/Sergeant Samuel F. Gifford, Recon Platoon, so she hadn't received the note Ray Mosby had written about the court-martial. I was stunned with desire and homesickness. But Gray's Landing was so far away, and Miles had promised that George Company men would be the last ones to benefit from the rotation plan. I hated Miles viciously then. I could have easily killed him if he had been present.

"We better get moving, Sam," Johnson said. I realized that he had been standing beside me for some time.

"Oh!" I fell in step beside him. "Didn't see you."

"Letters from your wife, huh?" he asked absently.

"Yes."

"I got a few to read after a while myself." He was preoccupied again.

We walked toward Angat in the hot, morning sun. To the east of Norzagaray a heavy, angry cloud was beginning to boil up, forewarning of a rain before noon. There was a soft breeze, but it wasn't enough to cool the sweat on my back. Johnson said nothing until we reached the bend near the first outpost, where he glanced at the top of the hill with absent-minded professionalism. Preoccupied as he was, Johnson, during his too many years as a combat officer, had become the professional soldier he hated so much, for he unthinkingly turned a sourly critical eye upon those functions under his command. I was sure, that morning, that his defense of Grimes had often been subconsciously one of loyalty to a fellow officer as much as it had been one of fair play.

"Savage'll be waiting for us in Angat," he said. "We're going to go see about the results of that air strike."

As we entered a dip in the road, where we were hidden from Jap observation, Johnson beckoned for me to follow and we made our way to the bank of the river. Following his example, I removed my boots and socks and washed my feet in the cool, fast water. To bathe them twice in one day was unadulterated luxury. I sighed with the keen pleasure of the cool water swishing over my calloused feet and ankles. So sensuous was my delight that I had almost forgotten about Captain Grimes.

"Grimes'll be in one hell of a lot of trouble," Johnson said suddenly, "before this day is over."

"Huh?" I recovered: "How's that?"

"Miles."

"Oh. What happened to Grimes?"

"Swanson's what happened to him." He began drying his feet with his handkerchief. "Miles sent Swanson out to keep an eye on Grimes. I'll have to admit that I didn't know that." He held his feet out to let them bake in the sun. "And it makes me think a little better of Grimes, knowing what he had to put up with. It must be hell, an Old Army man having every move watched by a mealymouthed little bastard like Swanson."

"Millard was nobody's angel."

"No, he was a prick all right. He's another example of the Old Army man getting all he can while getting's good."

We pulled on our socks and started lacing and buckling our boots.

"Something else—" Johnson said. "Grimes's trying to give up."

"Oh? He is?" I said evenly. The subject somehow embarrassed me. "Looks to me like he's trying to get shot by a sniper."

Johnson stood up. "He is," he said. "That's one way of giving up." Johnson spat. "Last thing Grimes said was, 'Wish to hell I'd never taken that commission.'"

7

The rain began when we passed the old church in Angat. Johnson didn't appear to notice it, but Savage, somewhat of a professional soldier himself, glanced irritably at the sky, pulled his cap down over his eyes to keep the mist away, and tried vainly to protect the action of the BAR. His shoulders were squared; he was quite angry.

Johnson led us along the edge of the paddy, in case of trouble, so we could easily fade into the woods and disappear. If he hadn't been so confident that the Japs had evacuated the woods after they had been discovered yesterday afternoon, he would have led us through the woods.

But the Japs hadn't evacuated and the woods had become their sepulcher. Some had no doubt escaped, for there had been a pause between the bombing and the strafing, during which the survivors could have fled, but the Japs had gambled that we wouldn't call planes in on them. The five-hundred-pound bombs had performed their function with a dispatch that their designers would have admired. The trees were mute bearers of a bloody fruit. Torn, slashed bodies had been thrown about with the abandon of a careless giant. It caused me to remember the readings I had done on Civil War history in which the streams had run red at the height of the battle. The familiar stench was beginning to rise already. The searing heat of the sun before the rain had hastened that. I shuddered because the rain, dripping through the trees, was often stained.

Savage, that model of marble calm, was so shaken that his voice trembled. "By god," he muttered, "this would be hog heaven for old Terry and his pliers."

"Cut out the talk," Johnson said curtly.

But Savage had been correct. The shredded corpses, in the last breath of their lives, had drawn back their lips in that last, horrible grimace of fear and pain to reveal gold that sparkled in grotesque contrast with the purple, bloated heaps of flesh.

I unexpectedly gagged and had to swallow rapidly to prevent vomiting. I cried out in alarm when a tree, its branches moved by the torrential rain, dropped a sleeved arm on my shoulder.

"Joe!" I cried imploringly.

"All right," he said. "It's enough for me too."

Savage and I fell in behind him eagerly; we were pleased when he abruptly broke into a trot. We jogged through the rain, our boots sloshing and sucking at the muddy paddy, and we didn't slow to a walk until we were a safe hundred yards from the woods.

After a while, Savage said, "I seen the bulldozers bury about four hundred Japs once."

"Leyte," Johnson said.

"Yeah," Savage said and glanced over his shoulder at the woods, "Leyte."

I spat, trying to force a bad taste out of my mouth. "That's something I wish I hadn't seen."

8

To the four points of the compass, the sky was clear and I could see the glistening stars, but directly overhead the moon was obscured by a huge, dark cloud. There was an illusion of light, but it was so dark I was never sure that I could see the line of trees that marked the boundary of the hill's bald knob.

Remembering last night's attempt, we had set up one of the mortars so it could drop shells into the river upstream. The other mortar pointed straight up, ready to use for flares. But there was no reflecting bar of moonlight on the river tonight. If the Japs attempted to float down, there was nothing we could do to hinder them.

The night was choked with wooly silence. It seemed to form a wall about me which hid a sinister apparition. I strained, feeling that I might have gone suddenly deaf—and heard the ticking of Johnson's wrist watch. It hung on the mortar sight, glowing dimly in the blackness.

The bark of the dog was like a flash of lightning in the black heart of night. I listened intently, but I couldn't tell whether the dog was in Angat or away to the north. He barked again, excited now, yelping. I tossed a stone into Johnson's fox-hole. He sat up immediately. Savage, Sellers, Terry and Willie also changed the rhythm of their breathing; then, while Johnson and I cocked our heads to listen into the night, the four men stood erect in their foxholes. The dog barked again, paused indecisively, and launched into a steady yelp of fear. Then, with a piercing cry of pain, he fell silent. Now it was plain that he was neither in Angat nor north of us. His bark had come from somewhere near Parade George three.

For thirty minutes, there was nothing. Patience, I thought hysterically, is the Jap's most effective weapon. We waited tensely, and I could hear the individual breath of each man. Johnson reached for the radio and punched out the warning signal, four longs, on the butterfly switch. The other outposts had heard the dog too, for they acknowledged the warning quickly. The night remained silent.

"Keep your eye on the trail, Willie," Johnson whispered.

Willie turned his back to the cliff and the rest of us watched in the direction of George three. My throat was dry and constricted. I had an overwhelming urge to cough and massaged my Adam's apple frantically in an attempt to squelch it. Finally, unable to hold it back, I emitted a short half-snort, half-cough that made the others jerk with alarm. I foolishly considered an apology.

I thought I heard the unmistakable rustle of clothing brushing against something, but it left my mind, for, away to the east, there came the somehow unexpected burr of a BAR, followed, after a short pause and another burst of fire, by the bursting light of a flare over the George four outpost. At the same time a voice, tenor with fear and cracked with haste, broke through the radio: *"Parade George four under attack by——"* And that was all he said. His voice broke, then he coughed and a second later the butterfly switch was released.

The flares continued to rise and burst over George four hill. "You're sending them up too fast!" Willie whispered tightly. From here the flares, when they burst, made almost inaudible puffs of sound before they exploded into a pin point of brilliance in a sea of blackness.

It was war-engendered instinct rather than superior hearing that caused me to detect the muted *clunk* as a sound different from the burst of the flares and the gunfire from George four. I whirled about and dropped a flare shell into the tube, but before it burst there was a bright flash and a heavy *KA-RACK!*, followed immediately by a heavy, hoarse gasp. During the brief flash of light I saw Sellers' body, half-severed at the waist from the explosion of the grenade, flop sluggishly from his foxhole. The Japs had exploded the grenade directly under him.

Grabbing the grip of the machine gun in front of my fox-hole, I jabbed it down toward the trail and searched the black-ness for a target. Then the light of the flare burst overhead. I saw nothing. The bald knob of our hill, basking in the eerie one-dimensional light, was empty. There was no movement among the trees. Indeed, the only motion on the entire hill was the queer fishlike gasping of Sellers' mouth. His eyes rolled and his mouth, flecked by an eruption of red foam, snapped shut with a click clearly audible in the onerous silence.

"Another flare, Sam," Johnson said clearly and calmly. And to all of us: "Don't look at Sellers."

Momentarily paralyzed, I hesitated almost too long to drop the flare into the tube and the first one was dropping into the trees before the new one burst.

"All right," Johnson said crisply. "Willie, shove those gre-nades along the line. Each man take a case."

In the bright silence, Willie heaved the heavily laden cases, using one to push the other, until each of us had a full case in front of his foxhole.

"No more flares," Johnson said. "Now, each of you get a grenade—pull pin—one—two—three—*throw!*" The trees and bushes were lashed to a fury by the explosions and the thousands of steel fragments whistled insanely overhead. "Grenade—pull pin—one—two—three—*throw!*" Again the trees dipped and shook with the blast. "Grenade—pull pin—one—two—three—*throw!*" We threw five more before Johnson said, "No more grenades. Machine guns! *Now—HOSE'EM DOWN!*"

During the instant before the machine guns began firing, I heard Sellers' breath stop in the middle of his last, desperate attempt to retain his grip on life. With a final, wistful sigh, he relaxed. Then I pressed the trigger and saw, lancing out ahead of me, the round fire of the muzzle blast and the arrowlike tracers.

My own machine gun hammered ruthlessly and I was aware that, to my left, Savage was methodically traversing his lane of fire with the other thirty. To my right Willie, having taken Sellers' BAR from beneath the body, was firing in evenly spaced bursts of four. Terry was chuckling and emptying clip after clip from his M-1. My machine gun was reaching a critical temperature when I heard shave-and-a-haircut banged out on the fifty-one Johnson fired. I released the trigger.

I listened for cries from the Jap wounded, but our grenades and machine guns had evidently done no good, for there was no sound other than our own hoarse breathing and the firing at George three. We waited. On the other side of our hill there came the sudden clatter of machine-gun and rifle fire from George one. Another second passed and there was a glow and the sound of more gunfire from George four.

Surely, I thought desperately, we at least wounded some Japs with all that violent firing. But the Japs—if they were there —made no sound.

But they were there and, because of the noise from the other outposts, I wasn't sure that I had heard the several sounds of *clunk* that came from the trees somewhat to the left of the trail, but I yelled, "*GRENADES!*" and waited. They came like a shower of gruesome hailstones. One of them, apparently having been arched high, smashed down on my foot. I leapt wildly from my foxhole and flattened myself against the ground. The explosion came then. It deafened me, made my ears ring achingly, but it was not the one that wounded me. A grenade, which had alighted near Sellers' body, exploded like a bolt of lightning and peppered my shoulder with tiny fragments and stones. I jumped back into my foxhole. Three or four of the Japs' grenades had rolled over the cliff and exploded with terrifying cracks behind me. Some of the grenades had been duds—not unusual with Japs—for I hadn't heard as many explosions as I had heard clunks. The Japs had a primitive cap on their grenades; to arm them they had to be smashed against something solid and the Japs usually used their helmets for that purpose.

"Anybody hurt?" Johnson asked quietly.

"I got peppered," I said. My voice was surprisingly strong and clear.

"If you're hurt bad," Johnson said, "come on over and I'll fix you up."

"I'm all right."

"You're sure?"

"Yeah."

"Good," he said. "Hang on. There's more to come."

Fumbling in the blackness, I examined my shoulder with my fingers. There were spots of blood and a few scratches, but I was still able to fight. It would be stiff tomorrow and there would be an infection if I didn't treat it as soon as there was daylight, but the arm was still strong and capable of doing its share. And it would be tested soon, for the main attack was yet to come. I stared into the blackness until my eyes bulged.

When the machine-gun fire began, it seemed that it was firing directly into my face—a common illusion during a night fight—and for a moment I thought I was going to die. During that brief lapse of time I was filled with a new exhaustion and, stranger still, an odd resignation, for it was foolish, I reasoned solemnly, to hope to outlast the war. I ducked and heard somebody grunt amazingly loud. It took me a moment to realize that the grunt had come out of me.

It was a Nimbu submachine gun. There was no mistaking the slow fire of the gun we had so often called a "woodpecker."

266

Bullets struck the tripod of my machine gun, sending a thousand sparks flying before the gunner moved his fire to sweep over the other foxholes. This was an old trick and, I said aloud, "You'll not fool *me,* you bastards!" I hated them insanely and their cheap, Oriental tricks. Japs seldom fired into a perimeter at night. They preferred the more suicidal tactics of rushing us. When they did fire, it was for but one purpose: they wanted to pin us down by firing from an oblique angle while another party moved in close enough to make a short, headlong rush immediately after the firing stopped. Taking a chance that the gunner was firing over the other foxholes, I jumped to my feet, dropped a flare into the tube and ducked. The Nimbu stopped firing.

Jumping back to my feet, I traversed the machine gun wildly across the slope of the knob. I didn't bother to aim. I realized absently that I was uttering a long, low grunt, as if I were straining to lift something heavy. I heard the men in the other foxholes firing too. The flare burst.

Only a few yards away, their shoulders low, their heads back to reveal the reflection of the flare in their amazingly slanted eyes, rushing at us with terrifying speed, were the Japs. They ran with their legs far apart, flat-footed. Leading them was the only truly big Jap I had ever seen. He was well over six feet. He wore a uniform of a darker hue than was on the others. My mind automatically registered that he was an Imperial Marine. I saw, too, that he clutched, in one big hand, two grenades, which he was in the act of throwing. They smashed against his helmet, the eyes darted about for a target, and he found me. The other Japs spread out and, running directly into our fire, sought their men to kill.

The big Jap had lowered his head now, pushing with brutal, fanatic courage, toward me. It had become a contest between my machine gun and my courage to keep it firing, and his brutal charge. With the same slowness that I had known for more than three years, I watched the ball-like tracers from my machine gun wheel toward him and feel for his chest. But he was too low. With the heel of my left hand, I held the machine gun steady and waited for him to run into the lane of fire. I was firing from ground level and he would have to run through a hail of steel to reach me. This Jap was going to die; I knew he was going to die. But he was laced with fiery fanaticism and, accepting death as inevitable, he was going to make certain that I died too. From now on it was my gamble: if his strength fails, my bullets will smash him down.

But I didn't kill him. He died at the hand of his own brutal courage. My first tracer to reach him jabbed at his shoulder, not where there was solid enough flesh to stop him because his kind had to be shot in the vital areas of the chest or head, but it deflected his charge. He missed my foxhole and, his head still down, he charged bull-like over the rim of the cliff and fell, silently. The two grenades in his hand killed him.

I didn't release the trigger. Two Japs, hidden by the big Marine, had been rushing Savage and they ran headlong into my fire. Both of them dropped like heavy sacks, their heads perforated by my bullets. The grenades they held in their hands exploded before I could duck and fragments sang angrily about my ears. My helmet rang dully with the impact of flying steel. Another Jap was so jarred by bullets from Johnson's fifty-one that his helmet fell over his eyes and he charged madly over the cliff and fell, screaming hideously until he was silenced by his grenades, into the river below. Willie, firing the BAR with its snout no more than a foot away from one of the bandy little creatures, was holding the Jap off by the sheer power of the BAR's muzzle velocity. It was the comic relief of a nightmare. The Jap, clutching crazily at the muzzle, finally crumpled at the edge of Willie's foxhole. Willie scrambled after the Jap's grenades and threw them, left-handed, over the cliff. Both of them burst no more than a yard from the edge, sending up a snarling canopy of fragments.

My entire body shook with one violent convulsion and I regained my self-control. I dropped another flare into the tube.

A Jap, so short that he appeared to be a child, was hit and he fell, as if he had been tripped, into Terry's foxhole. Terry, giggling merrily, hopped out of his hole and flattened himself against the ground until the Jap's grenades exploded, then he hopped blithely back into the foxhole with the shredded Jap.

I had one final glimpse of Terry's happy grin as he dumped the dead Jap out.

There were three Japs working on Johnson. One of them was already wilting under the fire of his fifty-one, which he held tilted back on the two rear legs of the tripod as he blasted a rapid arc in front of him. I whirled my own gun around and fired a blast at the Jap nearest Johnson and, while this one dropped, I changed my fire to the other one, who, caught between my fire and Johnson's, was held suspended for seconds before he slowly fell away to one side. Johnson leapt frantically from his foxhole as the Jap fell into it and dived headlong behind the protective body of Sellers. There were three grenade explosions under the Japs, whose bodies were tossed roughly aside, and there was the familiar whine of fragments; then there was silence.

"Another flare," Johnson rasped.

I dropped a flare and Johnson rose to his feet and stood erect. Huddled as I was in my foxhole, he appeared to me as a giant. With the mechanical precision of the most complex machinery, Johnson paced from one Jap body to the next, adroitly firing a shot from his pistol into each toothy, yellow face. He passed Sellers' body without a glance.

The flare flickered and its light dimmed out to leave us in blackness again. Eight corpses, one American, seven Japs. Five men alive, their breath rasping like the scratchings of monster crickets. I was bathed in burning sweat.

The fit of trembling struck suddenly, as if I had received a blow to the heart. It penetrated to my bones and smashed me down into my foxhole, where I lay, quivering and jerking, a useless wad of doughlike flesh.

"Oh my god," I heard myself say. "No more. No more. *Please*, no more!"

"Not so loud, Sam," Johnson said gently. "Try to hold it down a little, boy."

"I don't belong here," I said over and over. "I don't belong here at all."

Somebody dropped into my foxhole and gathered me into

his arms. I was rocked gently back and forth. "Take it easy, Sam boy," Willie murmured, as if to a child awaking from a nightmare. "Take it easy, boy. Easy now. You'll be all right pretty soon."

His voice murmured on into the impenetrable night.

9

Dawn broke and the sun came. We stumbled from our foxholes and surveyed the damage we had suffered. I instinctively ducked when I heard the distant crack of a sniper's rifle. His bullet, fired from a great distance, probably from another hill, droned past.

"Keep ducking," Johnson said, "if he keeps firing. Long's he thinks he's getting close, he won't change his sight readings."

I sat on the edge of my foxhole, trying to rub the aching smart from my eyes. The corpse of Sellers, which had been almost blown into two pieces by the initial blast, had received fragments until it was ripped and blasted from head to foot.

Johnson grimaced slightly. "Willie," he said quietly, "you and Savage bury Sellers. Sam, you and Terry get rid of the Japs." He picked up the microphone and began asking for casualty reports from the other outposts.

Willie took his entrenching tool and scooped up the crust by Sellers' body. Willie threw it over the cliff.

Terry didn't seem at all exhausted. He yanked his pliers from his pocket and, his eyes dancing with the prospects of great wealth, went about the business of pulling the gold from the Japs' mouths. While I rifled their pockets, Terry sat on their chests and, after having propped their mouths open with his stick, gleefully wrenched the teeth out.

The sniper fired and we ducked.

"Goddamn!" Terry shouted. "Sam, look at that!" He held

his pliers up to display a huge gold tooth. "Looks like a fuken elk's tooth!" He dropped the tooth into his ditty bag. "Another *banzai* like that one and I'll be rich enough to buy the Golden Gate Bridge! *Jesus!*"

Willie threw down his entrenching tool. "Terry," he said quietly, "if you don't shut your fuken mouth about them teeth, I'm going to stomp some of your own fuken teeth down your big throat, you hear?" Willie chewed his tobacco faster than usual, the only outward sign of his anger.

"Fuk you, Willie," Terry said casually, preoccupied with the joy of pulling teeth.

Willie spat carefully, toed the entrenching shovel out of the way, and walked deliberately up behind Terry.

"When I tell a man to shut his mouth," Willie said, "I ain't kidding."

"Damnit, Willie," Terry said with childish irritation, "don't bother me. I'm busy."

Willie reached down, took Terry's collar in a big, calloused hand, and twisted sharply. Terry tried to squirm and he said, "Goddamn you, Willie——" but he was hushed by Willie's jerking him roughly to his feet.

Willie shook Terry, easily, the way a pup shakes a rabbit. "Terry, I told you to shut up," Willie said. "I don't want to hear another word about them fuken teeth, you hear?"

Terry, his feet hardly touching the ground, tried only once to jerk free before he gave up and squeaked, "All right, Willie!" After he was released, he shrugged his jacket back around his shoulders and explained seriously, "You was choking me, Willie."

"You goddamn right I was."

"Well—it hurt."

Willie spat. "Next time, Terry, I'll do more'n choke you. I'm sick'n tired of hearing about them fuken teeth."

"Okay," Terry said tractably. "I'll remember."

Willie humped his shoulders in a shrug and went back to help Savage dig Sellers' grave. Savage, during the exchange between Terry and Willie, hadn't stopped digging. Nor did he

271

bother to listen to what had been said. By concentrating on Savage's taciturn ways, I managed to keep from looking at the corpse of Sellers.

While Terry continued with his dental activities, I stripped my jacket off and tried to get iodine on the places where I had been peppered by the Jap grenade last night. But I couldn't reach all of them. Johnson beckoned for me to sit in front of him and, while he talked to the other outposts on the radio, he smeared my shoulder. He patted my head when he was through.

Willie went through Sellers' pockets and stacked their contents in a neat pile at the head of the hole that was to become a grave. There was the wallet, the dog tags, a pocket knife, two olive-drab handkerchiefs, a carbine cartridge, a GI pro-kit——

We ducked as the sniper fired again.

——An empty key ring and an Australian florin. I was preoccupied with the peculiar fascination I had for the personal effects of a dead man. A man's pockets never seem to yield anything more than a rather transitory salute to small preoccupations. It was sad and it made the desire to go home become sickeningly acute. Sellers had done nothing that was important to anybody except the thirty-six men of his platoon: he had been a good man with a BAR, he was a cool hand on a patrol, he fought calmly and well. But Sellers was done. The thirty-six men would someday forget how he had looked and, later, many of them would not remember his name when they were relating the tales of the Pacific war. I was long accustomed to seeing death, but I was not now, nor would I ever be, the man to stop thinking about it.

The sniper fired again.

"Terry, goddamnit," Willie said, "you forgot to duck."

Terry looked up from counting his gold teeth. "Oh!" he said placidly. "Well, I'll duck next time."

"Make sure you do," Willie said. "Don't take chances at our expense. Joe said duck. You duck, hear?"

"All right, Willie," Terry said agreeably.

Pretending to go through the pockets of the Jap on whose chest he sat, Terry whispered, "Sellers'n Willie was close friends."

272

I hadn't known that. "Oh," I whispered.

I finished rifling the Japs' pockets and Terry had extracted the last available gold tooth. Johnson was still busy on the radio.

"Willie," I called, "what'll we do with these Jap bodies?"

Willie glanced at Johnson, who was too busy to be bothered. "Throw'em over the fuken bluff," he said shortly.

Terry and I dragged the Jap corpses to the edge of the cliff and lined them up neatly, like cords of fire logs, the heaviest one at the head of the line because Terry remarked that we should do the hard work first. I grasped the shoulders and Terry took the legs of the first Jap and we lifted him off the ground.

"On three," Terry said. "One—two—*three!*" The corpse sailed, his bloody uniform flapping about his body, over the edge of the cliff and down toward the river. Terry and I rushed up and looked over. The Jap corpse, diminishing in bulk, continued to fall for an eternity, and even after it had appeared to hit the water, it continued to fall. Finally, a speck now, it plunked onto the bank, its feet, as they fell into the edge of the river, making a tiny splash that caught the early sun for a small, momentary rainbow. Terry, his eyes dancing, gave me a look that expressed his gratification.

He added, "Hell, this's more fun than shooting'em."

"Oh certainly," I said wryly.

Each time we tossed a Jap over the cliff Terry rushed forward to watch the body fall. I waited patiently for him to come back and pick up his end of the next corpse. It took us quite a while to dispose of the last one, which, when we hefted it, Terry said, "Now throw hard, this time, Sam. I want to see what kind of splash he'll make when he hits the water."

I swung as hard as I could and, while Terry watched, I sat on the grenade case in front of my foxhole. I wiped my sweating face with my handkerchief. Not yet seven o'clock and it was already hot.

Savage and Willie had finished digging the grave and Savage sat down to rest. Willie approached Sellers' body and gently picked it up, cradled it in his arms, carried it to the grave and placed it carefully, full-length, in the earth. For a moment I thought Willie was going to speak over the body, but, instead, he turned to pick up his shovel, with which he began rapidly tossing dirt over the body. The hole filled, Willie wrenched a limb off one of the trees and, using his shovel as a sledge, pounded it into the earth at the head of the grave. With his trench knife, Willie broke the mortar tape that had bound the two dog tags together to keep them from jingling and put one of them on top of the neat pile of personal effects. The other dog tag, with the plastic necklace, he draped securely on the limb which served as a tombstone. This done, he dusted his hands on his trousers and gathered the personal effects into his big hands and stalked to his foxhole, where he placed them in his jungle pack. He dusted his hands again. He removed his helmet and dropped it on the ground. He dug his fatigue cap out of his cargo pocket, shook the wrinkles out, and placed it over his kinky hair. After having performed these rituals, he seated himself by me and wiped the sweat from his face with the sleeve of his jacket.

"Sam," he said, "you remember the time that the guy got up and called old Colonel Miles a murdering old bastard right in front of the whole regiment?"

"Yes."

"Well"—Willie spat with a quick side motion of his head—"that was Sellers." He picked up a clod and ground it between his fingers until it was dust, which he sifted between his fingers. "That Sellers was one hell of a good man. They wasn't a better man in the whole fuken regiment."

He stared thoughtfully at the grave for a long time before he said, "A *mighty* good soldier!"

"He sure was," Terry said brightly.

Willie snapped his head around and began furiously, "Terry, goddamn you, I'll——"

"I *meant* it, Willie!" Terry was sorely grieved because his good intentions had been misunderstood. "I meant it. I really did. Sellers was a *good* soldier."

The sniper fired and we ducked as his bullet droned past.

Willie finally believed Terry. "All right, Terry," he said. Willie flopped a hand toward the grave. "He never done nothing

274

more'n plant cotton and go to drill on Monday night. Worked hard on his crop too." Without pause: "Course you wouldn't know about how hard it is to bring in a good crop. But *he* did. He . . ."

No, I thought, I wouldn't know how hard it is to bring in a good crop. My civilian life had been one pleasant episode after another. It should've been, I thought ruefully, it was certainly mapped out carefully enough.

I remembered the day I had tried to drink coffee with Carr and Raker. Once that incident had been an island of unpleasantness in a sea of happiness, but now I understood the resentment that caused it. Nosir, Willie, I thought, I wouldn't know about bringing in a good crop, but there are a few things I do know.

I wondered now, were it possible for Colonel Cozzens to be alive, if he would have commanded the quality of unwavering respect today that was so easily his during those violent, innocent days of the first island campaign. Would he have commanded the same sort of respect that Little Joe Johnson got? I asked myself. Without knowing why, but at the same time caring intensely, I doubted it. For all those young men who had come to this war with an attitude akin to the romanticism of the Victorian soldier, there was nothing upon which they could hang the symbols of their accomplishments. Their officers were no longer the rich planters like Colonel Cozzens; instead they looked to men like Little Joe for their leadership. And they found it. It was always present.

So, on a hill where I had last night witnessed the death of a former cotton laborer, I, of Gray's Landing, had emerged from the final curtain of my isolation to become a man of the twentieth century, whether I liked it or not.

". . . Even if he never done much talking," Willie was saying, "specially after he come to George, he done his job right and carried his load—and more'n that—lots of times, without griping."

Too many young men, I thought, have carried more than their own load, and most of the time they didn't understand——

The sniper fired again and we ducked.

"Looks like we had a general shitstorm last night," Johnson

said. He glanced at his notebook. "George perimeter lost a man, George three lost one, George four got two wounded, George six got one wounded—and we lost Sellers." He snapped the notebook closed and placed it in his jacket pocket. "Next time I hear about some bastard general saying the war on Luzon's over, I'm going to stomp his fuken face in." He began rolling his sleeves up with short, angry motions. "Grimes says he can send a replacement to George four, but that's all he's got. The roadblock got it last night too and he had to send four men down there to beef them up." He began rolling the other sleeve. "Looks like the Japs're trying to save face and make up for the beating they took at the first of the campaign. Every one of our outposts've got a sniper firing on them." He cleared his throat and spat over the cliff.

"What's worrying me is that I can't figure out where they're all coming from," he said. "If they're moving around our flanks, those boys in King and Fox ought to be able to stop them. But the CO's of King and Fox both say they've had a little trouble too."

"How about the companies on the west end of the line?" Willie asked.

"They haven't heard a shot nor seen a Jap in the last two weeks. I guess the Japs were looking for the outposts the furtherest apart—and you can be pretty damn sure George would get those."

The sniper fired again.

"Anyhow," Johnson went on, "they don't have the men for a general break-through. They'll just have to be happy at doing a face-saving job by knocking hell out of a few bastards stashed out on a hill or two." He finished angrily: "I can't see what it is that makes them want to commit suicide by attacking when they haven't got the men and supplies. There's no purpose in dying like that."

I couldn't help thinking: And I can't see any purpose for dying like we're going to, either.

"Well"—Johnson picked up a rock and threw it over the cliff—"worrying about it only makes it harder to take." He got to his feet. "Willie, who's on water detail this morning?"

"Me'n Sam, if Sam's feeling up to it."

My heart lurched with the thought of having to leave the protection of the machine guns, but it was surprisingly easy to blandly lie: "Don't worry about me, Willie. I'll make out all right."

"All right then," Johnson said, after giving me a hurried study, "keep your rifles unlocked and your eyes wide open."

The sniper fired and we ducked.

"Terry!" Johnson said sharply. "Next time that bastard fires, duck like you really mean it. Leaning over a little bit isn't enough. Japs aren't that dumb."

"Sorry, Joe," Terry said, grinning sillily.

Willie gathered the canteens and hooked as many to his belt as it would hold. I carried the two jerricans. We struck out down the trail, walking as quietly as our heavy boots and the rolling rocks would permit, holding hard against the steepness. Willie led, acting as guard, his rifle held at an easy port-arms. My own rifle was at sling on my shoulder. I was very careful in keeping the cans from scraping on the brush.

Halfway down the hill the trail turned abruptly to the left and Willie stopped. I had heard it too, an almost imperceptible sound, like a man breaking wind. We waited. My throat ached for me to swallow its dryness. Sweat dripped from the tip of my nose; I brushed my sleeve against it, but the drop formed again almost immediately.

The sniper fired again. From this point on the hill his rifle sounded curiously like the sound of a bursting balloon. I remained squatted until Willie rose and proceeded cautiously on down the trail.

As we turned the next bend in the trail, Willie halted, grunted, and snapped his rifle to his shoulder. During the instant before he fired, I looked past him and saw a sickly Jap squatted at the side of the trail. He was relieving himself and his head was tucked between his knees as he studied the puddle of filth that had oozed from his body. He raised his head in time to face the muzzle blast from Willie's rifle. His face changed from veined strain, to the impassive Oriental mask, and then, unaccountably, he spread his face into a ridiculous grin.

He died with the grin still there, a figure toppled back into his own mess.

"Come on," Willie said and hurried ahead.

We didn't run because to do so down this grade would have made it impossible to stop. I hurdled the dead Jap and my nostrils were filled with an unbelievably bad smell. As we hurried along, I figured out why the Jap had let us walk up on him so easily: he had thought we were Japs too, which meant that, somewhere on this hill, there were more of his kind, either waiting until dark again or planning a daylight harassing attack.

Feeling that my back was the target for a Jap who would fire any moment now, I followed Willie to the banks of the river. I bent and filled the cans with water. I couldn't suppress a shudder.

"What's the matter?" Willie said.

"My back feels like a Jap rifle might be sighted in on it," I said shakily.

"Yeah," Willie said. "I know what you mean."

Downstream, resting in the depressions caused by the impact of their falling bodies, the Japs who had died in last night's attack lay in various grotesque poses. While I filled the cans, Willie stood at my back, his eyes searching the trees. It took the cans an agonizingly long time to fill. There were no sounds except the gurgling water and the quick spurt of Willie's spitting. The cans full, I stood guard while Willie filled the canteens.

"Back up the other trail," Willie said lowly.

I followed him. The cans were heavy; already my arms were aching at the shoulders and biceps. My rifle, now that the weight of the cans had made me so awkward that I could no longer hold a subtle balance, swatted solidly against my butt. As I threaded my way through the pattern of Jap corpses, I stumbled on a foot and fell. The cans banged against the rocks with a watery clatter.

Overhead, the Jap sniper fired again.

My right arm, sore from the peppering I had taken from the grenade last night, began to ache so hard after we traveled a hundred yards that I had to give it favor by leaning toward it. I was relieved when Willie noticed my predicament and whispered, "You guard, I'll take the water." He slung his rifle over his shoulder and, as easily as he would have carried an empty suitcase, grasped the water cans and followed me around the hill and up the trail.

Halfway up the hill I recoiled and crouched when, a few yards off the trail, there came the unmistakable sound of cloth drawn across the rough bark of a tree. It was impossible to run up the rocky trail. Curiously fatalistic, I plodded on up the hill, hoping that the Japs didn't want to reveal themselves by firing. I heard Willie panting, but he said nothing and I didn't slacken the pace. Three times before we reached the knob, I heard human movement in the underbrush.

Johnson met us before we cleared the trees and escorted us to our foxholes. Willie collapsed under the shade of his poncho and drank deeply from his canteen.

"What was the shot?" Johnson asked.

"Willie shot a Jap on the way down," I said.

"Caught'im taking a country crap," Willie gasped.

"Look, Joe," I said, "this hill's crawling with them."

Johnson nodded thoughtfully. "Did you hear them or see them?"

"Heard them."

"How many?"

"I heard them move four times," I said. "Don't know how many there were."

"After last night. . . ." Johnson stared in sad thoughtfulness. He roused himself: "Well—they'll probably think of something new for tonight." He let his mind drift again. Then: "Well—anybody got any ideas?"

"Hey, Joe," Terry said brightly. "There's a grenade launcher in the ammo hole. How about me putting it on my rifle and shooting a few grenades around the hill."

Johnson shrugged. "It might do some good—and then it might not. But if you want to, get busy."

Terry hurried to the little ammo dump and found the grenade launcher, a carton of thirty-caliber launching blanks and a number of antipersonnel grenade adapters. We watched absently while he hurriedly assembled his equipment.

"Shouldn't we fix up a few grenade traps before tonight, Joe?" I said.

Johnson nodded. "Terry, any telephone wire in that hole?"

Terry wasn't happy with the interruption, but he took time to find a roll of the new plastic-insulated wire. While the others went to work cleaning the rifles and machine guns, I prepared the booby traps. Carefully holding the spoons tightly against the grenades, I removed the pins and straightened the kink in them so they would fall out easily.

"You going to shorten the fuses?" Johnson said.

"No thanks," I said. "Not me."

The sniper fired again.

"Hand 'em over," Savage said. "I'll do it."

"Jesus!" Willie murmured. "I wouldn't do that for a fuken honorable discharge."

Savage, his gnarled, sure hands working slowly and steadily, cut the fuses, crimped them and put them back into the grenade cases. At no time did he show the slightest hurry or nervousness. He made me think, somehow, of Poppa. He placed the grenades into the empty case I shoved over, wiped his hands on his olive-drab handkerchief and nodded to show me that he was through.

"Savage," Johnson burst out, "you're a fuken iceberg. Don't you have any nerves at all?"

Savage shrugged. "Getting killed now or tonight—it don't make much difference." As soon as he finished speaking, he knew that he had said the wrong thing. He raised his head to add something, but, thinking better of it, he rose and shuffled away to his foxhole, where he eased himself under the poncho and promptly fell asleep.

We ducked when the sniper fired.

"Hey!" Terry said loudly. "That bastard's getting a little closer!"

Willie nodded and spat. "It musta hit pretty close around," he said. "I heard it plunk into something."

10

Terry passed a happy morning firing grenades down the hill. Because the launching rounds and the heavy grenades caused such a heavy recoil, he placed the butt of his rifle against the rim of his foxhole to fire. Each time after he pulled the trigger he would listen intently for the explosion and a scream from the Japs, but only once was he sure that he was enjoying anything more than agreeable sport: we heard a harsh scream that soon degenerated into a groan and finally silence, and that was the best Terry could get from his bright idea. He was very upset when Johnson made him stop because of the possibility of a grenade shortage.

"Aw hell, Joe——"

"That fifty-one's low on ammo," Johnson said. "No need putting us the same way with the grenades." He added: "Duck!" The sniper's bullet whistled past.

"Wind musta changed," Willie said. "That's the fourth time he's got close."

Willie fixed our lunch because he had bragged about his prowess with the frying pan on the deer hunts he had enjoyed as a civilian. He rifled the contents of four ten-in-one rations to make certain the meal was a definite variation from what we had been used to.

"Better take it easy on the ten-in-ones," Johnson said.

"Hell, might as well use 'em up," Willie said. "We'll be pulling out of here in not too long." The sniper fired and Willie said, "Bastard!" He handed each of us a can containing the first course of the meal. "Chow call."

I placed the can at the edge of my foxhole, fished my spoon out of my cargo pocket, wiped it with my handkerchief, made myself comfortable and ate. It was good. The sun had heated the food, meatballs and spaghetti, and even the water, with its lacing of purifier, wasn't bad.

"Not bad, Willie," I said. "That doesn't taste like ordinary meatballs and spaghetti. What'd you put in it?"

He grinned. "I spit a little tobacco juice in it," he said. "Here, pass this can along to Savage."

I handed the can to Terry. "Pass it on," I said.

Terry took the can and reached it toward Savage's foxhole. "Hey, Savage, you old bastard!" Terry called gaily. "Chow call, you sleepy-headed draft dodger."

Savage didn't stir. Terry tossed a handful of dirt into the foxhole, but Savage slept soundly. Terry, clutching the can, crawled out of his foxhole.

"Savage, goddamn you," Terry said cheerfully, "if that sniper gets me while I'm bringing your chow, I'll come back and haunt your fuken ass!"

Johnson smiled into his food. "Old Terry! He'd make a good ghost, wouldn't he!"

"Got a face on'im for it right now," Willie said. "Fact is, I've had my share of nightmares about Terry's face."

"Go ahead, Terry," I said, "keep fooling with him. He'll wake up in a minute and throw you over that cliff."

"Fuk you, Sam," Terry said. He lifted Savage's poncho. "Peek-a-boo, Savage! I see you! I'm about to catch you beating your meat, you old——" He dropped the edge of the poncho and scampered back to his own foxhole. "Oh shit," he said weakly. And at the same time he picked up his can of food and threw it over the cliff.

"What's the matter, Terry?" I said.

"Joe," Terry said. His voice had the peculiar timber of fear. "Joe," he said. "Joe—he's looking right at me."

Johnson paused, his spoon halfway to his lips.

"Joe," Terry said, "you better take a look."

Johnson gave Terry a searching stare. Slowly he lowered his spoon and replaced it in the can. "Dead?" he asked.

"Oh shit," Terry said. "He was looking right at me."

"All right," Johnson said gently. "You just don't look at him, Terry. Sam and I'll take care of it."

During that moment, Johnson's order became the most important words that had ever been spoken to me. "Let's go, Sam." Automatically, with a reflex born of training, I half rose before I stopped and sank back into my foxhole. A breeze caught the edge of Savage's poncho and revealed what the sniper had done. Savage, his head canted slyly to the side, was staring fixedly into blackness. The bullet had made only a small black and blue spot where it had emerged over his left eye.

This was the last picture I could see. There had been the raw beef of the Jap officer's face during my first night in combat. There had been the wild eyes staring from the stranger's face that had once belonged to Webster. There had been the surprised expressions on the faces of Meleski and Raker. And last night there had been Sellers. And now, Savage.

Gently, I began trembling. "I'd better not," I said.

Johnson exploded, "Now, see here, Sam——"

I held my trembling hands aloft for him to see.

"Oh," Johnson said. "I thought you said that didn't start till the fight's over."

I studied my hands, tried to control them. "This is the first time," I said evenly. "That's why I figure I'd"—I took a deep breath—"better not help with Sellers."

Johnson understood instantly. "Yeah, it sort of gets me too, Sam." He nodded to Willie. "How about you, Willie?"

Without a word, Willie got to his feet, spat, and came forward, leaning to pat my shoulder as he passed. He picked up his shovel, which he had wordlessly used to dig the grave of his own best friend, and began hacking and scraping at the stubborn earth. Watching him, I thought: Willie's the kind of man I needed for a friend when I was a civilian. And: He will be—if I'm ever a civilian again.

Johnson eased the corpse out of the foxhole and stretched it out on the ground. Carefully keeping my eyes away from the staring, sightless face, I watched while he removed the personal effects from the pockets. He picked up the wallet.

"Here," Terry said roughly, "leave that alone. I'll do it." Here, for the first time, Terry acted more like a man than a boy. I had seen his kind before; the perennial boy until that shadowy point is reached where something breaks in the soul. The eyes of the corpse had been enough, I thought.

Johnson rose without a word and let Terry take the personal effects. Terry hunched over the neat pile—the wallet and the pictures—as if he wanted to protect its mute privacy. Terry suddenly looked very young to me, and quite small too. He was a——

"BANZAI! BANZAI!"

Waddling like a crab, a Jap emerged from the trees, his legs far apart, running as if his crotch was so sore he couldn't get his feet together. He scrambled up the last few yards of the grade and directed himself toward Willie and Johnson, still croaking "BANZAI! BANZAI!" in a cracked, tenor voice. He sounded like a child playing a silly game. About his neck there dangled an antitank mine. Willie and Johnson, so dumfounded by a daylight attack that they couldn't move for an instant, stood and stared stupidly at the little Jap.

With one motion, I curled my finger around the trigger of my machine gun, pulled, and whirled it around as it fired. The tracers slanted across a short arc and the Jap met them full in the chest. With a deafening roar, he exploded and the concussion threw me violently against the back of my foxhole, almost knocking the breath from me.

Willie and Johnson were thrown sprawling. They jumped to their feet and raced to their foxholes, leaving Savage's body, its legs thrown wide apart by the blast, hands at its sides, to wait for its grave.

"BANZAI!" Another Jap burst out of the trees and this one carried a mine too. A faint trail of smoke drifted behind him; they were setting the mines off with dynamite cap and fuse. Before he had taken ten steps, the combined firepower of three machine guns and a BAR concentrated on him and he was thrown brutally backward, tumbling into the trees, where he exploded with another earth-trembling blast.

There was a pause. Willie spat with a flat, liquid sound that was curiously loud in the bright, midday silence. The muted jabber of Japanese could be heard from the trees—a series of inhuman sounds, urgent, commanding—and another Jap, stumbling as if he had been violently shoved in the back, emerged, only to be cut down before he had taken more than a few steps. Not waiting for a command from Johnson, we raked the trees where the Japs had appeared and, as our tracers darted among the leaves, the explosion of the mine came, followed immediately by the screech of a man suffering unbearable pain. Taking a hoarse breath, loud enough for me to hear plainly, the wounded Jap screamed again, but his vocal cords relaxed in midst of the scream and he died with a weird, horselike neigh.

Our ears ringing, we waited.

It took a long time, ten minutes or more, before the dust settled completely. And it was some time after that before Johnson said, "Well, I guess that's all of that." He coughed the dust from his throat. "Christ! A *banzai* right in broad daylight! How stupid can they get?" He cleared his throat, which dimly reminded me of the way Colonel Cozzens did when he was embarrassed. "Well—Terry, get your pliers! There ought to be a few teeth in that bunch."

"No thanks," I heard Terry say. My hearing seemed to be failing. "No thanks. I don't want nothing to do with it."

"What's the matter, Terry? You losing your——"

I heard no more of that. My hearing was gone and the bright sunlight began to fade to a mottled gray. Then I was unconscious.

The next thing I heard was Willie's voice: "Help me a minute here, Joe." It was some time before I realized that he was talking about me. "Put'im back in his hole or he'll walk right out again."

I roused myself to discover that, somehow, I was out of my foxhole and was close to the trees at the edge of the bald knob. Willie swept me into his arms as if I were a child. My head snapped back and my helmet fell to the ground.

"Get his tin hat," Willie said.

"How in the hell did I get——" But the question wasn't worth the effort. I relaxed and let myself be carried back up the hill.

Willie jumped into my foxhole and cradled me in his arms. I could smell his body odor. "Now listen, Sam," he said, his voice coming from close to my ear. "You *got* to hold on, hear? You got to hold on! We'll be pulled out of here tomorrow morning. *Nobody's* crazy enough to have us stay up here past tomorrow. No! No! Don't start that trembling, Sam! *You got to hold on!"*

Turning my heavy head aside, I vomited violently into the bottom of my foxhole.

"That's all right, Sam," Willie said gently. "That'll make you feel better."

11

My head ached dully and my hands felt bloated and smooth. I arose and leaned against the rim of my foxhole. The sun was achingly bright.

"Think you're going to be all right for a while, Sam?" It was Johnson.

"Oh god!" I murmured tiredly. "That was—" I tried again: "That was rough."

"He'll make it," Willie said. "Sam's a tough old bastard."

"Try to make it till tomorrow morn——," Johnson began.

"Parade George, this is Parade George Charlie. Tom Thumb speaking. Put Little Joe on. Over." Tom Thumb was the giant officer who had commanded the outpost before we had relieved it.

"Little Joe. Over."

"Tom Thumb. I am commanding this company till another officer is officially named. Over." The volume of the radio didn't seem to be as strong as it usually was.

We exchanged startled glances.

"Little Joe. Roger by me. But what happened to Waco? Over."

"This is Tom Thumb. Look, Joe—I mean, Little Joe, I don't know whether I ought to tell you this on the radio or not, but Waco took off this morning and told me he wasn't coming back. Over." Now I was certain that the volume of the radio was weaker.

286

"Best fuken news," Willie muttered, "I've heard since this war started."

"Shut up!" Johnson said irritably. Into the radio: "Little Joe. You haven't told me much, Tom Thumb. Can't you give me something else? Over."

"*Tom Thumb. Well—last night we had a perimeter attack and Waco was acting up in a way I'd never seen before, even if he has been acting funny lately. He charged out of the perimeter and killed a Jap that was throwing grenades from that clump of bamboo.*" Tom Thumb's voice was growing perceptibly fainter. "*This morning—after we got the big news—Waco got in the jeep and told me that he couldn't see any need of playing the goat to Indian Chief any more. Then he drove off. Over.*" During the last few words of the message Tom Thumb's voice became so faint that we had to bend low over the radio to hear him. The battery was giving up.

"Jesus christ, man!" Johnson shouted into the microphone. "What big news? Over."

"*Tom Thumb. Well—I shouldn't say on the radio, but well, anyhow—did you ever hear of a town in Japan called Hiroshima? Over.*"

Johnson, straining to hear, straightened and cried, "Willie, get another battery!" He pushed the butterfly switch. "Yes! Yes! I've heard of Hiroshima! What about it? Over."

The radio was dead.

"Goddamnit, Willie! Hurry with that battery!"

But Willie strode leisurely back from the supply hole. "Both them batteries, Joe, both of'em're tore all to hell and gone."

Johnson raced madly to the supply hole and wrested the batteries out of their cartons. Willie was right; both batteries had been ripped and torn by grenade fragments. But Johnson, without pause, ran back to the radio with the ruptured batteries and frantically removed the base of the radio. But the batteries, when he connected first one then the other, were ruined.

Johnson jumped to his feet and kicked the radio as hard as he could. "GODDAMN SONOFABITCH!" he shouted. "We'll sit up here and rust our assholes out while something big breaks loose down there and we won't know a fuken thing about it. I *told* Grimes he ought to string wire up here! But hell no! Not Grimes. Too much fuken——" He stopped. "Well, I'll be damn," he said thoughtfully. "Grimes took out on us."

"Ain't nobody going be mournful about that," Willie said.

Johnson pursed his lips and shrugged. He released his lips with a smack. "No," he said, "I guess not." He shrugged again. "That ought to prove something the army might learn some of these days: You can make a man act like a maniac just so long and no longer."

"Maniac," Willie said. "That's Grimes."

Terry said nothing. He didn't appear to be interested in the radio message at all.

"Christ!" Johnson said and slapped his thigh. "I wish to hell I knew what that big news about Hiroshima is!" He shrugged again. "Well, no need worrying about that. Let's get on with the grave-digging."

Willie and Johnson went back to work on the grave while Terry and I dragged the pieces of the Japs to the edge of the cliff, where I rifled their pockets. Two of them had been so blasted by the explosions that they were too messy for me to do much with, but one, the officer who had stood in the woods to direct the *banzai,* yielded a little leather book that might be a diary. He was an officer, a lieutenant, and he was fat, healthy and smartly uniformed. He had been killed, crouched behind a tree, when his last man had exploded so near that it got him too.

"I don't want his gold," Terry said with a strange hollowness. "I ain't throwing away what I got, but I ain't pulling no more teeth."

I was too sick to answer.

"Jesus, Sam, when I raised that poncho and saw Savage looking at me like that—jesus, I felt like I was going to jump right off that bluff! I've seen enough dead men to build a dam across that river, but Savage got me. Dead Japs don't bother me, but—oh jesus! Savage was looking right at me! Just thinking about it makes me want to run like hell. How about you?"

"I guess," I said, swallowing to prevent vomiting, "I'm getting like you: I'd like to see every Jap in the world dead."

"But not us, by god!"

"No, not us," I said. "Especially not us."

His eyes, which had recently been so bright and quick, searched my face slowly. "I guess," Terry said, "that's not really the way I felt till I seen Savage looking at me like he did."

The remainder of the afternoon passed quickly enough. Time was hurried by fear, which, although it remained unspoken, mounted in intensity as night drew nearer. I was sick, both in my stomach and head, and tried to take my mind away from this morning by working hard on the booby traps. While Willie stood silent guard over me, I arranged the grenades in the trees below our knob. I placed eight of the short-fused grenades so that a Jap, creeping toward us, would step on the wire which was tied to the pins. I chose spots as much as twenty yards into the trees so we would have adequate warning if the grenades weren't as effective as I hoped they would be. The remaining twelve grenades I taped to the trees, at head height, with adhesive from the mortar-shell cases. To the pin of each of these grenades I tied a piece of the telephone wire, the ends of which terminated in my foxhole. If, after dark, I heard a noise that sounded as if a Jap had managed to get past the booby traps, I could pull one of the wires and catch the Japs unexpectedly.

"Hey, Sam?" Willie said.

I looked up at him.

"What's so important about Hiroshima?"

For some unknown reason, the question irritated me. "I don't know," I said shortly.

He said nothing for a moment. "Quit worrying, boy," he said. "You'll make it."

And, as quickly as that, I was sorry for having spoken so shortly. "Let's hope so, Willie."

After having completed the traps, I returned to my foxhole and, as the others were doing, dug a shelf at the front edge. Upon this I placed grenades, the contents of a full case; I also put four canisters of machine-gun ammunition and several M-1 clips there too. Each of us shaved a week's growth of whiskers from our faces, but, because my hands were so tremulous and because I had no mirror, I cut myself several times. My cheeks, when I finished shaving, were amazingly smooth and oily and, as Johnson had suggested, I did feel somewhat better. I took a short nap while Willie, creeping carefully from one foxhole to another, prepared our supper.

Johnson, while he moved the mortars and flares to his foxhole, said, "Damnit to hell, I wish I knew what Tom meant about Hiroshima!"

As the sun touched the horizon, we removed our ponchos that had been serving as tents over our foxholes and folded them neatly in the supply hole. Each of us took his place in his foxhole and, when the sun was gone, waited.

"Jenny . . ." I whispered desperately, "if I can get through tonight, they'll come after us tomorrow. They'll come tomorrow, certainly they will." I wanted, more than anything in my life, to write her a letter.

By now the night was black.

12

The darkness was no more than thirty minutes old when Terry was killed.

We were warned that the Japs were near when two of my booby traps exploded, a nerve-ripping sound that was both times followed by gurgling groans. Johnson held back on the flares, letting the traps do as much damage as they could. I held the wires in my hands and waited. My breath was loud and unsteady, pulsed by my trembling chest.

There came a rapid sequence of clunking sounds as the Japs reached the edge of the trees and armed their grenades by smashing them against their helmets. I jerked two of the wires and, before I could duck, was answered by twin explosions whose flashes briefly silhouetted five Japs against the trees.

Four of them wilted, their grenades still in their hands, but one of them was not wounded, for during that brief flash, I saw him throw. There was a sound of the grenade hitting flesh and Terry uttered a half-grunt, half-sigh, then the Jap grenades began to explode. The one in the hole burst and tossed Terry neatly out of the hole.

"Grenades!" Johnson called softly. "Pull pin—one—two—three—*throw!*"

I heard the grenades hit and roll in the brush and then I heard a jabbered command and the sounds of the Japs scurrying frantically, either to find them and throw them back or to escape their fragments. The three grenades exploded deep in the trees and silhouetted three Japs, each bent in poses of frantic, fumbling search. Their screams were long and so loud that I heard a distinct echo. Then the night was quiet again.

My breath was loud, tremulous, and for one insane moment I thought of jumping over the cliff. Death seemed the logical means of escaping death. It took no more than Johnson's voice to stop me.

"Who got it?" he said.

"Terry," Willie said.

"Sam still with us?"

"Yes," I said. "Yes."

"How many of those short-fused grenades you still have out there?"

"Ten," I said.

"All right. They'll rest and think it over for a while. I'll watch. You two try to sleep."

I did try. I folded myself and huddled at the bottom of my foxhole as if I were trying to find shelter against an arctic wind, but the trembling, which lessened somewhat but never entirely left me, kept me awake. The hallucinations were the closest I got to sleep.

And they were intensely vivid. Carved on a log above the fireplace in Poppa's fishing cabin were the words "Sam loves Jenny," and they were encircled by a heart. There were once two young people who made love in a boat and tittered foolishly because they were nearly seen by two passing fishermen. There was a girl named Jenny and a boy named Sam. Sam's father was called Poppa and Jenny called him Poppa Felix. And there was the concerned face of a civilian named Cozzens who had by the incongruous circumstances of war commanded a regiment. And there were faces: the long-nosed, swarthy smile of a Yankee, Meleski. The defeated eyes of Webster. And the surprised death mask of Raker, father of four children. Those people, equally innocent, had arranged the termination of my own innocence. And there were explosions, crushed bodies, flames, half-severed bodies, glasses, eyes that seemed actually slanted, and long teeth. There was the pop of grenade fuses and there was the morbid whistle of steel fragments. There were flares and hoarse shouts and rifles. Too many rifles. Too much youth siphoned by fear. Too many patrols. Too many foolish little men ready to die because their emperor must live a thousand years.

"Hey, you guys up there!" It was an American voice, American accented, and it came from the trees. For a wild moment, I thought help had come. "Hey, up there!"

Willie whispered, "Joe—Joe, what's that?"

"Be quiet," Johnson said sharply.

"Hey, you guys up there! Hold your fire! We're re-enforcements."

At night? I thought. No, not at night.

"Lillie Lollipop," Johnson shouted, and waited for the countersign.

"Sorry, boys," the voice said. "Captain Grimes didn't give us the countersign."

"When did you talk to Grimes?" Johnson asked.

"Hell, Joe, not more than an hour ago."

"All right, come on out so we can see you."

"Oh no, don't fire that flare. There are Japanese soldiers all over this hill. You'll just have to let us walk up in the dark."

"All right, come on in."

I heard the slightest noise when Johnson traversed his fifty-one. "Wait for me to fire," he whispered.

There was a shuffle of feet on the hard earth and I saw a mass detach itself from the trees and move up the slope of the knob. They were coming up at squad front. Americans always move in single file, like Indians.

Both of my hands were jerking in uncontrollable spasms.

"We had a hell of a time finding you guys," the voice spoke from the mass of men. "How many men you got, Joe?"

"Seven," Joe said blandly. "How about you?"

"A full squad, nine men." American squads have twelve.

"Damn glad to see you," Johnson said.

I curled my finger around the machine-gun trigger.

"Damn, Joe, it's dark up here. How did you ever——"

I didn't intend to pull the trigger, but my hands were jerking so that I touched off a burst without being able to help it. Immediately there was the sound of Johnson dropping a flare into the tube and then all three of us were firing.

The Japs returned our fire. There were three Nambus and several rifles. But we were too much for them. When the flare finally burst, there were already several Japs sprawled and only three standing. One of them, tracers plunging into his belly, continued to stand and fire his Nambu until Willie and I dropped him. The Nambu fired another burst and at the same time the heavy blast of Johnson's fifty-one stopped. Willie and I continued to fire into the fallen Japs to make certain none of them was playing possum. We stopped when the flare fell into the trees.

"Willie?" Johnson said. There was a catch in his voice, as if he were about to cry.

"Yeah, Joe?"

"Willie, I've been hit." He was completely surprised.

"I'll help you, Joe, so you——"

"*Stay in your hole!*"

Willie moved in the dark. "Take it easy, Joe."

"Willie," Johnson said sternly, "get back to your hole. That's an order, Willie. That's an order. First one I ever gave you. So you'd better do as I——" Johnson stopped. Then: "Oh-oh! Willie, you're big brother from now on."

"Cut it out, Joe." There was the sound of Willie easing into Joe's foxhole. After a moment, Willie whispered, "Sam?"

"Yes?"

"Joe's dead."

13

It was some time between midnight and dawn when the next attack came. After Willie had announced Joe's death, there had been a muted scraping and rustling as Willie discarded the fifty-one. Its ammo supply was too close to exhaustion.

A Jap hit one of the trip wires on my booby traps and the flash revealed several others standing among the trees. Willie gave them a burst on his machine gun and I sluggishly jerked four of the wires to fire the head-height grenades. The surviving Japs suddenly charged us desperately, but Willie had a flare in the air before they cleared the trees and we cut them down before they fired a shot. We tried to hose them down, but they had taken cover behind the bodies of the men we had already killed.

"Think you'll make it, Sam?" Willie said.

"I don't know."

"You ain't sick, are you?"

"No."

"I can hear you shaking."

"Can you?"

"Yeah."

"I can hear you breathing."

Pausing between each exchange, listening, we talked for more than an hour.

"Are you a rich man, Sam?"

"No."

"You're pretty well off though, ain't you?"

"Comfortable, that's all."

"How's it feel?"

"Right now—it doesn't make much difference."

"I always wished I had money."

"Maybe you will have."

"Shit! I'm a fuken sharecropper."

"Croppers'll be better off after the war."

"Think so?"

"Mine will."

"You ever been in Walnut Creek?"

"Yes."

"What'd you think about it?"

"Not much."

"It ain't much of a town."

"I guess not."

"I ain't going back there after the war."

"Where're you going?"

"Gray's Landing."

"That's good."

"Can I get a job working for you?"

"Yes."

"What kind of job?"

"Any kind I have that you want."

"Any good-looking girls in Gray's Landing?"

"Lots of them."

"Think they'd go for me?"

"Sure they would."

"Even if I am a country jake?"

"They'd be foolish if they didn't."

"I wouldn't want no high-class woman."

"You can find the kind you want."

"I ain't got much education."

"You don't need it."

"Just fourth grade."

"That's enough."

"What kind of jobs you got for me?"

"Cotton farming."

"Yeah?"

"Gin mechanic."

"Yeah?"

"Truck driver."

"I'm a good truck driver."

"All right, you're hired."

"How much you pay?"

"I don't know. How much do you want?"

"Hundred dollars a month?"

"More than that."

"That so?"

"Poppa says salaries are higher now."

"How high?"

"Probably a hundred and fifty for drivers."

"That's a lot of money."

"Could you live on that?"

"I've lived on three hundred a year."

"You're kidding. That's impossible."

"Yeah, but it's the truth."

"How come?"

"Judge Wilkins starves his croppers."

"How'd you make out on three hundred?"

"Growed the vittles and Maw canned'em."

"That's no way to live."

"Lots of people do it that way."

"My croppers might have, but they'll never again."

"Good. What time is it?"

"Three forty-five."

"Think you're going to make it now?"

"Yes," I said, "I think so now."

For many minutes I stood in my foxhole and listened to the sounds of the night. There was the buzz of insects and the distant bark of a dog and a breeze murmured among the trees, but my ears noted and dismissed those. I listened for the swish of cloth against brush, the shuffle of split-toed boots, the insistent tap of Japs signaling by thumping their rifle butts. And I heard the abiding tremble of my own breath.

"Willie?"

"Yeah?"

"I wasn't kidding about giving you a job, hear?"

"Okay, Sam. Thanks. I'll take it."

"I'd be proud to have you working for me."

"Good."

"Jenny and I want to build a new house after the war. We'll build a special room for you."

"Aw—I wouldn't want to butt in your own home."

"You wouldn't be butting in."

"That pretty wife wouldn't appreciate me."

"Jenny would be honored."

"Aw, Sam——"

"Are you trying to hurt my feelings?"

"Aw, no, Sam—I ain't trying to do that."

"All right then, you'll live with us."

"Aw—maybe."

"Maybe, hell!"

"Aw, all right."

"Thanks a lot, Willie."

Willie said nothing for a long time. I could hear his breath, rapid but steady, and occasionally there was the smallest noise as he turned his head to listen.

"Getting close to daylight," Willie whispered. "See how them clouds is lighting up?"

"Do you think they'll attack after sunup?"

"Maybe. But at least we'll be able to see 'em coming. Besides, we'll be getting relief before long. After the radio went out"—he stopped to listen—"they'll get help up here fast as they can."

"I hope so."

"Think you're going to make it now, Sam?"

"I know I will."

"Thatta boy!"

When the sun first showed over the horizon, it lighted the hilltops with heavy, gaudy splashes of color, leaving the valleys as dark pools of cool purple. Willie's long solemn face, still clean-shaven, was wet with sweat and the yellow sunlight made it glow. He turned to look at the valley across the river behind us.

"Daylight looks pretty good, don't she?"

"It never looked better," I said.

He squinted into the shadows of the rice paddy across the river. "Sam, do I see something down in that paddy?"

It was a moment before I found them in the purple shadows. Five Japs, one of them evidently a high-ranking officer, stalking across the paddy. They moved with a slow, stately gait, their right hands resting limply on the handles of their sabers. The party halted at the edge of the paddy and the officer in charge turned to address the others. Leaving one man with the officer, three of the Japs departed. One came toward our hill and the other two started toward the other outposts.

"Well—" Willie said. "Well." He watched the strange spectacle for a moment. "Looks like they must be planning on really fixing us up, sending a big brass hat up to run things and all."

"Let's try them with a mortar."

"It'd be guesswork. We couldn't hit 'em before they had a chance to take cover. No, let's wait and——"

Clunk!

One of the Japs had played possum all night and now he had thrown a grenade. It came in a shallow arc and hit Willie squarely in the chest. He reared back to pick it up, changed his mind, and started to scramble from his foxhole. His body was clear of the foxhole when the grenade exploded, but his left leg, still in the hole, caught the full force of the explosion.

I killed the Jap with a long burst. I rushed to Willie's foxhole and knelt beside him. The fatigue trousers had been ripped almost completely away from his leg and the knee was severely wounded. The kneecap, strangely free of blood, dangled free, held only by a scrap of white tendon. I rolled him over and, jerking his first-aid pack from his belt, started to work on him.

"Ohhhhhhhhh," he said softly.

"Hurt?"

"No, it don't hurt, but it scares hell outta me."

The blood began coming then. Willie recoiled with fright and tried to get his fingers into the wound. I slapped him sharply across his cheek.

"Leave it alone," I said. "Look at it. It's seeping, not running."

Willie looked at me and grinned. "Blood scares hell out of me."

I removed Willie's belt and applied it as a tourniquet, and the seeping stopped.

"Did it get my balls?" Willie said.

His genitals were unharmed. "You've still got more than you'll ever need. Not a scratch." I pulled the bandage tight. Not knowing how much to use, I emptied the remaining sulfa crystals from Johnson's first-aid kit into the wound.

Willie sat up, his leg poked straight out in front of him. "Put one of them machine guns right here." He indicated the space between his legs.

I wrestled the machine gun to him. My calmness amazed me. I almost felt as good as I had during my first days of combat. When I held my hands up for Willie, he grinned and winked.

"Not airy a shake, huh?" He spat.

"Think you'll be able to make it, Willie?" I said.

"I feel a little funny," he admitted, "kinda cold. But I ain't hurting. Put three or four of them ten-in-one boxes behind my back so's I'n lean back and rest a little." He was quite pale and he was sweating heavily.

Willie looked at Johnson's corpse, which was still in its foxhole.

"Joe was a goddamn good officer," Willie said, "you know it?"

"Best I ever saw," I said. And he was. Better than Lieutenant Baxter, better than Ray Mosby. Maybe even better than Colonel Cozzens. A better officer, because the Colonel was never anything less than a civilian, while Joe had, in spite of himself, become somewhat of the professional; he was certainly the kind of man the Colonel liked.

"When Grimes busted me from Top Kick," Willie said, "Joe argued with'im for a week. Even threatened to resign his commission. Would've too, if I hadn't told'im to forget it." Willie spat.

The sound of the Japs' voices startled us and I hustled over to my machine gun. But there was no charge. A loud voice rattled off something in Japanese—it sounded like a command—and there was the rustlings of several other Japs among the trees. I heard them walking down the rolling rocks of the trail. I saw no Japs at all.

"Pulling'cm back," Willie announced. "Thinking up some new tricks."

We waited. I opened a ten-in-one and handed Willie a

breakfast of canned eggs and bacon. He tasted it, but he couldn't eat. He drank four canteens of water. The sun was soon hot and I rigged a shelter over him, but the ponchos were so riddled with fragments that they offered little shade. I placed the two canteens from Johnson's cartridge belt between the tripod legs of Willie's machine gun and he drank water while I finished my breakfast. Willie's breath was getting shorter.

He was in shock, but it wasn't severe. It takes a lot, I thought, to hurt a tough old sharecropper like Willie. A hell of a lot more than it takes for me and my kind.

"Them boys ought to be here to relieve us pretty soon," he said.

"They'll get here soon as they can."

"My leg's beginning to hurt."

I found a syrette in Johnson's first-aid kit and gave Willie a shot of morphine, hoping that three fourths of the tube wasn't too much.

"I wish we could bury Joe," he said.

"The relief will take care of that."

"Yeah," he said slowly and glanced at the wrist watch on the mortar sight, "I guess they will."

The sun got hotter. It burned like a fireplace at my back.

"My leg's ruined, ain't it?"

"It'll be stiff, Willie, but I've heard of stiff-legged truck drivers before."

He looked at the watch again. "They'll send me home," he said, "when they get me down off this hill."

"That's right."

He grinned weakly. "Don't that watch say five till ten?"

"Yes."

The big, dirty hands wiped sweat from his face. He sighed loudly. "They ain't coming."

"They'll be here after a while." But I knew I was lying. Oddly enough, the realization didn't frighten me as much as I thought it would. I was too preoccupied with my worries about Willie.

"No," he said, "they ain't coming or they'd be here by now." He took a deep breath. "Little short of breath."

"You're in mild shock," I said. "It does you that way."

"I guess so. Look, Sam. You're going to have to run for it."

"No, I'm staying here, Willie," I said firmly. "I have no intention of leaving you up here alone."

"You'll have to run for——"

"Willie, I'm not going——"

"Listen to *me!* I'm in charge here. Them Japs'll be trying something again after while. If you stay here they'll more'n likely get both of us. If you run for it, they's a chance you might make it and bring somebody up to get me. You got to try it."

"No, I'm staying here," I said. "I can't lose my best truck driver."

"Sam, you're just juiced up. You'll break down again after while, first time the Japs attack, and I'll be the same as by myself."

He was right of course. The coming of daylight didn't warrant such a rise in optimism.

"All right," I said, "if they're not here in fifteen minutes, I'll give it a try."

14

The corpses of Johnson and Terry rested where they had fallen; I couldn't bury them. I covered them with their ponchos. Terry's gold-tooth bag had dropped from his pocket. I picked it up, not knowing quite what to do with it, when Willie gestured for me to bring it to him. He tried weakly to throw it over the cliff, but it landed near the edge. I kicked and watched it fall until it was so small that I lost it in the rocks of the riverbank.

I said, "Terry's the only man I've ever seen to like combat."

"Yeah," Willie agreed, "but he pooped out before he got killed."

Terry had also lost his enthusiasm for gold, which, now, seemed a foreshadowing of what had come.

And Johnson. Some time in the future—I hoped it wouldn't be too soon—his beautiful wife would marry again because a woman of her beauty would have men after her. And this corpse who had once been a man would be a shadowy figure of her past. Someday there would be a time when weeks would pass without her thinking of him at all. And finally, she would forget what kind of man he had been, what he looked like. And, thinking of the moment when she would soon be in grief, it seemed cruel that six of us had known him better than she ever had.

"Sam, hold your hands out so's I'n see'em," Willie said.

"Don't worry about me, Willie. I'm all right."

"All right, my ass. Hold out them hands!"

I extended them toward him.

"What'd I tell you!" he said.

I shook my head stubbornly.

"Look down there in that paddy again, Sam."

Advancing, bandy-legged, across the yellow mat of rice straw, were at least a hundred Japs. At the head of the column, various brass devices agleam in the bright sun, marched another high-ranking officer. I quickly put my hands in my pockets where they were safely out of Willie's sight.

"We ain't got a chance with that many, Sam. You better be getting ready." He gave me no chance to argue. He was giving the kind of order Johnson and—earlier in the war—Ray Mosby gave: there was no room left for a question.

"Take the BAR," he said. "Put the ammo vest on. *Hurry!*"

I did as I was told. "Willie, I can't go running off——"

"Goddamn you, Sam! *Hurry!*"

From the trees there was silence. The Jap column was still moving across the paddy.

"I'll see you in Gray's Landing," Willie said. Urgently: "Now —*run!*"

I turned and trotted down the trail, my canteens bouncing at my butt. It was a mistake. A damn *foolish* mistake. Trotting was the wrong thing to do—wrong altogether. I couldn't slow to a walk; it required all my strength to keep from breaking into a run, for the hill was so steep and the trail, washed by a thousand tropical rains, was littered with stones that rolled under my feet.

Oh god, I thought, I should have remembered this.

I held the BAR at low port and, slipping, often staggering, tried to place my feet where there was a chance that I might have smoother footing.

There appeared, at the edge of the trail, the round face of a Jap, his eyes wide with alarm and surprise. His brown uniform took shape and he scrambled to his feet. As alarmed as he, I stopped trying to restrain my speed and raced directly at him. He stared foolishly at me for the briefest moment, during which I saw that he was unarmed.

Then, stupidly enough, he bowed.

As I hurtled past him I clipped him on top of his bowed head with the butt of the BAR. I heard a sickening crunch of bone, but I didn't look back, for it was taking all my powers of concentration to stay on the winding trail; I was running as fast, I thought, as my legs could operate.

I was running so fast that the wind whistled in my ears. My cap was blown from my head and rolled down my back. It was a certainty that I would fall soon; my legs couldn't possibly pound fast enough to keep pace with my hurtling body.

But, when I passed around a shallow bend in the trail, my legs served me well, for I saw a large group of Japs seated in a rough circle on the trail. They appeared to be chatting pleasantly about something. I even gained more speed and my legs, instead of trying to hold me back, actually strained for more speed.

The Japs reacted the same way the one above them had. They gaped in awe. Several of them were already in the act of rendering a servile bow when I pressed the trigger of the BAR. A burst of fire spewed hatefully at them and, a wild cry trailing behind me, I hurtled through their group and was out of sight around another bend in the trail.

I remembered the creek that drained into the river at the bottom of the hill and I worried briefly about how I was going to slacken my speed enough to wade it, but then I thought of that no more, for it appeared, slamming into view as if it had

303

been dropped across the trail by some cruel genie. And I jumped. I drew my legs up under me and sailed. It was only here that time slowed, for I seemed to have sailed forever and forever.

When I landed on the distant bank, my right foot folded under me and rolled with my weight. There was a tug and a crunch in my ankle and the landscape of gullies and trees slanted crazily and I was rolling. A rock smashed into my mouth and a smear of liquid splashed into my eyes. Whirling so fast that I could make my eyes register no more than a sliding blur, I tumbled down an embankment and rolled halfway up another one before my momentum died and I fell back into the gully.

I jumped to my feet, still grasping the BAR at port-arms, and burst from the trees like a startled deer. I sped across the rice paddy and into the ruins of Angat. Although my right foot felt slightly heavier than the other one, I seemed not to touch the crumbled paving at all. My combat boots were light as ballet slippers and I reached out and brought back giant, seven-league strides. Each time my weight was on my right foot, a chilling electric shock raced up my spine, but I didn't decrease my speed.

I didn't stop running until I reached the bend in the road that turns toward the George perimeter. Nor would I have stopped then if my right foot had not become leadenly heavy. I slowed to a hurried walk. My breath was so loud that I couldn't hear the heavy tread of my boots. And each time my heart gave an ear-filling beat, my head swelled and ached sharply. Each breath seared my lungs.

My right boot was laced too tight. That was a damn foolish thing to do, my mind registered. Any seasoned infantryman could tell you the most foolish of all mistakes is a tightly laced boot. With a rip of the laces of my boot, my ankle burst free and flowed with sappy fat until it reached the limits of the boot's tongue. The huge egg of fat around my ankle was warm and I could feel it jiggle with each step.

"Got to stop," I gasped aloud. "Ankle hurt."

But there was no need for me to stop. There was no pain.

Indeed, the only reason I was aware there was anything more serious than a sudden blob of fat was the peculiar little squeegy sound inside the ankle when I put my weight on it. It sent no protesting pain to my head. Why then, Sam, you old hard infantryman, you old professional soldier, should you stop?

"I'm not going to," I answered. "Willie can't last all day up there."

A very funny sound the ankle makes. I laughed aloud. Very funny.

I walked almost a half mile before my breath stopped choking me. Maybe I'm safe now. Maybe. Yes, maybe.

"Safe like hell," I muttered. "Gray's Landing is the only safe place in the world." I stumbled on the bad ankle. "In the whole fuken world."

15

When I entered the George perimeter, I was not certain that I had found the right place. For, instead of the sullen perimeter I had known in the days of Captain Grimes, there was a great hustle of men, trucks and jeeps. But they weren't George Company men. Some of the faces looked vaguely familiar, but. . . . Thinking only of finding Tom Thumb so he could send a patrol after Willie, I made my way through the perimeter. I had no idea of his whereabouts, but I was going to find him. Of that I was certain.

"Hey!" somebody called. "Hey, *Sam!*"

Must be somebody else around here named Sam, I thought.

A hand gripped my shoulder and tried to turn me about. I jerked away fiercely. It was insanely maddening for anybody to be so stupid as to interfere with my plans.

"Let go," I said. "Willie's still up there." I plowed on, my fattened ankle jiggling at each step.

"*Oh*-oh," the voice said.

"Get him," another voice said quietly. "That ankle—he'll mess it up good!"

The *sotto voce* intrigue, so merciless in its disregard of Willie's safety, threw me into a violent rage. I whirled and trained the BAR on the two men who stood behind me. One of them was bearded and dirty; he carried an M-1 at sling. The other one, a captain, was clean-shaven and rather pale.

"Just try it, you bastards!" I said. "Just move and see what happens! Just move one time!"

"Aw, take it easy, Sam," the bearded one said. "We ain't going to hurt you. All we want to do"—as he talked he moved slowly to my left—"is give you a little help with that ankle. You're hurt, Sam. You're hurt bad. No need of walking on it till we have a chance to see what's——"

The clean-shaven captain grabbed the BAR by the barrel and pushed it up. I jerked frantically at the trigger and emptied the clip. The bullets sprayed the top of the house that had been Grimes' headquarters.

"Get'im!" the bearded one said.

And both of them jumped me. In that instant I became a fatalist; if Willie must die because of the incredible stupidity of such people as these, then there was nothing I could do about it. I relaxed.

"What the hell's going on here?" a stern voice demanded gruffly.

I lay, relaxed, and stared at the blue, peaceful sky, aware only of the weight of the two men sitting on me.

"It's Sam Gifford, General," the pale captain said. "He wandered in here a minute ago, didn't stop, just kept going. He's out of his head——"

"No I'm not," I mumbled.

"Look at that ankle," the pale captain finished.

"Doctor Wingate!" the general's voice called loudly. "Come up here and see what's wrong with this man." I heard him whistle sharply. "That ankle's broken, I'd say."

The bearded face appeared over me. "Take it easy now, Sam," he whispered and grinned. I could smell his hot breath

306

plainly; he had been eating K-ration. "You'll be all right in just a minute." He waited for a reaction and then, seeing none, he said, "Don't you know me, Sam? I'm Kenny. Kenny Carr. Don't you know me?"

I blinked slowly, almost fell asleep, but I still had Willie to think about. . . . I spat into the bearded face.

He jerked back, grunted with surprise, and wiped his face with the sleeve of his fatigue jacket. "Jesus!" he said. "He's plumb off his marbles, General!"

"Yes," the general said. *"Doctor Wingate!"*

The pale captain bent over me. "I'm Ray, Sam. Ray Mosby. You'll be taken care of in just a minute."

I turned my head away. The sky was incredibly high. And blue. At the top of my field of vision, immediately behind the general's starred helmet, floated a puff of white cloud, as white as a burst of cotton.

I'm a cotton man. Back in a little town called Gray's Landing I am a very important individual. I am the heir to one of the town's fortunes; I own a lot of land, I own a gin, a house and an expensive car. I married the prettiest girl in town and she is still in love with me. She will be proud to meet my new friend, the only friend I ever had, and she will treat him like a brother. Willie, boy, you're my brother.

"General?" I said.

"What is it, Son?" For a moment I thought he was Colonel Cozzens masquerading as somebody else.

"Are you commanding this outfit?"

"Yes, what can I do for you?"

"There's a hill up there," I said, "and we call it Parade George. Willie Crawford's up there and he's badly wounded. Busted kneecap. I'd sure be much obliged if you would send somebody up there after him."

"Captain Mosby," the general said, "take Recon and the antitank platoon up to that hill. Find out from Intelligence where it is. Go as far as you can in trucks. If you meet resistance, start shooting. I want that boy off that hill and I want him off fast, so on the double. You have twenty minutes, Captain."

"Yessir. Stay with Sam, Kenny."

There was a shuffle of feet and the captain named Mosby left. The general bent over me.

"What did you say your name was, Son?"

"Sam Gifford," said the bearded one named Carr.

"He'll answer me, Sergeant," the general said. "Tell me your name, Son."

My ankle was grasped and somebody said, "*Cut* the boot off!"

"Samuel Francis Gifford," I said.

My sleeve was jerked up and there was a sharp pain in my shoulder.

"Doctor Wingate gave you a shot, Sam," the general said. "Do you know Doc Wingate?"

"There used to be a Doc Wingate in my home town."

"Is this the man?" A new face appeared behind the general.

"Nosir," I said. "I don't know that man."

"Are you married, Sam?"

"Yessir."

"What's your wife's name?"

"Jenny."

"What was her maiden name?"

"Jenny Cozzens."

The general looked inquiringly toward the bearded sergeant. "Cozzens?"

"Yessir," the bearded one said. "Sam's Colonel Cozzens' son-in-law, General."

The general looked down at me. "Do you remember Colonel Cozzens, Sam?"

"Yessir, I do."

"I hear he was a good soldier."

"The best, General. But he should've been commanding a regiment of Confederate infantry."

"Oh? Tell me about it."

It wasn't worth the trouble. I smiled benignly at the little cloud above the general's head.

"Keep talking, General," somebody said. "Tell him about the war."

I gave the general a thorough examination. He was a strong-faced man, about forty-five. There were three gray hairs in his right eyebrow and there were three parallel scars on his right cheek. Under his eyes were some wrinkles that looked like little relief maps of a gullied area. His nose had been broken and flattened. There was a fungus scab in the left corner of his mouth. His lips were thin. There was a huge cleft in his chin. He needed a shave.

"Sam," he said, "did you know the war's about over?"

I looked him square in the eye. "Don't lie to me, General."

He held up his right hand. "I'm not lying, Sam. That's what I'm doing up here. We're trying to contact a Jap general hiding up there in the hills and tell him to stop fighting. Hear the radios?"

I did hear the chirp of several radios sending on C-W. "Yessir."

"Well, they're trying to tell the Jap general that he's not to send any more attack parties out. If we can get him to agree, the war's over."

"First time I ever heard of a Jap giving up," I said.

"They will, though."

"I can't see why."

"We dropped an atom bomb on Hiroshima a day or so ago."

"What's an atom bomb?"

"I don't know, but it must be a big one."

"And you're not lying?"

He laughed. "You don't think a general would be up this close to the line if the war wasn't almost over, do you?"

"Nosir," I said seriously.

He chuckled before he got serious again. "Did they attack you last night?"

"Yessir. When we first went up there on the hill, there were seven of us. All but Willie and me got killed. Did you send somebody after Willie?"

"I sure did, Sam."

"Where's Colonel Miles?"

"He——"

"They're answering, General!" somebody shouted.

The general patted my shoulder. "Take it easy, Son. I've got a little work to do." He hurried away.

Carr bent over me. "Ankle hurting, Sam?"

I shook my head. "Where's Colonel Miles?"

"He got transferred back to the States, Sam. Ain't that fine?"

"No," I said, "no. I was planning on killing him."

My leg was lifted and I felt a tap on the tendon below my kneecap. I didn't feel a reflex. "It's going to be a bad ankle long's he lives, but he'll be able to walk on it."

"That was Doc Wingate, wasn't it?" I said.

"Sure was," Carr said.

"You're awful dirty, Carr," I said. "You smell worse than I do."

Carr grinned. "Yeah, we been out on an eight-day jeep patrol and I had to command. Didn't have time to take good care of myself with the commanding and all."

"You really are Kenny Carr, aren't you?"

He grinned down at me. "I sure am, Sam."

"What really happened to Captain Grimes, Kenny?"

"He tried to get at Colonel Miles with a tommy-gun," Kenny said. "A guard shot'im."

Doc Wingate said, "Get out of the way, Kenny. Help us put him on the stretcher."

I was rolled completely over and when I saw the sky again I was resting on the taut canvas of a stretcher. With a slight jolt I was lifted and moved along. I tried to sit up.

"Stay on your back, Sam," Doc Wingate said.

"Where're you taking me?" I said.

"Hospital." The open back of a field ambulance appeared. "You need a little rest."

"I'm not leaving here," I said firmly, "till they bring Willie in."

Doc appeared over me. "Now, Sam——"

"I mean it, Doc."

"All right," Doc said and gestured to the medics. "Put the stubborn bastard down."

I was lowered to the earth. A cold can was thrust into my hands. "General's compliments," Doc said.

"What is it?"

"*Don't spill it!*" he said sharply. "It's beer."

I raised it to my lips. Then I lowered it without having tasted it. "I'll save the first half for Willie."

"Go ahead," Doc said, "drink it. I'll get the general to give Willie a whole can."

I tasted the beer. It was so cold that it gave me a headache and it tasted almost as good as Uncle Ben's home-brew.

"Is the war really over, Doc?" I said.

"Looks like it," Doc said. "Isn't that right, Kenny?"

"All but the shouting," Kenny said. "The general'd been told all you guys'd been pulled off those hills late yesterday afternoon. I wondered where you were. What made you not come in?"

"Our radio was out."

"Jesus!" Kenny said. "All those guys got killed too. How many'd you lose last night?"

"Two. Terry and Little Joe," I said. "Little Joe was a good man, a good sonofabitch. Got shot right in the stomach and didn't moan or yell a bit. And he got the shitty end of the stick from the word go." I took another swallow of beer. "Did they bring Willie in yet?"

"No, but I'n see the trucks just coming around the bend."

"Willie's going to drive a truck for me when we get home," I said. "He's going to live with Jenny and me, too."

I could feel my ankle now. It was warm and tight and cold and flabby. Doc Wingate wiped my forehead with a fold of gauze. The beer was getting colder. It was the first cold liquid I had tasted since. . . .

"At least," I said, "I didn't lose my manhood like Morgan did."

"Jenny'll be glad to see you," Doc said delicately.

"When will I get home?"

"Three weeks. A month, maybe. Not long."

The general appeared over me. "How's it going, Son?"

I nodded. "Thanks for the beer, General. You think you can manage a can for Willie when they get here with him?"

"Sure," the general said. "Medic, get a beer for Willie." He looked back down at me. "If I had known you men were still up there, I'd've sent a patrol out as soon——"

"'Scuse me, General," Doc said. "Put him right here by Sam, boys." There was a rustle of uniforms and shuffling of boots. Doc said, "Well, Sam, here's your Willie."

Willie, his face pale, his eyes closed, lay beside me. There were tobacco stains at the corners of his mouth.

"Is he dead?" I asked anxiously.

"No," Willie said. He didn't open his eyes.

"He'll be all right," Doc said. "Fix those transfusion bottles up there." He turned to direct the erection of the plasma bottles.

"Willie," I said, "you old bastard, we made it! We outlasted the fuken war!"

Willie nodded weakly and, weaker still, a grin twitched at his mouth.

"I'll have Jenny lay us out a real banquet, Willie," I said. "We'll get some home-brew from Uncle Ben and really throw a wing-ding." That was a funny remark, a very funny remark. Oh, no doubt about it, I was a great humorist. And I had outlasted the war. I began to chuckle. But it got away from me; I couldn't stop. I laughed until my throat hurt. It was all very droll. I had outlasted the fuken war.

"Give Sam another shot," Doc said. "Not too much now, just enough to put him to sleep."

I continued to laugh hilariously until the morphine put me to sleep.